Praise

Deeply moving, *Nobody's Perfect* ultimately uplifting. The characters are so real a reader can't help but feel for Damián and Savi. The Masters at Arms world is one that will stay with you forever. Kallypso Masters gets to the heart of BDSM romance—the deep connection between Master and submissive and how each strengthens the other.

~ **Lexi Blake, Author**

~ ~ ~

...Kally Masters captured the heartache and pain that can drive a person to the lifestyle to fulfill their needs and, like a rose, she truly conveyed the beauty that can bloom from those thorns.

~ **Alyn Love, Guilty Pleasures Book Reviews**

~ ~ ~

Wonderful, emotional read about two wounded survivors helping each other heal and finding love.

~ **Cherise Sinclair, Author**

~ ~ ~

...(W)hen a book can move you, make you connect, engage you to the point that it feels as if you know these characters and you care so much for their well-being, not just for their happily ever after...then that is greatness!

~ **Francesca, Under the Covers Book Blog**

~ ~ ~

...(A)s a survivor it touches home. I've been with my husband 9 years, married for 6; to this day I have issues... He's currently reading it and it's helping him understand me. He's said sometimes he doubts my love for him because if I loved him we wouldn't have these issues. It's not something I could ever explain to him. He's about 30% through the book and he finally is getting it. So we thank you!!

~ **Chrystal, Reader's comment on her Amazon Review**

~ ~ ~

...(T)he Rescue Me series is a masterpiece of work because *Nobody's Perfect* left me glued to the pages, thinking about the book whenever I was not reading it and craving it as if I was having withdrawal symptoms. Most of all, the characters feel so real and the imagery of the scenes are so detailed that you truly feel that Damián and Savi REALLY do exist and are living life out there, somewhere, and you can't wait to see them again.

~ **Ollie, Bitten by Paranormal Romance Review**

Rescue Me Saga
Reading Order

Not stand-alone novels
(These love stories can't be contained within one book! In a saga, of course, characters recur to continue working on real-life problems in later books.)

These four titles are available in e-book and print formats, and will be coming in 2014 in audiobook form (digital only), narrated by the award-winning team of Phil Gigante and Natalie Ross.

Masters at Arms & Nobody's Angel (Combined Volume)
Nobody's Hero
Nobody's Perfect
Somebody's Angel

Next expected title in series:

Nobody's Dream

Also available in Spanish editions:

Sargentos Marines (*Masters at Arms* in English)
El Ángel de Nadie (*Nobody's Angel* in English)
El Héroe de Nadie (*Nobody's Hero* in English)

Additional titles are being translated into Spanish as quickly as feasible, but it takes time to do a good translation!

Nobody's Perfect

(Third in the Rescue Me Saga)

Kallypso Masters

Nobody's Perfect
Third in the Rescue Me Saga
by
Kallypso Masters

Copyright © 2012-2014 Kallypso Masters LLC
Print ISBN: 978-1480096950
Revised April 4, 2014

ALL RIGHTS RESERVED
Content edited by: Jeri Smith, Jacy Mackin, and Ekatarina Sayanova
Line edited by Meredith Bowery and Liz Borino
Cover art by Linda Lynn
Formatted by BB eBooks
Cover image licensed through Depositphotos and graphically altered by Linda Lynn

This book contains content that is not suitable for readers 17 and under.

Thank you for downloading this e-book. Please be aware that this e-book is licensed for *your* personal enjoyment only. It may not be reproduced, uploaded to share on Web sites, e-mailed, or used in whole or in part by any means existing without written permission from the author, Kallypso Masters, at kallypsomasters@gmail.com or PO Box 206122, Louisville, KY 40250, or within the sharing guidelines at a legitimate library or bookseller.

WARNING: The unauthorized reproduction, sharing, or distribution of this copyrighted work is illegal. Criminal copyright infringement, including infringement without monetary gain, is investigated by the FBI and is punishable by up to five years in federal prison and a fine of $250,000. (See http://www.fbi.gov/ipr/ for more information about intellectual property rights.)

This book is a work of fiction and any resemblance to persons—living or dead—or places, events, or locales is purely accidental. The characters are reproductions of the author's imagination and used fictitiously.

To discover more about the books in this series, see the *Rescue Me* Saga at the end of this book. For more about Kallypso Masters, please go to the About the Author section.

Dedication

To Dane Christopher Sattler, a brave American hero who lost his battle with PTSD in January 2011. What my nation has asked of its military service members and their families is monumental, and we need to reach out to them every chance we get to make sure they know we appreciate their sacrifices and are willing to help in any way we can. God bless you all. And, Sue, thanks for sharing your son with me—and for keeping his memory alive on Facebook and elsewhere so we will never forget his sacrifice, and yours.

Also, to my Dad, who suffered most of this adult life with PTSD from the horrors of his service in Korea. He's in heaven now. His battle over. But he'll always be in my heart and is the inspiration for the character of Damián Orlando. Love and miss you, Dad.

And to all my fellow survivors of incest and child sexual abuse—it wasn't your fault. I hope by reading about Savannah/Savi's journey and her courage to reclaim her body and her life you will see there is no one too wounded to find a happy ending, too. Believe me, if we can, so can you. Thank you to all of you who have shared your pain (sometimes for the first time) through private messages and e-mails. Know that you are not alone. Big virtual hugs to you all!

Acknowledgements

To my awesome beta readers who were tortured for months not knowing how the book would end (and were often left needing Xanax or serious aftercare after reading a particularly challenging chapter cliffhanger and not getting more of the story for days or months). They are Khriste Close, Kris Harris, Kathy Holtsclaw, Kellie Hunter, Alison K., Pix.E.Lee, Kelly Mueller, and Kathy Treadway.

To Toymaker and his submissive eirocawakening (their FetLife names) for helping me plan out the BDSM scenes for Damián and then for helping me get inside the heads of Damián and Savannah to take them even deeper into the scene. Knowing at least one scene even brought rare tears to the eyes of a Dom? Priceless.

To Jennifer P., Ekatarina Sayanova, and Jacy Mackin for helping me understand the psychological aspects of Damián and Savi's relationship and for advice on how this lifestyle might help them gain control over their PTSD triggers. And to Kathy Holtsclaw, Kellie Hunter, Ofelia Romero, eirocawakening, and Ekatarina Sayanova, who helped me understand Savi's triggers and the ways to help her overcome them.

To Top Griz, who always helps me get the Marine sayings I ask about correct, and even went beyond regs to help with some righteous retribution for Savi. After reading this book, I'll bet you'll see Frag Orders in a whole new light. Thank you, sir, for your help and for your service.

To Kelly Timm and her mother-in-law, who helped me get the factual parts of Solana Beach and Rancho Santa Fe correct. (Please note that San Miguel's, Savi's childhood mansion, the hotel in La Jolla, and many other aspects of these communities are *complete* figments of my imagination.)

To my Facebook friends and fans who chimed in on countless questions I asked on my Facebook Author Page and Facebook timeline. You always are there to help me out when I just don't have one more brain cell left! With thousands of Facebook friends and author-page followers, there are way too many to name here without leaving some out, but thanks for joining me on this amazing journey and for helping me whenever I got stuck on something.

To Corina Del Bene (Cori Db on Facebook) for helping me learn to swear like a Marine—well, in Spanish, at least, since I'd already mastered the English words. And to Jennifer A. Montes for correcting a couple of my Spanish phrases for the print version.

To Marine, wounded warrior, and model/actor Alex Minsky for confirming that, even with his amputation, Damián would have no trouble with the physical demands in scenes in this story.

To Kathy Holtsclaw for inspiration and suggestions. It was so nice to meet you in Denver this past summer.

To Rosie Moewe for keeping track of my series timeline and researching topics for me.

To the Kallypso's Street Brats (my street team) and Masters Brats (fans) who continue to pimp my books to anyone who will listen—even to some who probably would rather *not* know about your reading preferences. My career took off as a result of incredible word of mouth, and you continue to bring the Rescue Me Saga and the members of the Masters at Arms Club to the attention of new readers every day. My humble thanks for loving me and my Masters so much.

To my editorial team—Jeri Smith, Ekatarina Sayanova, Jacy Mackin, Meredith Bowery, and Liz Borino—who helped bring out the best book I had in me. I continue to improve and grow as a writer because of all you ladies teach me. Of course, it's those things I change *after* you and my subject experts sign off on them that usually lead to errors. So as always, all typos and errors are solely my responsibility and know that all of the above-mentioned people have prevented much embarrassment for me—and much frustration for you, my readers.

And to my awesome personal assistant, Leagh Christensen of Romance Novel Promotions, LLC, for her help in taking care of the business matters, promos, and marketing so that I could spend more time writing! You can't imagine how much time she saves me, even thought there's still so much to do.

Author's Note

This has been the most difficult book for me to write because it brought up so many of my own childhood issues, even though it's not autobiographical in any way. Now that it is finished, I am very pleased with how it turned out. I've heard from a number of survivors who also found healing within these pages. While the story takes readers to some very dark places in Savannah/Savi's life, it is primarily a story of hope and healing.

If you have a history of past abuse, you may be triggered by parts of the story. Please, before reading this book, be aware that it is primarily about an incest survivor dealing with the sexual aftermath of years of abuse. She has dealt with non-sexual issues with years of therapy but has tamped down anything related to sex. In this book, she struggles to find sexual healing through a trusting, consensual BDSM relationship.

The BDSM scenes in this book (some of them beginning and advanced sadomasochism techniques) are the result of many conversations with submissives and Dominants who have worked through similar abuse issues using activities in the BDSM community and lifestyle. I wanted to bring a level of authentic realism to the story rather than try to titillate readers. However, please don't try the techniques you read about unless you and your partner(s) are at that level of skill. Please remember that Damián has trained within the community for years to provide the service he does in this book.

This is a work of fiction, albeit realistically portrayed fiction. Follow the standards for safe, sane, and consensual (SSC) play outlined on sites like fetlife.com before you venture into real-world BDSM or activities that are beyond you and your partner's current expertise. You will find that Damián and Savannah don't play in this book for months. Instead, they spend that time building trust. I wanted to make that a very key part in telling this story, because when trust is shattered in childhood, it is very difficult to restore it and for the "adult child" to trust anyone again.

BDSM is not a cure or panacea for past abuse and trauma. However, for the people I've talked with in trying to understand how sadomasochism might be used as a means of healing, I've learned that it has been helpful to many on any number of levels. Do your homework before you explore further.

IMPORTANT: If you believe that reading about PTSD flashbacks of incest or combat, catharsis by whipping, mindfucks, and related topics might be triggering for you, please make sure you only read this book in a safe environment with supportive people available to you. Put the book down as often as you need to regroup or talk with someone. Be gentle with yourself, survivors.

Here are some web sites that can help if you need to talk with someone.

Crisis Services:
http://crisisservices.org/content/index.php/information-resources/

Rape Abuse and Incest National Network:
http://rainn.org/

To Write Love on Her Arms:
http://www.twloha.com/

And for military-service related PTSD, the Veterans Administration or any veterans group. I'm very impressed with the work done by these organizations for veterans and their families:

Hope for the Warriors:
http://www.hopeforthewarriors.org/

Snowball Express (for the children of the fallen, like Tracy Miller)
https://snowballexpress.org/

Cast of Characters for
Nobody's Perfect

Marisol "Mari" Baker—Savi Baker's daughter

Savi Baker (aka **Savannah Gentry** and briefly as Savita Diaz)—she met Damián Orlando as Savannah Gentry in *Masters at Arms* but changed her name to Savi Baker when she escaped her father's house. When he meets her again in *Nobody's Hero*, she goes by Savi.

Boots—a stray kitten

Gino D'Alessio—Marc's older brother; killed in action in Afghanistan; involved with Melissa Russo

Mama D'Alessio—Marc's mother

Marc "Doc" D'Alessio—Navy corpsman ("Doc"); co-owner of the Masters at Arms Club and owner of a Denver outfitter store. Dating **Angelina Giardano**.

Luke Denton—Marc's search and rescue (SAR) partner, an artisan who makes furniture, including pieces for the kink community, and does cabinetry

Rico Donati—Owner of daVinci's bar in Aspen Corners and a high-school friend of Angelina Giardano's and her brothers

José Espinosa—Damián's young nephew

Julio Espinosa—Rosa's abusive ex-husband and Damián's brother-in-law

Rosa Espinosa—Damián's older sister

Teresa Espinosa—Damián's teenage niece

Elise Pannier Gentry—Savannah Gentry's mother

George Gentry—Savannah Gentry's sadistic, abusive bastard of a father

Savannah Gentry (now Savi Baker)—an incest victim and sex slave who gave up hope until she met Damián Orlando in *Masters at Arms*; when she meets him again in *Nobody's Hero*, she is a social worker helping his niece Teresa and going by the name Savi Baker

Angelina Giardano—Marc's girlfriend and a submissive; nicknamed Angie by Karla and Angel by Luke

Lyle Gibson—business partner to Savannah Gentry's father and responsible for being her "handler"; nicknamed Cabron

Anita Gonzales—organist and church member at San Miguel's in Eden Gardens (Solana Beach)

Graciela—Cassie's pregnant alpaca

John Grainger—friend of Savannah's mother

V. Grant (Mistress Grant)—a Lance Corporal communications specialist on special assignment with Adam's recon unit in Fallujah and later in Black Ops. Now a Domme at the Masters at Arms Club and remains shrouded in mystery.

Victor Holmes—a Denver fire fighter who is a member at the Masters at Arms Club; with Patti

Gunnar Larsen—a sadist whip master who trained Damián, Grant, and others; retired Army Delta Force

Cassie Lôpez—Karla's Peruvian friend from college who now lives in Colorado; an artist living in seclusion

Father Martine—The parish priest at San Miguel's church in Eden Gardens (Solana Beach), the same church Damián attended in his youth

Doctor Robert McKenzie—a friend of Marc's who runs an inner-city clinic in Denver

Mrs. Miller—widow of the recon Marine killed on the rooftop in Fallujah during the firefight in *Masters at Arms*

Sergeant Thomas Miller—Recon Marine killed on the rooftop in Fallujah during the firefight in *Masters at Arms*

Tracy Miller—16-year-old daughter of the recon Marine killed on the rooftop in Fallujah during the firefight in *Masters at Arms*

Adam Montague (pronounced MON-tag)—retired after 25 years in the Marine Corps as a master sergeant; patriarch of the Masters at Arms Club "family"; surrogate father to Damián; husband and Dom to Karla Paxton Montague

Johnny Montague—Adam's great-great-grandfather; a Marine who served during the Civil War. His mother was Lakota and his father a French trapper

Joni Montague—Adam's first wife who died from cancer

Karla Paxton Montague—wife and collared submissive of Adam Montague; singer in the Masters at Arms Club; nicknamed Kitty by Cassie and Kitten by Adam

Kate Montague—Adam's great-great-grandmother; much younger than her husband Johnny. She emigrated from Ireland to the Black Hills of South Dakota

O'Keeffe—an abused mustang rescued by Luke Denton

Damián ("Damo") Orlando—served with Adam and Marc in Iraq; rides a Harley; Patriot Guard Rider; in love with Savannah Gentry

Mamá Orlando—mother of Damián; maiden name Diaz; deceased

Papá Orlando—father of Damián; deceased

Ian Paxton—Karla's brother who was killed in a motorcycle accident in *Masters at Arms*

Captain Reed—in this book, he isn't named but is the man Damián refers to as the Navy chaplain who married Adam and Karla

Mrs. Reynolds—the mother of one of Savi's clients

Melissa Russo—a woman Marc almost married before he joined the Navy; she cheated on him with his brother, **Gino D'Alessio**, becoming Gino's fiancée before Gino deployed to Afghanistan

Patti Varga—The unnamed bottom in a scene in *Nobody's Angel* involving Victor Holmes and Damián

Whiskers—Savannah Gentry's childhood pet cat

Marge Winther—Joni's mother

Playlist for the Rescue Me Saga

Here are some of the songs that inspired Kally as she wrote the books to date in the series. Because each book isn't only about one couple's journey, she has grouped the music by couple, except for the first one.

Spanning Multiple Rescue Me Saga Characters
Darryl Worley – *Just Got Home From a War*
Angie Johnson – *Sing for You*
Evanescence – *Bring Me To Life*
Dan Hill – *Sometimes When We Touch*

Adam and Joni
(backstory in *Masters at Arms* & *Nobody's Angel* and *Nobody's Hero*):
Sarah McLachlan – *Wintersong*
Rascal Flatts – *Here Comes Goodbye*
Aerosmith – *I Don't Wanna Miss A Thing*

Marc and Angelina
(*Masters at Arms* & *Nobody's Angel* and *Somebody's Angel*):
Andrea Bocelli – *Por Amor* (and others on *Romanza* CD)
Sarah Jane Morris – *Arms Of An Angel*
Fleetwood Mac – *Landslide*
Mary Chapin Carpenter – *The King of Love*
Air Supply – *The One That You Love*
Air Supply – *Goodbye*
Lacuna Coil – *Spellbound*
Air Supply – *Making Love Out of Nothing at All*
Styx – *Man In The Wilderness*
Keith Urban – *Tonight I Wanna Cry*
Michael Bublé – *Home*
Leighton Meester – *Words I Couldn't Say*
Halestorm – *Private Parts*
And a "medley" of heavy-metal music cited in the acknowledgements of *Somebody's Angel*

Adam and Karla
(*Masters at Arms* & *Nobody's Angel*, *Nobody's Hero*, and *Somebody's Angel*):
Tarja Turunen – *I Walk Alone*
Madonna – *Justify My Love*

Sinead O'Connor – *Song to the Siren*
Paul Brandt – *My Heart Has a History*
Rascal Flatts – *What Hurts The Most*
Marc Anthony – *I Sang to You*
Simon & Garfunkel – *I Am A Rock*
Alison Krauss & Union Station – *I'm Gone*
The Rolling Stones – *Wild Horses*
Pat Benatar – *Love Is A Battlefield*
The Rolling Stones – *Under My Thumb*
Lifehouse – *Hanging By A Moment*
Leighton Meester – *Words I Couldn't Say*
Air Supply – *Lonely Is The Night*
Beyoncé – *Poison*
Randy Vanwarmer – *Just When I Needed You Most*
The Red Jumpsuit Apparatus – *Your Guardian Angel*
Oum Kalthoum – *Enta Omri* (Egyptian belly dance music)
Harem – *La Pasion Turca* (Turkish belly dance music)
Barry Manilow – *Ready To Take A Chance Again*
Paul Dinletir – *Transcendance*

Damián and Savannah
(*Masters at Arms* & *Nobody's Angel*, *Nobody's Perfect*, and *Somebody's Angel*):

Sarah McLachlan – *Fumbling Towards Ecstasy* (entire CD of same title)
Johnny Cash – *The Beast In Me*
John Mayer – *The Heart Of Life*
Marc Anthony – *When I Dream At Night*
Ingrid Michaelson – *Masochist*
Three Days Grace – *Never Too Late*
Three Days Grace – *Pain*
Drowning Pool – *Let The Bodies Hit the Floor!*
Goo Goo Dolls – *Iris*
John Mayer – *Heartbreak Warfare*
Three Days Grace – *Animal I Have Become*
The Avett Brothers – *If It's the Beaches*
Leonard Cohen – *I'm Your Man*
A Perfect Circle – *Pet*
Pink – *Fuckin' Perfect*
Edwin McCain – *I'll Be*

Prologue

Savi Baker opened her mini laptop to update her résumé and write a cover letter for the "office clerk" position circled in the newspaper classifieds beside her. She'd need to hurry. Marisol's practice for the children's pageant at church would be over in an hour or so.

Her years of college and clinicals were irrelevant now. She just needed to find something fast to pay her student loans and keep up the house and car payments. She and Mari had never lived extravagantly, but losing her job last week—three weeks before Christmas—just added to her financial insecurity.

She'd bought and wrapped some gifts for Mari and tucked them away on the upper shelf in her closet. At least Christmas would have some special moments, but Savi would be lucky to be able to pay for groceries, much less the expensive ingredients needed for the holiday gifts she liked to bake for her friends. They would cut back this year by necessity.

After working so hard to achieve her goal of being a social worker and helping young abuse victims cope more easily than she had following her own years of abuse, the loss of her job hit her harder than ever. Another dream lost.

Don't think about Damián Orlando.

She still didn't know why she'd been fired. Her supervisor had seemed equally confused, so it couldn't have been because her daughter, Marisol, had been sick with the flu a couple of weeks before that. Everyone at the clinic was supportive of her being a working single mother. Her friend Anita, the clinic's receptionist and the only mother figure Savi had known most of her life, had even stayed home with Mari so that Savi had only missed two days of work.

Her supervisor had encouraged Savi to submit an appeal to the state agency responsible for her termination, which she'd done immediately. Was she fired because of the complaint the clinic had received from the mother of one of her new clients? Mrs. Reynolds accused Savi of being indifferent to her daughter's needs, but Savi and her supervisor had explained to the mother that wasn't the case at all. With the highly charged emotions in situations involving domestic and child abuse, all case workers had to remain professional, objective, and somewhat emotionally distanced. This was especially true for Savi. She couldn't let her own demons from the past come to the surface.

In the end, Mrs. Reynolds had hugged her, sobbing. The mother had claimed she understood, and Savi had thought that was the end of it. Maybe not. Had she gone to the licensing agency to complain?

Oh, what difference did the reason make? She'd been fired. It could take months, or even years, to get reinstated; unraveling bureaucracy took time. She didn't have a huge savings—or time. Her immediate concern was finding a way to support her daughter and herself until she got another job in the mental-health field—if that was even possible.

Absorbed in typing, she jumped when the doorbell chimed. She looked at the time on her screen's desktop. Too early for Mari to be dropped off—unless something had happened. Barely able to breathe, Savi nearly ran to the front door and opened it, expecting to see one of the youth leaders from the church group.

Lyle.

She gasped, nearly choking as bile rose in her throat. *Stupid! Why hadn't she glanced through the peephole first?* She tried to reverse the movement by slamming the door in his face, but it stopped abruptly against his Italian leather wingtip. The muscles in her arms quivered as she pushed harder.

"What kind of greeting is that for an old friend, Savannah?"

Enemy. Not a friend. Savi wedged the side of her bare heel against the door to keep him from opening it any farther. Her lungs burned as she tried to fill them with much-needed air. *Dangerous.* He couldn't stay here. He would hurt Mari. She had to get rid of him.

She pulled the door slightly toward her without moving her foot and then tried to slam it with all her strength. He didn't even flinch. "What do you want?"

He smiled at her and relaxed. "Let me inside. We'll talk."

Savi suppressed a shudder. "You're not coming in. Leave before I call the police!"

His eyes narrowed into slits. Fear crawled up Savi's spine unlike anything she'd experienced since she'd escaped this man and her father eight years ago. *Vile man.* Could she fight him off?

"Open this door, you dirty slut, or you and Marisol will regret this pathetic show of bravery."

Marisol. He knew her baby's name. Did he know where Mari was? *Oh, God,* she prayed. *Don't let Mari come home early.* Where was Savi's father? Had he gone after Mari while Lyle was here with her?

"I'm not letting you inside my—"

Without warning, Lyle rammed his body full force into the door, sending the edge of the wood into Savi's cheek. She hurtled backward until she lay sprawled on the floor, looking up at him. His navy-blue dress pants and wingtip shoes made her shudder as a distant memory tried to smother her efforts to regain her breath, but she tamped it back down. The angry man towered over her.

"Ah, just where a slut like you belongs, Savannah—at my feet." He reached for her. "Let me hear you scream, for old-time's sake, you filthy whore."

No! Memories of the night he'd placed her father's brand on her could never be erased, no matter how many times she'd tried. Neither could any of the degrading things Lyle had subjected her to at her father's orders.

She rolled onto all fours and scrambled to get away, sliding on the waxed floor. Lyle's savage kick slammed into her ribs as his wingtip impacted her left side. The air whooshed from her lungs, and she fought to catch her next breath.

"Your father asked me to bring you and your brat to him. But we're going to enjoy a little playtime first. What your father doesn't know…"

Another blow from his shoe struck her side near the same place. Panic set in as her breathing became more labored. Two more kicks followed in rapid succession. *The pain!*

Breathe!

Maman, help me. Give me the strength to fight him off. Help me protect Mari.

Savi pulled herself up using the hallway table and tried to inhale again. She turned to find Lyle smirking at her. *Bastard.* She picked up the wrought-iron candlestick from the table. In one swift motion, she swung it at his head, gouging his forehead. She hoped she'd more than stunned him but didn't wait for him to recover, following through with a knee to his groin. He doubled over and fell to the floor moaning as he held his privates. His blood trickled onto her floor.

Not unconscious yet. Cut off the blood flow to the brain.

She'd learned a number of self-defense techniques from a female Marine veteran in a study group at college. Savi cringed as her finger touched his neck, hating to place her hands anywhere on him, but finally she found the point she sought and pressed—hard. She counted. By thirty seconds, Lyle's body grew even more limp.

Escape! Now!

Running to the kitchen, she grabbed her purse and keys and stumbled out the back door. A black BMW sat parked behind her little blue Nissan. She glanced back at her bungalow. Her home, but no longer her safe place.

No sign of Lyle yet, but he wouldn't be unconscious forever. Breathing had become a struggle, but she refused to escape inside her head to that numb place where she could dull the pain. Mari needed her to stay in the moment.

Mari needed her. Period.

She filled her lungs with as much air as she could stand and held her breath. *Oh dear Lord.* Why couldn't she breathe? She pressed her hand to her chest and tucked her elbow against her left side, near where Lyle had kicked her repeatedly. Was something broken?

How had her father and his partner found her after all these years? She'd changed her name, her looks, *everything,* to keep from being found. No way would she ever let them anywhere near her daughter; they'd never do to Mari any of the things they'd done to her. In some ways, while Lyle had only been her handler, he was more sadistic than her father. Lyle had been the one to place her father's shameful mark on her. He'd enjoyed hearing her scream and often inflicted even more pain than what her father had ordered.

She opened the car door, got behind the steering wheel, and turned the key in the ignition. She couldn't zone out now. She needed to get to San Miguel's... To Mari.

Then what?

The images of Damián in her office comforting Teresa, his sixteen-year-old niece and Savi's former client, and of him later last month standing over the inert body of the girl's rapist father alternated before her eyes.

No. She couldn't get close to him again. He was dangerous in a totally different way from Lyle and her father—but still, oh, so dangerous.

What other option did she have, though? She could protect herself or die trying, but what if something happened to her and they got their evil hands on Mari? She couldn't risk that.

Mari needed Damián.

Chapter One

Damián wasn't home. What now?

Savi knew Damián lived somewhere in Denver, and she'd instinctively headed east after picking up Mari from San Miguel's. By the time Anita returned her call for help, they'd driven across California into Nevada, but she'd ditched the cell phone in Las Vegas to avoid being tracked.

She'd been in Denver a couple of hours with nowhere else to go. No one to turn to.

Please, Damián. Come home soon.

She'd come straight to the Colorado address Anita had retrieved from Teresa's file at the clinic, knowing that the farther away she could take Mari from Lyle and her father, the better their chances would be. Looking into a patient's confidential file was unethical, not to mention illegal. Even though Savi hadn't told Anita about the worst brutalities she'd suffered at their hands, Anita willingly took the risk to try and keep them safe.

Savi hoped Anita wouldn't lose her job. She owed Anita everything after that day so long ago when the older woman had taken a scared and pregnant runaway into her home. Savi didn't want her friend to become more collateral damage in her father's need to control his daughter—and now his granddaughter.

Looking into the backseat, she saw Mari still slept soundly. When Damián hadn't answered his door, she'd taken Mari to get something to eat at a fast-food place down the street and returned to knock at his door again. Still no answer. She'd decided to wait for him in the parking lot. Where else could she go to find him?

After an hour or so, she began to worry that perhaps he'd returned to California for a visit or gone somewhere else for the weekend. Didn't everyone in Colorado ski? What if he didn't come home at all tonight? She couldn't risk getting a motel room and using a credit card. Most decent ones wouldn't take cash without a credit card to back it up. She didn't want Mari to sleep in the cold car or in some "no tell" motel where predators might be a more imminent threat.

What if Damián brought a woman home? Awkward, to say the least. Unfortunately, she and Mari had nowhere else to go. Fear clawed at her, but she pushed it away. She needed to stay strong for Mari.

Off and on for the past hour, she'd run the engine a few minutes to keep the car's temperature comfortable. Mari had fallen asleep soon after dinner. Her beautiful baby had asked a thousand questions on the almost two-day drive here, but she seemed content when Savi told her they were going to visit the nice man they'd met at church after choir practice a while back. Savi couldn't believe Mari even remembered him, but she'd asked immediately, "Damián?"

Please, God, don't let this be an emotional disaster for either of us. Neither could afford to complicate her life with impossible emotional attachments, and anything having to do with a man would be impossible.

So why was she here on Damián's doorstep?

Simply put, there was no one else she could turn to. Everyone in California could be controlled or easily coerced by her father, except for Father Martine and Anita. Her parish priest had already put himself in danger by loaning her cash to help them make their escape. Both had promised not to reveal anything to Lyle if he tracked her to San Miguel's.

The roar of a motorcycle entering the parking lot drew her attention; her mind returned to a time when she'd ridden on the back of a Harley, her chest and thighs pressed against Damián's body while her arms were wrapped tightly around his waist. Her face grew warm.

She watched as the man in the leather pants and the Harley Davidson-emblazoned vest pulled into a numbered spot near the stairway. His lean, muscular body looked lethal. He set the kickstand, turned and removed the key, and swung his leg over the back of the bike. Then he unhooked the chin strap on his helmet.

Damián.

Before he pulled off his helmet, she recognized him. Her heart thudded, surprising her. His queue exposed below the helmet at the nape of his neck tipped her off before he turned sideways to reveal the familiar mustache and goatee. He didn't look in her direction but walked to the stairway. His shoulders slumped a bit as Savi watched him make his way up the steel staircase to the second floor of the old motel building. Was he limping? She hoped he wouldn't be too tired to deal with two unexpected and desperate guests tonight, because she was about to invade his world with a vengeance.

Again.

Damián rescued her once before, and he'd immobilized Teresa's father last month when the bastard had returned to try and hurt the teen a second time. Savi had been making progress as Teresa's therapist. At least until she'd been fired. Teresa was lucky to have a champion like her Uncle Damián. Now Mari and Savi needed him.

Glancing at her sleeping daughter, she decided to just lock her in the car rather than disturb her. Damián's apartment was in a converted motel complex with an exterior entrance. Savi wouldn't go inside or let the car out of her sight. She didn't know why it was important, but she didn't want to drag Mari up there only to be disappointed by him if he turned them away. If that should happen, it would be better to just leave and tell her Damián hadn't come home.

After summoning enough courage to proceed, Savi wrapped her arms around her side and took as deep a breath as possible. She opened the door and got out but shut the door quickly when hit by a blast of frigid wind. She hoped she hadn't let too much of the car's warmth escape. A quick check through the backseat window told her Mari still slept. Savi hoped she'd be able to tuck her into a real bed tonight.

She slipped on a patch of snow as she crossed the parking lot to the stairway, and a stab of pain ripped up her side before fading. These shoes weren't really suitable for winter. The wind out of the mountains cut into her thin jacket, as well. Father Martine had loaded them down with blankets and clothes from the church's clothing bank, but they didn't get weather like this in Solana Beach.

She didn't have money to spare for new clothes, but if they were going to stay here any time at all, she needed to get Mari a warm coat. She'd find a thrift store tomorrow.

As she climbed the stairs, she pulled out a pair of sunglasses. She must look ridiculous wearing them at night, but she didn't want to freak Damián out first thing by letting him see her bruised and swollen eye from Lyle's attack. She couldn't totally hide her cheek, but shades were better than nothing.

Steeling herself, she pressed the doorbell. Savi waited, crossing her arms to help keep warm when a shiver coursed through her. Concerned about Mari, she turned and looked back down at the car parked under a bright street light. Safe.

When the door opened, she was forced to turn toward him. A look of surprise, followed swiftly by concern crossed his face at seeing her.

"Did something happen to Teresa?"

"Teresa? No." Then realization dawned. She held out her hand with the palm facing him to allay his fears. "No! I'm sure she's fine."

Another blast of cold air caused her to wrap her arms tighter around herself.

"Come in." He stood aside and motioned her in.

"No, I can't. I…" Savi looked toward the car, then back at him, not knowing where to start.

"Why are you here? How did you find me?"

She lowered her head, wishing he'd give her more time to collect her thoughts. How did she answer those questions without getting the door slammed in her face? But she needed him, so she might as well be up front. She lifted her gaze to him. "I looked at the next of kin info in Teresa's file." She didn't want to implicate Anita in the breach of confidentiality. "We need your help."

"We?"

She glanced at the car again. His gaze followed. Time for the reveal—and to talk. Savi removed the glasses.

Damián's nostrils flared. While she detected no other sign of his anger, he seemed to be reining in his emotions. She fought the urge to back away. She needed him to help her, terrified or not.

"Who hit you?" He ground out the words as if he wanted to pound something.

"I can't say, but we need a place to hide out for a while, until I can figure out what to do."

"Marisol? Is she okay?"

Savi nodded. "She's asleep in the car. We drove day and night. I was afraid to fly or stay in motels. I didn't want to leave a trail."

He scanned the parking lot. "Look, that car's going to get cold PDQ. Why don't you get Marisol and come inside to warm up?"

She held her arm to her side, hating to admit weakness. "I can't lift her."

His gaze raked over her body, assessing her. "Give me your keys. I'll get her."

She hesitated a moment. *You have to trust him. You can't do this alone.* Then another blast of cold air hit her in the face and took her breath away. She looked down at the parking lot and pulled the keys out of her jacket pocket. "Follow me."

"No. You don't need to be going up and down those stairs. You look like you're about to keel over. Just tell me which car."

"The light blue Nissan." She pointed to her sedan parked under the light.

"Go sit down. I'll be right back."

Like hell. She watched him walk back down the stairs, holding onto the rail, and continue to walk across the lot to the car. Using the remote, he unlocked the car. The headlights flashed again as he opened the back door. Gently he lifted her baby into his arms and made his way back up the stairs carefully, one hand on Mari, draped over his shoulder, and one on the railing. Seeing him being so careful with her daughter made her think she'd made the right decision to come here.

At the top of the stairs, he seemed both surprised and annoyed to find Savi waiting for him, rather than going inside as he'd asked her. No, he'd definitely ordered her. She needed to be sure Mari was safe but didn't take orders from any man anymore.

Savi fell into step beside him and pushed the door wide open for them. Once inside, she locked it.

He turned to whisper to her, "Help me get her into bed. Then we'll talk." Damián led the way across the living room and stood beside what must be the bedroom door, which Savi opened for him. A blast of cold air hit them. Was there any heat in there? The living room had seemed wonderfully warm after being outside, but this room was freezing.

The bed was made, so Savi pulled down the vintage, apparently handmade Mexican-Indian designed comforter and watched as he laid Mari's head so carefully on the pillow. Then he lifted her legs onto the bed. When he reached to remove her shoes, Savi grabbed his hands, afraid he was going to undress her.

"No! I'll do that."

Holding up his hands, he backed off. While she unlaced the sneakers, Damián walked over to the wall near the doorway and adjusted the thermostat. She decided to leave Mari's jacket on for added warmth.

He whispered, "It'll warm up in here in no time."

Savi pulled the comforter and sheet over her baby and bent down to kiss her.

Sleep well, love. You're safe—for now.

Savi stood and turned, wincing as her chest muscles constricted. She held her hand to her left side again before noticing she'd attracted unwanted attention from Damián. She forced her hand back down. He motioned for her to lead the way into the living room.

When he started to close the door, she placed her hand over his. "No! Mari might wake up and be frightened to find herself in a strange bed."

He nodded and turned to proceed into the living room. "Can I get you a Coke, beer, tea, or something?"

She remembered a similar offer at Teresa's house in Solana Beach. "No Kool-Aid?" She smiled, then caught herself. What had come over her? This was no time for teasing.

"Sorry. When the munchkins aren't around, I prefer beer." He grinned.

"A Coke sounds good." She needed to keep her wits about her.

He went to the fridge and pulled out a can of Coke. "Glass and ice?"

"No. The can's fine."

He came back into the living room, popped the top, and handed it to her. "Let me take your jacket."

"No, I'm fine. I'll just keep it on."

His dubious expression told her he didn't buy her assurance, but he motioned for her to have a seat on the sofa. He sat down at the other end and reached over to pick up an open bottle of Dos Equis. The domestic scene was so normal, as if they hung out here every night.

His gaze targeted her. "Who hit you?"

Well, the time for polite pleasantries was over. Savi wasn't sure where to start. How much should she tell him? Stalling, she lifted the soda to her lips and tipped her head back, drinking long and slow. When she lowered the can again, she stared at it a moment, tracing a fingernail around the rim.

"Was it your husband?"

She looked up, frowning. Her *what?* She shook her head. "I'm not married." *What had made him think otherwise?* Then he looked at her left hand, and she remembered the wedding band she always wore in public to ward off unwanted male advances. He'd seen it on her at the clinic, but she never wore it at home and hadn't picked it up to bring with her when she ran. Of course, he knew she had Marisol. He'd drawn a logical conclusion.

He met her gaze again. "I have a friend who was a corpsman—a medic—in Iraq. Will you let him check out your injuries?"

No way. She squared her shoulders and sat up a little straighter, willing herself to show no sign of discomfort or difficulty breathing deeply. "What injuries?"

"Well, there's the black eye, swelling, bruising on your face. You've also been favoring your left side. Did he hit you there, too?"

She sagged against the sofa. "It's nothing."

"Let my friend be the judge of that."

She hadn't come here seeking medical help. She needed protection for her daughter. "I'm not leaving Mari."

"Who said anything about leaving? He'll come over here if I ask him."

"No. The fewer people who know I'm here, the better."

"Who are you running from, Savannah?"

A flash of anger sparked through her at his use of that name. "I told you not to call me that."

He grinned but just diverted the inquisition in a new direction. "I liked your hair better blonde. Why did you change it?"

She hadn't been a blonde in seven years. "None of your business."

He leaned toward her. Savi tried not to let him intimidate her, but he did. His nose had been broken. She remembered noticing that all those years ago and still wondered if it had happened in a fight. The man had a lethal aura about him.

"Hey, *chica*, you just showed up on my doorstep out of nowhere, beaten up and on the run. *You're* the one who asked *me* for help, so don't go getting all defensive. I'm just trying to figure out what the hell's going on."

When she didn't respond, he sat back and drained his beer, then lowered the empty bottle to nestle in his crotch. She averted her attention from that part of his anatomy and reached up to twirl a strand of her hair. Her physical discomfort from the stitch in her side equaled the emotional discomfort she felt. She hadn't been alone in a room with a man in almost forever.

"I felt safer changing my appearance."

"Marisol's father?"

Her hand froze on the curl as her heart thudded, robbing her of even more oxygen. Did he know? She looked up at him again, studying his face for some time. "What about him?"

"Is he the one who roughed you up and sent you running?"

He didn't know. She relaxed into the sofa and took another swig of the soda, buying time as she tried to will her heartbeat to slow down. "No. He's been out of my...out of the picture from day one." She looked away. She'd tried to find Damián when she'd gotten strong enough to function after Mari's birth, but she'd failed. Then she'd decided they were better off without a man to complicate things.

"Let me see where you're hurt."

She refused to make eye contact. "No. I'm fine."

"Bullshit, *chica*." His anger caused her to look up at him again, and he held her gaze. "Your choice—me or my friend? Which will it be?"

Anger ripped through her again. She hadn't come all this way to have him expose her to her father's hound dogs by leaving a paper trail, which is what would happen if he involved medical personnel. She glared at him for a moment, but he refused to back down. Leaning forward, she winced at the pain and tried to hide her shortness of breath. Her reaction times were delayed from the lack of sleep. She tried to mask her features as she set the soda can on top of a biker magazine on the coffee table.

She sat back against the sofa, putting more space between them. "It's nothing. Really. Just a bruise."

"I'll be the judge of that. I have some...expertise with bruising. Remove your jacket."

She continued to wage a silent battle of wills with him. However, after a few moments of determined silence, she decided they needed to get beyond this or she'd never get him to help. Savi raised a shaking hand to loosen the belt of her jacket, trying to control the trembling as she reached up to undo the top button.

Savi remembered those first months after she'd escaped her father's house, when she'd still fantasized about Damián finding her. Later, before she'd given up and shut down emotionally, she'd had fantasies about him being a daddy to Mari. Still, she'd always hoped he would try to find her. He'd broken her heart by not doing so.

Don't be ridiculous, Savi. He wouldn't have come looking for you. He'd have looked for Savannah Gentry; she was dead.

"I haven't ever hurt you, Savannah. Have I?"

Why did he insist on calling her that?

Choosing not to answer the question, she finished unbuttoning the jacket and peeled it off. She leaned against the back of the sofa and pulled the tail of her shirt loose from her slacks. His gaze went to her abdomen and she saw a flash of rage cross his face as his mouth tightened.

"Lie down."

His words sounded angry, and fear clawed at her throat again. She wouldn't let herself be placed in such a vulnerable position with him. "No." She took a deep breath and stood up, wincing as the movement robbed her of breath. "I'd rather stand."

He stood as well and leaned closer, reaching out his hand. She gasped even before he touched her. When he gingerly touched the bruised area on her left ribcage, below her breast, she held her breath and tried not to move. After a moment, he pulled away.

"I need to ask Doc what to do."

Didn't doctors here have to make reports of violent acts to the authorities? She couldn't risk that. But he didn't wait for her to express an opinion as he pulled out his phone and pressed a button. After a moment, someone answered.

"Sorry to wake you, man, but I need your help." He paused and glanced at Savi. "A friend of mine has been in…some kind of fight, and she has some bruising over her ribs." He seemed exasperated by the other person's response. "Look, this is serious. It's not from impact play."

How could violent impacts against someone's body be considered play?

"She's been punched by a fist, it looks like. Under her breast. Where the ribs are. The bruises are still dark in color. Happened at least two days ago." He looked to her for confirmation, and she nodded and held up two fingers. She wondered how someone who wasn't in the medical field became such an expert on bruising.

He listened a moment, then shook his head. "Can't do that."

Do what?

"What's plan B? What can I do?" Once more, he listened. A garbled voice came through the phone, but Savi couldn't make out the words. After a long while, he said "Hold on" and lowered the phone to the coffee table. Damián looked at her. "Take some deep breaths. Really fill your lungs."

Lost in his gaze, she did as he told her immediately. She caught her breath and winced again. The pain brought her back to the moment. She'd forgotten to be careful how she breathed. He picked up the phone again and said, "Might be a problem with her breathing, Doc."

Refusing to appear injured, Savi stood taller. "No, there isn't. I'm fine."

Damián glared at her until the voice came through the phone again.

"Shoot." He listened to the doctor's instructions. "I didn't take anatomy, Doc."

What had he asked? Damián's gaze lowered to her breasts and she grew uncomfortable. *Don't look at me like I'm a dirty slut.* She'd endured the unwanted stares and touches of more men than she could count during the year before she'd escaped her father's house.

"Be right back." Damián laid the phone on the coffee table again and moved closer to Savi. She fought the impulse to turn and run. "I need to check for a broken rib. Just try and relax."

No way. This time, she did take a step back.

"Hold still, *querida*." He maintained eye contact with her, but rather than calm her, she was overwhelmed with the need to escape, to go to her safe place.

Savannah ran along the beach, ignoring the broken shells that cut into the bare soles of her feet. Where were her flip-flops?

The cave. She'd left them at the cave. She needed to get back there. After climbing gingerly over the sharp rocks, she walked into the opening of the cave, then halted. Instead of her mother, she found Damián leaning against the wall of the cave.

No! Where was Maman?

Then she remembered how safe she'd felt with him here once upon a time. A very long time ago. She hadn't felt that kind of safety since before her mother had run away.

"Savi? Look at me."

She blinked and found herself transported instantly back into Damián's living room. She stared at him.

"Where'd you go?"

My cave. No! He couldn't know about that. "Go? I didn't go anywhere. Just check for the broken rib and get it over with."

Damián placed his left hand in the middle of her back, and she moved away.

"Wait! I'm not ready yet."

"You don't have to get ready for anything. Just look at me, *querida*."

No! Not yet! She tried to convey her fear with her eyes, but he didn't seem to notice.

"Take a deep breath, and let it out slowly."

She couldn't do this. Her respirations became shallow, rapid. She tried to force herself to release the tension in her shoulders and neck. *I can't do this!*

"That's it."

His words had a slight calming effect on her until he placed his right hand against her chest. Her breathing became even more shallow; her heart beat wildly. She drew another breath, sharper this time.

"Just relax. I'm going to press here, but tell me if it starts to hurt."

He applied what felt like an incredible amount of pressure on her chest wall, and she cried out in pain. She'd always been able to block out pain. Why hadn't she been able to stay in her cave? He abruptly let go of her and gave her a look as if she'd just landed on earth from outer space. He reached for the cell phone and picked it up.

"Doc? You still there?"

His tone conveyed he wasn't pleased with her. What had she done wrong? She'd tried not to scream in pain.

Only dirty sluts scream, Savannah.

She should have been able to take the pain without screaming. She'd endured so much worse at the hands of Lyle and the men in the penthouse. She'd trained herself not to scream until the pain was too unbearable to do otherwise. But she hadn't had to practice that skill in a very long time. Damián wouldn't want to help her if…*if he knew what I was. Control yourself, Savan…Savi. He doesn't know.*

Damián sighed. "We have a couple problems with that. One is that we need a babysitter."

Wait! What was he talking about? No one was separating her from Mari. Savi held up her hand. "No! I'm not going anywhere, and even if I did, I'm not leaving Mari with strangers."

He stared at her but spoke into the phone. "Doc, do you have any friends who can provide a medical assessment without leaving a paper trail?" Doc. She realized this was the medic friend. Not a real doctor at all.

Damián paused to listen, then said, "I haven't a fucking clue, but it's the only way I'm going to get her to cooperate."

I'll cooperate, as long as you don't take Mari away from me.

"No, nothing like that. Just call me back PDQ." He snapped the phone shut and just stared at her until her skin burned under the intensity of his gaze. "He's going to try and find someone to take a look at that rib. Do you want to lie down with Mari and rest a little?"

"No. I can't breathe when I lie down. I'm fine."

"You're *not* fucking fine, Savi."

She cringed and backed away.

"Who are you running from? Who did this to you?"

Without going into details Damián didn't need to know, she confessed, "My father." Bile rose in her throat at the mere mention of him, and she held her hand over her stomach to try and keep the nausea at bay.

"What?"

Savi tried to find the words to explain the unexplainable. She'd spent the last two days trying to make sense out of why her father had wanted her and Mari, but all she'd been able to come up with was that he'd wanted to hurt Mari the way he'd hurt Savannah. She wouldn't let him see her daughter, much less touch her. Ever.

They'd gotten all the way through Utah before she figured out how he'd found her. "He tried to take Mari from me. I guess he saw me on the news footage from Julio's arrest and tracked me down." Damián seemed puzzled. "I can't let him anywhere near her. That's why I came to you." She paused, trying to gauge how much she needed to say to enlist his help. "The way I saw you taking care of Teresa in my office. The way you were ready to kill her father, if necessary… We need that kind of protection right now. Will you help us?"

Savi watched and waited. Her side had been throbbing since he'd pressed on her sternum. Had she injured a rib? Why hadn't she zoned out? But hadn't she? A brief glimpse of herself in the cave at Laguna Beach flashed through her mind. In the past, Maman had always waited for her there. This time, she hadn't found Maman at all. She'd found Damián.

To say that had been disconcerting would be an understatement. How could she run from his touch physically and wind up running to him in her mind? Her safe place no longer felt safe. But he wouldn't hurt her. Would he? She had to trust him so he could protect her and Mari. That's what had sent her halfway across the country to find him, wasn't it?

"Why didn't you call the police?"

"He's friends with the police chief." Her father always made it a point to have something to hold over key people in power, including judges, several state legislators, and even a congressman. Her body had been offered to service many of them in the past. Apparently, he'd been exerting his control over her for weeks, beginning at her workplace.

Fired.

Until yesterday, she hadn't even put two and two together to figure out her father'd had a hand in her being fired. Her foremost thought had been to escape from Lyle. All her years of study and training, of giving her all for the children in her care to become the clinic's top victim specialist in such a short time were down the drain. Once again, her father had shifted her world on its axis.

She squeezed her eyes shut and lowered her head, worrying about the upheaval her sudden disappearance must have caused her young, vulnerable clients. Just thinking about the feelings of abandonment they must be experiencing...

"You're still in pain."

She opened her eyes and stared at him, realizing her face must have projected her pain. *Yes, but not the physical kind.*

"I'm fine."

A flash of anger in his eyes told her he wasn't buying her verbal assurances. Had she done the right thing coming here? Damián wouldn't be as easy to manipulate as the other men she'd had to deal with. Well, except for Father Martine, the only man she'd ever trusted.

How had Damián gotten her to reveal in a few minutes more than she'd intended to tell him?

So dangerous. But where else could she turn? Savi would do whatever it took to protect her daughter from her father and Lyle's sadistic ways. The other night, however, as she lay on the floor at Lyle's feet, she'd realized how difficult it would be to protect her little girl. Admitting failure or weakness, much less need, to someone else—especially a man—was incredibly difficult. She'd sworn she'd never be vulnerable to a man again. Yet she couldn't risk going it alone this time. The stakes were too high, and her father was much too powerful.

Damián's cell phone rang. "Yeah, Doc?" Pause. "You're sure?" Pause. "Appreciate it. Meet you there."

Savi tried to square her shoulders and stand straighter, but again, her breath was cut off. *Do not let him detect any weakness.* "I said I'm not going anywhere without Mari."

"Not a problem. My friend is meeting us at the clinic. We'll bring Marisol with us."

"She needs her sleep."

"She can sleep in the car. You need medical attention. Now. I'll drive your car. When we get to the clinic, I'll watch Marisol while the doctor checks you out."

No! She was losing control. Panic clawed at her chest, and sweat broke out on her upper lip. She cleared her throat. "Look, I said I'm fine. Just some bruises. I'll be even better after some sleep."

"You said you couldn't lie down. How do you plan to rest?"

Oh, God. What had ever possessed her to come here? She needed to leave, but she couldn't carry Mari down those stairs. Her gaze strayed to the open bedroom doorway where she saw her daughter curled on her side, sleeping peacefully. How could their lives have become so screwed up in such a short time? Everything had been going perfectly until…

Damián. He'd come back into Savi's life because of his niece's rape five weeks ago. Then she'd gotten called into the aftermath of the hostage situation at his sister's house when Teresa's father had returned, drunk and up to no good. If only Teresa hadn't called Savi to her house that afternoon to help. No, if only the news crews hadn't happened by and broadcast the incident.

It wasn't the girl's fault. She was another victim of a father's sick and twisted abuse. Who better to help Damián's niece deal with her father's assault than Savi, who knew all too well a father's depravity?

"Let's get your coat buttoned up…" When Damián's hands reached for her, she stepped back, her legs pressing against the sofa and nearly toppling her backward.

"No! I can do it myself." She scrambled with shaking fingers to close her coat and pulled the belt tight, wincing as she cut off her breath but hoping he wouldn't touch her again.

No escape. Trapped.

Damián frowned at her. "I'll get Marisol."

Savi followed him back into the bedroom, afraid to let him out of her sight, especially anywhere near Mari.

He turned toward her, not seeming at all surprised she was on his heels. "I'll just wrap her up in this blanket." He turned the Mexican blanket down first, then the sheet, uncovering Mari. Her little girl stirred, scrunching her nose and brows at the intrusion into her snug cocoon.

"It's okay, *querida*. We're going to take a little ride."

Mari opened her big brown eyes, so much like her father's, and looked up at him. "I remember you."

"You do?" Damián grinned, seeming pleased to know he had a lasting effect on her daughter. Did he know? "I remember you, too, *mi muñequita*."

Mari smiled and nodded at being called his little doll. Content that all was right with her world, she promptly fell back to sleep. Savi wished she could be that trusting, that innocent.

Never again—if she had ever been.

Damián picked Mari up and laid her down in the middle of the blanket; he wrapped it snugly around her. He lifted her into his arms with such gentleness, he made Savi's chest ache with a new and unfamiliar pressure. Letting Mari's little head rest on his shoulder, he started for the doorway. Savi blinked rapidly, then led the way. The sooner she could appease Damián and get her ribs checked out, the sooner she could…could what? She had nowhere else to go.

At the front door to his apartment, she looked out the peep hole, but she didn't see anyone near the door. After releasing the deadbolt, she held the door open for him, then reached into her pocket for her car keys.

She turned back toward Damián. "Wait! I need to find my keys."

"They're in my pocket."

"Oh." *Crap*. He hadn't given them back to her from when he went down earlier to get Mari, who was now in his arms. How was she supposed to…?

"Just close the door 'til it clicks. It will lock automatically." Damián walked through the doorway, and she did as he'd instructed. Following him toward the stairs, she watched him limp slightly.

What was wrong with his leg? Concerned he might not be able to support Mari's weight, she hurried to catch up. "Are you sure you can carry her down the stairs?"

He scowled at her. "What makes you think I can't?"

"You're limping." His fierce glare told her to back off, but she decided to get in front of them; if he lost his balance, she could break their fall. Thankfully, they made it down the stairs and to the car without incident, where Savi had to face facts. She needed to retrieve the keys. From his pocket. *Oh dear Lord.*

"Left-hand pocket."

Like hell. "Let me take Mari so you can open the car."

He ground out the words, "Reach in my pocket and get out the keys, Savan…Savi."

Still, Savi hesitated a moment longer, until he glared at her again. Did he have any other expression? Yes. He smiled and grinned when he looked at Mari. The glares he saved for Savi.

She looked down at the pocket. Leather pants. She supposed he'd worn leather because of his Harley, but she wished he'd changed into jeans or something else when he'd gotten home. Not that she'd given him time to change before she'd shown up on his doorstep.

"Get. The keys. Out of. My pants. Now."

How was she ever supposed to get them out without touching him more intimately than she'd touched any man since, well, since Damián all those years ago? Savi's hands shook as she placed one at the opening of the pocket of his lethal-looking, hip-hugging pants and pried it open. She could barely wedge the fingers of her other hand inside. The warm leather felt good against her cold fingers. Heat spread up her arms and into her face. Okay, the heat in her face was from a separate, mysterious source. She did not blush and did not let a man affect her this way. Ever.

What was happening to her?

Not wanting to prolong the contact any longer, she dug into his pocket almost ferociously and found the key fob. Thank God. She yanked on it until the key got hung up. *Shit.*

"Use both hands." Damián just grinned. *Damn him.* The bastard was enjoying her obvious discomfort. Heat spread to the pit of her stomach. She decided she preferred his glare to his grin.

Using her other hand, she opened the pocket wider and, with a slight tug, the keys popped out at last. She retreated several steps and took a few rapid, shallow breaths, trying to regain her equilibrium. Realizing she was just working herself up more, she remembered the Lamaze breathing techniques Anita had coached her on before Mari's birth and tried to control her response with slow, even breaths.

Better.

She clicked the remote to unlock the car doors and opened the back door, watching Damián sit Mari in the back seat. He looked back at Savi. "I need you to buckle her in while I hold her up."

Why was he forcing so much close contact? She'd managed to buckle Mari in without another set of hands. Of course, Mari had been awake those times. With great reluctance, Savi moved forward, but when her lower body brushed against his, she halted suddenly and took several rapid breaths.

I can't do this. Abruptly, Savi backed away and walked around the trunk of the car on shaky legs. Opening the other back door, she reached across the seat, ignoring the pain in her side and Damián's glare. She stretched the seatbelt over Mari's blanketed shoulder and waist, fumbling around until she found the buckle. It clicked into place, and Savi breathed a deep sigh of relief. Mission accomplished, minimal damage.

She looked up as Damián began to pull himself away from her daughter, and she was horrified when Mari held him tighter. "Don't go, Daddy."

Savi's heart thudded. Mari couldn't know. Why would she call him such a thing? *Because she's always fantasized about having a real daddy.* Apparently, Damián filled the bill for her. More likely, in Mari's deep sleep, she must be dreaming.

Savi ventured a nervous glance at Damián. His gaze focused on Marisol as he scrutinized her face. He closed his eyes for a moment, then turned to meet Savi's gaze with a question—no, an accusation—she didn't want to deal with at the moment. The grim resolve on his face revealed anger and something she couldn't name.

He knows.

Of course, she'd planned to tell him. Soon. But this wasn't the time or place. She needed to divert his attention. Reaching down to her side, Savi winced. Damián's face showed concern as his focus returned to why they were out here in the first place. He gently unlocked Mari's hands from around his neck. *Good.*

"Don't worry, *querida*," he whispered to Mari. "Daddy's not going anywhere." He cast a sharp look at Savi, as if to make sure she was aware he intended to keep his promise to his daughter.

Oh dear Lord. Why was he reinforcing her daughter's Daddy fantasy?

Only Damián wasn't Mari's fantasy Daddy at all.

Savi's heartbeat came to a halt for a second before slamming against her ribcage. She didn't need this complication. When he hadn't made the connection that he might be Mari's father at San Miguel's, she'd just assumed he never would figure it out. If Damián knew, would he try to take Mari away from her? Maybe telling him wasn't a good idea after all.

Unable to take his scrutiny any longer—his face showing a mixture of anger and pain that left her unsettled—she backed out of the car. By the time she reached for the driver's door, Damián's warm hand pulled hers away from the frozen handle. How had he come around the car so quickly?

He took her by the elbow, carefully but with a firm hand, and guided her to the passenger side. "I'm driving."

"But I drove all the way from the West Coast."

"Exactly. You don't need to be driving any farther until we get those ribs looked at."

No one had taken care of Savi since she'd moved out of Anita's house after graduating from college. That was the year she'd landed her first job at a mental-health clinic in San Diego. Even when Anita had tried to help Savi find a position at the clinic where she worked, Savi had refused the job until it was time for Mari to start school. She'd wanted her daughter to go to school in Solana Beach, rather than San Diego.

Savi had chosen independence, because she wanted to support herself and Mari. She didn't want to be a burden anymore. She took pride in not needing anyone—most especially a man.

What alternative did she have but to seek this man's assistance now? Damián held the passenger door open and waited for her to get inside. Her lungs constricted when she reached for the shoulder strap, but Damián blocked her hand and took the seatbelt, pulling it across her chest. His forearm brushed against her breast as he buckled her in like a child. She tried to press her back farther into the seat cushion to avoid the intimate contact.

Damián closed her door and was soon behind the wheel. Silence ensued as he drove across town, and Savi found herself consumed by memories of the decision that had started her on the long, twisted road that eventually led her back to Damián.

Chapter Two

*L*yle and her father would be at the hotel's party all evening. Finally, her first opportunity to escape since she'd arrived at the decision to run away two weeks ago.

She didn't have much time. The last thing she wanted was for them to find her walking along the road from Rancho Santa Fe to Solana Beach.

She'd managed to gather a few clothes and toiletries into a backpack, but she wanted very few reminders of her life in this exclusive community. When she walked out of her Father's gate this time, it would be like walking through the Pearly Gates into Heaven. She crept into Father's office to delete the video of her last client session in her father's penthouse suite at his hotel—the scene from which the bus-boy, Damián, had rescued her. He'd already lost his job most likely, but she needed to prevent her father from blackmailing the young man. Damián didn't need to be threatened with jail time for doing the right thing. Father was powerful enough to trump up charges against him, though.

Her stomach clenched as she approached the desk where so many of her punishment sessions had been carried out in recent years. Don't think about that time. That's in the past. Never again.

What if she ever needed evidence of what her father was doing? Rather than delete the video, she decided to remove the entire hard drive and went to work with a screwdriver. If her father had known that the computer specialist he'd hired to teach Savannah how to manage his second set of books actually had taught her more than how to create a spreadsheet, he'd be livid. Father was so sure Savannah would obey him always that he didn't even bother to put a password on his personal computer. She just hoped there weren't any other copies around of the video with Damián, but as far as she knew, her father didn't have the penthouse wired to the hotel's surveillance cameras, only to the secure Web feed linked to this computer.

Somehow her father had kept this sick-and-twisted part of his life secret from his hotel managers and staff—at least until Damián happened upon her that day almost three months ago, when she was being tortured in the penthouse.

After stowing the hard drive in her backpack, she started toward the massive front door. The fanlight cast prisms of light across the foyer. As a little girl, she'd loved waiting for the rainbows to appear each evening.

No time to get fanciful today. She had four or five miles to walk to reach her sanctuary. At least it all would be downhill. Still, she'd packed lightly. Carrying anything heavier than a backpack would be a strain and would slow her down. She'd lost a lot of weight in recent weeks because of her queasiness, weight she couldn't afford to lose. Ever since that morning just over two weeks ago, when she'd realized she was pregnant and made her decision to leave, the nausea had only grown worse. Part of it was worry about being able to escape to safety. She had to protect this baby from her father.

Damián's baby. She'd try to find him, once she'd reached safety. Maybe he could help her keep the baby. Savannah knew she couldn't do it alone, but she'd already grown attached to the tiny being growing inside her, even in this short time. She'd never be able to give her child up for adoption…or worse. Savi shuddered as she closed the door behind her, wondering what her father would have done if he'd discovered her pregnancy.

The evening air was cool for Southern California, but her quivering was more because of the monumental step she was taking than from the cold.

Escape.

If her father or Lyle caught her…she didn't want to think about how hard they would punish her.

"Oh, please, let this work." Maman would have prayed to God, but Savannah had stopped believing in God a long time ago. Yet when she thought about where to run to, she'd remembered a place her mother had taken her to as a young child. A holy place. She hoped it also would be a safe place for her and her baby. That's what their priest had promised in that sermon all those years ago.

Savi walked down the flagstone steps, her legs feeling like wet noodles. The patch of rubber Damián's Harley had burned on the driveway in late September had not yet faded, despite Father's attempts to have Savannah scrub it off. She hadn't tried all that hard, and she smiled seeing it there, feeling as if Damián was here to give her a huge dose of much-needed courage. Her father had been livid about the mark he'd left in the driveway. Apparently Damián had been more than a little pissed off at her father after dropping her off that night.

She took a deep breath. Her chest ached as she remembered how painful it had been to hear him ride away from her. Later that September night, she hadn't been able to go through with her suicide plan, hoping Damián would come and rescue her. But he'd never returned. Would she ever be able to find him again?

As she made her way down the drive and onto the roadway, she noticed traffic was heavier than usual. With no sidewalks, she constantly stepped onto and off of the curb. She hoped no one recognized her who would report her to her father, but few of their neighbors even knew she existed. He'd kept her tucked away with very little social contact for fear she might reveal his sick lifestyle. Now she would remain hidden by choice. She pulled her ball cap farther down to shield her face as much as possible while trying not to impede her vision enough to cause a misstep.

She just couldn't chance leaving any later this evening, as much as she'd like to have had darkness on her side. Her father's party probably wouldn't last much longer. Most evenings, he was home by eight. Her punishment sessions for whatever grievances she had incurred during the day always happened at night. Thank God he and Lyle hadn't done more than paddle or cane her lately.

Savi held her hand over her abdomen. If anything had happened to the baby because she'd been too afraid to leave sooner…

Darkness had fallen by the time she reached the Hispanic area known as Eden Gardens. She'd been fighting cramps in her left calf for the last mile and looked forward to finding a place to sit or lie down. The working-class neighborhood glowed with luminaries in waxed bags along the walkways; strings of white twinkle lights adorned many of the houses and shrubbery. Christmas. She hadn't kept track of the days very well—one day was no different from another. It must be close to Christmas. Her own house hadn't been decorated for the holidays since Maman left. Savannah hadn't minded. She didn't want to remember those happier times.

Savi's chest ached at how much she missed her mother, even knowing the woman had abandoned her. Her father said she hadn't wanted the responsibility of raising a child any longer. Tears pricked the backs of her eyelids. Her hand touched her abdomen. How could a mother abandon her child?

A few more blocks and the lights of the church beckoned her forward. She had nowhere else to go. Would the doors be unlocked this late at night? Would a dirty slut like her be permitted to come inside and seek refuge until she could get a job and support herself? As she neared the building, she remembered holding her mother's hand as they walked up these steps together that Christmas Eve when she was seven.

"Oh, Maman, why did you leave me with him?"

No. He's out of my life now. I don't need to think about him ever again.

Opening the tall, heavy, oak door, she stepped inside the vestibule. Poinsettias had been placed on mission-style tables at either end of the entryway. She stepped farther inside, blessing herself with holy water, as Maman had taught her to do before stepping into a Catholic church. It had seemed so much bigger when she was here the last time. Perspective. She'd changed in many ways, not the least of which was her increased height.

A statue of Mary, the Madonna, captured her attention. Savi walked toward it as if pulled by hidden strings. Looking up at the serene, smiling face of the teenaged mother, holding her chubby baby in her arms, more tears burned Savi's eyes. How would she be able to care for her own baby? She had nothing, and no one to help her. Would she be forced to give her baby to someone who could take better care of him or her?

No! She needed this baby. It was her lifeline, the only person she could count on to love her. That might not be a good reason to choose to keep the baby, but it was important to her. The baby had saved her life already, just as its father had done earlier. They had helped her maintain a tenuous hold on her sanity. She'd find a way to keep her child safe and to care for him or her when the time came.

Savi looked around more closely. Red and white poinsettias adorned the building, including those placed on either side of the white marble altar at the front of the church. Just the way she remembered it with Maman.

Her eyelids began to droop. So sleepy. She turned around and looked up, seeing a pipe organ in the loft at the back. Maybe she could go up there and sleep for a while without being discovered. She wasn't quite sure yet what she would do next. But with her brain so fuzzy, she wouldn't be able to make any big decisions for a while.

If ever. She hadn't been permitted to make decisions about anything for so long. Not about what to eat, what to wear, what to read, what to do. Savi began shaking. Suddenly being expected to make all of the decisions about her life scared the living hell out of her.

First decision—she needed to sleep a while. She'd figure out what to do about all the other things she'd need to decide later, like how to regain her power.

But how could she regain something she'd never possessed in the first place?

* * *

Que idiota soy.

A real fucking moron. Why hadn't he realized it sooner? Marisol looked just like Teresa. He'd noticed it before and still hadn't put it together. But at San Miguel's, Marisol had said she was in the third grade. Knowing his daughter would only have been seven, so naturally he'd assumed Savi must have been pregnant when he met her or already had a baby daughter at home. Hell, he knew next to nothing about her then—or now, for that matter.

Marisol must have started school earlier than most kids. Or skipped a grade. She was certainly smart enough.

So why hadn't Savi told him?

Mierda. She'd even named their daughter for the memory of the beach where she'd been conceived. Sea and sun. How better to describe Thousand

Steps Beach and their perfect day there?

Unfortunately, this wasn't the time or place to discuss it, but he would get the answers he wanted—soon.

As he drove through the downtown Denver area to the clinic Marc had referred them to, Savi remained quiet, looking out the passenger-side window. He hoped Marc's doctor friend wouldn't discover any serious injuries. He gripped the steering wheel as rage seethed to the surface. How could anyone hurt a vulnerable woman like that?

His woman.

Well, not anymore. Hell, not ever, if he wanted to be honest. Only in his dreams. They'd only been together one day. Best day of his fucking life. A day he could never have again. Not the way he was now. He'd only hurt her, and he wouldn't hurt Savannah—*Savi* now—for anything. She'd been through enough already.

Less than ten minutes later, he pulled into the parking lot. Lights were on in the front of Doctor Robert McKenzie's clinic. Marc's red Porsche 911 Carrera was parked beside a Ford Focus station wagon. Savi was out of the car before he could make it around to the passenger door, so Damián focused his attention on getting the blanket-wrapped Marisol out of her seatbelt. Awake now, she wriggled her hands free, reached up, and placed her tiny arms around his neck, tugging at his heart as no one ever had before—not even Teresa or José.

Could this little doll really be of his blood?

How could he process that kind of intel? Better to wait until he and Savi had a chance to talk. Alone. Damián lifted Marisol, blanket and all, out of the car, ignoring the pain in his stump. He kicked the door closed and followed behind Savi, noticing her slim legs encased in the skin-tight jeans. Hard to stay angry when just looking at her made him want to jump her bones. Again.

At the door, he met Savi's gaze. The hitch in her breath as she pulled the heavy door open wrenched his gut and wiped away all carnal thoughts. He needed to get Savi checked out—fast. They'd discuss Marisol's parentage later.

Inside the waiting room, the inner door to the exam rooms swung open, and Marc stood there in pale green scrubs. Damián did a double take at the get-up.

Marc grinned. "I'm assisting tonight."

Apparently, his buddy loved the idea of being in corpsman mode again.

He wondered why Marc hadn't pursued a career in medicine or healthcare when he'd gotten back from Iraq, rather than going into an outdoor-adventure and outfitter business. Then again, Marc volunteered in search and rescue, which probably enabled him to make use of his corpsman skills, too.

Marc looked from Damián to Marisol's face, then back at Damián. He quirked an eyebrow, then grinned. *Mierda.* His buddy was drawing conclusions Damián wasn't ready to acknowledge yet. Hell, he didn't even know for sure himself.

Yes, you do.

Yeah. He did. But he wasn't going to discuss it with Marc before he talked to Savi. He turned to find she had halted in the doorway and was looking warily at Marc. Damián adjusted his bundle, which wasn't nearly as heavy now that she was awake. Her tiny arms and hands held onto his neck as if she didn't want to let him go.

He just wished her mama would trust him like that again someday. Memories of Savi's body plastered against his back as they rode up the Pacific Coast Highway, and those of him carrying her to the beach cave, flooded his mind. Just thinking about her lying on the…

Focus, man.

"Savi, this is the friend I told you about. Marc D'Alessio, meet Savi Baker. She's from my neighborhood back in California." Marc walked toward Savi and held out his hand. She paused only a few seconds before reaching out to take his briefly. Quickly, she pulled back.

"Pleased to meet you, Savi. Looks like you've been in a bit of a scuffle." A shadow passed over Marc's face. Damián figured Marc was probably thinking about when Angelina had been attacked by some asshole who fancied himself a Dom. Abuser, more like it.

Self-consciously, Savi raised her hand to the right side of her face to hide her cheek, but she showed no sign of being in pain. In fact, she'd barely shown any discomfort. Either the woman's pain tolerance was through the roof or her injuries weren't too serious. He hoped the latter.

Damián shifted Marisol in his arms. "Check her ribs first. She's been favoring her left side and showed signs of some serious pain when I examined her the way you told me to over the phone." *Don't think about touching her right now, man.*

"Come, *cara*, let me get you into the exam room. Dr. McKenzie is setting things up for us in x-ray." Marc took her elbow and led her past the reception window to the door he had propped open. Savi looked back at Damián.

"Don't worry. We're right behind you."

Savi halted. "No. I don't want Mari to see."

Damián didn't intend to wait out here, but he couldn't just barge into the exam room if Savi didn't want him there. *Mierda*, she was right. Marisol didn't need to see her mama's battered body. Bad enough she could see the bruises on her face.

Savi's gaze shifted to Marisol. "Mari, honey, the doctor is just going to check and make Maman all better. You stay here with Damián. I think I saw some toys in the corner over there you can play with while you're waiting. I shouldn't be too long."

Marisol looked from her mother to Marc. "Don't hurt Maman." The fierce tone in her high-pitched voice made Damián smile. Protective of her mama. He liked that, although he was saddened that his little girl felt the need to protect her mother. Parents were supposed to protect their kids, not the other way around.

Marc smiled his understanding. "Don't worry, Mari. The doctor and I will take very good care of her. She'll be back with you in no time."

Marisol scrutinized Marc a moment longer, taking his measure. Seemingly satisfied with his buddy's ability to care for her mother and return her safely, she nodded. Heaven help Marc if he didn't follow through on that promise, though. This *muñequita* would be a force to be reckoned with.

Already the little doll had breached a major wall in Damián's defenses.

"Come, *querida*, let's go check out the toys."

"I'm not a baby. You can put me down now."

Yes, ma'am. He grinned as he put her down, feeling instant relief in his stump. He hadn't even realized the strain his leg had been under until now.

Marisol placed her hand in his and led him to the table laden with Legos and books. He remembered the last time he'd played with the plastic blocks, with his ten-year-old nephew José at Teresa's birthday weekend a few months ago. Those were happier times with his niece and nephew, sorely missed during his last visit to Eden Gardens when they'd had to deal with the aftermath of what Julio had done to Teresa.

He figured a little girl would be more interested in dolls and books, but this one surprised him when she sat at the table and began playing with the plastic blocks. He soon discovered she was quite adept at building intricate structures. Like a construction foreman, she instructed him on what he could do to help and soon they had built four castle walls, complete with a drawbridge that could be lowered and raised. Next she began working on a tower.

Marisol's fingers stopped moving, and she looked up at him. "Do you like princesses?"

Damián wasn't sure how to respond. "Well, I haven't met too many princesses, but the ones I know, like my niece and you, I like a lot."

She smiled, but only briefly. "Not me, silly. I mean Maman. An evil knight from a kingdom far away put a spell on her; she doesn't know she's a *princesa* anymore. She needs to have a prince kiss her so she can remember."

Mierda. The calculating expression in the little girl's eyes told him he was being sized up to take on the role of her maman's rescuing prince. He imagined having Marisol's approval would make it easier to get close to Savi.

Fuck that thinking. No way was her mother going to find her perfect prince inside this man's broken body and soul. Besides, his days of scaling towers to rescue princesses—especially ice princesses—were long gone. Hadn't he tried to rescue Savannah once, only to be shown in no uncertain terms she'd wanted nothing more to do with him? Apparently, she'd never looked for him. Didn't even find him to tell him he was going to be a father.

Damián's focus lifted over Marisol's head to the door leading back to the examination rooms. How the hell long did it take Marc and his doctor friend to figure out if Savi's ribs were cracked?

Damián could use a little rescuing here, too.

* * *

"How about here?"

The physician pressed his cold, hard fingers into her abdomen. Savi shivered as memories of Lyle's touch bombarded her mind, including the many ways he'd managed to place bruises on her body that her father wouldn't notice. She'd avoided male doctors in the past, because she couldn't bear the thought of being touched by a man. No choice this time. She hated having her choices taken away.

Having Damián's Italian friend staring at her from the other side of the examination table didn't help. His thumb stroked her upper arm as if trying to calm her, but his touch only made her skin crawl even more. Sweat broke out on her upper lip.

Breathe, Savi.

She was marginally successful at keeping herself from screaming in fear and revulsion. These men weren't trying to hurt her. Not yet, anyway. Still, she wanted to crawl into the nearest dark corner to hide but could only escape in her mind.

Go to your safe place, Savi.

Surf.

Sun.

Safety.

Damián waited there, holding out his hand to her.

No!

"That's it, *cara*. I know it hurts, but don't tune out the pain. Dr. McKenzie needs to assess where it hurts first. We'll get you something soon to deal with the pain."

Marc brushed the dampened hair back from her temple. Tears? No, she never cried. Must be perspiration.

Despite him cautioning her against it, she continued to try to block the pain from her consciousness, afraid Dr. McKenzie would send her to a hospital if she was too severely injured. Then he pressed against her ribcage, and Savi screamed, lifting her knees involuntarily to protect herself. *Oh dear Lord.* She hadn't gotten back to her safe place and had fought so hard not to give in to the pain. Her body was wound tighter than an overstretched rubber band. *I can't take much more.*

"Slow, even breaths, *cara*." She couldn't draw a breath. Panic filled her. "Inhale. Now, Savi."

She looked up at Marc and found herself doing as he instructed. Maybe him being in scrubs reminded her of giving birth to Mari. She remembered her Lamaze training, and her body sank against the examination table as she forced herself to release the tension. She could focus on him and…

Dr. McKenzie patted her arm. "Good girl."

She shrank away from the doctor's hand. Those haunting words caused renewed panic to bubble up. Savi tried not to let his unfortunate choice of words do a number on her psyche. He couldn't know they would trigger something in her, and he hadn't meant anything by it. Both Anita and her therapist had worked with Savi for so long on how to stop letting someone's innocently spoken words send her spiraling down into the abyss.

"Eyes on me, *cara*." Again, Savi turned her head toward Damián's friend. He leaned a little too close to her face for comfort.

"I can't do this," she whispered.

"You don't have to do anything but relax. Dr. McKenzie's only trying to see where you're hurting." His words were firm, but gentle. Still, Savi couldn't let go and relax.

"Marc, help me sit her up. I need to listen to her lungs."

"*Cara*, I'm just going to put my hand behind your shoulders, and we're going to lift on three. Are you ready?"

No! Don't touch me! Fear clawed at her chest, and she raised her hands to ward them off. *Wait. They just want to help.* Savi forced herself to nod. Breathe. She just wanted to get this exam over with as quickly as possible so she could get back to Mari. She didn't like having her baby girl out of her sight with a stranger for so long. Okay, maybe stranger was a bit of a stretch when it came to Damián. Still, Savi needed to hold her daughter. Mari provided her soul with everything she'd ever wanted or needed.

"I want you to breathe in and out once, as deeply as you can before we lift you."

Savi did the best she could before a stitch in her side caused her too much pain. Why couldn't she zone out the pain as she'd done for so long? Feeling numb was better than feeling pain.

Marc seemed satisfied. "Very good. Now, on two, I want you to inhale, and then you'll exhale on three as we lift you. Okay?"

She nodded.

"One. Two." Inhale. "Three." Exhale. In one fluid motion, they lifted her until she was sitting upright. The pressure on her ribs and side was excruciating.

Oh, sweet Jesus, Mary, and Joseph!

Savi panted, trying to regain her equilibrium and to control the pain response. She masked her discomfort as best she could. She needed to get out of here, not be put in a hospital where her father could track her whereabouts.

Marc cupped her chin with his hand and made her look at him. "Still with us?"

She nodded, unable to speak through the pain. Marc held his arm across her chest to support her. She fought the instinct to pull away. *Get it over with.*

The doctor placed the stethoscope in his ears and stood beside her, holding the cold, flat disk against her back through the hospital-type gown she wore. "Breathe as deeply as you comfortably can." She breathed in.

"Exhale through your mouth." She released the breath, forcing herself beyond her limits, hoping to show him she was fine.

"Again."

Oh, great.

He moved the instrument to the other side of her back and repeated the breathing instructions. When he brought the stethoscope around and pressed it against her chest, he said, "Just breathe normally."

Easy for you to say.

The doctor stepped in front of her field of vision again. "There's definitely something going on with that rib, Ms. Baker. I'm going to need to get an x-ray to know for sure, but it might be fractured."

"I'm not going to the hospital."

"No worries. I have everything we need here at the clinic. Not the latest technology, but I can take a chest x-ray." He smiled.

"What if it's broken?"

"Well, there's not a whole lot medicine can do. It'll just take time to heal, but I'll want you to be extremely careful so you don't injure it further. I also can prescribe some narcotics to help with the pain."

"No. I can't take anything like that."

"Allergies?"

Savi glanced away. "Yeah."

"To which medications?"

"All of them."

He chuckled. "I see. Well, you might get some relief from over-the-counter meds, but you're going to be in quite a bit of pain for the next couple of weeks if it's broken. I'll write you a script anyway, in case you change your mind."

I won't. "I have a high tolerance for pain."

Marc laughed. "I'll say, if you drove halfway across the country with a probable fractured rib."

She only hoped she'd driven far enough away to protect Mari.

"Marc, help me get her down off the table, and we'll go take that picture."

Thirty minutes later, Savi made her way back to the waiting room. How a possible hairline fracture could cause her so much pain was beyond understanding. Dr. McKenzie said nothing definitive had shown up on the x-ray, but he still suspected a fracture. He explained hairline fractures didn't always show up right away. She was supposed to come back in a few days for another image.

If she was still here.

She opened the door and her breath caught in her throat, this time not because of pain to her rib. Mari was sitting in Damián's lap.

"Savannah, you crawled into my lap...you know you wanted me to touch you there."

Savi clutched the doorway and fought the memories that threatened to consume her.

Damián looked up and concern registered on his face. He started to stand, but he couldn't get to Savi because he held Mari. *Thank God.* Savi didn't want him to touch her.

"Whoa, *cara*. Let me help you." Unfortunately, his friend reached out to steady her, touching her arm.

Savi held onto the doorjamb a little longer, wanting to be sure she was steady before letting go. She pushed Marc's hand away. "No! I'm fine. I just...felt a little dizzy. It's over." To prove her point, she stood taller and forced herself to place one foot in front of the other as she walked over to where Damián cradled her innocent daughter in his lap.

Savi relaxed a bit, seeing Mari's droopy eyelids, her dark, loose curls lying against Damián's massive chest, and her tiny hand resting on his forearm. Mari trusted him. The tightness in her chest loosened. Damián's hand rested protectively on her daughter's hair, where he'd been stroking it gently. Comfortingly. He wasn't touching her...there.

Mari trusted him enough to fall asleep in his arms, and she'd definitely taught her daughter what to do if anyone ever touched her in a bad way. Mari even had a rape whistle on a necklace she wore under her shirt, but hadn't used it.

Savi trusted her instincts, honed from dealing with many victims over the last two years, and knew Damián wasn't a threat to their daughter. He could never be the monster her own father had been.

Damián held an open copy of *Goodnight, Moon* in his lap that he'd obviously been reading to Mari before she'd fallen asleep. The book had been one of her little girl's favorites when she was younger, but ever since she'd learned to read, she preferred to read to Savi at bedtime now. Mari cherished her growing independence from her maman—and yet she sat curled up in her daddy's lap. She must have been feeling insecure to let herself be babied again.

Savi missed those simpler times with a much younger Mari, going from window to window in their bungalow to find the moon and say goodnight before Savi tucked her into bed. She blinked rapidly, trying to ward off the sting of tears.

Had she been wrong to deny Damián knowledge of his daughter all these years? *No.* She couldn't know who to trust. Besides, she hadn't been able to find Damián when she'd made that one attempt after Mari had been born. He'd moved and left no forwarding address.

Her emotional side warred with her rational one. She still didn't know if she could trust him completely with Mari, even though the way he had comforted his niece and the way he now held Mari certainly silenced most of Savi's emotional alarms.

At the moment, though, his warm, chocolate-brown eyes were filled with worry for Savi. Her stomach lurched. She wasn't prepared to acknowledge whatever that response meant and turned away.

Savi opened her purse to pull out some cash, hoping she wouldn't deplete the small amount Anita and Father Martine had given her.

"Put that away." Marc said, still standing at the doorway. "Everything's taken care of."

"You don't have to do that. I can pay."

"I said, everything's taken care of." His tone brooked no argument. Of course, she was in no position to argue with him. She'd make a donation to this clinic later, after she got her life back in order.

Marc crossed the room holding a slip of paper, then his attention shifted to Damián and he handed it to him. "Here's the script for pain. She probably has a cracked rib and says she's not going to take any pain meds. I'll let you persuade her otherwise." He grinned at her then, thinking he'd outmaneuvered her. Well, she'd just see about that.

Marc's focus returned to Damián. "Unless she's asleep, you also want to make sure she coughs as deeply as possible every hour or so to prevent pneumonia. The pain meds can help her cough more deeply, too. Don't tape her up, even if it helps with the pain." To Savi, he added, "You don't want a collapsed lung. Trust me on that."

Her chest muscles tightened, and she already felt as if her lungs were collapsing. *Escape.*

"I need to get Mari into bed."

Marc walked over to a chair near the door and retrieved the blanket Mari had been wrapped in and brought it over to Damián. "You want me to carry her out to the car, Damián?"

"No. I have her."

Marc gave him a questioning look that puzzled Savi. "Here, let me take her from your lap so you can get up." Damián glanced at Savi, then he took the blanket from Marc and wrapped it around Mari's now-sleeping form. He let Marc lift Mari into his arms, and Savi watched as Damián grimaced when he rose to his feet. Maybe the doctor should check *him* out, too. However, he quickly reached out to take Marisol into his arms again.

Savi reached out, suddenly concerned he might not be able to carry her all the way to the car. He stared at her, daring her to try and take Mari away. She decided they'd better get to the car as quickly as possible, so she headed in that direction. "I'll get the door."

Marc waved her away. "I'll get it. It's heavy, and you'll just aggravate that rib." Desperately wanting to get some fresh air, Savi waited impatiently for Marc to open the door. He looked at her jacket. "Where's your coat?"

Damián responded before she could. "That's all she brought with her. Doesn't get this cold in Southern California."

Looking at Damián, Marc said, "Bring them both to the store tomorrow. I'll be giving ski lessons to Angelina, Rosa, and the kids, but I'll tell Brian to outfit them fully for their stay." He turned back to her. "Get everything you need."

"Just take us to a thrift store. I don't want to owe any more than I can..."

Did he just growl at her? "Don't argue with me, Savi. You won't match the quality I stock anywhere else, and you have enough health problems without adding pneumonia to the list. Besides, Mari can't run around Denver in a blanket during your stay."

Savi's attention moved to her daughter. She'd provided everything Mari needed since she'd left Anita's home and embarked on her career. Sure, they'd frequented thrift stores, but there was nothing wrong with used clothes. They didn't need to waste money on new ones.

Once again, the actions of Savi's father had taken away her autonomy, making her feel weak and helpless. She didn't like that feeling one bit. Now these two domineering men were telling her what she could and couldn't do for her own daughter.

Marc opened the door and held it for her. A blast of much-welcomed, cold air whooshed in, spurring her to action. Needing to get away from the men in the room, she nearly bolted through the door to the parking lot.

How was she going to get used to accepting help from others, especially men, without feeling like a...*filthy whore*?

The words Lyle and her father had drummed into her psyche invaded again. She'd learned early on that her body was not her own. It was only good for one thing—a business deal in exchange for the sexual torture of a slave's body.

If Damián expected her to repay him with sex, he might as well stop being so kind to her. No way would he ever get her into his bed—well, not when he was in it, anyway—whether he thought she owed him sex or not.

* * *

Damián tucked the still-sleeping Marisol into his bed when they returned to the apartment after finding the all-night pharmacy to get Savi's pain prescription filled. He still hadn't managed to get her to take one of the damned pills, though. Stubborn girl. What was she afraid of—that he'd attack her while she slept? Why the hell had she come running to him, if all she wanted to do ever since was run away?

Damián ached to massage his stump. He hadn't expected it to be so raw from carrying Marisol. Of course, he'd carried Karla's bridal litter down the stairs at Marc's earlier today, too. Clearly he was getting out of shape. Maybe when he was working again he wouldn't sit around on his ass so much.

He walked back into the living room where Savi was seated at one end of the couch. No way was he going to remove his prosthesis while she was here. Okay, he might have to buy himself some private time at some point or risk irritating it to the point of doing some serious damage. Right now, though, he was the one irritated. He sat down and glanced over where Savi had wedged herself into the corner of the couch, as far from him as she could get. Someone sure must have done a number on her since they'd first met as teenagers. She'd had no problem trusting him that day. He still remembered her lying beneath him with her head pillowed by his leather jacket and her body stretched out on a towel to protect her fair skin in the beach cave.

He hadn't been back there since he'd left for Fallujah. With his stump, he doubted he'd be able to take those stairs ever again, most definitely not with Savi in his arms. He remembered how he'd practically carried Savannah all the way to the cave that day and how they'd spent the rest of the day having sex.

His dick grew hard just thinking about it. He'd better start thinking about something else or she really would think he was up to no good tonight. He looked at Savi's thin frame in the long-sleeved shirt. How much weight had she lost? She looked almost boyish. That someone could hit her defenseless body the way that bastard had done more than pissed him off. If he ever got his hands on the shithead who'd done it...

Control yourself. Justice would come. Later.

"How's your pain level?"

"Fine."

Doubtful. He could see the strain in her eyes. "What did the doctor say?"

She looked up at him, a quirk in her eyebrow. "About?"

"About how long it'll take your rib to heal."

"If it's fractured, six weeks. But I'm sure it's just a bruise. They'll take another x-ray on Wednesday."

"How do you plan to sleep if you don't take the pain meds?"

"I'll be fine."

She'd probably go to her zone and deny the presence of the pain. *Been there, done that.* "I'll prop up some blankets and extra pillows when you're ready to get into bed with Marisol."

The mention of her daughter—could she really be his daughter, too?—sent her gaze toward the bedroom. She seemed satisfied with what she saw and turned her attention to the bottle of water in her hand, studying the label intently. Her thumbnail dug at the paper as if she was picking at a scab.

Damián needed to know. "She's mine."

Savi looked up at him. He saw not only pain reflected in her eyes but fear. She didn't fucking trust him.

"Why didn't you try to find me? Why didn't you tell me about Marisol?"

She sighed but didn't relax a muscle. He had to lean closer to hear her when she began to speak. "When I left my father's house, I was...a mess. Father Martine at San Miguel's Church helped, and I was taken in by one of the parishioners there." She looked down at the bottle again and picked at it some more. "I was hospitalized for a while." *Pick.* "Anita, the woman who took me in, helped me a lot." *Pick. Pick.*

She paused and looked up at him. "After Marisol was born, I did try once to locate you, but you'd moved away from your apartment in Eden Gardens. I didn't realize you had lived there until then."

He couldn't believe she'd run to San Miguel's, just blocks from his old apartment. Maybe if he'd gone to church more, he'd have seen her. "I got evicted. Joined the Marines." She nodded and looked back down. "Why didn't you tell me about her last month when I was out there for Teresa?"

Savi stopped breathing for a long while. She swallowed and drew a shaky breath; her voice barely a whisper as she said, "I was afraid you'd try to take her away from me. She's all I have. She gave me…a reason to live."

Sounded like she'd been about as far gone as he was after his foot had been blown off in Fallujah. His scars were more visible, but mental scars could be a lot more painful than any physical ones. They'd both been pulled back into life—Damián by Adam and Marc, Savi by Marisol and the folks at San Miguel's.

Now they'd found each other again. He didn't have a fucking clue what that was going to mean for him and Savi, but he did plan to be a part of Marisol's life.

Hell, in all honesty, he doubted he'd have been any help to her or Marisol while in Fallujah or even the next couple of years. He'd been too fucked up. At least she'd been able to keep their daughter and take care of her. She'd done a damned good job, too. That couldn't have been easy for someone so young.

"You're a great mom. I'd never do anything to come between you and Marisol." She looked up at him, and he saw the relief in her sad, beautiful blue eyes. He still couldn't get used to her as a redhead. She'd been blonde in his dreams and fantasies—a helluva lot of fucking dreams over eight years.

Mi sueño. My dream.

Fuck that shit.

"But I'm her father, and I'm going to be a part of her life now."

Savi remained still. After a long while of silent deliberation, she nodded. "Mari's always wanted a daddy."

Damián didn't want to think about any other men who might have tried to fulfill his obligations over the years. He hoped there hadn't been many—but if there had been, he'd sure as hell make sure Marisol knew who her real daddy was.

"I know she's calling me daddy already, but I want her to know it's more than wishful thinking, to know I'm not just a temporary daddy."

Savi winced as she leaned forward slightly and pierced him with her gaze. "If you ever do anything inappropriate to her or hurt her in any way, I'll make sure you never touch anyone ever again."

Mierda.

Obviously, he had some work to do to win her trust. Nothing but time and a track record would achieve that. But he wanted her to know one thing going in. He leaned closer to her face to make sure she heard his deadly promise.

"If anyone ever touches *either* of you inappropriately, I'll rip their fucking balls off and cram them down their throats."

Chapter Three

"**M**aman, did Santa come yet? Daddy said he would find me all the way in Colorado."

Savi groaned to herself. Damn Damián for making promises like that. All of Marisol's gifts were back at their house in Solana Beach. Savi had found a few things at a local thrift shop and a discount store this week, but there was nothing nearly as nice as the toys she'd purchased over the last six months with whatever remained from each paycheck. All had been left behind when she'd had to run. Savi damned the bastard who had fathered her, this time for ruining Christmas for her daughter. She hoped he would rot in hell one day soon.

"Maman. Are you awake?"

"Yes, baby. Just resting my eyes." Savi blinked several times, stalling for time. "*Feliz Navidad*, sweetheart. Why don't we go fix Dami…*Daddy* some breakfast before we open presents?"

Savi still couldn't get used to calling Damián "Daddy." But her daughter certainly had no problem latching onto the name once they'd explained that Damián was her father. Heck, Mari had called him that even before she'd known there was a biological connection.

Not having experienced a father's love, Savi wasn't sure how to analyze the bond forming between the two of them. She'd fought hard not to impede their relationship, but she still kept a watchful eye on them. Men could change, just as her father had done when Savi was eight. Watching Mari's face light up whenever Damián called her his little doll or teased her about something made Savi long for that kind of love and acceptance.

Her chest tightened as she watched the light go out of Mari's eyes because mean old Maman wouldn't let her dive into the mountains of presents she expected to find under the tree they'd decorated together last week. Mari's disappointment would only grow worse when they went into the living room and saw that Santa hadn't really found her in Colorado, after all.

"Can I look under the tree before we go to the kitchen?"

Savi swallowed against the lump in her throat. "May I?" Savi prompted, still hoping to postpone the inevitable.

Mari sat up on her heels and stared down at Savi. "May I look, Maman? May I?"

Savi tossed the blanket off and fought back a moan as she swung her legs over the side of the bed. She sat until she could get the pain in her side under control. She still couldn't believe that Lyle had broken her rib.

"Please, Maman?"

Not sure she could stand to see the disappointment coming, Savi nodded and let Mari scamper off the bed, get into the wooly slippers she'd gotten at Marc's outfitter store, and pad to the door. It was still dark outside, but when she opened the door to the living room, the lights of the Christmas tree illuminated the bedroom. Damián certainly had used a lot of lights on the little tree. The smell of fresh spruce wafted to her. The tree they'd cut was so much more beautiful than anything Savi would have found back home. Mari had been half-asleep when Damián had carried her into the apartment after they'd returned home from midnight Mass not so many hours ago, but he had turned the lights on for her to see before they tucked her into bed. He was sweet to leave the tree on all night for their daughter, in case she got up and peeked.

Their daughter. She couldn't wrap her mind around having to share Mari with anyone.

The squeal she heard from Mari set off warning bells, and Savi rose more quickly than she should have. After regaining her equilibrium—and her breath—she held her side as she hurried into the living room. Her eyes opened as wide as Mari's at the sight. Around the tree were dozens of gifts—including an enormous wooden dollhouse Mari was checking out at the moment. Many of the other gifts were wrapped, but there were so many more than the few Savi had placed there. She turned her head only to find herself staring at Damián's bare shoulders over the back of the sofa where he sat, a sappy grin on his face as he took in the experience of his first Christmas with his daughter.

"How did you...?"

He turned toward her shaking his head as he placed a finger against his lips. Savi rubbed her chest to ease the unexpected ache there.

"Maman, Daddy was right. Santa did find us! Look what he brought me!" Her daughter peeked inside the dollhouse shaped like a log cabin and began moving tiny pieces of furniture around. The look of awe and wonder on her face reminded Savi how resilient children could be. Her whole world had been upended two weeks ago, but this morning, all was right in her little girl's world because Santa hadn't forgotten her. Savi blinked against a burning in her eyes. An image of a past Christmas flitted across her mind.

"Maman! Look what Santa brought me. Barbie's house!"

Maman, dressed in her maroon silk robe, sipped hot tea and watched seven-year-old Savannah open her presents. Father read the newspaper, disconnected from the females in the scene, but Maman's brown eyes shone with happiness. Maman loved Christmas more than any other holiday.

"Open another present, chére. *What else did* Père Noël *bring you?"*

The blonde-headed little girl pulled another box from under the enormous tree and opened it to find a Holiday Barbie doll in a sparkling green-velvet gown. A big bow was set at an angle on the doll's blonde head. She looked like a princess, without a tiara.

Her mind flashed forward to what might have been the next Christmas…

The little girl crawled under her bed, clutching the blond-haired princess in her hands, trying to hide from Father…

The pad of Damián's thumb brushed against her cheek, and Savi nearly came out of her skin.

"Whoa, *querida.*" Damián reached out to steady her, grabbing her by the upper arms.

Savi looked up at him, drawing a few ragged breaths as she fought to regain control. His hands were so strong. For one weak moment, she wished she could lean on him, but she needed to pull away instead. She followed the instincts that had kept her safe for so long.

His look of hurt made her feel guilty after all he'd done for them, but she wasn't ready to have any man touching her. She'd never give her body to another man, especially not as payment for services offered. Never again.

"You were a million miles away."

She blinked and wondered where that flashback had come from. She hadn't thought of those Christmas memories in…forever. Even now, Savi felt as if she was watching a scene from a Christmas classic movie, not remembering a part of her own life. *No, not her life. Savannah's.* All emotional ties to that tragic little girl had been severed for a very long time.

"You okay, Savi?"

She nodded but needed to put some distance between them. "What can I fix you for breakfast? Pancakes? Mari's probably hungry."

"She won't be thinking about food for a while." He studied Savi's face with concern in his eyes, and she had the feeling he was seeing more than he should. "You sure you're okay? You look like you've seen a ghost."

Savannah's Maman disappeared when she was eight. The little girl's spirit died soon after, right after her father molested her and began more than a decade of abuse and torture on the innocent little girl's body and mind.

The only person in the flashback scene who had survived unscathed was Savannah's father—and she wished she could send him and all monsters like him to the pits of hell where she could watch them burn.

* * *

Well, at least he'd brought a smile to the face of one of his girls this Christmas morning. Damián tried to hide his disappointment. Last week, when he'd heard Marisol chatter to Santa at the mall about the things she wanted to receive, he'd gone to work trying to make his daughter's Christmas dreams come true. That Josefina doll had taken a chunk out of his dwindling checking account.

He'd hoped Marisol's happiness would bring a little joy to her mama, too, but no such luck.

Clearly, Savi wasn't interested in anything he had to offer. The look on her face made it obvious the holiday wasn't as special for her as it was for him. Maybe sad memories from her past clouded the joy of the season for her. The holidays weren't happy for lots of people. Adam—well, Dad now—for years had gone into a funk in the fall until he got through the holidays. Damián hoped he and Karla were making new memories this Christmas morning to replace the sad ones.

While he didn't think he could do anything to change Savi's state of mind, Damián was determined for Marisol to have nothing but pleasant memories, and he was ready to start celebrating.

He'd never managed to go to sleep last night partly because of his excitement at seeing Marisol's face in the morning and partly because he'd had a helluva lot of toys to assemble. When Luke Denton, a new member at the club and Marc's SAR partner, had texted him to come down to the parking lot, he'd helped the carpenter carry up the log-cabin dollhouse he'd made for

Marisol. Luke, also an artist, must have worked on the house night and day all week. He'd heard about Marisol from Marc and, like a man on a mission, wanted to help make her first Christmas special. Damián had been blown away by the gesture.

Today, Damián had a lot planned, including playing Legos again with Marisol. He hoped he'd connect with Savi on common ground at some point.

First, he needed to answer the call of nature and take care of his stump. "I'll be right back."

When he returned to the living room, Savi was smiling, sitting on the floor and watching Marisol unwrap another gift. Ah, the set of American Girl books. He remembered how much Teresa had enjoyed reading Josefina stories at that age and hoped Marisol didn't already have them, or the doll, for that matter.

"Josefina stories!"

Damn. She probably already had them.

"How did Santa know I wanted these?"

Score. Pride swelled his chest. Savi glanced over at him and mouthed the words "thank you," but he didn't miss the pang of regret in her eyes. He hoped she didn't see him as competition for their daughter's affections. Hell, he had some asinine notion about sharing the responsibility of raising her now. Far-fetched, given how Savi hadn't wanted to have much to do with him since she'd shown up on his doorstep. They'd co-existed, but Savi avoided being alone with him—not easy to do in this tiny apartment with the three of them practically on top of each other.

But he couldn't believe how much he had enjoyed having them both here. *Mine.* Family was the most important thing of all to him. If Savi thought he'd turn his back on his daughter, well, she had a lot more to learn about him.

Damián limped into the kitchen to start a pot of coffee. His stump ached this morning. It had looked redder than Santa's suit when he'd been in the bathroom, but he'd be damned if he'd remove the prosthesis and show Savi what he'd become. Of course, if he ever did get anywhere with her, he'd have to reveal he was a cripple. He'd look pretty damned stupid if he refused to remove his pants in bed, and he couldn't get them off without first taking off the prosthesis.

"You should have Marc or Dr. McKenzie take a look at that foot."

Damián spilled coffee grounds on the countertop and turned to find Savi standing in the doorway.

"Nothing they can do." Determined to veer this conversation off in another direction PDQ, he went back to loading the coffeemaker. Marc should be here soon, but he hoped she wouldn't mention the foot to him. He hadn't told Marc she didn't know about the amputation yet.

Savi reached for a paper towel and began cleaning up the mess. Too bad she couldn't clean up the mess in both of their lives as easily.

"Thank you for making this day so special for Mari."

Damián measured the grounds again. "No big deal."

"Yes, it was. You helped keep the magic of Christmas alive for her another year. I just want you to know I appreciate it."

He turned back to her, noticing that the bruising around her eye had faded to yellowish green. Almost healed. Anger that someone would hurt her seethed beneath the surface, but he regained control and picked up the conversation. "She's my daughter, too. That's what daddies do."

A flash of pain crossed her eyes, but she masked it and went to the cupboard to pull out two mugs. "How did you know about the Josefina books?"

"Teresa loved her at that age, too."

"Mari is fascinated by Hispanic history. She was always asking me about her heritage." Savi smiled, but her eyes remained so fucking sad. "Maybe you can fill me in on your family's background, so I can share that with her."

No, Savi, we. He looked forward to sharing Marisol's roots with both of them.

The coffeemaker hissed and gurgled to life. He reached for the coffee pot and filled her mug, as he told her a little about his grandparents who had emigrated from Mexico back in the Thirties. He'd never thought he'd carry on the Orlando name with children of his own. Sometime soon, he wanted to talk with Savi about having Marisol's name changed legally. He was proud to claim what was his.

No chance in hell would Savi ever take his name.

"Have you thought about enrolling Marisol in the Catholic school here?"

"I can't afford it."

"The public schools are good, too, but she's so smart, she may even get a scholarship. Why don't we look into it after New Year's?"

If anyone had told him a few weeks ago that he'd be discussing where to send his daughter to school, he'd have told them they were seriously fucked up or smoking some funky weed.

"In case I haven't said it, I'm glad you're both here, Savi, even under the circumstances." In the short time they'd been here, they'd made his apartment into a home, rather than simply the place where he crashed at the end of the day. "I wish you could stay forever."

Savi's hand began to shake so badly, she sloshed coffee onto her chest. He grabbed the mug from her with one hand and placed it on the counter as he pulled her scalding-hot shirt away from her skin with the other. Damián reached for a paper towel, but he waited for the liquid to cool before he let the fabric touch her skin again.

"Did it burn you?"

"Did what burn?"

The fucking hot coffee, that's what. "The coffee you spilled on your shirt."

She looked down at his hands, and Damián let go of her T-shirt as he continued to dab at the wet fabric. His fingers pressed against her firm tits. *Fuck, yeah.* Too soon, she stepped back and took the towel from him.

"I'll do that."

His dick tried to rise to a full salute in his jeans, and he turned back to the counter to hide his body's response to touching her. He poured his own coffee and refilled her mug.

At the table, he decided to push for more intel. "Why were you wearing a wedding ring when I saw you at the clinic that day with Teresa?"

Savi turned her attention to him, and her expression grew steely. He tried to ignore the fact that her nipples protruded against her wet shirt, large and inviting. He needed to control himself better.

"So that men wouldn't hit on me."

"Men like me?"

She shrugged and took a sip of her coffee. *Fuck.* The woman sure knew how to hurt a guy's ego.

"You haven't been in touch with the clinic you worked at, have you? I don't want you to leave any breadcrumbs."

"No, there's no reason to contact them."

"Still I know how much you cared about your clients; it must have been hard for you to leave them behind."

"I was fired from my job."

What the fuck? If she'd told him her best friend had just died, she couldn't have sounded much sadder.

"But you're so good at what you do."

"I got caught up in some…politics. The politicians won."

"Well, I'm sure you could get a job in social work here in Colorado."

"Not that simple. There's state licensing and…"

Realization dawned on him. "Your father's the politician who had you fired."

She glanced down at the table. "No, but he must have had something on the legislator who did. The clinic is funded almost entirely by state and federal grants. The director couldn't afford to lose that money and keep me."

Wanting to provide some comfort, he reached out his hand to her, but she pulled away and stood, taking her mug to the sink. "I told Mari to play with what she'd already opened until we got back. I'm sure she's dying to see what else Santa brought her." She made her hasty retreat into the living room.

"You might flit from me now, *mi mariposa,* but you can't evade me forever."

* * *

Savi watched her daughter open another box, still not one of the gifts she'd placed under the tree after Mass last night. Mari would be so disappointed in the inexpensive presents Savi had gotten her, after all these beautiful new ones from Santa. Well, Santa Damián, anyway. At least hers would be seen as Santa gifts, too, albeit much simpler ones.

"Oh, Maman, look! My own Josefina doll!"

The reverent awe in her daughter's voice made it difficult to feel jealousy over Damián's ability to buy her such nice things. Of course, Savi had a wrapped Josefina doll in her bedroom closet back home. Mari had wanted one since she was six, but money had always been tight and it wasn't until getting the job at the clinic last summer that Savi had been able to splurge on something that extravagant. Savi had bought it too long ago to return it, though. If she ever returned to the bungalow, she'd donate it to the annual toy drive at San Miguel for next year.

A chill ran down her spine. Where would they be next year? Clearly, she couldn't take Mari home as long as her father and Lyle posed a threat. If something happened to Mari—something even one iota like what her father had done to her all those years of captivity—Savi would die.

Sweat broke out on her forehead, and her heart began racing. Time to face facts—her life had changed irrevocably. The bastard held too much power in Southern California. She needed to think about starting over. *Here.* In Denver.

Mari picked up one of the packages from the thrift store. Savi held her breath, hoping her daughter would like it as much as the other gifts. When she ripped the paper open and found the black, plush animal, Mari's breath caught in her throat and her eyes grew to the size of saucers.

"A kitty!" She lifted the stuffed animal to her face and rubbed it against her cheek, as if it were a real kitten.

Savi cleared her throat and blinked a few times. Marisol had always had a fondness for kittens and cats. They couldn't have one at the house they rented, but Savi tried to provide her with inanimate ones whenever she could.

Toy ones can't die.

Savi pushed away the stray thought, instead choosing to remember the expression on Mari's face when they were at Marc's outfitter store the day after her visit to the clinic. Her little girl discovered the litter of kittens the store's manager had harbored when a pregnant cat had been abandoned outside the shop. He'd been surprised with four baby kittens a couple weeks before Thanksgiving. Luckily, the kittens were too young then to be separated from their mama, or Savi would have had a problem getting out of the store without one.

Placing the stuffed kitten on one side of her and Josefina on the other, Mari reached for another package from the thrift store. "A Hello Kitty purse!" Mari opened the clasp and started pulling out the dime-store trinkets Savi had stuffed inside. "Look, Maman! Purple nail polish! Can I paint your fingernails?" Mari loved to paint her maman's fingernails, just as Savannah had for Maman. Savi had bought the polish just for that purpose.

"Yes, you *may*—but let's wait 'til tonight." Of course, Savi would paint her daughter's nails, as well. It was one of the things they enjoyed doing when they vegged out on the sofa on Friday nights. She glanced over at Damián, who smiled back at her.

Why she'd been worried about her inexpensive gifts, she didn't know. Mari had always appreciated anything she'd been given, probably because she, too, remembered those early years when things hadn't been quite so good for Savi while she was in school and first starting to counsel clients. Or maybe it was because her daughter had been taught about gratitude. Savi had encouraged her to start a gratitude journal as soon as she was able to cut pictures out of magazines. Later she'd learned to use words along with pictures to show what she was grateful for each day.

Savi admitted to feeling insecure these days. Her life had been turned upside down with no sign of righting itself anytime soon. Damián was right. She needed to see about enrolling Mari for classes here in Denver as soon as they got through the holiday break.

"Here, this is for you." Damián held out a long, black-velvet jewelry box to her with a tiny red bow on top.

Savi and Marisol had only baked and decorated cookies for him. They'd agreed no gifts for each other, only for Mari. "Why did you—?"

"Ulterior motives. Go on. Open it first. I'll explain afterward."

Opening the lid, she saw matching necklaces each with a delicate-looking, filigreed silver whistle hanging from the end of a thin, brown leather cord. There were several unique trinkets of silver, along with a few clear glass beads, dangling from the cord.

She looked up at him. "They're beautiful, but why two?"

He grinned. "One for each of you. You can use the whistle to call for help. There's also a GPS chip in each one. I'm not taking any chance on losing either of you ever again."

His words held a double meaning, but she chose to think he meant the obvious. While her father was a threat, this would give them a little added protection, in case either or both of them needed to be tracked. She shuddered. "These had to have cost a fortune."

Damián shook his head. "*No es nada*, and Marc added the chips for free."

She moved closer to Mari and placed the smaller necklace around her daughter's neck. She wouldn't need the enormous rape whistle if this one was loud enough, but for now, she'd keep them both on her. Better safe than sorry.

"Marisol, anytime you need Daddy to come, you just blow that whistle and I'll be there. You can use it anytime you're scared, too."

Mari put the whistle to her lips and blew. The shrill sound would certainly attract attention. She wouldn't need the other one. What kind of man gave a GPS tracking necklace? He could have just given her the tracking devices. But the necklaces were beautiful pieces of art, and the matching mother-daughter aspect made it an even more special gift.

She looked at Damián and wished she could convey her thanks in a more special way than merely saying the words, but she didn't want him to get the wrong idea if she hugged him.

"Thanks, Damián. They're very special. I want you to know I appreciate you taking care of us like this."

He shrugged. "That's what families are for."

Family.

A knock at the door made her jump, instantly putting her on full alert.

Damián stood up. "Now I wonder who that could be?" The theatrical way he asked made it perfectly obvious to Savi he knew exactly who it was. Still, he looked through the peephole before opening the door, reminding her he knew they weren't safe yet here, either.

The door swung open and there stood his friend, Marc, wearing a green elf's hat on his head and a big grin on his face. He looked perfectly ridiculous but didn't seem to mind at all. Beside him was a beautiful Italian woman with long black hair and big brown eyes. Savi wasn't sure if she was his wife or just a girlfriend, but the way his arm was draped around her shoulder almost possessively told her they were in a close relationship.

"Merry Christmas!" they said in unison, then laughed.

Marc carried three large, long festively wrapped boxes under his other arm and the woman held a red box with a gold-colored bow on top. She held the box out to Damián. Were there holes cut in the top?

"We were on our way to Mama's in Aspen Corners, but we think Santa might have delivered these to the wrong address, so we thought we'd be Santa's elves and get them to you and Marisol first."

"*Feliz Navidad.* Come in," Damián said, stepping aside.

Marc's hand guided the woman to precede him out of the cold. After he introduced Angelina to Savi and Mari, he said, "We'll only intrude for a minute or two. Her mama likes to serve Christmas dinner promptly at noon, I hear, and with the way she cooks and Angelina's brothers eat, well, we don't want to be late."

Angelina nudged him in the side. "Marc, all you think about is food."

"If you and your mama weren't such good cooks, maybe I'd have more time to think about something else." The look he gave Angelina made Savi uncomfortable.

"Oh, you have no trouble thinking about other things when you want to." The woman's eyes were filled with love for him; Savi felt the electricity sparking between the two of them.

Squirming inside, Savi came toward them and reached for the boxes in Marc's hands. "Here, let me take some of those."

He turned to her and grew serious. "Just the top two. The bottom one's too heavy for you with that injured rib."

"Yes, sir." The man certainly had a protective streak in him. Not nearly as strong as Damián's was toward her and Mari, but it was more than enough to leave her feeling…uneasy. She'd never been under the protection of a strong, caring man. But she'd hate having a man tell her what to do, as if she were a powerless child.

The boxes she took from Marc were very light. Savi wondered what was inside, then a glance at the box in Damián's hands confirmed her suspicions. A tiny black-and-white paw poked out of the top through one of the holes.

Savi looked at Damián, hoping to get his attention to try and stop this train wreck before it happened. Mari didn't need to get attached to a real kitten. What if something happened to it and her heart was broken?

You need to learn your lesson for kicking me last night, Savannah. Whiskers is going to the pound today.

The blonde-haired girl began to cry, begging her father not to take away her precious pet. Maman had given her Whiskers as a kitten one Easter when Savannah was only six. The two had been inseparable and she felt closer to Maman whenever Whiskers was in the bed beside her. But last night Savannah had kicked her father as hard as she could to keep him out of her bed. To keep him from hurting her…again.

Savi's hands began to shake. Her face grew warm, then cold, causing her to break out in a clammy sweat. Suddenly, she lost all feeling in her hands and feet. As if the sound reached her ears through a tunnel, she heard the boxes she'd been holding hit the floor, one after another.

* * *

Damián's gaze zeroed in on Savi's pasty-white face. She stared at the box he held as if she expected all the evils of the world to spew forth when the lid was removed.

"Angelina, hold this." Damián shoved the box back into her hands and gripped Savi's upper arms. He stared into her glazed eyes. "What's wrong, Savi? Does something hurt?" He resisted the urge to shake her. "Look at me, *querida*." She blinked, a glazed look in her eyes. Suddenly, she tried to push him away, but he refused to release her.

Her hand went to her throat. "I…can't…breathe."

"Come with me." Damián led her across the room with his arm around her back. "Sit." He eased her onto the center cushion of the couch.

Marc sat on her other side and pressed his fingers against her wrist to feel for a pulse. "Inhale slowly, *cara*."

Savi shook her head, opening her mouth, but nothing came out.

"Maman? Are you sick?"

Marisol's presence seemed to jar her but caused her to shake her head even harder. She held her hand up to keep their daughter away.

"Come, sweetie," Angelina said. "Show me this awesome log house of yours. I always wanted one like this." The woman shepherded Marisol toward the tree, but the little girl's eyes didn't leave Savi's face.

Damián went into the kitchen and grabbed a bottle of water from the counter, twisted off the cap, and returned to Savi's side. Her color was still gone. "*Querida*, drink this." Damián held the bottle to her lips, and she drank a few sips. He brushed the hair back from her dampened forehead. "Good girl."

She focused on him and spewed out with great vehemence, "Don't *ever* call me that again."

"It's just an expression, Savi. I didn't mean anything by it."

"I am nobody's *good girl*. Never again." Savi closed her eyes tight, as if in pain.

Clearly someone she didn't care for had called her a good girl in the past. Had it been a Dom or maybe some client she'd had in the hotel?

Marc placed a hand on her arm. "Take a deep breath, *cara*. Let me make sure you haven't reinjured that rib."

"Maman, look! A real kitty!"

Damián looked over at the tree in time to see a ball of black and white fur scamper out of the box and up the tree.

"No, Daddy!" Savi whispered, a look of horror on her face. "Whiskers can't climb!"

Whiskers? She'd named the kitten already? How did she even know he got one of the kittens at Marc's store? Still, hearing her call him Daddy in front of his friends did something to him, publicly acknowledging his role as Marisol's father.

But when Damián turned toward Savi, he knew instantly she wasn't referring to him, even if they had agreed to let Marisol call him that. Savi had the same glassy-eyed, blank stare he'd seen on the faces of his fellow veterans at the amputee rehab centers where he'd undergone physical therapy during his recovery. Old timers called it the thousand-yard stare. She looked at the tree with unseeing eyes, as if in a trance.

He needed to bring her back. "You're okay, Savi." He reached out and stroked her arm.

Savi blinked, looking from Damián to the tree as she seemed to try to regain her bearings. She whispered, "Whiskers was declawed. He couldn't survive out there. He knew that."

"Who knew?"

Savi looked at him with anguish on her face. She brushed Marc's and Damián's hands aside and pushed herself up from the couch with a grimace and a groan. Damn it, if she wasn't careful, she *was* going to reinjure herself.

"I need to be alone."

"Savi, stop! Don't run from it."

She shook her head and nearly careened into the wall before she veered through the opening to the bedroom, closing the door behind her with a thud. He glanced at Marc and said in a voice only for his friend's ears, "Keep an eye on Marisol—don't let her go in there."

"Sure thing."

Damián followed Savi, giving a cursory knock before he opened the door. He glanced around the room. No Savi. She must have gone straight into the bathroom. He heard the water from the faucet.

Damián knocked on that door. "You okay in there?"

"I'm fine. Just leave me alone."

Fuck that shit. Savi wasn't fine, and he was tired of hearing her say she was while masking—or blocking—her real feelings. He opened the door to find her curvy ass facing him as she bent over the sink. She straightened up and turned toward him, holding a washcloth against her cheek and blinked. Her hand still shook.

"Go away! I said I'm fine."

"Savi, you're not going to shut me out anymore. Tell me what's going on."

Savi closed her eyes and winced when she tried to swallow. She turned back to the sink and cupped her hands, letting water from the faucet fill them, then bent over and slurped the water into her mouth.

He reached around her and held the bottled water in front of her. "Here. Drink this."

She grabbed it like a lifeline, stood, and tilted it back against her lips, gulping down half the bottle as if she'd spent a week in Iraq without a drop.

Damián's hand stroked her back in what he intended as a comforting gesture, but she shrank away from his touch as far as she could with the sink in front of her.

"Savi, what happened in there?"

"I don't want to talk about it. I just need a few minutes alone to regroup."

Damián leaned his pelvis against her backside, pressing her into the sink. He'd given her personal space for two weeks, but he recognized the signs of PTSD when he saw them. Clearly, she needed to face whatever demons pursued her before they'd let go of even a fraction of their hold on her.

The bottle shook in her hand.

"I can help, Savi. I have been through some of my own living nightmares. It helps to talk about them. Takes away their power."

He allowed her enough room to turn and face him, but she stared up into his eyes for so long he didn't know if she was trying to formulate words to respond or was planning to wait him out in silence. Then she shook her head.

"He still has all the power," she whispered.

He brushed a wet strand of hair off her soft cheek and curled it behind her ear. "Who, *bebé*?"

She shook her head again. "I don't want to talk about it. I don't want to remember." She held a shaking hand to her head and pressed her fingers against her temple. "Why do these memories keep bubbling up? I dealt with all this stuff in therapy years ago."

"They don't come up until your mind feels safe, until it knows you can handle them." At least, that's what his shrink had told him. Maybe it would give her more comfort than it had him. If Adam hadn't been there for him…

"Of course. I know that." She was still shaking and clearly rattled by whatever memory she'd relived. "But I don't *want* to handle them. I don't *want* to feel anything!" Her voice grew louder. "Why can't they just leave me alone?" She tried to push him away, but he kept her body trapped between his and the vanity.

"I care, Savi. I understand. Let me help."

She shook her head, keeping her gaze cast toward the sink. "No one can help me."

"Bullshit. I'm living proof everyone can be helped. Dad…*Adam* and Marc dragged me back from the brink more times than I can count." He ran his hand through his hair, realizing he hadn't tied it back yet this morning. "Savi, just talk to me. Tell me what he did to you."

She pushed against him, but he couldn't back down.

"I need to get back to Mari."

"She's fine with Marc and Angelina. Talk to me. What did he do to you?" He was pretty sure it had something to do with a pet cat from what she'd said in the other room. Had her father abused her pet in front of her? Whatever had been done, it clearly had been to torture his daughter, maybe to ensure her silence or compliance.

Savi needed to remember, to say the words. He brushed his hands up and down her arms trying to infuse warmth into her chilled limbs.

"I take it the flashback was of your father."

She closed her eyes and lowered her head, but she didn't deny it. "What did he do to you, Savi?"

In barely a whisper, she answered, "It's not what he did to me."

He leaned down so he could hear better, but she didn't continue. The beast stirred within. Had the bastard hurt Marisol, too?

"You're hurting me."

Damián was gripping her arms too hard and released her. *Get ahold of yourself, man.* He ground out the words, "What. Did. He. Do?"

She looked up at him, her forehead wrinkled more in confusion at his emotional response than a reaction to her own anguish. She gave the response he had demanded, but without any emotion. Her voice was matter-of-fact. "He killed Whiskers. He didn't take him to the pound. He told the little girl he would dump her out in the desert, too, if she ever told anyone about what he did to her when they were alone." He could feel her body quaking, could see the cold, blank stare as she continued in a whisper, "She never told. She kept his secrets. All of them."

He couldn't let her stop now, even though he wasn't prepared to hear her say the words. He reached up and stroked her cheek. "What little girl? What kinds of secrets?"

"Savannah's. He hurt her so badly. She shriveled up and died."

What the fuck? "You're Savannah. You didn't die."

Savi struggled to get out of his arms. "But she had to die. She couldn't live with her shame."

"The shame wasn't yours. You weren't to blame for what he did."

"No! You don't understand!" She dug her nails into his chest and pushed against him, but he didn't budge. She needed to release this misplaced guilt and shame.

"Then help me understand, Savannah."

The vehemence in her eyes was at least an emotion, not the dead look he'd seen since this flashback had started. She was feeling something—finally.

"Don't *ever* call me that again."

With a force that nearly knocked him on his ass, she shoved at him, but he quickly reset his feet and regained control. He was just glad to see her fighting back.

"It's your name, Savannah."

"No! She's dead!"

"You're not dead."

"No." She shook her head again. "I'm Savi Baker. He didn't hurt me. He hurt Savannah." She gasped on a sob. "Oh, God. I had to do it."

"Do what, Savannah?" She hung on the precipice of really letting go of the tight rein she held on her emotions and memories. Her mouth moved to speak, but no words came out. "What did you have to do?"

After a moment of struggling to form the words, she leaned back and looked up at him. "Oh dear Lord. I had to leave her with the monster."

What the...? "Leave who?"

She whispered, "Savannah."

Madre de Dios. What did that bastard do to her? How could he get through? "Savannah isn't dead. She escaped. *You* escaped. I'm holding her right now. Holding *you*." God, this conversation was fucked up. "Savannah grew up to be a wonderful mommy and to help other kids who were hurting like she'd been hurt."

She shook her head, a wild look in her eyes, but didn't say anything.

"*Bebé*, you just had to put Savannah into hiding for a little while. To let your body and mind heal. To make a new life for yourself and take care of Marisol."

She splayed her hands against his chest and grabbed his shirt. "Don't let him near her. You have to promise me you'll protect her if something happens to me."

He wrapped his arms around her and pulled her closer. She didn't fight but stood rigid. "He's never going to hurt either of you again, *mi sueño*." Encouraged that she wasn't pushing him away this time, he held her tighter, trying to enfold her into his body where she could absorb some of his strength, his heat.

Her body shook for what seemed like forever. When she spoke finally, it was in a ragged whisper. "I got away."

Damián doubted she'd ever escaped emotionally, but she had gotten away physically.

"Yes, you did."

"All thanks to you, Damián."

Bullshit. She'd had no help from Damián's sorry ass. Hell, he hadn't even stayed around for her when she'd needed him the most. Instead, he'd dumped her on the rat bastard's front steps and ridden away. He hadn't even been there for her when Marisol had been born.

But he didn't want to shut her down again. "What did I do?"

"You gave me Marisol. Without her, I never could have left that house. You gave me the courage to leave."

"If I'd known…" How much abuse was Damián responsible for after returning her to the monster's house that night?

She placed her finger over his lips. "It's not your fault. You're not to blame." Hearing her throw his own words back at him told Damián he'd at least gotten through to her mentally, whether she accepted the words for herself yet or not. Hell, she probably didn't believe them any more than he did. But guilt could eat a person alive. Man, did he know that.

Damián's gaze lowered to her full pink lips. Having her body pressed against his like this wasn't such a great idea at the moment. *Control yourself, Chico.* He'd spent more than six years regaining control of his life, his body, after Fallujah. Why couldn't he maintain control over one long-neglected part of his body at the moment?

He wasn't going to make a move on her, though. He'd only hurt her if he pushed her too far sexually and abandoned her. Again.

Which he would have to do eventually. She needed a whole man.

That didn't mean he couldn't fantasize about being with Savannah again. Savi. Whatever the hell she wanted to be called. She was the woman he'd dreamt about for more than eight years.

Mi sueño.

Chapter Four

Savi had too much to lose to get involved with Damián. So why did she feel the need to comfort him? She didn't want him to feel responsible for what her father had done to Savannah all those years ago.

She shuddered.

To her.

But she hadn't told Damián about her father back when they were two desperate nineteen-year-olds just seeking one day of perfection in each other's arms. There had been no need. She'd planned to end her life that night after he'd dropped her off at home. How could he know what horrors happened to her in the stately, sinister mansion on the hill in Rancho?

Damián's gaze warmed her lips, and she held her breath. She needed to get back to Mari. Now. Before it was too late.

Don't panic. This is Damián. He won't hurt you.

His head came toward hers, and she shivered. How could she be hot and cold at the same time? Was she about to go into another panic attack? She opened her mouth to tell him she didn't want to do this, but Damián seemed to take it as an invitation, and his lips brushed hers.

Savi's heart pounded. Fight or flight kicked in. Why couldn't she just enjoy the sensation of his kiss? Part of her wanted to respond and enjoy it. Heat pooled in her lower abdomen.

No!

I can't do this.

Damián pulled away and looked down at her. "You okay?"

She shook her head, but no words came out when she opened her mouth to speak. How had he known she needed to stop? No matter. The point was that he'd stopped, even without her needing to tell him to stop.

"I'm sorry, Damián."

"Sorry about what?"

"I can't." She couldn't even say the words, but surely he knew what she meant. She looked into Damián's deep brown eyes.

The pads of his thumbs brushed along her still damp cheekbones. "Tell me what you're feeling."

Feeling?

"Nothing."

But she had. And she didn't like it at all.

Savi shook her head and looked down in shame, trying to negate her body's response. She didn't want to feel anything sexual ever again. Kissing led to sex. Sex was dirty. Sex hurt. She splayed her hands against his chest and gave him a gentle push, but he didn't budge. Again the feelings of panic started to bubble up.

"Talk to me, Savi."

"I can't."

"Yes, you can. Look at me."

Her gaze rose to meet his. Why did he keep pushing? Worse still, why did she respond to him so docilely?

"Better." He smiled. "Now, when's the last time you were kissed—by a man, not Marisol or some air-kiss from a girlfriend. I mean the wet, heart-pounding kiss of a man."

Well, that was easy to answer. It had only happened with one person. "At Thousand Steps Beach."

Damián didn't mask the look of surprise on his face. He grinned and pointed to his chest, the obvious question in his eyes.

"Don't let it go to your head. I'm not interested in men for kissing or…anything else."

His grin widened. "I think we've made enough progress for one morning. I'll let you flit back to Marisol, *mi mariposa*, while I take a shower. A very cold shower."

Savi didn't want to think about him being aroused right now, and she tensed.

Damián placed his hands on the tops of her shoulders. "What was that thought?" He seemed upset with her reaction. She shuddered and tried to pull away.

"You want more than I can give."

"But I'm not going to take it, Savi, if you aren't giving it. I can control my body. I will never force you to do anything. I'm not like those other men."

She hoped not. She didn't think he was, either. How else would she have been able to come to him for help? But she'd only wanted his protection—not his kisses, his affection, his advances. How had this morning turned into such a chaotic mixture of emotions? Her head swam, as if she were careening on the Tilt-o-Whirl Mari loved so much at the annual church festival.

"We'll go play with Marisol and her toys. This afternoon, I'm taking you both out for Christmas dinner with some friends of mine at a nice local place I think you'll like."

Not waiting for him to change his mind about letting her go, Savi slid sideways. Pressure from his hips and his arousal, which she was trying in vain to ignore, caused her to suck in her stomach. He chuckled.

Savi nearly ran from the bathroom needing a moment to compose herself. She held her cold hands to her warm face and tried to regulate her breathing. Slowly, her heart rate returned to something resembling normal, and she planted a smile on her face. The thought of facing Damián's friends after that panic attack embarrassed her. They must think she was unbalanced.

When she opened the door and walked into the room, Marc was kneeling on the floor next to Angelina and Mari, who was holding a squirming bundle of black-and-white fur in one hand and her new plush stuffed kitty in the other, introducing the two to each other.

Marc looked up at Savi and scrutinized her. When they smiled warmly at her, Savi relaxed. Marc stood up and reached down for Angelina's hand. They came over to her while Mari continued to enjoy two of her Christmas presents.

Savi couldn't meet either of their gazes. "I'm sorry about that…"

Angelina held her hand up to halt the words. "No apology necessary. I'm just glad to see you're feeling better."

Marc looked toward the bedroom; Savi felt compelled to explain Damián's delay. "Oh, he needed to take a shower." The grin that widened across Marc's face told her what he thought, but Savi wasn't comfortable with him thinking that about her. She didn't arouse anyone, not on purpose anyway.

"With Mari and me taking over his bedroom, his bathroom time can be a little hard to schedule." His eyes told her he didn't buy a word of it. "Anyway, thank you for bringing Mari the kitten, but I know you need to get to your Christmas dinner." She wished she could return to having a quiet Christmas alone with Mari. Okay, she wanted Damián to be a part of the day, too. For

Mari.

But they could never be a real family, even if Mari connected them by blood. Savi was damaged goods.

"Oh, we're fine," Angelina assured her. "Mama makes enough food for an army." She paused a moment. "I hope you enjoy the meal at Adam and Karla's."

Savi figured that must be the restaurant Damián had mentioned where they'd be joining his friends later. "I'm sure it will be wonderful."

Angelina smiled. Maybe she'd recommended the place to Damián.

"Maman, I'm going to call him Boots. Is that a good name?"

Thank God she didn't choose Whiskers.

Savi looked at Mari's tiny hands and the ball of fluff curled up, sound asleep. The little fella trusted his new mama. She remembered how this kitten had taken great interest in Mari when they were at the outfitter's store two weeks ago. Its white paws and leggings looked like knee-high boots.

Mari crooned to her new little friend and an ache broke loose in Savi's chest. The two had bonded already. Savi would fight like a mama grizzly to make sure no one separated them. Ever.

Damián came into the room wearing black jeans and a black T-shirt with a Harley emblem on it, looking positively sinful. His hair had been drawn into the neat queue she'd come to expect. He came over to Mari and hunkered down, reaching out to pet the kitten for a moment.

Achoo!

Savi reached automatically for the box of Kleenex and handed it to Damián. "God bless you."

"Thanks." *Achoo!*

Ruddy splotches broke out on his face, and he was hit by another sneeze. Angelina dispensed the blessings this time.

Savi began to have a sick feeling in the pit of her stomach. "Damián, you aren't allergic to cats, are you?"

Please tell me you aren't.

"Of course not." *Achoo!* His gaze went to the kitten, and he squinted as the possibility dawned.

No way could she let him take Boots away from Mari. Her little girl needed something stable in her life after all the turmoil she'd been through the last couple of weeks. Mari needed this kitten. She'd already lost all the things they'd had to leave behind—all of Mari's photos, memorabilia from school, books, and toys.

She hoped she didn't lose those things forever. Savi had nothing left of her own childhood, not even from the happier years before Maman left. Having something she could call her own would make her little girl feel more secure.

After all, she couldn't impose on Damián forever, especially in his small place. They were practically climbing over each other as it was. Memories of the tight quarters in the bathroom with Damián sent an unfamiliar tension through her and a flush of heat into her cheeks. She'd imposed on Damián long enough. Maybe this was the impetus she needed to get her and Mari into a place of their own.

First things first. The first step would be to pursue legal channels and check into creating new identities for them. Then she could look into getting licensed in social work, finding a job, and renting a separate place where she and Mari could live.

But Savi didn't want to separate Mari and Damián completely. Guilt over not trying harder to unite the two of them sooner ate at her conscience again. Savi owed him the chance to get to know his daughter, to let Mari get to know her daddy.

"Sure looks like allergies to me," Marc said, pulling Savi away from her thoughts. "Do you have any Benadryl?"

Damián nodded, wiping at his eyes. "Bathroom." Marc headed in that direction, while Savi went to the kitchen to pour him some water.

Please let it be a mild allergy. Please.

* * *

Damián pulled in next to Luke's new gray Dodge Ram in the driveway. Judging by the amount of mud on the fenders, he'd been off-road somewhere this morning. It hadn't looked like that last night when Luke had delivered the dollhouse. Marc's friend was becoming a regular at the club. Of course, Luke had worked on the cabinetry and carpentry at the club a few years ago when they were trying to get the place ready to open. The man was a helluva woodworker, but his work creating the beautiful equipment in the club was his real gift.

Lately, Damián had been training the "baby Dom," as Marc liked to call him, to wield a bullwhip. The man had finesse with butterfly kisses, and Damián doubted he'd want to go any harder on a sub or bottom—not unless she needed him to. Lately, the newest Dom at the club seemed more interested in learning Shibari from Dad.

Damián wondered how Adam and Karla were getting along on their honeymoon. Hard to believe the wedding had been only a couple weeks ago, given all that had happened since then.

Savi and Marisol had happened. His life would never be the same again. He opened the back door of the Nissan and helped unbuckle Marisol while Savi eased out of the passenger side. She still moved stiffly, favoring her healing rib, but Marc assured him it was just going to take time. There was nothing much they could do. He hated feeling so fucking helpless.

Normally, Damián would be in California for Christmas, but he couldn't leave Savi and Marisol—and sure as hell wasn't going to take them back there. Good thing he'd been able to give his sister Rosa the presents he'd bought and made. They'd left a few days after Savi showed up. He would give them a call later today to see how their day went. He felt torn between two families now. But Rosa and Teresa were healing, and Savi and Marisol needed him more at the moment.

He glanced up at the old brick mansion they had fixed up. It held sentinel on this block in the rejuvenated Five Points neighborhood, its wrought-iron fence a bit intimidating but also giving the place a militaristic feel that fit the Masters at Arms Club perfectly.

Damián motioned for Savi and Marisol to precede him onto the back porch. He didn't expect anyone but Grant and Luke to show up today. He'd told them Savi had no idea half this building housed a kink club, but they were only going to be in the private residence today. No sense mentioning it.

Still he braced himself before opening the screen door. Savi would probably roast his nuts if she knew what went on here three nights a week. But it was also Dad's home, at least until he and Karla found a more appropriate place to raise a kid.

Savi held the screen door as Damián opened the inner one into the kitchen. He was assaulted with the smells of the season. Italian seasonings. Ham. Cinnamon.

Leather.

Whoa! Mierda. He could smell the club's leather all the way out here in the kitchen. Not to mention a little sweat. He'd never noticed it before but had probably just gotten used to it. He looked down at Savi and saw her cute little nose scrunching up as she appeared to sniff out the unexpected scent as well.

The confusion on her face was evident. "Adam and Karla's is…someone's home?"

Either she hadn't noticed the leather or was too polite to point it out. "Yeah. This is my adopted dad's place—Adam Montague. Do you remember meeting him and his now wife, Karla, at Rosa's house last month?"

"Oh, yeah."

"They were married the day you…arrived, but they are still on their honeymoon right now. Angelina made dinner for some of…some friends so we wouldn't have to fend for ourselves this Christmas." Damián looked down at Marisol and back at Savi. The original plan was for Angelina to cook for those who didn't have family to spend the day with—but it turned out that he *was* with his family—both his new family and his adopted family at the club.

"Now you're included. I know Dad…Adam will love seeing you again, Savi, when he gets back next week."

"Maman, why does it smell like horses in here?"

"Shhh, Mari," she whispered, bending down to Marisol to whisper, "That's not polite." Still, Damián hadn't missed the question in Savi's eyes.

Okay. How to explain this?

"Hope I didn't smell the place up too bad." Luke came down the hall drying his light brown hair with a towel. He wore a western-cut plaid shirt, jeans, and cowboy boots. "Been on a mustang filly all morning and didn't have a chance to change."

Horse leather. Damián grinned, relaxing his guard a bit.

"Haven't gotten the water hooked up at my new ranch house yet, so I just came up here a little early to take advantage of the facilities."

Marisol leaned a little closer to Damián's leg, reminding him that introductions were in order. "Savi and Marisol Baker, I'd like you to meet Luke Denton. He's a…friend of mine. He does search-and-rescue with Marc."

Luke had just bought a little place in Fairchance, near Aspen Corners, where he was setting up a workshop for his carpentry and a training facility to turn rescued mustangs into SAR horses.

Luke shook Savi's hand, smiling, before he hunkered down to Marisol's level and extended his hand to her, as well. "Hello, darlin'. You're cute as a button."

Marisol still seemed reluctant to warm up to this stranger. *Good girl.* Damián put a protective hand on his little doll's shoulder to reassure her that she was safe. She released her grip on his leg, not as scared, and drew herself up a little taller.

"Buttons aren't cute."

"Hmmm. Well, maybe that's true." He grinned. "But you are. Pleased to meet you, Marisol."

Luke waited for her to become comfortable enough to make the next move. Damián's thumb stroked her shoulder, and she stretched her tiny hand out to be swallowed up in Luke's much bigger one.

The back door opened, and a blast of cold air swooshed through the room as Grant came inside. "Merry Christmas, everyone!" Grant's blond hair was pulled into a Marine-style, above-the-collar bun the way she'd worn it in the Corps. At the club, she wore it loose or in a ponytail when in full Domme mode. Dark circles under her eyes told him something was up. The fact that she wore mock desert-digital pants like what they'd worn for physical training, along with a black, long-sleeved shirt, made her look like she was ready for a mission. A glint of something almost bitter showed in her eyes, though her smile tried to mask it. Maybe he could lift her spirits.

"Cute PT duds you've got on there, sweetheart."

Grant pounded him in the bicep with a mean hook. She laughed. *Better.* But they wouldn't be able to talk around Savi and Marisol. Maybe later.

Damián made quick introductions.

Grant looked over at the kitchen area. "Something smells great. Angelina's a lifesaver. I'd be at a fast-food restaurant, otherwise."

Damián figured he was serving as host today, so he crossed the room and approached the stove. Inside the oven, he found a hot pan of lasagna.

Luke headed to the fridge. "Angel said there's a salad and some other sides in here."

"I'll get the drinks." Grant preferred to tend bar in the club when she was without a partner or needed her physical space. She soon had drinks poured for everyone, including a glass of milk for Marisol.

"Mari, why don't you help Maman set the table?"

Within minutes, they were sitting down to a feast of traditional Italian and American Christmas dishes. Marisol said a simple grace that did something to his heart, and they began passing platters and bowls until everyone's plate was filled.

Angelina had cooked up a storm. Marc's girl had a big heart, making sure the unattached members in this community of lost souls—Damián, Luke, and Grant—celebrated the day in style with each other while Angelina was with her family in Aspen Corners.

Marc was a lucky man.

Now, Damián had Savi and Marisol.

Family. Nothing was more important to Damián.

* * *

Savi listened to the three friends catch up on their lives. They were all so different that she wondered what tied them together, though they did seem to genuinely enjoy each other's company. She especially felt the undeniable connection between Damián and Grant. He'd called her sweetheart, but it seemed more like a brother-and-sister rapport than a sexual or romantic one. A strong bond, nonetheless. Then she learned Grant—an odd name for a woman—was a Marine who had served with Damián's unit for a short time in Iraq. That explained why Damián called her by her last name. But Savi wasn't military.

"I feel funny calling you Grant. Is there a first name your non-Marine friends call you?"

Grant's hand froze in midair, and she stared blankly at Savi. Surely she'd been asked the question before. "No, ma'am. Just Grant."

The "ma'am" made Savi feel old, even though the two women were about the same age. Grant had the demeanor of someone who never left the military behind, even though she'd apparently been discharged.

"Good try, Savi," Damián said with a grin. "I thought you were going to be the first person to pull it out of her. I've known her almost seven years and have never heard anything but Grant."

Grant grinned. "Adam knows."

"Yeah, well, he's our master sergeant, too. He knows a lot of things he'd never share with a grunt like me."

As the talk at the table went on, Savi felt Mari's head lean against her arm and looked down to see her daughter had cleaned her plate and now was nodding off. She'd gotten up awfully early to see what Santa had brought her.

Damián leaned across the table toward Savi. "Let's get her upstairs to bed, so she can take a nap." He always seemed so in tune with her and Mari's needs, without her having to ask.

Savi nodded. "A sofa downstairs will be fine. I don't want her to wake up scared in a strange place."

Damián's expression grew shuttered. "The bed will be more comfortable. I can stay with her until she wakes up."

Savi didn't really have much in common with Luke and Grant, and she was feeling a need for some quiet time herself. She'd much rather escape than try to be social. "Actually, if you wouldn't mind, I'd like to lie down with her for a while. All this food has made me really sleepy."

Mari's sleeping form leaned against her until Damián came around the table and gently pulled Mari's chair out. Suddenly, it hit her. *Wow.* Once, she might have used taking a nap as a ruse to keep Damián away from her daughter, but this time she genuinely wanted to take a nap. For the first time ever, she hadn't panicked about leaving Mari alone with a man.

Of course, Damián was different, but having any man being alone with Mari would have sent up warning bells a couple weeks ago, and it hadn't. The realization that she'd come to trust him alone with her daughter, even in a bedroom, surprised the hell out of her.

As he lifted Mari into his arms, she smiled.

When Damián looked at Savi again, he frowned. "What's so funny?"

"Nothing."

He paused a moment, then he turned his attention to Mari. He was so gentle with her. Savi yearned to have him hold her with such tenderness, too.

Whoa! Where had that thought come from?

She turned to Luke and Grant. "In case you aren't here when we wake up, I just wanted to say how nice it was to meet you both." After saying their goodbyes, Savi followed Damián down a brick-lined hallway. The house was huge and very old. She imagined the furniture in the front rooms would be period pieces, possibly Georgian or even Victorian. Formal. She could understand why Damián would suggest a comfortable bed instead.

Damián seemed to be favoring his right foot or ankle again. She wished she'd thought to ask Marc to take a look at it this morning, but—with all the Christmas commotion and her meltdown—it had slipped her mind completely.

Damián preceded her into a room near the end of the hall. "It's quiet in here. I slept here when I first…when I moved to Denver."

Warm brickwork along the outer wall, a beautiful walnut bureau that matched the cannonball bed, and a log-cabin quilt on the bed made her feel instantly at home in the room. The scent of lavender enveloped her as she turned down the quilt and sheet. She grabbed Mari's legs as Damián eased her body onto the mattress. Her baby didn't even whimper.

Damián brushed the hair back from their daughter's face and looked at the sleeping child a moment. He turned to Savi to whisper, "I'll be down in the kitchen cleaning up if you need anything. Think you can find your way back down there?"

Savi met Damián's gaze. "Sure. Thank you."

"No problem." He left the room, not limping as much now. Maybe it was just lifting Mari that aggravated whatever was bothering his foot.

A sudden lethargy came over Savi. She slipped out of her shoes and walked around the bed to the side near the window and slid between the sheets. Curling onto her uninjured side and facing Mari, she let sleep claim her.

* * *

While Savi and Marisol rested, it was just Damián and Grant left in the kitchen. Luke had headed back down to Fairchance, determined to make more progress this evening with his new mustang. Damián poured two mugs of coffee. "Why the PTs?"

Grant looked across the kitchen at him. "Just missing the good old days, I guess. The holidays make me all sentimental." She smirked to lighten the mood, but her left leg shook involuntarily. She seemed more restless than nostalgic.

Was she dealing with some shit from Fallujah? Not many women Marines were placed into a combat situation, but her expert communications skills had been needed on that rooftop in the waning days of the Second Battle of Fallujah. She'd gotten a glimpse into the bowels of hell up there, something every man in the unit deeply regretted—well, those who had survived, anyway.

Yet, after her discharge, she'd hooked up with some defense contractor—or worse—and gone back to that shithole. Said she had unfinished business at the time. As far as Damián could surmise from the bits and pieces she'd shared with him over the years, she hadn't joined with an agency publicly sanctioned by the government. He wondered if she'd gotten any satisfaction.

Damián handed Grant a mug, and they moved back to the table, sitting across from each other. Lost in thought, she held the dark-blue ceramic mug between her hands as if to infuse some warmth into her fingers.

Damián didn't know anyone who loved the military life more than Grant did—well, except for Dad, maybe. Damián and Grant had kept in touch after Fallujah. Still bugged him that only Grant and Dad had gone on to finish the mission during that deployment; Damián and Marc had been sent stateside and medically discharged. He wondered if she'd been more forthcoming with Dad about that part of her life. The man had a way of worming secrets out of a person.

Damián could use some practice with mining a few secrets himself. Savi sure as hell had been harboring a shitload of them since she'd shown up here. Hell, he didn't really know much about Savi's background at all. They'd wrapped themselves in a cocoon during that one perfect day at the beach, not letting the world intrude in any way.

Even though he'd known Grant a lot longer, she'd kept her background unknown to him as well. Maybe she'd talk if she really was in a nostalgic mood.

"What did you get into after you left the Corps?"

"Trouble, mostly." She laughed harshly and looked back down at the black liquid in her mug. "Made some bad decisions. Connected with the wrong people." She lifted the mug to her mouth, holding on with one hand, two fingers curled through the handle. Setting it down, she looked at him. "Got into contracting."

"You went back to Iraq."

She nodded. "Mostly Anbar Province. My knowledge of Fallujah was a bonus to our missions."

"Fucking shithole."

"Actually, I got to know some people there who, at first anyway, changed my opinion of the place. A former Army National Guard soldier in my group got me to take a closer look. Learned more about their religion, their economy, their culture. Made locating and dealing with the friendlies a little easier."

"Problem is, you could never tell a hundred percent who the friendlies were."

A shadow passed over her eyes. "Yeah. Sometimes, though, the traitors were right in your own group. Needed to watch out who you lowered your guard with, no doubt about it."

Damn. Someone had betrayed her, broken her trust. He hoped she'd settled the score with the asshole.

"What made you leave?"

The grim set of her mouth told him this conversation was nearing an end. "Bunch of reasons." She stood and picked up their near-empty mugs. "Refill?"

He nodded.

She walked over to the counter. "How about some of these Italian cookies? They're fucking awesome." She poured the Joe and returned to the table carrying the steaming mugs, and then she went back to retrieve the platter.

Damián wasn't sure why, but he didn't want to let the conversation veer off track. Practice for upcoming talks with Savi, maybe? No, he just wanted to know what had happened to Grant to bring her here a year ago, looking lost and not a little pissed when she'd shown up here.

"What kinds of missions were you assigned?"

Grant bit into a cookie as she thought. Still maintaining silence, she took a sip from the mug. Finally, she turned her gaze to his. "Counterterrorism. Black ops. We could do things—get in and out of places—that legit personnel, especially female ones, couldn't."

Damián grinned. "Borderline legal?"

She smiled back. "Way past the border."

"You miss it." It wasn't a question.

Those storm clouds formed in her eyes again. "Yeah. I miss it."

"Why'd you leave?"

"Didn't really have a choice. Some dickhead got me booted."

Mierda. He'd never have guessed. No wonder she was so pissed. He could ask if she wanted to talk about it, but she'd just say no. Open-ended questions. He also needed to push her a bit, if he wanted her to get riled up enough to respond. "What did you do to get kicked out?"

Grant slammed the mug onto the table. "I did my fucking job. Maybe too well. He must have been jealous. I don't have a fucking clue. All I know is that, if I ever see him again, he'll regret the decision he made for the rest of his life."

Bingo. He wished he could get Savi to lose her cool like that. She had a lot of anger and hurt buried deep inside.

Later.

"So do you plan to hunt him down?"

"Oh, I've looked. He went off the scope last summer. And he's a master of disguise. I'm sure he's just gone to ground somewhere. Deep cover." After taking another sip, she continued. "Like all rats, he has to surface sometime. I'll get mine."

Damián had no doubt she'd succeed ultimately at her mission. Grant was nothing if not tenacious.

Could he help Savi deal with some of the rats from her past, too? He'd like to plug the rats' holes until they fucking suffocated and rotted. Or plug them with a bullet. Made no difference—as long as the outcome was they couldn't hurt Savi ever again.

Something Grant had said made him think. "How easy would it be to get Savi and Marisol documented? Savi had to leave all her legal records behind. For their safety, it would probably be best to change their names altogether. Know anyone who can help?"

Grant smiled. "Damo, I have more connections with the feds than you can shake a stick at. Just tell me what you need and how deep you want them buried."

* * *

A tiny hand on her face caused Savi's eyes to shoot open.

"Hi, Maman. You slept a long time."

Not nearly long enough. Dear Lord, Savi hadn't slept so peacefully in…forever. This room had an incredibly calming effect on her. She half rolled over and glanced toward the window. It was dark outside. What time was it? She didn't wear a watch. Reaching to retrieve it from her purse, she realized she'd left it downstairs. Another lapse. What if she'd had to escape again?

"Can we go home and see Boots now? He's probably lonely."

Savi blinked. Home. Children had such an amazing way of adapting to their surroundings. Just meet their basic human needs, and they thrived.

"Sure, honey. Let's go find Dami—Daddy."

Mari jumped up, slipped into her shoes, and was nearly out the door before Savi could even sit up. "Hold on, Mari! I need to put on my shoes." Savi quickly straightened up the quilt but abandoned making the bed fully when she chased after Mari. She caught up with her rambunctious daughter outside the bedroom door looking confused. *Join the club.* Mari had been asleep when she'd been brought upstairs and had no clue which way to turn.

"This way, honey." *I think.* Savi walked back down the hallway and hoped she was heading the way Damián had brought them up here. The stairway ahead confirmed she had remembered correctly.

At the foot of the stairs, she found a closed door to the left and an open archway to the right. She didn't remember Damián opening a door when he carried Mari upstairs, but she was curious about what was beyond the door. Her mother had passed her fascination with antique furniture and architecture on to Savi. The house had such beautiful furniture in the bedroom upstairs; the downstairs would be equally decorated, she was certain.

She walked over to the door and placed her hand on the doorknob. Just a quick peek…

Locked. How odd. Maybe it didn't lead to the living room after all, but still, having it locked just made her more curious.

"Daddy!"

Savi jumped and turned to find Damián staring at her, a scowl on his face. Guilt washed over her for snooping, not that she'd seen anything. Hell, he was the host. He could have offered her a tour.

"I was dying to see the rest of the house. It's beautiful, and I have a thing for Victorian houses."

He glanced at the door and back at her. "Dad keeps that part of the house locked off." He smiled down at Mari. "Angelina made some great cookies. Who wants some?"

"Me!" Mari took his hand and glanced back at Savi to see if she was going to say no.

"Go on. I'm right behind you."

Damián turned and led the way back to the kitchen.

"Grant and Luke left a while ago." He took the plastic wrap off the plate of cookies and pulled some saucers down from an overhead cabinet. Savi went to the fridge to get the milk out, but the pot of coffee smelled so good. That's all she wanted right now.

"You two must have been worn out."

As they sat at the table with their treats, Savi nodded. "I haven't slept that well in ages."

"Sorry my digs aren't quite up to this speed."

Savi reached out to touch the top of his hand but pulled back surprised at how natural it had been for her to do so. "No. It's not that. I don't know. I just had a very relaxing afternoon and the room was so…comforting."

Damián stared at the untouched cookies on his plate. "Yeah. It was good for me, too. This place was my haven when I first came to Denver."

"When did you move here?" She wanted to know more about the missing years.

"Six years ago. Adam took me in. Treated me like a son. Well, sometimes he treated me like he was my master sergeant." He grinned. "That's the rank he held when I served under him in Fallujah."

"Ah. I wondered how you two came together; why you called him Dad." Savi could hear the emotion in his voice when he spoke of the man. She'd met him briefly following the altercation with Teresa's father in Solana Beach. He seemed like a nice man. Definitely someone people would take orders from out of respect and not fear.

Well, people other than Savi anyway. She didn't bow to authority figures if she could help it.

Damián nodded. "That sort of just happened. I think he regretted never having kids of his own. And I sure was fu…" He stopped and looked at Mari who was poking her finger into the jam filling in one of her cookies. "I was messed up back then." She got the distinct impression he might be thinking he was still "fucked" up. She grinned that he was policing his language around their daughter. She imagined he could get pretty colorful at times, if he was like any of the Marines she'd met near Pendleton.

"I'm glad you found someone, Damián." Nothing worse than being lost and alone in the world. Savi had been blessed, too, she supposed, with Father Martine and Anita. She still remembered the day they'd discovered her hiding in the choir loft at the church that Christmas Eve so long ago.

"Merry Christmas, Father!"

Father? No! He couldn't have found her so soon! Savi's head bolted up from where it rested on her backpack, and she tried to take in her surroundings. Pipe organ. Two long pews covered with red-velvet cushions, more than a little frayed and stained with age. Who woke her? At first, she didn't see anyone.

Then a priest with dark black hair and olive-colored skin, wearing an ankle-length black robe—or whatever they called it—walked across the choir loft to fiddle with some buttons on the organ.

"I think it'll make it through our Midnight and Christmas Day Masses, Anita, but we're definitely going to have to see about getting a repairman in here to look at the old girl. She's getting tired, I think."

"Don't worry, Father. I'll coax her to make beautiful music once again." A Hispanic woman in a pretty Kelly-green dress set her purse down on the floor beside the organ and removed her jacket. Grasping the red-rimmed eyeglasses that hung on a chain around her

neck, she lifted them onto her face and scrutinized the organ.

The priest looked at the organist and smiled in a non-threatening way, as if he meant it. "I'm sure you…" His gaze drifted to the corner where Savi sat huddled, trying to be invisible. "Who do we have here?"

Savi's heart pounded, beating like a fist. Would he make her leave? Where could she go? Her hands began to shake followed by her arms and legs. When he came toward her, she fumbled to her knees, hoping to get away before he touched her.

"Whoa, don't be afraid. I won't hurt you, little one."

Savi grabbed her backpack and stood, but her head swam from rising too quickly. The priest reached out to her and she screamed. "No! Don't touch me!"

He held his hands up to show he meant no harm and would comply, but she only began to shake more. Her teeth rattled, and a knot formed in her chest.

The woman he'd called Anita came around from behind the priest. "It's okay, sweetheart. Father Martine and I won't hurt you. We just want to help." Her calm voice released some of the tension from Savi's chest, and she filled her lungs with much-needed air.

"I-I-I didn't take anything. I j-just wanted to sleep a little bit before I moved on."

The priest smiled, his brown eyes crinkling at the corners. "You're most welcome to stay, but I'm afraid sleep will be impossible up here soon, with Midnight Mass just a couple hours away."

"It's Christmas Eve?"

"Of course it is," Anita answered, a puzzled look in her eyes.

They must think I'm an idiot, not knowing it's Christmas Eve.

The woman turned to the priest. "Father, why don't you go on and get ready for Mass. I'd like to talk with our Christmas visitor a bit more—alone."

Father Martine nodded at the woman and smiled at Savi. *Don't trust him. Men smile to get what they want.* She'd learned at a very young age that they always wanted some part of her she wasn't willing to give. Never again.

His smile faded, as if disappointed to see smiling would get him nowhere with her. "Welcome to San Miguel's, little one. Please stay as long as you like. We have an open-door policy, and we're glad you came to us."

Savi regarded him warily until he turned to the organist and nodded, an exchange passing between them Savi couldn't decipher. After he left, Savi's focus zeroed in on the woman. Anita. Her warm brown eyes showed compassion. Or was it pity? She wasn't sure which. They reminded her of Maman's eyes.

"Would you like to sit and talk a bit?"

Savi shook her head. She didn't want to reveal anything to this woman or anyone else. If they knew who she was, where she'd come from, they might send her back. No way would she go back. Ever.

"I'm good at listening. I work at a mental-health clinic."

A shrink? Oh, perfect. That's all she needed was someone getting inside her head. No thanks.

"I should go."

"Where will you go?"

Savi's glance shifted to the floor before she raised her gaze again. "San Diego. Maybe LA." *Surely those cities had places for teenage runaways. No, wait. She was nineteen now. An adult. She wouldn't be eligible or welcome in those places.*

She had nowhere to turn. The face of the woman swam before her eyes, and Savi's shaking began again. Oh Lord. What was she going to do?

The woman came closer, and Savi stepped away until her back came against the wall. Trapped. Her breathing became shallow, rapid.

"Please...Don't...Touch...Me." She sucked in a breath between each word, then drew a deep, ragged one and said in a rush, "I don't like to be touched."

"I understand. Come. Let's sit down a minute and get comfortable. My knees have been bothering me today." *She smiled and walked over to the front pew, sitting and looking up at Savi. Waiting.*

Savi's gaze went from the worn pew cushion to the brown-haired woman. There was a space of a few feet between Anita and the end of the pew. She wouldn't feel hemmed in. Maybe the woman could help her find a shelter or someplace to stay until she could get a job.

Doing what? She had no training or skills. All she'd thought about was escaping from her father and Lyle. But how could she support herself and her baby? Her hand went automatically to her abdomen.

"Are you in pain?"

Savi shook her head and let her hand drop to her side. She didn't want to reveal her condition to this woman for fear she would make her give her baby away. No one was going to take her baby. Not as long as she could stop them.

The woman patted the seat. "Come. I promise not to bite or claw." *She smiled, her eyes growing even warmer, if possible. Maman had warm brown eyes, too. Anita didn't seem like a threat. Maybe...*

Savi took a step toward her. To keep her arms from shaking, she wrapped them around her waist hugging herself. Another step. Another. Almost there. Her gaze homed in on the empty section of the pew cushion.

When she stood inches away, Savi braced herself. Anita didn't make a move toward her, so Savi relaxed in small degrees and eventually slid onto the cushion, pressing her back against the end of the pew as far from the woman as she could go. Slowly, she raised her gaze to the woman's face again.

"You're safe now, sweetheart. Whatever you're running from, we won't let it touch you here."

How could the woman make such a promise? She didn't even know from what—or whom—Savi was running.

"Are you on any illegal drugs?"

Savi was surprised by the blunt question, but shook her head.

"Good. That always complicates things. My name's Anita Gonzales. And yours?"

Savi sized her up a moment. Should she reveal her name? She wasn't planning to use her birth name. Savannah Gentry didn't exist any longer.

"Savi Baker." When she'd given herself a new name to coincide with her new self, she'd chosen Baker—the English translation for her French-born maman's maiden name, Pannier.

Anita smiled, revealing slightly crooked eyeteeth. "Nice to meet you, Savi. How old are you?"

Savi was an infant, birthed in her bathroom the day she'd discovered she was pregnant. But that response would only invite more questions. "Nineteen."

Anita studied her a moment. As if satisfied with her response, she nodded slightly. Did she think she was a runaway? Well, Savi guessed she was. Just not a juvenile one.

"Do you have a place to stay?"

Savi looked down at the cushion and reached out to pull a loose thread. "Sure."

"Don't lie to me, Savi."

Her gaze returned to the woman as Savi shrank away, but she'd already backed up against the pew and had no place to go. Anita was angry at her. Savi knew that meant trouble. She didn't want to give this woman or anyone else a reason to punish her. When her hand began to shake, she pulled it back and wrapped both arms around her abdomen. She had to protect the baby in case the woman hit her.

Savi flinched when the woman reached her hand out and laid it on the cushion between them, much as Damián had done in the hotel room, like someone might do while training a dog to accept them and not to bite. Anita just let it lie there. What was that all about? Was Anita afraid of Savi? How ridiculous. Savi had no bite. She was a victim, not an attacker.

No, that was Savannah. She was dead. But Savi could be or do whatever she wanted. The thought was rather freeing.

Terrifying. Tears burned her eyes. She didn't know who she was or wanted to be. All she knew were the actresses in the movies she watched to escape into, like Novalee from "Where the Heart Is" or Slim from "Enough." And the heroines in the books she devoured. Two strong women she admired for making a life for their babies. They hadn't let their victim status get them down. They'd fought back.

Savi wanted to fight back, too.

But how?

Chapter Five

Damián watched as Marc gave Marisol her first ski lesson on the slope twenty yards away. The New Year's weekend was in full swing here in Aspen. Marc had insisted there was room for Damián to bring Savi and Marisol up to enjoy a much-needed break at his family's resort.

Savi stood on the slopes nearby, ever watchful of their baby girl. She rarely let Marisol out of her sight. Not that Damián or Marc had let Savi even think about putting on skis. The doctor had said another three or four weeks before that broken rib would heal, and Damián would make sure she followed those orders.

For years, Marc had told Damián about special equipment he could use to learn to ski with his stump, but he'd never wanted to try. Until now. Marisol fell on her butt, and Damián almost came off the bench wanting to run over and pick her up to make sure she hadn't hurt herself. Then she started giggling as Marc reached down and took her arm to lift her up onto her skis again.

"Marc's an incredibly patient teacher."

Damián looked up as Angelina sat down beside him on the bench. "Why aren't you out on the slopes with them?"

She shrugged. "Didn't feel like it today. How about you?"

Damián looked down at his foot and back at her, but he didn't state the obvious.

"You know Marc has equipment that would get you out there."

So he'd heard.

Damián had been too busy with Savi and Marisol to take the time to learn to ski when Marc had taken Rosa and the kids to a resort near Denver. *Hell, 'fess up, man.* Even before Savi and Marisol showed up on his doorstep, he'd had no intention of joining them. He didn't want to show Teresa and

José their uncle was a cripple. Off the slopes, he was able to hide his disability pretty well.

However, sitting here on the sidelines didn't sit well with him. He wanted to be the one Marisol looked to for help getting up, not Marc. Not that he'd be able to show her how to ski. He'd never been on skis before in his life.

Beside him, Angelina sighed. She'd seemed subdued at breakfast, too, but he reminded himself it was none of his business.

Old Dom habits die hard, though. At the club, he needed to look out for all of the subs and that need didn't end outside the club's doors. "What do you think of Marc's family?" This was Angelina's first time to meet them since she and Marc had moved in together a few months ago.

Her smile seemed genuine. "They're wonderful. I can see where he gets a lot of his personality traits. They've been very welcoming…" Her smile faded; her voice drifted off.

"Except…" She sighed even more heavily. "His late brother Gino's fiancée is driving me crazy. There's something…I don't know. Something Marc hasn't told me about his relationship with her."

Okay, so this was a conversation she needed to be having with Marc. "Have you talked with him about her?"

Angelina shook her head. "We haven't really had a chance."

"Bullshit, and you know it."

She looked taken aback at first, then nodded and smiled sheepishly. "Yeah." She looked down at her lap. "I think I'm afraid of hearing the answers to my questions."

"You know he'll tell you the truth. He's already been bitten in the ass once for lying. I can assure you that the man learned his lesson."

Angelina stared out at the slopes, and Damián followed her gaze. While she thought about it, Damián refocused his attention on Marisol as Marc taught her a new move on the bunny slope. Savi glanced in his direction and flashed him a smile that stirred his dick to life. *Madre de Dios*, she was so fucking beautiful. So perfect.

He hated the reason she'd come back to him, but he was so damned glad she had turned to him and not someone else.

"I sometimes feel that Marc wears a mask."

He turned to Angelina again. "He hasn't worn one at the club for a couple months."

"Well, he didn't stop wearing it voluntarily." She glanced down. "I…um, well, Karla and Cassie and I were…oh, hell, I destroyed his wolf mask last October."

Damián raised his eyebrows. *Damn.* He fought the urge to laugh out loud, not wanting to encourage a sub's bratty behavior, but it was about time someone got rid of that asinine thing. Marc needed to admit who he was, no matter who might have a problem with it. Chances of any of the people he said he was hiding from, especially his parents, ever seeing him in the club were nonexistent. Maybe he wasn't hiding from them at all, though, but himself.

Realization struck Damián. Just like—

"Marco taught me to ski in college."

Damián looked up at a stunning Italian woman dressed in an expensive-looking ski outfit he'd guess had never come near touching the snow. She sat down on the bench on the other side of Angelina, who stiffened and inched closer to Damián. Was this the woman Angelina had just been talking about?

"You went to college with Marc?" Angelina asked. He heard the tremor in her voice.

"Yes. I'll never forget that September he brought me up here to meet his family."

Angelina clenched and unclenched her hands. Was she debating whether she should deck the woman or just run away from her?

"Mama D'Alessio invited me over last night to welcome Marco home, but I hardly got to speak with him the way you monopolized his time."

Angelina's body tensed.

The catty woman bared her claws as she tried to get a rise out of Angelina. Damián hadn't heard Marc talk about anyone special who had gotten under his skin before he'd enlisted, certainly not like Savannah had affected Damián.

He reached over and squeezed Angelina's hand. Surely, she knew Marc thought the world of her. How could she think this woman had any influence over Marc anymore, if she ever had?

Angelina sat up taller. "Marc's his own man and can decide who he wants to spend his time with."

"Well, I'm just saying you shouldn't try to keep Marco away from us. We missed him at Christmas especially."

The woman made it sound like she was more important to the family—or had more of a right to be here—than Angelina.

"Family is very important to both of us, Melissa. I've enjoyed meeting his family very much this weekend, but we couldn't be in two places at once. He spent Christmas with my family."

Now it was the bitch's turn to clench her fists. Apparently, Angelina had hit a nerve. Good for her.

Melissa stood and pranced off in a huff, and Angelina's body relaxed. Soon she began shaking. He caged her chin and forced her to focus on him. "Breathe deeply." She didn't respond. "Now, Angelina."

She took several shallow breaths, but it didn't erase the tears in her eyes. At least her shaking stopped. He released her face but took her hand and squeezed it. "Just ignore her. She's only trying to make trouble. Marc's with you, not her."

"Thanks. I'm okay."

"Talk to Marc. Tonight."

She nodded. "I'll try."

"Don't try. Do it."

She pulled away. "I'm going up to the room. I'll probably see you at dinner."

Damián watched her walk toward the chair lift and wondered if she had any intention of dealing with the issue. Ultimately, that was between her and Marc. He had his hands full with Savi and Marisol.

Damián looked out at the slopes and saw Marc skiing backward down a slightly steeper grade, Marisol facing him, her eyes wide and excitement mixed with fear evident on her face. He appeared ready to catch her if she fell.

She placed all her trust in Marc at the moment. Damián wanted her to look at him like that.

His gaze drifted to Savi and met hers for a minute, but she quickly turned away.

He wished Savi would place her trust in him, too. It would probably be a lot easier for Marisol to do that than his *savita*.

* * *

Damián looked up as Marc strolled into the bar area, ordered something, and slid onto a barstool. Marc ran his hand through his hair and sighed. Something must be up, but Damián wasn't sure his friend wanted company. If he did, he'd either be upstairs with Angelina or have joined him. Marc valued his solitude and privacy more than anyone Damián knew.

Maybe Angelina had brought up the subject of Melissa.

When the redheaded bartender set a glass and a bottle of white wine in front of him, Marc waited for her to pour a sample but didn't bother to go through his usual ritual of tasting. He picked up the bottle and filled the glass nearly to the rim, and then downed the contents in a few swallows.

Marc was going to be shitfaced if he kept chugging his wine like that. Damián picked up his beer and headed over to see what was up.

"Where's Angelina?"

Marc looked up at him. "Upstairs." He looked around to see if anyone was with Damián. "How about Savi and Marisol?"

"I think you wore Marisol out on the slopes today. They said they plan to soak in their Jacuzzi and go to bed early."

Damián was disappointed that their last night at the resort would be spent apart. Savi didn't even want to have dinner with him; she'd said they'd order room service instead. For *their* room. They'd been apart most of the day, and he missed them like crazy.

Funny, a few weeks ago he'd have been fine being alone. Situation normal. Now the thought of them not being in his life hurt. An actual physical pain.

Damián took a seat next to his friend and a swig of his now-warm beer. The bartender placed several bowls of salty snacks between them. She reminded him of the redhead he and Marc had played with at the kink club in LA, just before they'd been deployed to Iraq. Marc had insisted Damián come along that night. It had been the first time Damián had experienced BDSM in a positive way since he'd dumped his kinkster girlfriend after juvie.

Damián reached for a handful of pistachios and laid them in a row in front of him. He opened one and set the shells aside. Marc seemed pissed about something. "Anything you want to talk about?"

"Not particularly."

So much for that.

Marc paused, grabbing a nut and cracking it open. "Tell me more about you and Savi. Where did you meet her?"

Damián washed another nut down with a swallow of beer. "At the hotel where I worked a long time ago. She was in trouble, and I happened to be the only person around to help."

"You played the hero, huh?"

"Something like that."

Some fucking hero. He'd taken her back to the very man she was on the run from now.

"Why didn't you tell me you had a kid?"

"Didn't know myself until a couple weeks ago."

"*Merda!* She's the Savannah you were always talking about in Fallujah!"

Damián nodded. "Yeah, but don't call her Savannah. She'll bite off your head and spit it back at you."

"Duly noted." He drained his glass and refilled it.

Damián ordered another Dos Equis, definitely his last of the night. "We'll be shoving off tomorrow about noon. If I don't see you here before that, thanks for everything. Seeing Savi and Marisol laughing out there today was great."

"Glad to have you all here. Looks like we'll be leaving tomorrow, too."

"I thought you were going to stick around and visit with your family more."

"Change of plans."

That didn't sound good. The bartender set another bottle in front of Damián. "Angelina said she liked your family."

Marc grinned, first time since he'd walked in here. "They like her a lot, too. I tried to tell her she had nothing to worry about."

If his family and Angelina weren't the problem, then the Italian barracuda must have said something to upset him. Clearly, Marc wasn't going to talk about it, though.

Time to change the subject. "Adam and Karla should be home sometime tomorrow afternoon. I want to stop by and see him before we head home. Fill them in on what's going on."

"Tell them we'll invite them over later this week. Angelina would love to cook something up. Why don't you all come over, too?"

"I'd like that, but I'll have to check with Savi."

Marc nodded. "*Merda*." Abruptly, Marc stood up. "If you'll excuse me, I need to go check on Angelina. We may come down for drinks and appetizers later, unless she wants to just go have dinner. You want to join us?"

"No. I'll finish this one and head back upstairs."

Motioning to the bartender, Marc signed for both checks and told the bartender to charge anything else to Marc's room.

Damián felt like a fucking freeloader but after his Christmas splurge, he didn't have the funds available to even cover the drinks for this weekend.

At least this week he'd get his sorry ass back to work at the Harley shop and get some money coming in again so he wouldn't have to dig even deeper into the money he'd saved for the dream of starting his own Harley repair business someday. *Fuck that dream.* Despite years of putting every spare cent into his savings, he needed to face reality. He had a daughter to support now, and she came before any biker dreams.

But her mother had been a major part of his dreams for a long time.

Mi sueño. Talk about a fucking pipe dream.

* * *

Savi leaned against the head rest and let the wintry scenery fly by without paying much attention. The weekend in Aspen had been fun but exhausting.

Marisol certainly had taken to the slopes and her new environs. Savi wished she could adjust as quickly. She wanted to regain control of her life, or some semblance of it, as soon as possible. They'd been away from California for three weeks, mooching off Damián. While he'd gotten called back to work this week, he still didn't have the resources to put them up indefinitely.

She wished she'd taken her legal papers before fleeing the house in California during Lyle's attack. How many times did she counsel families with domestic-abuse issues that they needed to have things like that ready to take with them, if they had to leave and find shelter? She'd been too terrified to think of anything but getting to Mari. There was no going back to her house for them now. Lyle and her father surely had the place under surveillance. Maybe even Mari's school wouldn't be safe. And how could she register her without her immunization and school records?

Oh, Lord, what was she going to do?

"Mind if I stop off at Adam and Karla's before we head home, Savi? They just got back from their honeymoon."

Savi remembered the nice house where they'd spent much of Christmas day and the couple she'd met at Teresa's house. She'd rather go back to Damián's and decompress in a long, hot bath, but she couldn't even control something that simple in her life anymore.

"No, that's fine." Mari would sleep most of the way to Denver, so she should be well-rested by the time they got there. Thoughts of what she was going to do when she went home drained what little energy she had, and she closed her eyes.

No, not home. Damián's…

Savi awoke with a start when they hit a bump, and she looked up. She'd fallen asleep. It amazed her that she trusted Damián enough to make herself that vulnerable. Maybe it was just exhaustion.

"Sorry about that rude awakening, *querida*."

Savi wiped the sleep from her eyes and looked out the passenger window to see they'd pulled into the drive of Adam and Karla's, next to a white Hummer generously dusted with road salt. She wondered where they'd honeymooned. Savi turned around and looked into the backseat to find Mari rubbing the sleep from her eyes, as well.

"Where are we, Maman?"

"Remember the house where we had Christmas dinner? Well, we're going to visit some of Daddy's friends here for a bit."

"Can we go home soon? I want to see Boots."

As Savi opened the back door and unbuckled Mari, she assured her daughter they'd be home soon. *Home? No, Damián's place.*

"Damián!"

Savi held onto Mari's hand as she looked up to watch a woman with long, black curly hair catapult herself across the porch and into Damián's arms. Karla. Savi remembered thinking this young woman and Damián were a couple the first time she'd seen them sitting next to each other and holding hands in the waiting room at her office. They'd been holding hands again when she'd seen them later at her church after choir practice.

Not that it mattered to her.

Damián reached up and touched a pink-and-green filigreed choker around her neck. "What's this?"

She beamed at him. "One of my Christmas presents. Adam had it designed especially for me."

He smiled at her. "Congratulations, sweetheart."

Congratulations didn't seem like something you'd tell someone for receiving a Christmas gift, but Savi soon forgot that when Damián bent down and kissed the young woman's cheek. Savi wondered if they had ever been anything more than close friends. An unfamiliar emotion bubbled up, leaving her unsettled. She chose not to explore it any further and walked up to them.

"Ms. Baker?" Karla looked from Savi to Damián and back again, but quickly recovered. "What a nice surprise. Happy New Year!"

"Same to you. Please call me Savi. And this is my daughter, Mari."

Karla took one look at Mari, and her gaze riveted toward Damián with a question in her eyes. He grinned and nodded, and Karla beamed as she hunched down to Mari's height and exchanged hellos.

A male voice interrupted the scene. "Who do we have here?"

Savi looked up at Adam walking across the porch, his stride almost pantherlike. She shuddered, trying to control her fight-or-flight response. *He doesn't want to hurt you.* His smile was warm. Savi relaxed.

"Dad, you remember Savi?"

So he really did call the man Dad.

Damián cupped the back of Mari's head. "And this little doll is our daughter, Marisol."

The older man's green eyes twinkled as he grinned ear to ear. "You had to beat me to it, huh?"

Savi watched as Karla's hand went to her abdomen and the young woman smiled at Adam. The newlywed couple was expecting. Their easy acceptance of Damián's being the brand-new father of a seven-year-old made it clear these people shared a close bond with nonjudgmental, unconditional love.

Adam pointed the way to the door. "Let's get inside before you all freeze to death." The man wore black jeans and a black, short-sleeved, USMC-imprinted T-shirt, but he didn't seem to be cold at all.

Inside the house, the warmth of the kitchen enveloped them. Such a friendly home, it exuded a welcoming vibe. Savi wondered if she'd get a tour of it this time. She still wanted to check out that mysterious, closed-off living room.

When Damián placed a hand at the small of her back, Savi froze and stepped away to put some much-needed space between them. She ignored the look of sadness that crossed his face. Surely he didn't think spending a weekend together—in adjoining rooms, of course—would have changed anything. What did he want from her? When would he demand more than she could give?

Karla offered everyone a warm drink and soon had a pot of milk heating on the stove for cocoa. Damián asked if he could talk with Adam in the office, and Savi watched them walk down a hallway toward the front of the house. So much for the grand tour.

"Um, how was your honeymoon?"

Oh, what an invasive question. But Karla just grinned and didn't make her feel nosey at all for asking.

"Wonderful." The woman blushed and touched her choker. "We went to his family's cabin in the Black Hills. It was a nice escape after a few crazy months around here."

Savi knew Karla and Adam had gone to California after Teresa's attack in early November. Because they were so close to Damián, she could imagine that incident would have affected them all profoundly.

"Damián called us earlier to say he was in Aspen. I just assumed he'd gone up with Marc and Angie."

"Yeah, they were there, too." Savi reached out and stroked her daughter's hair. "Mari got some ski lessons."

"How about you?"

"No. Doctor's orders." She realized the woman didn't know what had happened. "I broke a rib a few weeks ago. It's still healing."

When she looked back at Karla, the woman's eyelids had opened wider. "I'm so sorry! I hope you're feeling better."

"Much. Thanks."

"Did Damián go skiing?"

"Oh, no. He seems to have an aversion to the slopes. He just watched."

The disappointment in the other woman's face puzzled Savi, but she didn't pursue it. There were lots of things Savi didn't want to try, usually out of fear. For whatever reason, he wanted to avoid skiing. She'd respect his choice. If not for Mari, Savi probably would have stayed in the lodge and read a book by the fire.

"How long have you and Adam known each other?"

"Nine years." She didn't look old enough to know him that long. "We met when I was sixteen." Karla smiled. "He rescued me from my own stupidity."

Karla told her the story of how she'd run away at sixteen to find fame and fortune but had wound up close to being kidnapped by a pimp. Savi shuddered. How many times had her father and Lyle threatened that fate for her if she hadn't obeyed them? Toward the end of her enslavement, she'd wondered if perhaps the life of a street hooker might have been preferable to the treatment she'd received at their hands and those of their sadistic clients.

Feeling unwanted emotions roiling to the surface, Savi took a sip of her cocoa and found it still too hot to drink. The back door opened, and Grant walked in. The woman exuded a quiet power.

Grant took one look at Karla's necklace and grinned.

"Congratulations, Karla. You've been collared by one of the best."

Collared? It sounded like a police term, nothing to do with Karla's receiving a pretty necklace.

Karla laughed and touched the necklace Adam had given her. "Some days, I wonder what I've gotten myself into."

What was it about this necklace that had everyone in such awe? It was beautiful, but it was still just a necklace.

Grant moved to the coffee pot and poured herself a mug. "You so deserve this, after all you've put up with."

Savi felt like an outsider and glanced at the doorway through which Damián had disappeared with Adam. How long would they be gone? She just wanted to get back home and decompress for a while.

Yes, she was beginning to think of his apartment as home, a safe haven. She only hoped it would remain one. How long could she hide from Lyle and her father?

* * *

Damián watched Dad clench his fist after he told him what had happened to bring Savi to his doorstep. Well, he'd shared as much as he'd been able to determine about what had happened. Getting Savi to talk about it was like pulling teeth from a shark. She'd much rather bite his head off than answer him.

"Bastard ought to be castrated."

"Yeah, well, stand in line for those honors. Listen, part of what I need to talk with you about has to do with these *dos cabrones*. I just got called back to the Harley shop part-time starting on Tuesday. I'm going to need some help keeping Savi and Marisol safe while I'm at work."

"You know we'll all do what it takes—Grant, Marc, me. Family comes first. Is she going to let us do our jobs, though? She looked like she was afraid I was going to tear her limb from limb when I first approached her on the porch."

Damián looked down at his hands. "Yeah, well, getting her to trust anyone—especially men—could be a problem. But until I know those shitheads have been neutralized, I want my girls under twenty-four/seven watch."

"Can do. While I'm at it, I'll contact a few retired recon Marines and see what they can dig up in California." Damián knew Dad wouldn't bring any active-duty Marines into this operation. They'd have to answer to the Uniform Code of Military Justice if they got caught, a system that would come down on them a helluva lot harder than the civilian criminal court system would on those no longer serving actively.

Back in master-sergeant mode, Dad continued. "Grant's the best when it comes to communications, or I wouldn't have had her up on that goddamned roof in Fallujah."

Dad had never forgiven himself for putting Grant into a combat situation. Women Marines, like all women, were to be protected even if they *had* trained alongside the other Marines. Not only was it the right thing to do, but from Dad's, Damián's, Marc's and every other Marine's perspective, there was a good reason for it, too. With a woman present in a firefight, a man's focus would shift at a critical moment from the mission to trying to protect the woman in harm's way.

Damián had to admit his thoughts had gone to Grant even before thinking about Miller on that rooftop. Maybe if he'd focused on Miller sooner, he could have... *Enough.* Dad would kick his ass if he took that thought to its logical conclusion.

The chain of command had thought the worst of the hostilities were over at the time; unfortunately that had been far from the case. All the men who'd survived that attack on the rooftop carried that guilt of Grant's having to experience combat. Then she'd gone and volunteered for covert missions that they knew beyond any doubt had put her into much more dangerous situations. *Damned warrior-woman.*

"I've already talked with Grant, Dad. She's on board for whatever we need. I've also asked her to obtain some new identities and documents for Savi and Marisol, so they can start a new life here."

"Good thinking. We can pull in some discreet bodyguards. Besides us, I'm sure Victor would take a shift, if he can get away from Patti. Some days, he has his hands full with her. There are some others, too. Make sure Savi knows she and Marisol are under constant guard, so they won't think they're being followed."

Damián nodded. Dad had more connections than Damián would have been able to muster, evidenced by the retired and former military men who had attended his wedding. Knowing Dad could enlist help in putting up a safe perimeter around Savi and Marisol helped Damián relax for the first time in weeks. Even so, how the hell was he going to concentrate on work while he was away from them?

He felt out of control, a feeling he'd fought hard not to experience again.

"Aw, fuck. That reminds me." Dad opened the center drawer of his desk and pulled out something wrapped in pink tissue paper with tiny bows. "What with the wedding and honeymoon and all, this completely slipped my mind." He slid the package across the desk.

"For me?" *Pink?*

"Yeah. I stopped by to see Mrs. Miller and the kids in Illinois."

Blood pounded in Damián's ears. He looked at the package as if it were…the grenade.

Paralysis. He fought the incoming memories but found himself catapulted onto the rooftop in Iraq. A band of steel tightened around his chest, cutting off his air. No fucking way out. The roaring in his ears from that fucking explosion nearly drowned out the fucking high-pitched screams.

He realized the screams were his own.

"Madre de Dios! *No! Sergeant, don't you fucking die!*"

He knew Sergeant Miller was gone, but kept yelling at him as if he could bring him back by the sheer volume of his voice. He looked up and watched as Grant and Wilson, on either side of him, lifted the body off him.

"Damián. You're in my office in Denver. You're safe now, son."

Damián drew several ragged breaths as he fought to regain control and bring himself back into the moment. He felt the pressure of Dad's hand on his shoulder rock solid, comforting. The older man sat on the edge of the desk, and Damián looked up and focused his gaze on his eyes.

"I'm okay. SNAFU." Situation Normal, All Fucked Up described his normal to a T.

"I didn't mean to spring that on you like that. Tracy, Sergeant's oldest girl—God, she's sixteen now, if you can believe that—anyway, she asked me to give this to the Marine who was with her dad when he…" He stopped and cleared his throat. "Go on. Open it."

Damián stared at the pink package, trying to control the shaking in his fingertips, then reached over and picked it up. Not wanting to put it off any longer, he tore away the paper to reveal a long, coiled piece of thin leather.

"She said there's an inscription."

Damián picked up the brown leather and stretched it out to a couple feet in length. He ran the strap between his hands a few times, warming it up.

Stalling. He wasn't sure he wanted to see what the daughter of the Marine he was responsible for letting die would have to say to him.

"You can read it when you're alone, if you want."

No, he was going to do this in here, in case he went off the deep end again. He turned the leather over and saw the marks where a message had been forever burned into the leather, much like the image in his head of Sergeant Miller bleeding out on Damián's chest.

The words swam in front of his eyes, and he blinked.

For Daddy. For Damián. Semper Fi.

A tear splashed onto the leather before he realized he wasn't alone. *Damn.* He'd already messed up the gift, too. Without a word he handed it to Dad, unable to read it aloud.

After reading it, Dad reached out and squeezed his shoulder again and cleared his throat. Damián looked up. *What the fuck?* Seeing the sheen of tears in the man's eyes about undid him. His master sergeant had taken hard the deaths of the three Marines killed under his command, no doubt about it, but Damián had never seen him with tears in his eyes before.

"No one ever blamed you, son, but you."

Dad handed the leather back to him and returned to his chair. "I think you're supposed to wear it on your wrist. Guess you could use it in your hair, too."

Damián took the leather and wrapped it around his right wrist several times, entwining the strip of leather the way he and Sergeant would forever be entwined.

Something else that had been bothering him came to the fore after that episode. He never shied away from asking this man anything, but he was a little nervous to bring up this topic.

Dad reached over to pick up the tissue paper and bows and tossed them in the trash bin. "I think it's time to change the subject. Think it's about time you married her mama?"

The man wasn't one to pull any punches. Damián had thought about it, but Savi didn't seem to want to have anything to do with him, other than as her protector. "Jury's still out on that one."

Dad leaned forward. "That kid needs a full-time dad."

Tell me about it. "Yeah, well, tell her mama that."

"Happy to, but she might go to ground again if I issue a direct order like that."

"She's not going anywhere for a while." Not if Damián had anything to say about it. "I'll work on her, but she's got more baggage than this latest incident. She just needs time."

Dad waited. Normally Damián wouldn't reveal someone's personal story without permission, but Dad needed to know there would be some issues with triggers for Savi.

"When I met her over eight years ago, she was some kind of masochist-for-hire for some pretty sadistic bastards. They worked her over pretty good."

"What the fuck's a masochist-for-hire?"

"Hell, I don't know. I never got the full story, but the guy she was handled by seemed to be pimping her out to businessmen. He was setting her up with the clients, then disappearing and letting total strangers restrain and torture her." Images of Savannah tied to the bed in the hotel flashed across his mind's eye. "Money must have changed hands, although I don't think Savi saw any of it. She was more like a sex slave."

Damián closed his eyes and rubbed his face, wishing he could blot out those images. If only he'd known how much deeper her problems were then, he'd never have left her. "I don't know that she's dealt with any of that trauma yet."

"What do you plan to do about it?"

Love her. Yeah, as if he was what she needed—or wanted. "I don't have any intention of letting her know what I've become."

Dad scrutinized him, and Damián sat back to put some space between them.

"Just what is it you've become?"

Why Dad needed him to state the obvious was beyond him. "A cripple. A sadist. A freak—and not the good kind, either."

"First off, I'm going to pretend I didn't hear you call yourself a cripple. That's bullshit. If I ever hear you say it again, you'll have one whip-wielding former master sergeant wearing out your ass with a singletail." He paused. "You know that's not an implement I'm particularly well-trained on, either."

Even so, Damián had no doubt the man would follow through on that promise—with predictable results. Fine. He'd just keep those thoughts to himself.

"As for being a sadist, you know you've never hurt anyone who didn't want or need the pain you've dished out. I've never seen a Dom with more self-control than you have."

Yeah, for Damián, sadomasochism had always been about control—regaining what had been taken away from him in Fallujah.

"Now, you want to tell me what you mean by a *bad* freak?"

Damián stared down at his biker boots and let the silence drag out between them. He'd never told anyone this before. He had no secrets from Dad; it just hadn't come up in the conversation before.

"What are you afraid of, son?"

Hurting her. He wasn't sure how to bring it into this conversation either.

"Spill it."

Damián raised his head and looked across the desk. "I haven't slept with anyone since," he looked down at his boot, "...before deployment." The blood pounded in his ears, and he almost didn't hear Dad's response.

"That's a fucking long time, but there's nothing wrong with a little discernment."

Okay, the man had missed the point, whether intentionally or not, Damián didn't know. Dad probably just wanted him to speak the words out loud. Take away some of their power, as Damián had tried to get Savi to do. Might as well come right out and say it, because Dad wouldn't take silence for an answer.

"I didn't say I haven't had sex. I just haven't let a woman I've been intimate with sleep with me. For two reasons."

"Number one being?"

"My stump."

Damián didn't think he'd ever have caught Adam Montague off guard, but the look on his face clearly said he hadn't expected to hear that.

"Wait. Let me get this straight. I know you only play publicly with Patti to help Victor out, but I've seen you go upstairs with some of the willing bottoms before."

Damián had topped fellow veteran Victor Holmes's slave Patti Varga many times in the great room, giving her what she needed—a level of pain Victor couldn't deliver—but there'd never been anything sexual between them.

"I only had sex with bottoms when I knew and they clearly understood there would never be anything more than a physical release."

"Sounds familiar." Damián looked up at Dad who glanced away without elaborating.

"Anyway, there haven't been any interested in more than a superficial connection with me."

Savi didn't meet his criteria for no connections, because they were way beyond superficial already. They'd formed a bond years ago that he'd never been able to break, even with no expectation of ever seeing her again. Now he'd discovered they shared a daughter. How did you keep something like that on the superficial level?

Dad found his voice after a few moments. "I thought you said Savi's been living in your apartment for the past couple weeks. How the hell hasn't she seen you without the prosthesis?"

Now it was Damián's turn to avoid eye contact. "I haven't taken it off around her."

Dad nearly came out of the chair again as he leaned forward. "What the *fuck* do you mean you haven't taken it off? It's not like you live in Marc's monstrosity of a house and can fumble around without seeing each other for a fucking week. You have to be living on top of each other in your place. Are you bucking to get the rest of your damned leg amputated when it gets infected?"

Dad was right, as usual. Damián was asking for trouble by not giving the stump a longer break every day than his half-hour or less of bathroom time twice a day. He continued to avoid Dad's gaze, but he tried to reassure him. "I had my own room in Aspen and had a chance to rest the stump a bit more there. And I check for signs of any problems a couple times a day."

When Dad grew silent again, Damián ventured a glance his way. The scowl on his face spoke volumes, but he added a few choice words, anyway. "Pride goes before the fall."

Who said anything about pride? He just didn't want to gross her out looking at a man who'd had his foot blown off. "Look, I don't think she's looking to have any kind of serious relationship."

"You share a kid together. Sounds fucking serious to me."

"That was one day at the beach eight years ago for two lost, horny teenagers."

"Bullshit, and you know it. That girl's been on your mind a lot, at least since rehab. I heard you scream out her name a few times during nightmares."

Dad had been the one to wake him from dozens of night terrors and bad dreams during that first year he'd lived here, and off and on for a couple more years before Damián had moved to his own place. The man had saved his life. Damián had been so fucking close to putting in place a suicide plan when Dad had come into that hospital room in San Diego the day before Damián had been discharged.

"Look, I plan to be a part of Marisol's life now that I know she's mine but that doesn't mean her mama wants to have any kind of relationship—kink or vanilla."

"You two need to work on your communication skills." Dad, who never had trouble speaking his mind, looked a little sheepish and glanced away again.

Damián sighed. "Look, I can barely touch her without setting off a dozen triggers."

"Give her time. Sounds like she's been to hell and back. Now, what's Number Two?"

He could never get anything by Dad. He took a deep breath. "I'm afraid to sleep with her."

"I thought that was Number One."

"No, not sex—*sleep*. What if I have a bad episode? I could hurt her if she's lying in the bed next to me."

"Son, there are never any guarantees, but when I was home with Joni recovering from that ambush in Afghanistan, I had plenty of nightmares."

The man sure had loved his first wife, but he'd lost her to cancer after twenty years of marriage. Damián wondered what it was like to be committed to one woman that many years.

"Even though I lashed out at night a couple times and insisted on moving to the couch, she refused to sleep anywhere but beside me every fucking night. We'd slept together so seldom over the years, we decided it was a risk worth taking. Thank God I didn't miss those last few opportunities. We didn't have that many left."

Dad was lost in memories a moment before looking at him again. "I have a feeling the two of you are going to be able to help each other on the nights when the nightmares return. Just warn her not to touch you when you're sleeping on the couch. Have her call out to you first and make sure you're awake before she gets too close. That's not PTSD, just your training as a warrior—always having to be on guard. But if you go to bed with each other, I think your mind will continue to function on some level most nights. You'll know she's not the enemy."

He paused to give Damián time to absorb the information. "Look, you'll never know for sure unless you try. What've you got to lose?"

Savi. Marisol. Everything.

Well, he had plenty of time to worry about getting into bed with Savi. "Speaking of being there, or not in this case, I'm going to have to steer clear of the club a while. She doesn't know about that either, and it's nothing I'm going to talk about except on a need-to-know basis. Right now, she doesn't need to know."

Dad moved in on him again, leaning forward. "Fine. But if I hear any more bullshit talk about you not being good enough for her because of kink or your foot or whatever excuse you drum up, I'll blister your butt good. She won't find anyone more honorable and worthy as a husband or a father."

"Yeah, well…" Damián looked away.

Dad stood up. "Get back out there and figure out how you're going to win her over." Damián relaxed, glad this talk was over. "Besides, I have a bride in the kitchen who hasn't been out of my sight this long since our wedding day, so I'm getting a little itchy to get my hands on her again."

Damián smiled. There was a time when Dad would have hidden out in here to avoid Karla. "I'm glad you two have each other."

"Not half as glad as I am that she'd have me after what I put her through."

"No, I guess you aren't the easiest man to live with."

Dad came around the desk and slapped Damián on the back of his head. "Don't be insubordinate. I still outrank you."

Damián grinned. "That you do, Dad. You always will."

"So tell me what fatherhood's like."

Damián grinned. "Well, I'm no expert, but hearing Marisol call me Daddy the first time was just about the sweetest thing ever."

"I'll bet it was. Can't fucking imagine it—but I guess I'd better. End of July there will be a little Montague running around here. Well, not here—and maybe not running right off the bat." Dad grinned. "We're going house hunting, but will probably stay here through June or so. Grant's agreed to move in after us, and she's finishing out her lease."

"She'll take good care of the place, I know."

"Yeah, but it's not like any of us are going anywhere. This place is home."

* * *

After tucking Mari into bed later that night, Savi felt a restlessness come over her that kept her from being able to sleep. She left the bedroom, easing the door nearly shut so as not to disturb her daughter, and found Damián thumbing through a motorcycle magazine.

Keeping her voice low, she asked, "Would you like something to drink?"

"Coffee sounds good." He tossed the magazine onto the coffee table and pushed himself to his feet. "I'll get it."

"No, I can do it. But let's make decaf, or I won't get any sleep tonight." She'd probably get damned little sleep as it was.

He followed her into the kitchen. They wouldn't have to be so quiet here. Ten minutes later, they sat across from each other, each with a steaming mug. Hers had a Harley emblem on it. Memories of the ride he'd taken her on to Laguna Beach tried to edge into her consciousness, but she tamped them down. Her heart pounded as she tried to decide how to start this conversation. Might as well just jump in.

"I don't know how I'm going to get Mari registered for school tomorrow. I don't have her immunization records, past school records, nothing."

He set his mug down and smiled. "Don't worry. Grant got the documents we need. They were in the mailbox when we got home. She even managed to enlist Father Martine's help in getting records from the school there and had them revised to reflect your new names."

Savi blinked. "New names?"

"You can't use your real names, so we've created entirely new identities for you both. To make it easier for Marisol, we just shortened her name to Mari Diaz. Diaz was my mother's maiden name." He sat a little taller. "It means a lot to me for her to carry Mamá's name, even if it's only temporary."

The backs of her eyes began to sting, and she cleared her throat. "She'll like knowing she's going to have her grandmother's name."

He grinned. "Don't you want to know your new name?"

"Sure." Her third identity. Anita had helped her get her papers for Savi Baker. Who would she be now?

"Savita Diaz."

Little Savi.

She smiled. "I like it."

Some of what she'd worried most about since making her decision to stay in Denver had been handled without her having to ask. She'd never had a man take care of her needs before. She thrived on being autonomous because, in the end, she only had herself to depend on. Still, she couldn't trust herself to keep Mari safe without help.

Fear began to claw at her throat, though, as the real reason for her restlessness tonight surfaced. "Damián, I'm scared."

He pushed his mug aside and reached across the table to squeeze her hand. "No one's going to hurt either of you."

As much as her body told her to pull away, she chose to accept his comforting touch. She needed to feel connected, for a little while at least.

Soon, the fear resurfaced. "How can you promise that? We've barely let Mari out of our sight since we got here; sending her to school where we can't keep her safe terrifies me."

He looked away a moment before locking his gaze with hers. "You have nothing to worry about. I wasn't going to mention this, though I don't know why it didn't occur to me that you'd be concerned. Listen. Dad and I were just talking, and we're going to have you two on round-the-clock protection. Between Dad, Grant, Marc, and me—and whoever else's help Dad enlists—neither of you will be without a guard."

"Like a prisoner."

"That's what I thought you'd think, but surely you…"

Savi held up her hand to halt his words. "No, I'm sorry. I know this isn't about me feeling hemmed in; it's about protecting Mari. I'm just used to having more freedom. In California, I had Anita and Father Martine as a support net, but I still made all my own decisions. I had a job. I could pay my own way." She blinked away the sting in her eyes. "It's not easy for me to accept help without feeling weak."

"Savi, sometimes admitting we can't do it all alone is a sign of strength. I don't know where I'd be if not for Dad and Marc being there for me when I needed them at the darkest point in my life."

"Do you want to talk about it?"

He looked down at his coffee mug, and then back at her. "Not really."

Typical man. She smiled. "Well, thank you for taking such good care of us."

Damián sat back in the chair and stared at her a moment until she nearly squirmed in her seat. She didn't like to have a man stare at her.

"Savi, you came to me for help. For protection. Just know that I always take my responsibilities seriously."

Responsibilities. Of course, there could never be anything more between them. She didn't want anything more. Did she? She was too broken to give any man what he needed and wanted from a woman.

But this was the first time her inadequacies bothered her.

Chapter Six

Damián towel dried his leg thoroughly and massaged the stump after getting out of the shower. Two months of limited prosthetic-free time and the skin was becoming a little sore. His time in the bathroom—and sometimes at work, when he didn't have to be on his feet—had been the only chances he'd had to get some relief. Slowly he rubbed the skin, wincing at the red spot on the inside of his leg. Pushing the pain away, he let his mind wander.

He still couldn't believe all that had happened since New Year's weekend. Now in the third week of February, life seemed to be going by in a blur. In other ways, the three of them had settled into a routine. Like a family.

Mari was thriving at school where she was finishing up third grade. Savi didn't even seem to mind that the only available option had been public school, but she had put Marisol's name on the wait list for the Catholic one, just in case there was an opening. The Navy Chaplain who had married Dad and Karla had promised to put in a good word for them at his parish's school.

Savi had been looking into what hoops she'd have to jump through with the State of Colorado to get licensed and continue to work toward certification, as she'd been doing. He could see how much it bothered her not to be able to help kids deal with their emotional and physical traumas. Her work as a therapist probably had helped her deal with some of her own issues from the past. Problem was, she couldn't produce the credentials she'd earned under her legal name in California, so Colorado wasn't going to even think about allowing her to practice. They'd talked about it and agreed that her need to work took a back seat to their need to protect Savi and Marisol from the bastards who had sent her running in the first place.

Damián had been working at the Harley shop on an as-needed basis, but the repair and maintenance jobs had been steadily increasing since January as the fair-weather riders started thinking about getting their bikes road-ready. Apparently, the shop had fallen behind since Damián had been fired last year for running out to California after Teresa's rape. The new man hadn't cut it, so there had been a backlog for a while. The owner knew Damián's mechanical skills were solid.

Coming home to Savi and Marisol in the evenings felt right, like having a family again. He hadn't realized how much he'd missed being with Rosa and the kids after moving here. But it was even more special than that. Getting to know his daughter had been a blessing he'd never expected and probably didn't deserve. He was so grateful.

Getting to know Savi was another matter. The woman was shut down tighter than a gnat's ass. He hadn't pushed her for anything more than what she was comfortable with—cohabiting without benefits. He told himself just having the girls near him was enough, but he'd be lying to say he didn't want more. He wanted to be a real family, *with* benefits.

Not that Savi would agree. She seemed to be down lately. Maybe it was because she couldn't work. He'd known that feeling himself, many times. She had to miss the kids she'd been counseling back at the clinic. He'd talked with Rosa, and she said Teresa was doing okay with her new therapist, which lifted Savi's spirits some. Clearly, Savi was worrying about the kids she'd been working with, too.

Savi had tried to volunteer at Marisol's school, but when the question of a criminal background check came up, she'd withdrawn the request. She hadn't wanted to point her father in their direction, knowing he'd probably have access to government record-keeping systems. So she'd tried to find other things to keep herself busy. Savi wasn't one to be idle. Karla had given her an electronic device for digital books, and she'd been doing a lot of reading lately. He wondered what she read, but when he mentioned it, her face turned eight shades of red. He probably didn't want to know.

He was glad she and Karla had hit it off so well. But Savi remained emotionally distant with him, and it frustrated the piss out of him. It might be a pipe dream, but he wanted to rekindle what they'd had at the beach eight years ago. Hell, he'd be happy just to have a simple kiss. Of course, with Marisol sleeping beside Savi every night in his bed and him sleeping on the couch, there wasn't a whole lot they could do intimately even if Savi decided to let him get closer.

What was he thinking? He ought to be thanking Marisol for providing a buffer, because Damián had no business putting the moves on someone like Savi anyway. She deserved a whole man. Until she found one, he'd be her protector and give her shelter, but it could never go any further.

Providing protection had been a concern since January, but Dad had managed to line up a number of non-active-duty Marines to provide unobtrusive surveillance for Savi and Marisol when Damián couldn't be there to protect his girls. Of course, Damián knew Dad and his friends took their watches, too. So far, there'd been no hint that Lyle or her father had traced them here, though.

Savi hadn't had any more flashbacks, not around him, anyway. Maybe she was feeling more secure. He hoped so, happy that the haunted, hunted look he'd seen that first month in her pretty blue eyes had finally gone away. She laughed more, too. *Dios*, he loved hearing her laugh. She didn't do it often enough. So fucking serious most of the time.

Thank God for the kitten. The playful antics of Boots helped to lighten the mood in the apartment, transforming Savi into a relaxed, happy person for longer stretches of time. Damián just knew not to pick up or touch him. If he did, his allergies got the best of him. He'd only needed to take a pill once. It had made his brain fuzzy, and he'd had to call Dad to provide backup until it wore off. Now, one sneeze and he'd back off, content to watch his girls giggle while he left the kitten to them.

Tomorrow he'd turn twenty-eight. Damián had no idea who had tipped Karla off that it was his birthday—probably Grant or Dad—but she'd insisted on having a party to celebrate. He'd tried to get her to call it off—Friday nights weren't good for most of them because of the club.

Damián hadn't played at the Masters at Arms Club since Savi and Marisol arrived, but Marc, Dad, and Karla needed to be there by seven. It would have to be an early party tomorrow.

Tonight, Damián and Savi had the apartment to themselves. When Karla mentioned the party to Marisol, she'd screamed and said she wanted to make him a cake. Damián cleared the knot in this throat just thinking about her excitement over doing that for him. So Karla had taken Marisol over to Marc's tonight, where they and Angelina were preparing for the party. Marisol had insisted on taking Boots along to help, whatever the hell that meant.

His daughter was one of the greatest joys in his life at the moment. Damián's eyes burned when he thought about how fucking blessed he was to have found her before she got any older. Seeing Dad and Karla looking forward to their new baby, though, he realized he'd missed out on a lot already. He wouldn't miss anything more.

Damián and Savi rarely found themselves alone in the tiny apartment. Here they were alone on a Thursday evening—but in separate rooms. He decided now would be a good time to see if there could be something more with her. Hell, he'd been living a celibate life with her for two months. He'd never slept around, but he wasn't a monk, either. Having the woman of his dreams within reach and not being able to touch her was…

The smell of cinnamon and coffee invaded his mental ramblings, and he glanced down at his pinky ring. With a sigh, he sat on the john to put on his prosthetic foot and adjusted the black stump sock over it. His stump didn't hurt too badly today. He'd try to go without the device more often, maybe while at work, so he didn't wind up with trouble he didn't need.

Damián left the bathroom and made his way through the bedroom and living room into the kitchen where he found Savi pouring two mugs nearly to the brim. They'd been enjoying their evening decaf and chats about the day's events for a while now.

Her ass was molded into a tight pair of faded jeans. He fought the urge to walk up behind her and place one hand on each denim-covered cheek, figuring he'd wind up with the contents of the coffeepot poured over him if he tried anything like that. Still he couldn't keep himself from wanting to touch her.

A tray of cinnamon cookies hot from the oven lay on top of the stove. He'd loved the smell of cinnamon since he was a kid.

Walking up beside her, he placed a hand lightly on her shoulder. She grew tense. Ignoring her discomfort, he bent down and gave her a peck on the cheek. Damn, her skin was soft. "You're an angel of mercy. How did you know I needed that?" He wasn't talking about coffee or cookies, either.

Not wanting to send her into a full-blown panic attack, though, he released her and took the mugs to the table, setting them down in fairly close proximity to each other. She followed with two cookies on her saucer and three on his.

He waited for her to sit and did the same, close to her. "Any plans for tomorrow?"

Savi moved her chair farther away. Still running from him. "I thought maybe I'd do some shopping while Mari's in school."

No fucking way was she going anywhere alone. "Sounds good. I'll tag along. They're waiting for some parts to be delivered at the shop and are supposed to call me when they come in."

"No, you can't go with me!"

Why the fuck not?

She blushed, and his dick went into overdrive.

"I mean, well…" She took a sip of coffee but grimaced and pursed her lips to blow into the mug. His dick strained against his jeans, imagining how it would feel to have her lips wrapped around his hard-on.

Cool it, Chico.

Savi avoided his gaze. "I mean, I can't take you with me. I, um, well…"

Spit it out, savita.

She nailed him with her sky-blue eyes. He'd take what he could get. If that's all she'd nail him with, so be it. For now. "I didn't know it was your birthday 'til yesterday, and I need to get you a present."

Now this could work to his advantage. "You don't have to buy me anything."

"But I want to give you something. You've been so generous to put us up all this time."

Hell, he didn't want her to give him something out of a sense of obligation. "You don't owe me anything. I have a lot of lost time to make up for…with Marisol." He saw the hurt look in her eyes, but he didn't want her to give him anything out of guilt, either. "Hey, I didn't say I don't want a present. I just said you didn't have to *buy* anything." He grinned.

She quirked an eyebrow before a wary look crossed her face. She sat farther back into the straight-backed chair. "What do you mean?"

"Do you want to know what I'd like from you for my birthday?"

If she could've pressed her back any farther into the chair, she would have. "What?"

"A kiss."

Her gaze went to his lips, then back to his eyes. "Damián, I'm serious. I want to give you something special but that's too…personal."

"I'm not talking about a curl-your-toes, take-your-breath-away kiss…unless that's what you'd like."

She shook her head like a scared little bunny in Marisol's cartoon movies. He grinned, even though he wished she did want that because *he* sure as hell did. "I just want to kiss you and have you kiss me back. A mutual give and take. No tongues. No hands below the waist."

Sounded like he was ordering an oil change off the quick-lube menu—top off the fluids, check the air filter, change the oil.

"Neck."

Neck? She wanted to neck? *Fuck yeah!* He grinned. "I'd love to neck."

Her eyes grew wide. "I mean, no hands *below* the neck. Well, shoulders, maybe."

Damián's spirits deflated a bit. *No, wait.* It sure sounded like she was agreeing to kiss him, despite having narrowed down the playing field. There was a lot he could do in that region encompassing her face, neck, and shoulders, so the battle wasn't lost yet. "Sounds good to me. I think that would be a fantastic present, Savi."

"When do you want me to give you your…present?"

"Why don't you let me surprise you?"

The wary look returned. Savi didn't like surprises. How fucking sad was that?

Without responding, she lifted her mug to her mouth and took a cautious sip, then a bigger one. She avoided looking at him when she set down the mug. Her lips were wet with coffee and Damián just about leaned over to kiss her then and there.

But anticipation would be good for them both, even if Savi didn't agree. He'd wait for the perfect moment to claim his birthday kiss.

* * *

All day Damián's birthday, Savi had been on edge. Every time he came near her, she steeled herself for the kiss she'd promised him. What had possessed her to agree to something as ridiculous as that? Well, that had an easy answer. Money. She didn't have any. What could she possibly buy Damián for his birthday that he'd actually want?

But a kiss? Could she afford the cost that gift would have on her psyche? She'd long ago stopped bartering parts of her body to men.

Damián entered the living room, where she'd been reading the same paragraph over and over for the last half hour. She held her breath. Would he claim his kiss now? Her heart drummed in her ears, and she had to remind herself to breathe again. When she looked up, he just grinned at her. The bastard knew the effect he was having on her. Why didn't he just take his damned birthday kiss and stop torturing her?

Instead, he walked into the bedroom, pulling off his shirt as he went, giving her a glimpse of his well-muscled back. The scales and plates of what looked like a dragon covered his left shoulder blade, its tail slithering over his biceps and down his upper arm. She shuddered and looked down.

Lately, he'd been limping worse than he had when they'd first met. When she asked about it, he said it was nothing. Maybe Marc could take a look at it when they were at his house tonight for the party.

She looked through the doorway into the bedroom. Oh, this was totally ridiculous. Mari would be home in a couple of hours, and Savi would not let him kiss her in front of their daughter. All she needed was for Mari to think Savi and Damián were going to get married. She could never fulfill her daughter's childish, princess fantasy. So not going to happen.

Savi got up from the sofa and walked into the bedroom. Expecting Damián to be in the bathroom getting ready for a shower, she was surprised to find him lying on the bed. Half naked. Luckily, the top half.

He grinned. "I'm ready for my kiss."

Savi's heart stopped, then pounded back to life with a vengeance. *No way. Not on the bed.*

"Remember, though, *querida*, you can't put your hands anywhere below my neck, even if you want to touch."

What? If *she* wanted to touch? She hadn't set the rule to restrict *her* hand movements, damn it. Her gaze roamed to his bare chest, tracing with her eyes a long silver scar that curved to his side. The menacing dragon seemed to roar to life across his left pec. Did it just jump at her? His mischievous grin told her he'd intentionally flexed his muscle to make the dragon move.

This room usually was on the chilly side, but Savi's face grew hot. "I don't think…"

"Good. I don't want you to think. I want you to feel." He held out his hand to her.

After searching her mind to find a plan of attack, or retreat, she surrendered and walked over to him, her feet growing heavier with each step.

Damián's smile faded, and he stared at her lips. She imagined how it would feel to have them touching her lips again.

Whoa! She needed to stop thinking those things!

"Don't be afraid of me, *mi mariposa*. You know I won't hurt you."

He waited patiently for her, but she still wasn't sure what he expected her to do. She wasn't going to get onto the bed with him. *No way.* Savi retreated a step. In an instant, Damián swung his legs over the side of the bed and stood up, closing the gap between them in one easy motion. The room closed in on her.

"Breathe slowly, Savi."

She hadn't realized she was practically hyperventilating until he'd spoken. Damián placed his hands firmly on the sides of her head, tilting it back to meet his gaze. "Look at me, *querida*. Breathe in." She did so. "And out." Slowly, the dizziness left her, and she remembered how to breathe without instruction.

Her face grew warm with embarrassment. Or was it because he held her so tightly? Having his hands on her head hadn't triggered anything bad for her. Men definitely had held her head before but apparently not at this angle. She was floored there actually was a touch-safe zone on her body.

Before she had time to think about what he intended to do, Damián's face lowered to hers. He stood at least half a foot taller than her five-four frame, and it took him a while to get close enough for the warning bells to go off.

She tried to wrench herself free of his hands. "I can't."

"Yes, you can. It's just a simple birthday kiss." He hovered just inches away, and his breath was warm on her nose. His hands continued to cage her head. She needed to get away and tried to pull back. He released her head, and she gasped for air.

Her gaze was drawn inextricably to his lips, and a stray thought had her wondering what they'd feel like against hers. Again. No, she didn't really want to know that.

Or did she?

Damián's fingers brushed the loose strands of her hair behind her ears, leaving a trail of tingling skin in their wake. His hands meandered down to her shoulders brushing the pads of his thumbs in a circular motion against the lines of her jaw.

"So soft. Just like I remember."

Distant memories of their time in the beach cave niggled at the edges of her mind. She'd tamped down those good memories along with all the bad ones from her past. They'd only emerged during times when she sought refuge in that place to escape the pain in the present. Not having Damián in her life beyond that one perfect day had been one of the hardest things to survive. But she'd gotten over him. Even forgotten him.

Hadn't she?

Well, except for every time she looked at her daughter and found herself staring into his dark-chocolate-colored eyes.

But she didn't want *any* man in her life. She needed to focus on Mari's safety and on getting her career back on track. Becoming any more involved with Damián would just complicate things. She had enough complications already.

But he's just asking for a kiss—not for you to have sex with him.

An unfamiliar heaviness pervaded her lower body, and several pulse points began throbbing as her heart thrummed its erratic beat. *No!* She wouldn't let her body override her common sense.

His head remained still, but his lips brushed hers as he slowly turned his head back and forth. He captured her lower lip and sucked gently before releasing her, keeping his word and not forcing his tongue into her mouth. Instead, he covered her mouth with his and ground his lips against hers. When she tried to refill her lungs, his lips broke free and blazed a trail to the side of her neck. Oh, dear Lord, she didn't want him to do this. She parted her lips to tell him to stop but moaned instead. Her face grew even hotter with embarrassment.

Damián's right hand skimmed along her shoulder and she tensed, expecting him to break her rule and maul her breast—or worse. He surprised her again when he just rested his hand on her shoulder, which nearly made her knees buckle as she melted against him like chocolate left in a hot car.

What was he doing to her?

His lips burned her skin wherever they touched—and they seemed to be touching her everywhere. Everywhere above the neck, at least. Who knew limiting him to that part of her body could produce this much…

No! Savi pushed him away with all the force she could muster, and he staggered back, thrown off balance. She'd vowed long ago to never let a man play her body like this again. Never let a man make her body respond sexually.

The hurt and confusion on Damián's face made her feel a pang of guilt, but she refused to let it dissuade her.

He sighed. "Another trigger?"

She didn't trust her voice and just shook her head. *Well, maybe.* Her entire freaking body was a trigger.

When he smiled, it was her turn to be confused. "That's got to be the hottest birthday present I've ever gotten."

She hadn't really given him anything, had she? She didn't even remember kissing him back. One good thing, though. At least he considered the gift delivered, and she didn't have to worry about kissing him anymore.

* * *

"...Happy Birthday to you." He listened to them sing to him hearing lots of Damiáns but that one sweet "Daddy" in the chorus was the second-nicest birthday present he'd gotten today—the first being that mind-blowing kiss he'd had with Savi earlier today. He looked across the table at her smiling face. Damn, but the woman sure had cranked up his libido with that kiss. Still made his knees weak. Good thing he was seated.

Not the right time to be thinking about kissing Savi. Damián grinned and looked around the table. Being surrounded by his new family was high on his list of unexpected presents today, too. Marisol, Savi, Dad and Karla, Marc and Angelina, and Grant had been able to come over to Marc's for his last-minute party.

"Blow out the candles, Daddy!"

Damián pulled his mind away from the carnal thoughts that had been hounding him all day and looked down at the slightly lopsided chocolate cake.

"You made this for me, *mi muñequita*?"

Marisol nodded and smiled, rightly proud of her accomplishment. Most beautiful cake he'd ever seen. She stood beside him, her little hand resting on his leg, and looked across the table. "Karla and Angie helped, too. And Boots!"

The kitten heard his name and came over to rub against Damián's leg.

Why me? All these people in here and he picks me?

Karla stood by ready to cut the cake. "Mari did all the hard parts. I just read the instructions on the box while Angie was busy working on dinner prep."

Angie smiled. "Marisol has some serious talent. Baking will never be my expertise."

Damián shook his head. "Anyone who cooks like you do doesn't need another expertise."

He noticed the dark circles under her eyes and wondered what was wrong. He glanced over at Marc who also looked like hell and remembered the conversation with Angelina back in Aspen about Marc's wearing a mask.

Damián suddenly realized Marc wasn't the only one of the Masters at Arms Club owners wearing a mask. Damián hadn't revealed himself to Savi, either.

Before he had much time to think about how to remedy that, Marisol reminded him about the candles. Damián met Karla's and Angelina's gazes and mouthed a silent "thank you" to them over Marisol's head. Then he tweaked his daughter's nose. "Thanks, doll-baby, for making this beautiful cake for me. Best present I could get."

He looked across the table at Savi and winked. Her face turned pink. At least she hadn't forgotten yet.

Marisol crawled up into his lap. "Do you want me to help blow them out, Daddy?"

"I thought you'd never ask." He wrapped his arm protectively around her and they leaned toward the cake. "One, two—"

"Wait!" Her tiny hand yanked at his ponytail, jerking his head back. "You have to make a wish first, Daddy."

A wish? Damián hadn't made a wish for anything since he was twelve, sitting in the ER waiting room along with Mamá and Rosa to hear how Papá was doing after several farm workers had found him face down in a field he'd been harvesting for the rich bastards up in Rancho.

That wish hadn't been granted. He pulled back and looked across the table at Savi as he placed his arm more firmly around their daughter. Maybe his answer would be the same, but, then again, maybe God would grant him a positive answer this time.

Under his scrutiny, Savi nibbled on her lower lip, reminding him for the millionth time today of the special birthday kiss she'd shared with him earlier. Yeah, there was only one thing he wanted but that was impossible.

So as not to disappoint his daughter, he formulated the wish in his mind. Thank goodness birthday wishes had to remain a secret in order to have any chance in hell of coming true. "Got it." He and Marisol leaned forward again. "One, two, three." They blew out all the candles together—all twenty-eight of them. *Mierda*, some days he felt more like fifty-eight.

Then his daughter pulled his chin toward her face and kissed his cheek, content to live in the moment without a care in the world. His childhood had been taken away from him; he wouldn't let that happen to Marisol.

After Karla cut the cake, Angelina brought a container of chocolate ice cream from the kitchen. He almost asked for a bottle of cinnamon but resisted. Having a birthday party just made him think of Mamá, who always sprinkled a little of the spice on his chocolate ice cream.

Whoa! What was with all the trips down memory lane tonight? He hadn't thought about that in a long time, but somehow he felt closer to Mamá as a whiff of cinnamon reached him, anyway. *What the...?* She'd been gone since he was fifteen, but her spirit stayed close to his heart. Mamá and Papá were enjoying their well-earned rest. They'd worked long hours so that he and Rosa could have a better life than they'd had, which only wound up putting them both six feet under long before their time. He'd also lost two older siblings much too early. Mamá told him—one of the few times she'd spoken about her dead children—their deaths could have been prevented if life hadn't been so hard for the family.

He knew none of them could come back. Still he wished Mamá and Papá could have been here to share this birthday with him and see how his life had turned out, despite a few bumps along the way. He also wished they could have gotten to know their newest granddaughter, but they hadn't lived long enough to meet any of their grandchildren.

He glanced down at the pinky ring—Mamá's wedding ring that had been passed down on Papá's side of the family to the oldest male, Damián being the third generation to be entrusted to pass it on. He'd never thought he'd be able to fulfill that legacy. He looked across the room at Savi and wondered if he'd ever see it on her finger.

No, he'd already been granted his quota of impossible birthday wishes for one day. But Marisol might one day wear it. Traditions could be changed to fit the needs of a new era.

Marisol jumped off his lap and ran to help Karla serve the cake. She brought Damián the first piece with a huge scoop of ice cream, watching the plate intently and being very careful not to drop it. A lump formed in his throat, and he wasn't sure he'd be able to swallow past it. When she placed it in front of him, the triumphant expression on her face just about did him in.

"Hurry, Daddy! Taste it!"

He picked up the fork and took a big bite of the chocolate-on-chocolate cake. *How the...?* He tasted cinnamon. With some difficulty, he swallowed and looked at her. "How'd you know Daddy likes cinnamon in his chocolate, doll-baby?"

She shrugged, but beamed. "I just had a feeling."

Karla piped up, "I told her I'd never heard of putting cinnamon in chocolate cake, but she insisted that's the way it had to be."

Damián was speechless.

"Daddy, your eyes have tears. You don't like it?" Her little chin quivered with her distress and disappointment.

Damián blinked the moisture from his eyes and shook his head. "No, honey, it's the best cake I've had in a long time. Just like *mi mamá* made for me when I was your age. Thank you, Marisol."

Thank you, too, Mamá. He didn't know how she'd communicated his love of cinnamon in chocolate to his daughter, but he had no doubt that she had. He leaned forward and placed a kiss on Marisol's cheek and whispered, "Daddy loves you."

She wrapped her arms around his neck and hugged him tightly, whispering back, "*Te quiero*, too, *papi*."

Damián's eyes burned to hear his daughter speak those words so naturally in Spanish. She must have picked them up at her school at San Miguel's or from her Hispanic friends. He wasn't sure she was going to let him go, so he lifted her into his lap again and took another bite of his cake after Karla placed a plate in front of Marisol.

Damián looked across the table again at Savi and saw her cheeks had red splotches on them as she fought back tears. As usual, none fell. She had an iron grip on her emotions most of the time. He wished he could wrap his arms around her and hug her until she let the tears spill, but she wouldn't stand for that. Instead, he just smiled at her and mouthed a "thank you" to her, too. Even better than the birthday kiss, she'd given him Marisol.

No fucking way could he let either of them go. First, though, Damián had a confession to make. He should have said something sooner. He couldn't run the risk of her counting on him to do more than he was able to do if they were in a dangerous situation. What if he failed her or his baby girl when they needed him most? Sure, he could get all macho and promise to protect them from harm, but could he? Could he fucking protect them with his bum leg? She needed to know the score.

Yeah, it was time to come clean about who he was—well, that part of him, anyway. He hoped she wouldn't take Marisol and run. Not that she'd get far. He wasn't going to let her go back to California before they'd managed to neutralize the threat out there. But he didn't want to make her feel she was a prisoner.

He couldn't let anything happen to either of them. They'd quickly become a major part of his life. *Mierda*, they *were* his life.

He fought the urge to mouth "I love you" to her because he didn't want to scare her off. So he just mentally tattooed the words on his heart, instead.

* * *

Savi rubbed the towel over her hair as she came out of the bathroom, not paying attention to her whereabouts as she tried to sort out her feelings about what had happened at Marc's last night. Watching Damián with Mari left an ache in her heart. She'd never known a father's love, but she was happy her daughter wouldn't experience what she had. She trusted Damián to never harm their daughter, no matter what.

She tried to think about what she'd do with herself this morning before she went back to Marc's to pick up Mari, who had stayed there with Angelina last night to help clean up after the party. Everyone else had plans to go to a club. She and Damián just came back to the apartment and retreated to their separate rooms.

Maybe she'd read a little. Karla had gotten her addicted to reading again. Unfortunately, most of the books on Karla's e-reader were sexually explicit and about things Savi had no interest in—bondage, whips, and such. Savi couldn't imagine Karla being interested in such books. When Savi recently had discovered the mystery series of a forensic anthropologist, she'd bought one after another until she'd run up quite a bill. She really should stop, but escaping into that world had helped fill her long days alone, and Karla told her not to worry. Just enjoy herself.

"Savi, I need to tell you something. About me."

She stilled the motion of her hands as she opened her eyes, surprised to find Damián sitting on the side of the bed in her room. Well, technically it was *his* room. *His* bed. *She* was the interloper.

She lowered the towel in front of her chest, as if it could shield her from his gaze. Thank the Lord she'd gotten dressed in the bathroom rather than coming back into the bedroom wearing only a robe. Either one would have hidden the scars on her arm, but a robe seemed more intimate.

Not that he could be interested in her sexually. She'd fought to keep her body very thin, almost boyish, not wanting to attract any man's attention. Warmth suffused her face as she thought about Damián seeing her naked. Again, she hoped he would be repulsed by her thinner body. Savannah had been slightly more filled out.

"Sit down, Savi."

She held her breath. He seemed so serious; his jaw and body remained rigid, guarded.

Savi looked around. The only place to sit was on the bed. That didn't seem like a good idea.

"Sit. Down." He pointed at the bed, clearly upset with her. She wasn't sure why that bothered her so much. "Savi, I'm not going to…touch you. We're only going to talk."

Savi crossed the room slowly and sat on the same side of the bed, keeping a safe distance away. She wasn't sure what she was afraid of. Intellectually, she knew Damián wouldn't hurt her. He'd been extremely gentle and supportive since she and Mari had arrived here.

But he was still a man. Sometimes they changed into monsters. *No. Not Damián.* He wasn't one of the bad guys.

He raked his hand through his hair, pulling it back from his face. She wondered why he hadn't tied it back. She didn't see his hair loose like this, except when he got up in the morning. What was it he needed to tell her that made him so uncomfortable? She didn't want to know anything bad about him.

"When I got out of Iraq, I was fucked up."

"Damián, that's not unusual. You saw gruesome things. War is…"

He held up his hand and halted the string of words she had intended to be supportive. She supposed they sounded trite. Still, she hadn't meant them to be.

"Don't go into therapist mode on me, Savi." He grinned slightly, so maybe he wasn't upset with her for trying to put him at ease.

He was such a gentle soul. War had to have been an enormous blow to his psyche. Last night, when Mari had presented him with the cake, he'd had unshed tears in his eyes. Processing the horrors of war would be difficult for someone who was much better at making love than war.

Don't think about his lovemaking abilities.

His grin faded, and he looked down.

"I fucked up a mission."

Savi's heart went out to him. She knew how hard it was for a Marine to admit failure concerning a mission.

"We lost our sergeant because I couldn't act fast enough…"

"Damián, you can't blame yourself for…"

He stared at her. "Hear me out. This is hard enough to admit as it is."

"I'm sorry. Go on."

"I still have nightmares about it, especially around my Alive Day."

"Alive Day?"

He looked down at his feet again. "That's the day I should have died. But I surv…I didn't die."

Savi knew not to interrupt anymore. He needed to talk, and she needed to be quiet and listen. He held his body so stiffly; he barely breathed. She waited.

After several moments, he continued, "A grenade landed on the roof where we'd held our position all day. I saw the damned thing, but I froze until it was too late to get away. When it went off, Sergeant Miller was killed. He…" Damián's breathing became rapid, and she scooted closer to him on the bed, laying her hand on his thigh. She squeezed, hoping to help him focus on the present and not get lost in the memories. She knew how much it helped to have someone keep her in the moment when the past threatened to take over. He placed his hand over hers and squeezed her back as if she were a lifeline.

"He died on top of me."

"Oh, God, Damián. I'm so sorry!" Savi shuddered. Beads of sweat broke out on her upper lip. She couldn't imagine the horror of watching someone die in front of her eyes and shuddered as the cold fingers of some unknown horror crawled down her spine.

What a sad thing to have in common, neither being able to stand having weight pressing on their chests, albeit for very different reasons.

"I'll never block out that image as long as I live. I could have saved him, but I…"

Hearing him take the blame for something beyond his control broke her heart. Not unusual for those in combat situations, though. They were trained to watch out for each other. Nothing she could say would help assuage his guilt that a member of his unit was killed, even if she could come up with the words to say. She just squeezed his thigh again, knowing there probably was more to come. She braced herself mentally.

"I came to in a military hospital in Germany. When I realized what I'd lost, I didn't want to go on."

"Lost?" He wasn't talking about his sergeant now.

He avoided making eye contact but nodded, his gaze remaining on his feet. *Oh, God, no!* In an instant, it became clear to her why she'd seen him limping so many times. She looked down at his feet. This was the first time she'd seen him without his boots on. Odd, considering they'd lived in such close quarters for two months.

Dread washed over her as she slid off the bed onto the floor. With shaking hands, she sat in front of his feet and reached out to touch his legs. Starting below his knees, which were flesh on solid muscle, she ran each of her hands down the backs of his legs until her left hand bumped into straps on his right leg. On the other leg she felt sinew and muscle. Unmarred.

She reached down to the hem of his jeans leg and folded up the right one. Damián reached out and halted her hand. She brushed him away. "Please, Damián. I need to see what they did to you."

His hand went to her chin, and he lifted her face to his. The pain—no, the torment—she saw there told her how hard this was for him. She needed to back off and give him time to prepare himself. This wasn't about what she needed. She had to do what Damián needed.

Savi held onto his wounded leg, wrapping both arms around it and laid her forehead against his knee. She wished she could shed tears for him, but she hadn't been able to cry in…forever. Her chest ached as she mourned the loss of his limb. She grieved even more for the loss of the gentle innocence that had been the younger Damián. He shouldn't have had to go through that.

What if she'd found him again before he'd enlisted? What if she'd tried harder to let him know about her pregnancy? He might have made a different decision. He might not have joined the Marines.

He might not have been injured.

His hand stroked her hair and brought her back to him. She looked up again, seeing him through her own emotional pain.

"I need to see, Damián, but I think you need for me to see it, too. It's part of who you are now." A shadow crossed his face, and she squeezed his leg above the straps of the prosthesis to let him know she wasn't afraid to touch him, to see him. "I'm sorry you felt you needed to hide this from me…" She pulled back. "My God! How did you wear this thing twenty-four/seven for two months straight?"

Dear Lord, she and Damián were both so fucked up—to use Damián's expression—each hiding so much from the other. How could she push him to reveal his secrets if she couldn't tell him about her own?

"I found times to rest the stump. I didn't wear the prosthesis in the shower and usually found some time each day to lock myself in the bathroom and massage my stump."

Savi grinned, before catching her errant thought.

"What?"

Her face must be as red as a tomato. "I thought maybe you were massaging something else those times."

He smiled. "Well, that, too, sometimes."

Suddenly aware of how close she was sitting to Damián and that her hands were touching his legs, Savi grew rigid. As if expecting her to retreat, he put light pressure on her shoulders, and then he gently pushed her away from his leg. She thought he was going to stand and walk away from her and realized she didn't want him to leave.

Instead, he reached down and pulled his pant leg up until he revealed the sock-covered prosthesis. She asked him with her eyes and a motion of her hand if she could touch him, and he nodded.

With shaking hands, she reached up and pulled the black sock down. At first, she saw only the straps of the prosthesis. His calf and most of his leg were still intact, and she breathed a sigh of relief.

When she rolled the sock down to where his ankle had been, she encountered where the prosthetic foot was attached to his lower leg. He'd lost his foot and ankle. Again, she experienced an odd sense of relief that it hadn't been worse, but she mourned the pain and agony he must have gone through as he'd learned to walk and to live without such a vital part of his body.

His beautiful body. She remembered their time in the beach cave and how she hadn't been able to keep her eyes off him. He'd carried her down the stairs, across the sand and rocks.

How many activities had he been unable to do since he'd been injured? Yet he was still so strong and brave. She'd never noticed any fear or reluctance on his part to protect her and Mari, either.

Looking up at him, she thought he was even more beautiful now. Damián was still the gentle, caring man she'd known back in that cave. Only now he also was the father of her daughter. *Their* daughter. How could he have thought she would reject him because he'd been injured in the war?

Maybe because she'd done nothing but push him away since she'd shown up here. Savi removed the sock and stared at the flesh-colored plastic prosthesis that had supported him so well all these years. Did he still have phantom pain? He'd said he had nightmares, but she hadn't witnessed any during the time she'd been with him.

Alive Day.

He'd almost died. She shuddered and looked up. "What's your Alive Day?"

"Fifteen November 2004."

Mari had been almost five months old when he'd been injured. At that time, Savi had been trying to learn to be a mother, keep up with college classes, and process what had happened in her fucked-up childhood. Damián had been fighting for his life.

"I'm sorry, Damián. I didn't know. I wish I'd been there during your recovery." Not that she'd have been much help. There were so many times she'd been barely able to function for herself and Mari back then. She wouldn't have been able to help him. But they could have held each other and…

Damián took her elbow and pulled, indicating he wanted her to stand. She did so, and he tugged until she landed in his lap, where she was seated before her mind registered that this was a very bad idea.

But then, why did it feel so nice—not scary, as she'd expected? She'd stay here a moment.

"*Mi sueño*, you *were* there. Every night, I escaped with you to our beach cave. I carried you down all those stairs, as if I was still a whole man. You held onto me, trusting me not to drop you. We made love."

Something broke loose in Savi's chest, and she released a dry sob. He pulled her head to his chest. "Shhhh, *bebé*."

She should be comforting him, yet he was stroking her hair, rocking her, crooning to her.

How many nights had she escaped to their cave when she needed his support to get through the night, or the days for that matter? There had been so many times she'd questioned her decision to raise a child on her own, only to find Damián there every night telling her she'd done the right thing. That she was the best mother their daughter could ever have.

"You said you had nightmares."

His hand stilled on her head, and he stopped breathing for a moment. "A few. Over time, though, I chose to dream about you…us…and the nightmares faded some."

"So that's why you call me *'mi sueño.'* Your dream. Oh, Damián." They'd missed so much over the years. Now, it was too late for them.

How could she and Damián have anything together? She was too screwed up. Damián didn't know half of what Father had done to Savannah yet. Or how Savannah had responded. When he found out, would he still want to hold her like this? Touch her? Would he still want someone like her in his life? In his daughter's life? She shuddered again.

"Shhh. It's okay, *querida*. It's just new to you right now. I adjusted to what I've become long ago."

The jury was out on that given that he'd hidden his prosthesis from her until now, but it certainly didn't seem to be holding him back from living his life. She'd only detected a limp a few times, usually when he was carrying Mari or overly tired.

Savi reached up and stroked his jaw. So strong. The man had a calm reserve she envied. Nothing seemed to faze him. Of course, she hadn't seen him in the midst of a PTSD episode. He said he still had them. She wondered what triggers set him off.

Damián took her hand and turned his head to bring his lips to her palm. Savi pulled her hand away, as if bitten. She hadn't meant anything sexual by touching him.

"Savannah, you crawled into my lap...you know you wanted me to touch you there."

She pushed herself upright. "Let me off your lap."

Chapter Seven

Damián knew the moment he'd lost her to another bad memory. Her breathing stopped for a moment, before growing rapid and shallow. She struggled to get off his lap, but Damián held her tighter.

"Let me go."

"You're okay, Savi. You're safe. I'm not going to do anything to hurt you."

"I didn't do anything to make it okay for you to touch me there."

Touch her? Where? When? Suddenly, he realized she wasn't talking to him. Damián wasn't sure which of her tormenters she *was* talking to and hated asking for details about something she'd probably kept bottled up a very long time, but she needed to say the words. He just hoped he could handle whatever she revealed. "Touch you where?"

"You know where. You molested me. I didn't do anything to make it okay for you to hurt me like that."

She sounded more like she was trying to convince herself than she was her abuser.

"Shhh, *chiquita*. You're right. I shouldn't have touched you like that. I'm sorry."

She blinked and pulled away, staring him in the face. "Damián?" She pulled even farther away, as if just coming to the realization she wasn't trapped in a scene from the past with whoever had molested her.

Damián ran the pad of his thumb over her full lips and fought the urge to cage her jaw and draw her mouth open to shove his thumb inside, the way he'd seen Victor take control of Patti so many times. *Damn.* He needed to get her off his lap. Or rein in his libido. Both, actually.

But she needed to talk with him about this, or it would stay locked up inside her.

"Who were you talking to a moment ago?"

She blinked a few times before casting her gaze away from him. "Let me up." Again she tried to get up, but he wanted to push her a little further. Maybe he could get her to tell him what he needed to know. Who was she fighting in her mind still? He had an idea but needed for her to say the name. Maybe he could help her send the bastard into the bowels of hell if she'd allow him to get that close to her demons.

If she'd trust him that much.

"Who was he?"

"Don't ask me that. Please."

"He hurt you. Took advantage of your innocence. Who hurt you, Savi?"

Her chin began to shake, and he pulled her closer, sinking back onto the mattress and taking her with him. For a moment, he had to fight the roar of the beast within as her body's weight pressed against his chest, much like Sergeant Miller's body had.

Slow, deep breaths. In…out.

He held her as tightly as she'd allow him. "He can't hurt you now. He'll have to go through me first. That won't happen."

Savi grabbed onto his T-shirt and clenched it in her fist, shaking her head.

"Tell me, Savi." *Trust me,* mi mariposa.

She released his shirt and sat up, straddling him. He hoped she couldn't feel the raging hard-on he had for her. Suddenly, she hit his chest with her right fist and soon struck him repeatedly with both fists, each impact harder than the last. She wasn't hitting him—Damián—anymore but one of her abusers.

"That's it. Let him have it, Savi. Let go of some of your hurt, your anger."

She walloped him a good one in his left pec and Damián grinned. The woman had some serious upper-body strength. She must have worked out back in California, because he hadn't seen her doing that here.

"Again. Harder. Hit him like you mean it."

She closed her eyes and pounded him several more times in quick succession. "I hate what you did to me!" Lost in the past, she continued to pound on him, her hair flying with each swing.

"Let it out, *bebé*."

A moan of anguish tore from her throat. "You fucking monster! How could you do such despicable things? I was only eight! You raped me when I was eight years old! You goddamned bastard!"

Puta madre. The animal within him stirred to life wanting to seek vengeance, but he reined in his emotions. Savi was the one who needed to unleash her anger. *Eight fucking years old?* He'd known Savi's handler was a *cabrón* from the day he'd seen him in the hotel restaurant but raping an eight-year-old kid? If he ever got his hands on that goddamned son-of-a-bitch, he'd burn his balls off. Heaven help him if he came anywhere near Savi or Marisol. He'd get his eventually—for Savi—and would make sure old-man Gentry and his *cabrón* lackey were never allowed to walk free or hurt anyone else ever again.

Savi continued to beat on his chest, but he could tell by how hard she was hitting him that the fight was leaving her. "I prayed every night you would die! I wished *you* had left me, instead of Maman! I hate you, Father!!!"

Madre de Dios. *Her father?* Damián tried to imagine what kind of man would rape his daughter—a daughter about the age of Damián's own daughter, Marisol. His heart hammered in counter beat to Savi's fists. Why hadn't he realized it before?

He'd thought his ex-brother-in-law Julio was the biggest shithead on two feet for raping sixteen-year-old Teresa. And Savannah...Little Savi had been half her age. *How the fuck...* A roaring in his head distracted Damián from his thoughts as the beast within sprang to life. *No.* He couldn't lose control, not now. He let Savi pound on him with renewed vigor.

"Let him have all your rage, *savita*."

Thank God she'd finally been able to speak the words she'd needed to say. Moments later, her fists slowed. He pulled her against his sore chest and wrapped her in his arms. When the familiar panic rose up at having pressure on his body, he refused to give it a handhold. He needed to maintain control and stay in the moment. For her.

He'd be sporting some serious bruises tomorrow. The woman didn't hit like a girl, that's for sure. The rage had to have been building up inside her for almost twenty years.

After a few moments, the ache coming from around his heart hurt a helluva lot worse than had any injury ever inflicted on his body. He didn't want the images in his head of little Savannah being raped by her father, but they kept flashing across his mind, anyway. He'd need those images later, when he was ready to release the beast and exact justice for Savi. No doubt in his mind that opportunity for justice would come one day, but not now.

Damián wouldn't do anything to jeopardize Savi's and Marisol's safety. He needed to remain calm and protect his girls right now.

Savi clung to his T-shirt with her right fist as her body convulsed. Was she crying? He hoped so. She needed to let go of her tears as much as her rage, but he hadn't seen her do that yet either. He reached up to stroke her hair. "Shhh. You're safe, Savi. I have you. Just rest now."

Holding her like this reminded him of aftercare following an intense SM scene. She would probably benefit from some controlled, mild SM play to help her regain a sense of the power she'd lost as a child. But she'd never agree to anything like that. He probably was trying to project his own baser needs onto her. Of course, he was in no condition for an SM session right now. His own demons were too close to the surface tonight. If he couldn't control himself, hell, he'd be no better than her father. Right now, she just needed comfort and a safe place to heal. Nothing more.

Maybe that's all she'd ever need from him. A safe harbor.

Fine by him. He couldn't give her more, anyway. Still, he liked being needed. He'd always liked that, even as a teenager. Maybe losing his dad so young and having to be there for his mom and sister had made him into the type of guy who needed to protect others, the guy people leaned on when times got tough.

He rested his chin on the top of her head. After a few moments, her body sagged against his. Sleep. That's probably what she needed most. He'd just hold her. *No la molestes.*

"Just sleep, *bebé*. I have you."

As long as you'll have me.

He eased her onto the bed and curled her body into his.

Damián startled awake sometime later and found himself looking into Savi's sleepy blue eyes. He'd dreamt of waking up with her in his bed so many times that it took him a few moments to realize she was real. He wondered how long he'd slept. Hell, he never slept that soundly.

He reached out to stroke her velvet-soft cheek. She didn't flinch as she'd done most of the times he'd touched her. Emboldened, he let his finger trail along her jaw to her neck.

"Damián, I don't think…"

"Don't think. Just feel."

He saw the distress on her face, and his heart ached for her. He barely heard her as she whispered, "I don't know how to feel anything. It's been so long."

"Let me do the work. You just focus on my hand. If you want me to stop, say...hot tamale."

He hoped the silly safephrase would be non-threatening enough for her to lighten up, even if she didn't know that's what it was.

Savi grinned. "Hot tamale?"

"*Si, mamacita*. I will stop if you say those two words, unless, of course, you're referring to *me* as a hot tamale, in which case...hmmm." Thoughts of her getting carried away like that kicked his long-dormant hormones into overdrive. "Maybe I should let you choose a word or phrase you might not normally use."

She visibly relaxed and laughed. "I assure you, hot tamale rarely comes up in my vocabulary."

His finger continued its journey along her collarbone, lightly trailing over the top of her shoulder. He wished she wasn't wearing a long-sleeved T-shirt, but it didn't matter really. He wasn't going to be getting her naked anytime soon. He'd just use his imagination.

He traced the joint where her shoulder met her arm. She was so much thinner than she'd been at nineteen; her bones jutted against the fabric. He needed to get her to eat more. Hell, if they ever did have sex again, he didn't want to have to worry about breaking her. Not at first, anyway.

"What are you smiling about?"

He'd smiled? He was so lost in finally being able to touch her, he'd zoned out a bit.

"How much I love touching your body. How much I've missed you."

A cloud crossed her face. *Crap.* That wasn't the right thing to say. Hoping to get her attention back to where it belonged, he leaned forward and captured her lower lip between his and sucked until he heard her hiss. He sucked even harder, and she placed her hands on his shoulders, as if to control how close he could get. He noticed she wasn't pushing him away, so his tongue traced the curve of her upper lip. She shivered. He took her full lower lip between his lips again and sucked gently. Savi's body shuddered with an intensity that set off the responsive jerking of his dick.

Sorry, Chico, you aren't getting any. So behave.

He wished he could see her eyes to tell if she was as aroused as she seemed to be, but he didn't want to pull away. His lips released hers, and he nipped a trail along her cheek to the column of her neck. Her pulses tripped

123

against his lips and fingers.

Emboldened, he let his finger trail down her bra strap. Her nipple protruded against the underside of his wrist, but he fought hard not to zero in on the target too quickly. He'd just scare her off.

Damián sat back and leaned his head in his hand as he looked down, watching his middle finger trail a path around the side of her breast. Not overly large, but didn't they say more than a handful was a waste?

His dick strained against his zipper, and he made sure he wasn't pressed against her leg. Didn't want to send her running. Savi was letting him touch her; he'd do nothing to make the moment end.

His fingers cupped the underside of Savi's shirt-covered breast, and he brushed her nipple with the pad of his thumb. She drew in a sharp breath, but her pupils dilated.

"That's it, *bebé*. Just feel."

He stroked her nipple again, and it hardened against his thumb. Her breathing became shallow and rapid.

"I can't do this." He heard her fear, but she didn't push his hand away or use her safeword, so he continued to stimulate her.

"You don't have to do anything, *bebé*. Just feel."

"I don't want to feel like this."

"What's wrong with feeling pleasure, Savi?"

She tensed and turned her head away. "It's dirty."

"There's nothing dirty about two consenting adults wanting to touch each other. I'm a consenting adult. How about you?"

She nodded.

"Then there's no problem." He took her swollen bud between his thumb and middle finger and rolled it gently, the fabric of her bra probably adding additional friction. Her hips bucked toward him.

Yeah, bebé. *Just feel.*

He started to lower his head to her nipple, but she scooted away. Leaning back, his gaze locked with hers.

Stay with me, mi mariposa.

He moved his hand up to her shoulder again and stroked it until she relaxed. Her mouth opened as she fought to get more oxygen.

That's it, savita. *Open for me.*

She closed her eyes.

Emboldened, he lowered his face and wrapped his lips around the swollen peak. He expected her to push him away but heard a distinct moan instead. The shirt and bra must have provided a safety barrier for her. Taking advantage of her lowered defenses—and just needing a fucking taste—he slid his body down the bed and took the hard bud between his teeth. Pulling, nipping…teasing.

Her hands pushed against his shoulder. "Stop! What are you doing to me?"

He looked up her body and made eye contact, gauging her response. "Did you mean 'stop' or 'hot tamale'?"

She groaned in frustration. "I don't know what I mean anymore."

"If you say 'hot tamale,' I'll stop immediately."

Not waiting for her response, Damián bent down again and tugged her nipple with his teeth as his hand explored her other firm breast. Her breath hitched. She was responding to his touch, rather than running away. *Better.* Even with a protective covering, the bud swelling even larger against his tongue sent his dick into spasms.

So sweet. So responsive.

So mine.

Unable to stop himself—as if he wanted to—he draped his leg over both of her thighs and pushed her lower body into the mattress as he devoured her nipple with his lips. He'd waited so long. Missed her so much. He brushed his hand over her midriff to her lower abdomen and wondered if her belly had stretch marks from carrying his baby. He longed to trace the path of each one with his tongue, but they would only remind him of all he'd missed from that time in Savi's life. Instead, he continued to suckle as his hand kneaded her flesh.

His hand moved toward the juncture of her thighs. The tight jeans kept him from getting inside them, so he stroked her clit through the denim.

Savi tensed and stopped breathing.

Before he could back off to give her breathing room, she shoved him away with more force than he would have expected and scooted to the other edge of the bed, crouching on all fours and gasping for air in fear rather than the arousal he'd hoped to see.

Damián forced himself to regain control of his libido. What the hell had happened? He hadn't intended for things to move that fast; he just hadn't been able to stop himself. He was acting like a fucking horny teenager. Again. He fought to regain control of his own breathing. Damián hated losing control like that.

The shuttered look in her eyes told him she'd gone to ground again. Clearly he'd hit another trigger. No wonder, given the way she'd been mauled by the men in her past.

"Savi, you're with me. Damián. You're okay. I'm not going to hurt you."

He forced himself to keep his voice calm but raged inside at the men who had abused her beautiful body and stolen her innocence. He wished he could drive his fist through each of their goddamned faces.

Her chest heaved as she also fought for control. Soon, the wild-eyed look left her gaze.

"That's right, *bebé*. It's just me." He pointed to his bare chest. "I won't hurt you, *mi sueño*." He waited for her to focus on him again. "Where did you go?"

She blinked again. "Go?"

"You zoned out on me when I touched your clit."

He'd never have believed it possible, but she grew even more stiff. "You touched me…there?"

Mierda. He'd like to think she'd noticed. A flush blazed a path across her cheeks. She continued to inch away from him until she got off the bed, turned, and ran into the bathroom, slamming the door behind her.

Fuck.

Damián pounded his fist into the mattress, but he gained no satisfaction from the impact with such a soft surface. He needed to maintain control of himself, especially when everything else was spiraling out of his control. *Damn it*. Savi didn't need for him to be in barbarian mode when she came back to him.

Dios, he hoped she'd come back and give him another chance. Discovering her triggers was like walking through a fucking minefield.

Could he ever reach her sexually, break down the walls she'd built since he'd left her at her mansion on the hill in Rancho all those years ago? What the hell had they done to her there?

The chances of her ever letting him get close enough to explore an intimate relationship with him were about as likely as his regenerating his foot.

* * *

Savi splashed cold water on her face and sucked air into her lungs, trying to regain control. Her body's traitorous responses to Damián's mouth and touch confused her. Something stirred that had long been buried deep inside. Something ugly. She didn't want to respond to a man's touch ever again. Just now, in his bedroom, her body had betrayed her for the first time since…

Father and Lyle had forced her to orgasm with beatings and sex toys until she lay emotionally and physically exhausted. They'd pimped out her body to their potential business clients with only one restriction—no penetration. The sadists beat her until she screamed, ejaculating on her body afterward. She shuddered, her stomach heaving against the memories.

When Damián had touched her clit, images of her father, Lyle, and the endless succession of men in the hotel penthouse swirled through her mind. She felt like she was in the throes of a spell of vertigo. Dizzy, sick at her stomach.

She stood up and looked at herself in the mirror. *Slut.* She'd enjoyed the touch of those men at times, even if unwillingly. How could she face Damián again? Did he know what she was? Maybe if she just told him. She shook her head. *No.* If he knew, he'd kick her out. No decent man would want to be associated with someone who did the things she'd done. Besides, she couldn't risk placing Mari in harm's way in order to reveal her true self to Damián.

She could never say those words aloud. He could never know.

Dirty slut.

No! Bile rose in her throat and her image swam in the mirror. She squeezed her eyes shut. Savi needed to get out of here. She glanced over her shoulder at the door. *Smart move.* She was in an interior bathroom with no means of escape, unless she faced him again. She wished she had her phone. Maybe her therapist could give her some advice about what to do. They'd never really dealt much with the sexual issues during her recovery, because Savi'd had no intention of ever being a sexual creature again. She'd flatly refused to go there.

But with Damián…

Oh dear Lord. He did things to her mind and body she wasn't prepared for.

Pain. A piercing pain stabbed her chest. She needed relief. The room spun…

Crouched in the corner, she became chilled with the tub at her back and the floor tiles against her leg. Savi looked down at the steel razor blade lying on the floor beside her. How had she gotten here? Had she cut herself? She looked at her sleeved arm. *No. Not yet.* No visible blood.

A fire burned beneath her skin, but at the same time, she had chill bumps over her entire body. Pain. She couldn't escape the pain.

Don't cut yourself.

Focus on your breathing.

Her therapist's and Anita's voices played in a continuous loop in her head. The pain would go away if she could just focus on her breathing. She'd succeeded in controlling it that way for years. Why wasn't it helping this time? The pain screamed at her; she needed release. Nothing else would help.

Dirty slut.

Damián had to know the truth now. She'd responded to his touch like the dirty slut she was. Part of her hovered near the ceiling, watching the scene below, as if she and her body had separated. Slowly the woman rolled up the sleeve of her T-shirt. She fought to control the shaking of her hand.

Over her forearm.

You wanted me to touch you there.

Beyond her elbow.

You asked for it.

Higher and higher she raised the sleeve until she'd exposed the tracks of skin where she'd cut herself before. The twisted coping mechanism had begun when she was a teenager, soon after she'd escaped from her father's ungodly prison, and had continued until Mari was three.

Breathe.

Her hand shook even harder as Savi reached for the razor blade.

No, don't! Breathe!

She fought to reconnect with the woman huddled in the corner, sweat pouring from her forehead, gooseflesh all over her body. Despite the disconnect, Savi knew the fires of hell burned beneath the woman's skin.

Relief. She needed relief.

The woman picked up the razor blade. Her hand stopped shaking as it moved closer to her arm. It had been so long since she'd gotten relief this way from the pain, so long since she'd needed to escape this badly. Perhaps the only way she'd managed to avoid cutting herself all these years was her need to keep the promise she'd made to her therapist never to have razor blades around, but Damián used them to shave. She'd found a new pack of them in the medicine cabinet soon after she'd sought refuge in here.

She'd never been able to stand the sight of blood. Why did she choose this means of hurting herself?

Not hurting. Helping.

Her heart raced, the hammering almost deafening. Would her heart explode before she could ease the pain? *Hurry.* Savi couldn't shed tears for herself, but her blood weeping from her skin would help ease the pressure. The pain.

Please. Wash away my pain and shame.

No!!! She pulled the blade away before she'd connected with her skin. She couldn't do this, never again. Mari needed a mother who was strong, in control. This was a sign of weakness.

Breathe.

She drew a deep breath and leaned her head against the wall, watching the razor blade fall in slow motion, hearing it clatter against the floor tiles as if she stood at the opposite end of a long tunnel.

"*Madre de Dios!* What are you doing, Savi?" Large brown hands grabbed her upper arms and tried to lift her from the floor. "Stand."

Damián.

Her legs felt like hot rubber. Her gaze remained fixed on his hand on her arm, covering many of the tracks she'd made so many years ago.

He released her and walked to the sink. She heard water running, then he knelt beside her. She tore her gaze away from her arm and looked up at him. Disappointment. Fear. Determination. He took a white washcloth and wiped her face. The wet cloth against her numb skin didn't ease the ache. He went back to the sink to rinse it out. When he returned, he pressed the cloth on her head, draped over her forehead.

"I stopped this time."

Damián looked at her as if she'd just sprouted a second head. She couldn't bear the look of disappointment in his eyes and focused once more on her arm. He would send her away now. Perhaps he should. She never should have brought her problems into his world.

Too broken. She'd thought she'd healed, but she'd only buried the biggest hurts deep down inside, hoping they would never be uncovered.

"Savi, look at me."

She hadn't learned to cope with her shame one bit in all these years.

"Now."

Savi dragged her gaze from her arm to Damián's intense scrutiny. Something inside shriveled up and tried to die.

But he wouldn't leave her alone.

"Why did you try to cut yourself, Savi?" He looked at her arm, and her gaze followed in horror, but she *hadn't* tried to cut herself. She'd succeeded in putting the blade down. She'd kept herself safe.

"*Dios*, it's not even the first time." His hand cupped her chin and forced her to look at him. "Did I do this? My God, if I'd known, I wouldn't have touched you like that." The pain in his eyes hurt. She'd never wanted to hurt Damián.

"No, it's not your fault. It's me."

Dirty slut.

He'd only done what the dirty slut had wanted him to do. To touch her. To connect with her. She'd let him lie on the bed with her.

You asked for it.

When he moved away from her, she convinced herself he was going to leave her, as he should. She'd tried to do a bad thing. She should be punished. Still, the thought of him leaving her left her feeling lost. Scared.

She didn't want to be alone anymore.

Damián picked up the razor blade and dropped it in the wastebasket. He removed the cloth from her head and went to the sink to scrub his hands with soap and water, washing away the filth from touching the dirty whore she was. After drying his hands, he returned and bent down.

"Come on. Stand." He took her by the elbows and tried to lift her. Frustration tore across his face. "Savi, I can't lift you from the floor. You'll have to help me."

Help him what? When he pulled at her elbows again, she realized dazedly what he wanted. She wanted to help him, to please him, and pushed his hands away as she scrambled to her knees. When she stood, she swayed on her feet from rising too quickly. Damián caught her and lifted her into his arms.

"No! Put me down. Your foot!"

A low growl emitted from his throat, and Savi knew not to protest any further. She didn't want him to get angry. He passed the bed and carried her into the living room, putting her back on her feet in front of the sofa. He sat down, pulling her into his lap.

"No. This is wrong!" She struggled to get away, but he held her firmly.

"No, *bebé*. I need to feel you in my arms right now. This is very, very right." He guided her head to his chest and wrapped his arms tightly around her upper body. She held herself rigid, expecting him to touch her again. But he didn't move, just held her.

"You scared the hell out of me, Savi. I didn't know you were hurting this badly. I'm so sorry."

Don't be kind to me. I don't deserve it.

Now that he knew she was a dirty slut, why did he still want to hold her?

His hand stroked her upper arm, and she relaxed a little. There was nothing more she could do. Maybe this was good-bye. Needing to be in control, she decided she'd speak the words first. "We'll leave soon. Just don't tell Mari why we couldn't stay." Savi didn't want her daughter ever to find out what her mother was. When she started to get off his lap, he stopped her again.

Damián lifted his head off hers and tucked his index finger under her chin until she met his gaze. "What the fuck are you talking about leaving for?"

She looked into his eyes and saw…confusion? Anger. "I thought you wanted me to leave."

"What gave you that idea? You two aren't going anywhere."

Of course. This Marine had accepted a mission and wouldn't stop until he'd met his objective. It was his responsibility to protect Mari and her. Thank God he was such an honorable man. Savi had done a very poor job of keeping Mari safe. Lyle had come too close for comfort to her daughter. They needed Damián. He wouldn't abandon them, even if he wanted to.

His voice was gentle, understanding. "We need to talk about what happened in there."

Savi shook her head and shifted on his lap. What on earth was she doing in his lap? She was broadcasting the wrong message, if she didn't want him to touch her.

You know you wanted it, Savannah.

No! I didn't!

"We're only going to talk, *mi mariposa*." He cupped her chin and gently tilted her head back until she met his gaze. "Don't even think about flitting away from me—physically *or* mentally. *¿Comprendes?*" She nodded. "We'll talk about the bathroom incident in a minute, but first I want to know what led you to run like that. What happened in the bedroom?"

"I told you it wouldn't work. You should have listened to me."

"Oh, everything was working just fine, if you'll recall."

Her face grew warm, and she pulled away from his hand, looking down at her hands in her lap. He was right. She *had* responded to him. Why now?

She'd buried those feelings for so long, hoping never to experience them again.

Why are you doing this to me? I don't want to feel anything for you—for any man—ever again.

Savi turned toward him again. His eyes were nearly black, pupils so large they obliterated his chocolate-brown irises. A shiver danced down her spine, definitely from a response other than fear.

Too intense.

"It's going to take time for me to discover your triggers, Savi. Maybe if you tell me about what you can remember those men doing to you, I can avoid some of the obvious ones."

No, she could never tell him about the despicable things her father, Lyle, or any of the sadists had done. For the most part, she'd dumped those memories into a black hole long ago, where she wanted them to remain. So why did they keep resurfacing into her consciousness now? It was enough to know her father had raped her too many times to count from when she was a little girl until she'd turned eighteen. What purpose could recalling the details serve in her healing? She'd thought the disgusting memories would disappear entirely, but they were still there, buried deep inside. Only now they seemed to be closer to the surface than they once were. She didn't want to see or feel them.

But one memory had never gone away. The branding. She shuddered, tensed, and firmly stomped on the memory with the fervent hope that this time it would go away. No such luck.

Damián's hand stroked her back until she relaxed again. She hadn't even shared that incident with her therapist. No one knew except Father, Lyle, and her last two sadistic clients at the penthouse who had photographed her mark of shame.

Her therapist and Anita knew generally about the sadistic torture she'd endured, and she'd admitted to both of them that she'd been raped repeatedly by her father, which was horrific enough. She'd just never allowed herself to acknowledge or deal with any of those deeper feelings or the more vile memories on an emotional level. *Just the facts, ma'am.*

"I remember the scene with the two sadists at the hotel the night when I heard you screaming. I can imagine you'd be triggered by the violet wand, the quirt, and maybe even being restrained with ropes."

Ropes, quirt, electricity.

Savi shivered. She didn't remember the pain of that night but was thankful he could focus on that incident, which had been mild compared to the ones at her father's house. She'd had no emotional connection to those two men, so it held much less power over her. She relaxed against him.

"You responded when I touched your breasts. You seemed to enjoy that."

No! I didn't mean to!

Sex was ugly, dirty, bad.

Savi was ugly, dirty, bad.

No, not Savi. She'd never even had sex.

It was Savannah.

Then why had Savi's body betrayed her in Damián's bedroom, stirring up feelings of Savannah's arousal that Savi had tamped down for years? Why had those feelings returned now and with such a vengeance?

Savannah isn't dead.

She gulped air into her lungs, not realizing she'd stopped breathing until her chest began to burn.

"Slow, deep breaths." She did as he instructed, and the burning went away. "Talk to me, *mi sueño*."

Tell him. "I don't like sex. I don't want to have sex—ever." Maybe he'd give up on her when she realized he wasn't going to get anywhere with her in that area.

"What you experienced with those men wasn't sex, *bebé*. It was sadistic torture." He clenched his fist. She could almost feel the rage seething within him, boiling just below the surface.

Savi pulled away. She didn't want to absorb his rage. She'd dealt with her own anger; she didn't need his. She'd moved on.

Or had she?

He relaxed. "Remember our day at the beach, Savannah? In the cave?"

"Savannah's dead."

He frowned.

She has to remain dead. I can't survive if she lives. She knows too much.

Why did he refuse to understand that woman didn't exist anymore? If he wanted Savannah, well, then… She moved to get off his lap, but he didn't release her. Panic flared within her.

"Savi, we aren't finished." He stroked her arm. "Breathe deeply."

She did as he told her and relaxed again, but her nerves remained on the defensive. "I'm finished with sex." *I've been finished sexually since I was nineteen. Since our time in the beach cave.* "I can't be that promiscuous girl for you again. She doesn't exist."

Savannah is dead. Savannah is dead.

He raised his eyebrows. "I never thought of you as promiscuous, Savi. We both just needed someone that day. We connected, were there for each other."

She'd never considered the notion that Damián had needed her that day, too. She'd thought he'd only tried to fill her brokenness with his tenderness, that he'd taken pity on her for what she'd experienced in the hotel.

She stopped fighting to get away from him. Finally.

Chapter Eight

What the fuck was going on? Since the moment he'd walked into the bathroom and found Savi huddled on the floor, razor blade lying beside her, her eyes lost in a trancelike state, Damián felt like he'd been dumped into a combat zone without a clearly defined mission.

Obviously, his touch had triggered something that had been done to her all those years ago. He wished he knew what, so he would know not to do it again. He'd touched her nipple, but she hadn't responded negatively to that. Total opposite, actually. Then he'd touched her mons and clit through her jeans. That seemed to be when all hell broke loose.

Now she was talking about leaving. That wasn't going to happen. Still, how could he keep her safe—not from the outside threat he'd been so focused on the past couple of months but safe from herself?

He needed to help keep her in the moment, get her mind to interpret his touch as something positive instead of the pain and degradation she'd known in the past.

A cutter. *Mierda*. That complicated things. Patti at the club had been one, too. He'd been able to help her with SM sessions when needed, even though most Doms knew to steer clear of cutters and just get them the mental healthcare they needed. Victor had assured him Patti was in counseling and begged Damián to help her, too. Victor couldn't inflict the amount of pain she'd needed to take away the pain exploding inside her body.

Apparently, Savi also needed that endorphin release if she'd been that close to using the razor to cut herself to counteract the psychological pain she was feeling.

Guilt washed over him. This time, it was from pain Damián had inflicted without even knowing it. Hell, the irony of it was that he got relief from his own psychological pain by inflicting pain on women he topped in controlled sadomasochism scenes. He always knew the bottom's limits. He hadn't intended to hurt Savi today, though, in any way. He thought he was being gentle, sensual.

Maybe he couldn't be that kind of man anymore.

"Tell me what it felt like the last time you cut yourself."

She shook her head. "I don't want to talk about it."

"Tell me, Savi." He needed her to define the feeling. She'd clearly resorted to the cathartic behavior before, judging by the scars tracking across her upper arm.

He didn't want her to hurt herself like that anymore, but there was only one way he knew to help. Damián was a mechanic. He needed to fix things. He also was a sadist and a Service Top, but his sweet Savannah had been tortured by sadistic monsters much of her life. She wouldn't want to be around another one, even if he was nothing like those others. Sure, he'd helped Patti and other masochistic bottoms who needed more than they could get from any other Dom in their life or at the club, but he had no emotional attachments to those subs.

Savi looked down at her lap, picking at the skin next to her middle fingernail. Was this another way she mutilated herself? He placed his hand over hers to still them. She tried to extricate her hands from his, but he wouldn't let her escape.

"Tell me."

He'd about given up on her responding when she said, "A rush."

"You get high off cutting."

She shook her head. "Not high. It's just a…rush. The pain would build up inside until I couldn't stand it anymore, then when I cut myself all that pain gushed out and I just felt a rush. Afterward, I was incredibly relaxed and the pain was gone."

"Do you know what endorphins are?"

She nodded. "Yeah. I know that's the clinical term for the rush I'm trying to describe."

"Would you like to find other ways to get that rush without cutting yourself?"

Savi pulled away and looked at him; hope flashed in her eyes but faded as quickly. "If you're going to suggest curing me with rough, hot sex, it won't work."

He grinned and brushed a strand of hair from her cheek. "Too bad. But that's not what I had in mind. I want to help you overcome some of your aversions to being touched. Help you connect with your body again."

When she tried to scoot off his lap, he placed his hands on her upper arms. "How do you feel about being restrained—but this time by someone you trust?"

He couldn't imagine how she could have gotten any more tense. She did. She placed a hand on his chest to keep him at bay but didn't use enough resistance for him to feel she was in a full-blown panic. Yet.

"I don't give up control to anyone."

Well, he sure knew that feeling. "Even if you trusted the person you surrendered your control to? Even with me?"

The wary expression in her eyes told him she didn't trust him either, and it hurt to think he still hadn't gotten anywhere in that regard.

"*Mi sueño*, I know you've had some awful experiences with men." She held her breath. "What I want to try won't be about sex, Savi. It might eventually make sex less frightening for you, but I'm not trying to get inside your pants."

Her face flushed, and she looked down at her hands again. "I'll never be ready for sex again, Damián."

"One thing I've learned in recent years is never say never." There had been a time when he'd thought he'd never walk like a normal man again. Okay, he still wasn't normal, but he sure as hell could fool most people. If he could adjust to an artificial foot, Savi could learn to enjoy sex.

"I'd like to plan a scene for you where you would have ultimate script control over what would happen. A scene you could call off at any moment if it became too intense or uncomfortable."

"You want to do a play?"

He grinned. "Not *do* a play—just play. Hear me out."

She placed her cool fingers on his lips and shook her head. "I'm sorry, Damián. I can't trust anyone enough to let them restrain me. Even having someone touch me sends me…"

He fought the urge to suck her fingers into his mouth and moved her fingers off his lips, trying to regain his self-control. "I'm talking about a role-play scene." His heart tripped over a couple beats. It was now or never. "I know of a club where you would be safe to explore this scene with me. There would be other people there whose job it is to protect you from harm—not that you'd need them. If you use your safeword, I'd stop immediately and we'd talk about what you were feeling."

"Safeword?"

He forgot not everyone knew the lingo of his kink community. "It's a word or phrase you could speak during a scene when you needed the action to stop—like when a director says 'cut' in a movie." He winced. Okay, cut wasn't the right word. "Remember in the bedroom when I told you I'd stop if you said 'hot tamale'? Well, tamale could be your safeword. Of course, if you said 'hot tamale,' I might think you were referring to me." He grinned, hoping to lighten the mood.

She didn't relax even a tiny bit, but he continued, anyway. He'd come too far now. "You would use your safeword to signal me that you needed to stop what we were doing. To take a break. Regroup. Even stop the scene for good."

"I understand what you're saying, but it's still not going to happen. No one will ever restrain me again."

How could he explain this without sounding like the Marquis de Sade? "I'm told it's different when it's consensual restraint. There's a sense of freedom you find when you give up control willingly."

"How can being tied up make someone feel free?"

"I'd have to show you in order for you to understand."

She shook her head again. "So not happening."

Damián steeled himself. He had to tell her eventually, but he hadn't planned to do it so soon. But he needed to be honest with her, if he expected the same from her. "What if we went to my club? There would be monitors present to put an end to the scene if I didn't stop when you used our safeword." He decided that referring to these people as dungeon monitors might not be what she needed to hear right now.

"What are you talking about? What kind of club did you join?"

Slow down, man. You're moving too fast for her. Someday he'd tell her what he'd become, but right now, he'd just talk about the club. "I'm not just a member. I co-own the club." She raised her eyebrows. "After our active service ended, Adam, Marc, and I started a kink club here in Denver."

Her eyes opened wider. "Kink? As in bondage, whips, and stuff like that?"

"Yeah."

"Whoa. I don't think I can picture you in such a place."

He wondered what she thought such a club was supposed to be like. "To be honest, I'm not sure how I got roped into it." He grinned and she groaned at the pun. At least she didn't seem as freaked out. He needed for her to understand what the place was all about. "We run a nice, safe club. Everyone there signs a contract and agrees to follow the rules. We're all consenting adults just looking for a safe place to play. Our club provides equipment most people can't install in their homes and a place to explore their power exchange more deeply, maybe even learn some new techniques or improve a skill. Some just stop by to hang out with like-minded people who understand this part of their nature."

People who won't think of us as freaks, even if we may call ourselves that.

"Power exchange?"

He took it as a positive sign she hadn't jumped off his lap and hightailed it back to Solana Beach. Yet. "Yeah, couples negotiate rules within their relationship. One or more partners relinquish control to one or more others."

"I'm not into group sex. Hell, I'm not into sex. Period."

"I said it doesn't have to be about sex. It's mainly about control—the giving and receiving of control. Of course, that power exchange turns some people on, and we provide private rooms for those wanting a more intimate experience with each other, but the main gathering room is pretty tame. Even scenes in the theme rooms often don't involve sex."

Well, that was true enough—up to a point. He had no clue what happened in most of the theme rooms. He spent most of his time in the great room or the dungeon.

"Theme rooms?"

"Those rooms are set up mostly for fulfilling fantasies. Medical, harem, office, and the like."

Damián appreciated that she still seemed to be considering his words without freaking out like most people would have if they'd been in this conversation. It gave him hope. He brushed a lock of hair off her forehead. "What do you fantasize about, *savita*?"

Her gaze focused on him, shooting daggers at him. "Nothing."

"Everyone has fantasies. It's normal. Healthy."

* * *

Savi's chest grew tight, a stab of pain radiated outward from her heart. She might as well confess her inadequacies to him now, to avoid embarrassment and disappointment later. If there would be a later.

"I'm not normal or healthy when it comes to sex. You're wasting your time, Damián." She moved to get off his lap, but he wrapped his arms tightly around her. Tendrils of panic snaked through her.

She looked into his warm brown eyes and calmed a bit. "What's in it for you?"

"Savi, I'm a Dom."

A what? She cocked her head.

"Sorry—a Dominant. I like to be on the end accepting control from a submissive. But what I really enjoy is being able to give a sub what she needs. What no other man can give her."

She shivered. What was Damián trying to tell her? He liked to tie women up and beat them—because they needed it? "What she needs. What does that mean?"

He placed his hand over her arm just above her elbow and she grew warmer at his touch. His thumb made lazy sweeps over that tiny patch of skin, short-circuiting her ability to follow the conversation for a moment. *Focus.*

"A submissive has an innate need to surrender to a Dominant. It's only then that she feels a sense of fulfillment and completion. There are also male submissives, but we'll focus on female ones—because that's my favorite kind." He grinned. She couldn't believe he was telling her these things. Damián was into bondage and sadomasochism? "There's also a lot of pride a submissive feels in pleasing her Dom."

"I won't be a submissive plaything for any man." Never again.

"In a healthy Dom/sub relationship, it's symbiotic. You will receive as much as you give, maybe even more. It could help free up your mind and body from the things that are holding you back. Not that I can vouch for that feeling of freedom from my own experiences at being restrained." He grinned.

Great. She couldn't get out of her head the visual of Damián chained to a bed.

"Why would you let someone restrain you?"

"Part of my training. It's important for me as a Dom to experience what I'm going to do to a submissive, mainly so I can keep her safe when she's in my care and know what to look for if something goes wrong. I've experienced everything I've done to a sub."

"You've had a lot of submissives?" As much as she hated to admit it, the image of Damián dominating other women bothered her.

"As one of the club's owners, I have to be available to unattached subs wanting to experience various…techniques I'm good at. We also do demonstrations with models we've practiced with before. Sometimes I provide a needed service to a Dom's sub when he is unable or unwilling to provide what's needed—with permission, of course. It's always consensual. Again, I'm not talking about sex—just bondage, impact play, and the like."

He made it sound as if they were talking about Damián offering personal training services at a gym. Savi couldn't believe she was having a conversation about bondage, S&M, and submission with a self-proclaimed Dom. She didn't want to think about participating in anything of the sort but was inexplicably fascinated by it. To make herself that vulnerable to a man again would be unthinkable.

And sadomasochism? Not long before she'd come to Denver, she'd accidentally tuned into an episode of a popular network crime show where a sadomasochism ring kidnapped women, broke them down in every degrading way possible, and sold them against their will as sexual slaves to the highest bidder—to rich men like her father who had more money than morals. She'd turned the television off as soon as she'd realized what was happening to the women, but the nightmares plagued her for days.

She'd been enslaved like that much of her early life. To return to that kind of existence was unfathomable. She'd never put herself at risk of that happening again.

How could someone as gentle as Damián want to be involved in degrading and overpowering women like that?

"I can see you're trying to sort this out in that pretty little head, but don't assume you know what we do just because of a label."

He was only teasing her. She was too boyish to be pretty. She'd fought hard to keep her body as thin as she could; even her breasts had shrunk to almost non-existent after she'd stopped breastfeeding, they were still a little larger than pre-pregnancy. Having men look at her sexually always creeped her out; most didn't notice her if she kept her body as thin as a young boy's.

But Damián noticed. She squirmed inside her skin. The smoldering looks he gave her when he didn't think she'd catch him, and the way he'd touched her breast a little while ago, stirred feelings she'd kept tamped down for so very long. She wasn't ready to remove the lid on the box where she'd kept those feelings hidden.

"*Savita*, your experience with BDSM wasn't consensual. What we do at the club is always with the consent of both parties. Tell me, what questions do you have?"

She wondered what special techniques he was referring to.

"Go ahead. Ask me."

He read her like an open book. She captured her lower lip between her teeth until she noticed Damián's gaze zoning in on her mouth, then she turned her lip loose. She didn't want to send him any sexual signals.

Why was she so morbidly fascinated by this subject? She was no doormat. She was a strong-willed, independent woman. Maybe he'd taken her vulnerable state these past couple months or what had happened to her in the past as a sign she was submissive. Savi needed him to know she'd never succumb to a domineering man again.

"Questions, Savi."

She sighed. First she needed to learn more. "You're co-owner of an S&M club. I can't get past that."

"Not just an SM club. We prefer to call it a kink or BDSM club. There's a whole spectrum of kink that our members and their guests are interested in. Bondage, discipline, dominance, submission, Master, slave, sadomasochism, and fetishes. Only a small number of the membership is into hardcore SM."

"You keep saying SM. I've always heard it called S&M."

"To most in the lifestyle, it's just SM."

Just SM. *Wow.* "There's a lifestyle?"

He nodded. "For some. Most just role-play in their homes or when they come to clubs, but others live their Dominant and submissive roles twenty-four/seven—not just with sex and role-playing, but within all aspects of their lives."

"That sounds like slavery."

"There are submissives who relinquish total control to a Dom or Master, and they are referred to as slaves in the Scene. Most Masters still honor a slave's hard limits. Just depends on their agreement."

Willing slaves? Was he serious?

"But no matter the intensity or duration—lifelong or for an evening—participants negotiate very specific boundaries in their power exchange."

"How long have you been doing…this?"

He thought a moment. "Actively, almost five years, I guess. I trained with a whip master west of here for a couple years prior to opening the club but much more since we opened."

"Why haven't you been going to the club these last two months?" She pulled away again. "Or have you?"

He shook his head. "I told Dad I was taking a break while you two were here."

She'd kept him away from something he loved. Now, he wanted to coax her to join him there. She didn't want to share that part of his life. "I'm not a submissive."

"What makes you so sure?"

She opened her eyes wider. "I've got a career. I don't bow down to any man."

"You'd be surprised who the submissives are—nurses, housewives, teachers, business executives. You wouldn't recognize most Doms or subs on the street as being in the lifestyle. In our society, they have to keep this part of themselves hidden so they don't lose their jobs, custody of their kids, and such. People outside the Scene don't understand this subculture."

No shit, Sherlock.

"Savi, I think submitting to a Dom can give you a sense of control you don't feel right now."

She hadn't been in control since Lyle had broken into her house. No, in reality, she'd only had the illusion of control even before then. She hadn't been in control of her world or her life for a very long time—since she was eight. She tensed, not comfortable thinking about that time in her life.

What was Damián offering her? Should she find out more? Could it help her?

He rubbed some of the rapidly vanishing heat back into her arms. "Look, I know you've had some bad experiences with men who took what they wanted without your consent."

Having him believe and validate her helped some but didn't make the pain go away.

"What I'm proposing is an experience where you would have total control. You'd consent to give your submission to me before each scene—as a gift, if you will."

Controlled surrender. Sounded like an oxymoron. "I'd have to have a tendency toward submission in order to give you that gift—and I don't."

"Let's try an experiment."

Savi narrowed her eyes. "What kind of experiment? I'm not a guinea pig or some kind of sacrificial lamb."

He grinned. "Not *that* kind of experiment." He indicated that she should get up and helped her to her feet, then he followed to stand in front of her. "Turn around."

He guided her until her back was to him. The heat from his body surrounded her and made her feel warm. Safe. She waited on tenterhooks, not knowing what he planned to do. After what seemed an incredibly long time, he placed his hands at the back of her neck and over her shoulders. Her knees buckled.

Savi gasped, but he caught her before she fell. She wrenched around in his arms to stare at him. When his hands had touched her like that, she'd lost all control of her body. If he hadn't caught her, she'd be puddled at his feet.

Like a doormat.

"One more test."

"No. I don't want to be tested any further." Not after obviously failing the first one. Or had she passed? Depended on who you asked—her or him.

"Humor me. Hold your hands up like this is a robbery, palms toward me, hands open."

"I don't think…"

"Shhh, *bebé*. Just do it."

Something inside her stomach flip-flopped. How could she resist him when he looked at her like that? She raised her hands, as he'd instructed.

He took a step back and stared intently into her eyes. She stared back, not wanting to back down or show submission. Something unfamiliar heated in her core. The place where he'd touched her a moment ago, behind her neck, prickled with awareness. After an interminable pause, he raised his hands and pressed them against her forearms. Rather than push him away, or back up, her body nearly melted toward him.

Realizing by his grin that was exactly the response he wanted, what he'd expected, she finally had the wherewithal to push back. Too late. She'd failed both tests. What was he doing to her body? She could take down a man his size if she'd been threatened in any way, but she hadn't taken him down. She hadn't felt threatened at all. He'd played her like a puppet. Had he hypnotized her?

He smiled and nodded. "There's a good chance you'd respond well to submission."

"I told you, I won't let anyone tie me up."

"There are lots of ways to submit to someone without being restrained, if that's what you're most afraid of."

She raised her chin, cringing when she felt it quiver. "I'm not afraid."

He tweaked her nose. "Too bad. A little fear in a submissive is attractive as hell to a Dom."

But I don't want to be attractive to any man, Dominant or not. Not even you, Damián.

Feeling the once-firm grip on her control slipping away, she took a step back, but his hands on her arms locked her in place.

"Please hear me out, Savi."

Damián doesn't want to hurt you. He wants to help.

Why couldn't he see that no one could fix what was wrong with her? Her therapist had tried for so many years. She'd helped some, getting Savi to where she could at least function as a mother and as a therapist. However, Savi hadn't wanted to tackle the issues revolving around sex. There'd been no point. She wasn't looking for a sexual relationship with anyone ever again.

Then Damián had touched her.

She'd only come to him seeking protection for Mari. She didn't want to rekindle some long-dead physical attraction between them.

But she'd learned today that the feelings weren't dead. Something long dormant had stirred back to life a little while ago in his bed. Oh, dear Lord, she didn't want to feel anything—but she had.

Still, she couldn't afford to tick him off. There was nowhere else she and Mari could turn. What exactly did he want in exchange for sheltering and protecting them? Could Savi pay the price if it were too high?

The silence became uncomfortable. A surreptitious glance told her he was watching her. Her heart began to beat more rapidly.

Damián's firm hand released her left arm, and he moved closer, stroking her back. Her throat and lungs constricted. Panic clawed at her, and she tried to wrest herself away.

"Breathe slowly, *querida*. Don't fight me."

Savi swung her hand at him, hoping to push him away, but he wouldn't let go. She pushed harder and he released her. *Escape.* She started toward the door, but before she reached it, Damián commanded, "Savi, stop. Now."

Her chest heaved as she fought to fill her lungs, but her feet obeyed him. *No!* She needed to get away. Heat from Damián's body alerted her that he was standing close behind her, but still she couldn't move.

"I'm not going to hurt you, Savi. I need you to stop running before you hurt yourself."

Savi began to shake. What was happening? She wrapped her arms around her midsection trying to comfort herself, but it didn't help. Then Damián's strong arms covered hers, and he pulled her against his body, snuggling his face into the hollow of her neck.

"Don't worry, *mi sueño*. No one will ever hurt you again. I won't allow it."

How could he make such a promise? Savi tried to pull away from him, but he only held her tighter. Smothering. She began to fight him, elbowing him in the upper arm, kicking his shin with her heel; he only grunted and held on tighter.

"I can't breathe."

"Yes, you can. Inhale, Savi."

She shook her head frantically at the same time she filled her lungs with a shaky breath. Why was her body responding to his commands like this?

"You're hurting me." Her plaintive cry sounded like a weak little girl's. She didn't want to feel pain. She didn't want to feel anything. Why was he forcing her to feel?

"Shhh. I have you. You're safe, *mi sueño*. I won't harm you."

She'd never be able to put all these feelings he'd resurrected back inside their hidden box where they belonged. "But you already have," she whispered.

Damián let her go as if she'd become red hot—or ice cold, more accurately. She had to reach out to grab the doorjamb to keep from falling. The loss of his arms around her left a void in the pit of her stomach. She should be relieved to have his hands off her; instead, she felt the loss in the most intense way. What had he done to her?

He made me vulnerable. Weak.

She leaned forward until her forehead touched the cold door. Damián's warm hands brushed lightly from her shoulders to her upper arms and back again. "Savi, it's going to be okay. We'll work on this together."

Savi shook her head. "It will never be okay. *I* will never be okay. I'm too broken."

"Nobody's perfect, Savi. Hell, look at me. But you'll always be perfect to me."

Chapter Nine

Hearing the hopelessness in her voice crushed something in Damián. How could she think she was broken? She was fucking perfection. She had been from the moment he first saw her across the restaurant at the hotel. Hell, *he* was the broken one.

He reached up to brush a hank of hair from her shoulder and resisted the desire to press his lips against her neck. "So perfect, *mi mariposa*. Don't ever let me hear you call yourself broken again. Do you hear me?"

"You know nothing about me. About what I am."

"I know all that is important."

Savi caught him by surprise when she turned around and looked up at him. Her anguished face tore at his gut. So tiny, petite. He hated that men had taken advantage of her just because they were bigger and more powerful than she was. Maybe he should take her to the downstairs gym at the club and help her gain confidence and strength by working out, so that no one would intimidate her again.

Hell, he couldn't do that. Judging by her response tonight, she'd freak out if she went anywhere near the club. Besides, the dungeon lay just beyond the weight room. He huffed to himself at the ridiculous thought. Yeah, if she caught sight of that, it certainly wouldn't allay her fears about how honorable his intentions were.

He stared at her eyelashes brushing against her cheeks; then she opened her eyes, drawing him into their sparkling blue depths. The mixture of vulnerability and defiance only made her more irresistible to him.

"I'm scared, Damián."

He brushed her cheek with his thumb. "What are you afraid of, *mi sueño?*"

"Everything. Everyone. My father. You."

Damián flinched and pulled his hand back. How could she compare him to her father? The bastard had raped and abused his own daughter. Damián might be a sadist himself now, but only in consensual situations. He would never harm her to get his rocks off.

Did Savi suspect what he'd become? If she did, why didn't she run away from him? He didn't know of any sadist who would stoop to the level of depravity exhibited by her father and her handler at the hotel. Damián would never go that far.

After what she'd experienced at the hands of those sadistic clients in the penthouse, he didn't picture her submitting to another sadist in this lifetime.

Best to remember that the next time he got the urge to get all carnal with her.

But the trembling in her body beckoned. He wanted her to tremble for him. How could he get her to lower the wall and let him in?

One technique might help her in this moment without freaking her out completely.

"Will you trust me to demonstrate something to you—how I can control you without restraints?"

She looked up at him, furrowing her brows. "I don't know."

"Trust me. I won't harm you. I just want to help relax you."

She took a long time to think before she responded but finally nodded.

"Speak the words."

"Yes. You can try."

He smiled. "Close your eyes, Savi."

"I can't relax with you this close."

Damián wished she meant that in a different way, but he knew the fear was still talking.

"Close your eyes, *savita*."

* * *

Savi's heart rate ramped up as his intense gaze bore into her. She felt so…

Before she could name the elusive emotion, he lowered his head to hers. She placed her hands on his chest to push him away, but he just held onto them as if to steady himself and continued to move closer.

"I don't want you to kiss me."

"This isn't a kiss."

The words had barely left his mouth when he pressed his lips against hers. If this wasn't a kiss, then what was it? His left hand released hers and caged her chin, opening her mouth totally to his will. He didn't move but applied steady pressure, closing off the airway. Even though she could breathe through her nose, panic set in. She clenched his hair and tried to push him away. His response to her distress was to draw her breath from her lungs with his mouth making her panic even more.

Then he pushed the breath back into her mouth.

What on earth...?

Again he drew her breath into his mouth and lungs, and then repeated the process. A wave of dizziness swept over her, and she slumped against him. Damián pressed her harder against the wall, sandwiching her between his unyielding body and the hard wall, the only reason she could remain standing.

The tension and anxiety she'd been experiencing released, and she floated in his arms. Her focus became riveted on the back-and-forth play of their breathing. He pressed even harder against her body, depriving her chest of any room to expand on its own. Her breathing was controlled totally by Damián.

Giving up control of something so very basic—and vital—to life should have terrified her. But it didn't. She was able to gain the oxygen she needed through her nose, but a large amount of carbon dioxide was going straight to her head.

He pulled back. "Take several deep breaths."

They each filled their lungs several times, his breath warm and moist against her face. Then his hand went to her nose and pinched off her airway as he lowered his mouth again.

"No, wait! I'm not..."

Ready.

The sensation of having both airways completely obstructed sent panic through her, and she pushed harder against him, but he filled her lungs with another breath. She inhaled his breath deeply into her lungs, needing more. Needing...him.

Damián's penis pressed against her lower abdomen, sending warning bells clanging. His thumb brushed her jaw, and her fear receded a tiny bit.

Relax. Don't fight him. You'll only make it worse.

Only this feeling wasn't bad, as much as she expected it to be. Having him take control of her freed her mind and body in a way she'd never experienced before. She didn't want him to stop. The dizziness increased, and she allowed herself to float, drift away.

* * *

Damián felt her body relax and laid his free thumb against the pulse in her throat, gauging her body's response. Just a little while longer and she'd be in subspace, if she wasn't already there. He wanted to feel her body pressed against his a little longer before he pulled away. He breathed into her mouth again, feeling her breasts push against his chest as he filled her lungs with his breath.

While he could still breathe through his own nose, he definitely felt a little lightheaded himself from the amount of carbon dioxide he'd sucked into his lungs. Savi's breaths. Her very essence. He felt a little heady at the thought of sharing something as intimate as a breath with her.

It might be the most intimate moment they would ever share again.

Fuck.

Damián pulled away. This wasn't what he needed to be doing with Savi. He needed to keep his fucking hands off her. What the hell was he thinking?

Placing a hand under her chin, he raised her head. Dazed. Her eyes had glazed over. Thankfully, he had her on her feet. He bent and scooped her into his arms, then carried her the short distance into the bedroom without aggravating his stump. He laid her on the bed, and she moaned, wincing as if in pain.

Fuck it all.

Damián reached down and pulled the Indian blanket over her, then walked around the bed and crawled in on the other side. With the heavy blanket between them, nothing would happen. But how could he not administer aftercare to her when he was the one who had put her into subspace? Turning her onto her left side, he wrapped his arm around her waist and pulled her against him, infusing her with his body heat.

Her hair moved as he breathed on her. She moaned again and tried to pull away, but he held her tighter. "You're safe, Savi. I have you."

With a sweet sigh of surrender, she stopped fighting him.

"Just float." She'd certainly earned this relaxation time, a chance to drift away in her head to some neutral place between reality and dreams. He hoped she'd avoid the dark places.

When she awoke, he'd explain what had happened. He hoped this breath-control play helped her see that there were ways for him to exert control over her without restraints—or pain.

But he needed to be careful. Savi would want nothing to do with his world. He was playing with fire introducing her to any control techniques.

Mierda, just being around Savi was the equivalent of playing with fire.

Maybe he should talk with Dad about sending Savi and Marisol over there for a while, as far away from him as possible, for her own well-being—and his.

* * *

Maman's screams woke Savannah from a deep sleep. She looked toward her open bedroom door, drawn to the hallway. Tossing the summer bedspread back, the eight-year-old stood on shaking legs. Placing one foot in front of the other, she crossed the room, the cold floor sending a chill up her spine. Or was it Maman's screams causing that?

Near the end of the hallway, the light to her parents' bedroom shone under the doorway. Should she go in there? She'd been told never to go in when the door was closed. But it sounded like Maman needed her.

Where was Father? He should protect Maman. Maybe he wasn't home yet. Still, what could a little girl do if someone had broken in and was attacking her mother?

Slowly, quietly, Savannah turned the door knob. Everything moved in slow motion. Then she saw Maman thrashing on the bed, a man on top of her...

"Nooooo! Stop hurting her!" Savannah pounded her tiny fists against the man's arm.

She heard the bedroom door open behind her, and someone grabbed her flailing arms in mid-air. The man turned toward her. Father?

"Savi! You're dreaming, *querida*. Wake up. Now."

"What's wrong with Maman?" Mari's cries filtered into her brain. She needed to protect Mari from Father. "Run, Mari! Run! Don't let him catch you!"

"Daddy won't hurt me, Maman."

But he will. He's evil. All men are evil. "Don't let him touch you, Mari. Please, run!"

"Savi. Wake up. That's the past. You're here in Denver."

The hands holding her arms down began to hurt. She whimpered. "Don't hurt Maman!"

The strange man's voice was upset as he barked orders. "Marisol, go on the coffee table and get my phone." The deep, masculine voice had a Spanish accent—not like Father's at all. "Press the number 2 and hold it until Grandpa or Karla answers. Tell them we need Grandpa to come get you."

"But, Daddy, I want to stay with my maman!"

"*Muévete rapido*, Marisol. Do as I say."

"Yes, Daddy."

"Good girl."

At Father's words, Savi fought against the arms holding her. "Noooo! Don't call me that! I'm bad. I didn't stop you."

Strong, warm arms pulled her up and held onto her. "Shhh, Savi. It wasn't your fault. You couldn't stop what happened. You were just a little girl."

"Choking."

"Oh, *bebé*. Just let it all out."

"Hands. Choking. Won't stop."

"He choked you?"

She shook her head. Why didn't he understand? Savi sobbed, then realized her face was pressed against a bare chest. A man's chest.

He stroked her hair. "That's my girl. Just let it out."

Damián. He lay stretched out beside her. How did she get into bed? The last thing she remembered was Damián's mouth on hers, stealing her breath. She turned away and saw Mari's Josefina doll. Mari had come home at some time. What time was it?

Damián's hands stroked her hair as he crooned to her, uttering words of comfort. But there could be no comfort. She would never heal from the images branded on her mind.

"Oh, God!" The brand. Her shame. How could Damián ever want to touch her again if he saw her shame? She tried to escape his arms. "Don't touch me!"

When he didn't release her, she panicked further. She needed to get away. She pushed the heels of her hands against his chest, but he just held on.

"I'm not going to hurt you, Savi. I'm not going to let you go, either. You might hurt yourself."

"Mari? Is she okay?"

He nodded. "She's fine. She got home a couple hours ago. You were sleeping and just had a nightmare. It's over now."

"Oh, Lord. I'm…so…broken." She'd been branded a slave by Lyle and her father. She'd done horrible things, but didn't want to have anyone touch her ever again. Yet being held in Damián's strong arms felt so good. So safe.

He brushed the hair from her cheek, curling it behind her ear. "You're perfect for me, *mi sueño*."

The words, whispered in her ear, sounded so sincere. But she wasn't perfect. He deserved someone better. Someone whole. Not a broken, dirty slut like her.

She pulled away and searched his eyes. "I can't stay here any longer, Damián. Mari and I need to leave. Tonight."

The look of pain in his eyes hurt her, too, but she couldn't run the risk of Damián ever discovering her secret shame.

* * *

They were gone. Savi and Marisol had packed and gone to Dad's after her nightmare. Damián had wandered around the apartment for a week, feeling their presence everywhere he looked. Boots didn't help. The damned kitten missed them, too, and kept curling up on his lap. Dad didn't want a cat around his house while Karla was pregnant. Damián polished off another Dos Equis and wiped away the moisture from his eyes. *Fucking allergies.* He reached down and petted the ball of fluff purring against his crotch.

Achoo!

Damián laid the kitten on the sofa beside him and carried his empty bottle to the kitchen. He opened the fridge to reach for another but decided against it. Three were enough. He should just go to bed. Maybe he could get some sleep.

That would be a first. He had barely slept in a week.

Inside the bedroom, he looked at the bed, still rumpled from where Savi'd had her nightmare last week. Had she figured out what he'd become? Dreamed about him? When she yelled for him not to touch her, he'd wondered, but thought she was still fighting whoever was in the dream. Then she'd demanded to go away. If she knew, it would be no big surprise she'd want to get away from him.

He'd avoided the bed all week, knowing it would make the separation even harder. He removed his clothes and the prosthesis and crawled into bed face down in the pillow that still carried her flowery, clean scent. He inhaled deeply, then rolled onto his side and grabbed the other pillow, hugging it to his chest.

Sleep claimed him…

"Madre de Dios! No! Sergeant, don't you fucking die!"

He knew Sergeant Miller was gone but kept yelling at him…he looked up and watched as Grant and Wilson, on either side of him, lifted the body off him. Damián turned his head away, watching in horrific fascination as Sergeant's blood ran down the rooftop toward Damián's feet, where it mingled with another pool of blood. The one forming around his own mangled foot.

No, not the rooftop. He was in bed now. What the fuck?

On the bed in front of him, the Barbie doll from the restaurant was trussed up in a grotesque position. The soles of her feet were red. Her naturally blond pussy was splayed open for God and everyone to see. Red, angry welts covered her inner thighs. White nylon ropes suspended her knees in the air, attaching her to the headboard.

Her eyes were closed, but her face was red, with tracks of tears down both cheeks. The sight of her ravaged body tore at his gut.

Damián jumped off the bed, forgetting his foot had been blown off, and fell to his hands and knees. He needed to help Savannah. He needed to escape the rooftop. Damián scrambled away from the bed, his heart about to pound out of his chest.

He low-crawled on his forearms into the living room. Safety. But where was Savannah? How'd she wind up with him in Fallujah?

The demons followed. Blood. Sergeant's blood. Damián's blood. He wouldn't be able to keep the demons at bay.

Where the fuck was Savannah? He needed to save her.

Reality slapped him in the face, and he huddled next to the sofa. He'd never mixed his nightmares like that before. He needed to regain control. Everything was so fucking out of his control right now.

Dad.

He reached for the cell phone on the coffee table and hit the speed dial. Glancing out the window, he saw it was daytime. How long had he slept? Was Savi okay? Marisol?

Fifteen minutes later, Damián answered the knock on the door.

"How are you doing, son?" Rock solid. Dad never let anything faze him. Damián wished he could be like that.

"I've been better. Sorry to bother you again, but—"

"Fuck that shit. If you hadn't called and I found out, you know I'd ream your ass but good."

Damián nodded and motioned him toward the couch, but Dad headed for the kitchen instead. "Let's get some Joe brewing first." Damián followed. Of course, Dad had things under control, having been through this routine enough times, so Damián just sat at the table and held his head in his hands.

Every time he closed his eyes, his mind flashed images of that rooftop in

Fallujah mixed with Savannah's battered, abused body in the hotel penthouse. What had triggered the latest episode?

Dad placed a mug of coffee in front of him, and the smell of the strong brew brought him back to the present.

"Which particular nightmare are you dealing with right now?"

"Same old, but with a twist this time."

"Spill it."

Damián knew silence wasn't an option. Not a good one, anyway, if he valued his ass. These talks with Dad usually helped him process shit from a combat PTSD episode, but what the fuck was he supposed to do with that scene with Savannah?

"Now, not tomorrow."

Damián looked up at Dad. "How are they doing?"

Dad blinked, then seemed to follow his train of thought. "Fine. No school today. A professional-development day for the teachers, so Marisol and I played in the snow all morning."

Damián should have been the one playing with her in the snow. He'd been avoiding them all week, figuring Savi wanted nothing to do with him. She'd made it clear she didn't want to be around him when she'd moved in with Dad and Karla.

"Savi? Is she okay?"

"She's quiet and stays in her room a lot. I can't get a read on her. Plays it close to the vest."

"She doesn't like to let anyone get too close."

"Did the twist in this episode have something to do with her?"

Perceptive man. Damián nodded. "One minute, I'm on that rooftop with Sergeant Miller, the next I'm finding Savannah—Savi—tortured and restrained in a hotel room. I froze. Both times."

"We've been through that before. You sure as hell didn't freeze in Fallujah, and I doubt you did with Savi either."

"Maybe not, but I hesitated. Waited too long trying to assess the situation. I could have gone in there and helped sooner, but didn't want to get involved."

"You're talking about Savi now."

Damián nodded. "They fucking tortured her. She was screaming and I kept thinking maybe it was consensual. I had a girlfriend once who liked that stuff."

"But you did rescue her, didn't you?"

"Yeah. Finally. But I sure didn't rescue Miller."

"No one could have."

"So what's the connection? Why am I being bombarded by my two worst nightmares now?"

"I think the two incidents are connected in your mind. You're feeling a loss of control."

Damn straight. "I'm not sure I ever had control."

"Sure you have. I'd hazard a guess you're the most controlled Dom I've ever known. Gunnar trained you well."

"Takes a survivor to know one, I guess."

"When you plan a scene at the club and execute it perfectly, giving the bottom what she needs, you're in total control."

"It's been a while."

"You've been missed, for sure, but you have to do what's best for you and those you love. I've never known anyone who could get his priorities straighter than you. Country. Family. Friends. Work. You just have a lot to juggle right now. But maybe being out of the club for months hasn't been a good thing, after all."

He'd certainly stayed on an even keel longer when he'd had regular scenes with pain sluts at the club. "How's Patti been doing?"

"There've been a couple times she probably could have used you, but we helped her and Victor work through it best we could. Even called Gunnar to town one time."

Guilt assailed him. Patti was a masochist who had come to expect Damián to be there when she needed him, to deliver the level of pain she needed during the dark times. Damián had fulfilled the role of sadist Service Top for her many times.

During the years before their own club opened, he trained under the expertise of Gunnar Larson, the most highly respected sadist Service Top and Whip Master in the area. Gunnar ran a dungeon in a ski-resort town west of Denver. But here at the Masters at Arms, there were only a few hardcore sadists who attended regularly. Damián was probably the most sought-after one, though, because a lot of the masochists had issues like Savi's. They didn't want some man getting turned on by their pain—they just wanted to work through a pain session and get on with their life. Being able to help Patti and others who needed him and his well-honed skills had given him a real sense of purpose, of being needed.

But the one woman he most wanted to help wouldn't let him near her. Rightly so. She'd been abused by a lot of sexual sadists and predators in the past. No wonder she'd run to Dad's place when Damián revealed he was a sadist himself. She'd wanted nothing more to do with him.

"Why don't you come to the club tonight? I think you're due for a visit."

Maybe that was what he needed. At least he wouldn't run into Savi or Marisol there. Yeah, maybe it was time. If he could get into a scene in the dungeon, he might be able to regain some sense of control.

* * *

Savi stared out the bedroom window at the snowy scene below. A knock on the door sent her across the room. The bedroom she and Mari had been staying in the past week had a calming effect on her, from its lavender-scented sheets to the antique walnut furniture. The room made her think of Maman.

She opened the door to find Karla carrying a tray with a teapot and matching bone china cups.

Savi reached out. "Here, let me take that."

Karla executed a half-turn to keep Savi's hands from the tray. "Don't you start that, too. Adam's driving me nuts. I'm pregnant, not a freaking invalid."

Savi smiled, but didn't want to tell her how lucky she was to have a man wanting to take care of her like that. Being pregnant and single was so much harder, even if Savi did prefer to keep men at arm's length. There were times when she'd even wished she'd had Damián there to lean on. At least she'd had Anita when the time came to deliver Mari. Being alone in that situation would have been even worse.

"Savi, would you like to come across the hall and share a cuppa with me? Adam has ordered me to sit with my feet propped up for the rest of the afternoon while he's over at…I mean, to get ready for the club hours tonight."

Savi glanced over at the bed where Mari was enjoying an afternoon nap after Adam had worn her out playing in the snow all morning before he'd been called away. "Sure, I think she'll be out at least another half hour."

She followed Karla across the hall into the master bedroom. The hunter-green walls gave the room a relaxing feel, too. Karla put the tea tray on a small table near the rise of steps leading to the French doors. The patio and hot tub were covered with the newly fallen five-inch snow. Savi had never seen as much snow in her entire life as she'd seen these few months in Denver.

Karla motioned for Savi to have a seat in the wingchair while she sat in the cushioned glider. After Karla poured them each a cup of berry-colored herbal tea, they both relaxed and enjoyed sipping the soothing brew.

"So how are you settling in?"

Savi didn't want to be impolite, but she actually missed being in Damián's apartment. When Adam had come over to the apartment the night of her last nightmare, Damián had abruptly announced that she and Marisol would be going home with him. Savi couldn't very well argue. She'd practically insisted it was time to leave. And it was more than crowded over there. Mari didn't even have a yard to play in, as she did here.

Still, for reasons Savi didn't understand, she missed being at Damián's place.

Missed him, too. He'd avoided them all week. Savi never thought she'd be thinking such a thing, but she really wanted to see Damián again.

But Karla didn't need to know that.

"We're doing fine. Thanks for letting us stay here."

"It's been great *having* you here. Seeing Adam with Marisol…" Karla's voice cracked with emotion, and she cleared her throat. "I can't wait 'til the baby comes. He's going to make such a great daddy."

"Do you know if you're having a boy or girl?"

Karla shook her head. "We want to be surprised. Neither of us is much into traditional baby colors, so that won't make a difference as far as clothes or the nursery. Don't you just love that room you're staying in? I think the colors are so relaxing. It was a wonderfully healing place when I came here after…" Karla looked down at the teacup in her lap. "…after my brother was killed."

"Oh, Karla, I'm so sorry!" Savi hadn't heard that she'd lost her brother.

Karla took a sip, then held the shaking cup in her lap. Her protruding belly pressed against the teacup's rim. "It's still hard to think about him being gone forever."

"I can't imagine."

But she could, in a way. While Savi didn't have any siblings, her Maman had walked out of her life, never to return. Only Maman had left intentionally. The details of that night nineteen years ago were sketchy, at best. She and

Maman had spent a perfect day at their beach cave, the same one Damián had taken her to, ironically. Savannah remembered their picnic and watching the sun set before Maman took her back to the house.

The next day, Maman was gone. Savannah's life had never been the same.

Time to change the subject from loss to life. "How far along are you?"

"I'm due the 11th of July. Seems like an eternity."

Savi laughed. "You'd better pace yourself. You do have a ways to go."

Karla bit her lowered lip, then focused on Savi's face. "Adam says we can't have sex anymore until the doctor gives the all-clear *after* the baby is born."

Savi didn't know anything about sex during pregnancy, but she'd only heard of it being a problem for someone on bed rest. "Are you having difficulty with your pregnancy?"

"Far from it. Everything's going perfectly." She smiled and rubbed her belly and smiled enigmatically for a moment. "We couldn't have asked for more, but he blames himself for somehow causing his son to be stillborn because he likes it a little rough." Karla blushed and grinned. "Sorry. Too much information. But no amount of logic and scientific evidence will get through that stubborn man's head."

Oh dear Lord, Savi did not want to continue this conversation, either. So out of her league.

Karla grew serious. "But I'm not going to wait that long." She grinned. "I have a plan to batter down his defenses yet again. I'll drive him crazy, until he reaches his monumentally high breaking point. Then, I'll bring that man to his *knees*, he'll want me so badly."

The sheer determination in her voice made Savi worry for Adam. He didn't stand a chance.

"Sex wasn't an issue I had to worry about during my pregnancy." *Thank God.* If Savi had been with Damián or any man during her pregnancy, she probably would have welcomed a reprieve from having to have sex. As she'd grown stronger away from Father, she'd wanted to close off that part of her nature forever.

Karla's eyes opened wide. "Oh, no, *I'm* the one who's sorry! I totally wasn't thinking. All of my brain cells must be going straight to the baby lately."

Karla must have thought she'd *wanted* Damián in her life back then. "No, don't apologize. It is what it is—and everything worked out just fine." Until Lyle and her father found her and Mari.

"You're stronger than I am, Savi. I don't think I could have faced becoming a mother without Adam by my side, even if I do want to wring his neck at least once a day." She smiled, again placing her hand over the baby cocooned in her belly. "The man can't communicate worth a darn, but at other times, well, let's just say I'll always know where I stand with him. He shoots from the hip, just like the ancestor he keeps telling me stories about. That's him on the far right in those photos on the dresser."

Savi looked over at a line of framed portraits of six men in uniform. The one Karla referred to looked like a 19th-century photo—probably Civil War era or soon after. The man inside the picture looked young and handsome in his uniform. "Adam's mom gave him those photos for Christmas. They're duplicates of the ones she has of his relatives who served in the Marines."

Savi's eyes stung. Karla's baby would have a whole ancestry and lots of love from both sides of the family. Savi hadn't been able to share the details of Mari's heritage with her daughter. Not only had she known nothing about Damián's background, but her own family's mementos were lost to her, too. Of course, Savi could care less about her father's side, but being able to share Maman's French heritage would have been…

Karla's hand squeezed Savi's. "You okay?"

Savi forced a smile to her lips and raised her hand to rub her eye. "Yeah, I'm fine. Just got something in my eye."

"Listen, why don't you come down to the club tonight?"

The abrupt change of topic caught her off guard. "No, I don't think…"

"It's pretty laid-back on Wednesdays—more social than anything. You'll meet a lot of great people. We run a really nice club. You can have a couple drinks, listen to my show, meet some of Damián's friends."

"No, I need to stay with Mari."

"Grant and I can take turns watching her. Adam only lets me do two sets a night now when the club's open, so I'll just start the first one later on when things start hopping. One of the other members can tend bar for Grant tonight."

"No, I don't want anyone to go to any troub…"

"No trouble at all! If I'd known Marc would be on another overnight expedition, I'd have asked Adam to bring Angie back to the club." Karla rolled her eyes. "Adam's fit to be tied that Marc's let Angie move back to

Aspen Corners. They're so perfect for each other. Wish I knew what happened, but neither of them is talking." Karla glanced down at her cup, lost in thought, then she gave herself a mental shake and looked up, smiling. "Sorry. Anyway, Grammy Karla would love to spend some time with Marisol—and Auntie Grant would, too. We love that little girl like crazy. And I'd love for you to see our club."

Savi decided to put an end to this notion immediately. "Thanks for the offer, but I'm really not interested in…that kind of thing."

Karla leaned toward her. "If you're like me, you probably have a lot of preconceived notions about this BDSM stuff. Believe me, most of my notions were far from reality. If you met most of our members at their jobs or on the street, you'd never guess what they do in private."

Damián had said the same thing.

"And if you stay in the great room, there really isn't anything too kinky that goes on there—not most of the time, anyway. We don't have any demos planned for tonight, either, as far as I know."

"Really, Karla. I appreciate the invite, but I'd feel too uncomfortable there."

"Uncomfortable where?"

Savi turned to watch Adam walk in and suddenly the walls of the room closed in on her. The man's size and presence seemed to suck all the energy from the room.

"Adam! I didn't expect you back so soon." Karla stood and walked over to him, giving him a hug.

She turned her face toward him, clearly wanting a kiss on the lips, but he kissed her on the cheek instead. Karla didn't hide her disappointment.

Adam smiled and patted her growing belly. "Turned out everything's okay."

Karla's face and body relaxed visibly, but Adam didn't elaborate about what or whom he'd been checking on.

"Adam, I was trying to talk Savi into coming to the club tonight."

"Excellent idea. What's the problem?"

"She won't say yes."

Savi wished they'd quit talking about her as if she weren't here—and that they'd quit trying to get her to go to their damned club. The last place she was going to be found in was a sex club.

Adam turned to her, his expression stern, as usual. "What are you afraid of?"

Savi pulled herself up in the chair. "I'm not afraid of anything." He grinned and might as well have called her a liar. When he smiled, his entire face changed. He should do that more often. Of course, he usually smiled for Karla, and sometimes Damián.

"I need to stay with Mari."

"I told her Grant and I could alternate babysitting for a couple hours."

"Problem solved. I don't expect a big crowd tonight, just the regulars."

How could she get out of this? "I don't have any…of those kinds of clothes."

She thought she saw a twinkle of laughter in his eyes. "What kinds of clothes would that be, hon?"

Her face flushed. "I don't know. High heels, latex, fetishwear."

He grinned. "Why don't you just wear a pretty blouse and a pair of jeans?" He looked down at her athletic shoes. "The shoes you have on now are perfect. Bare feet are fine, too. Everyone chooses their own style of dress and comfort. You'll fit right in."

Really?

"But I don't know how to act…kinky."

Adam laughed heartily now. She was glad her discomfort provided him so much entertainment. "Hon, you leave kink to the rest of us. Just be yourself."

Why was it so hard to argue with the man? Because he wouldn't take "no" for an answer. Like Damián. She shivered.

Adam kissed Karla on the cheek again. "I have some paperwork to draw up."

Good. Maybe he would leave this ridiculous idea alone. Then he turned to Savi. "Come down to my office when you finish here, and we can go over the guest contract. No one gets into the club without reading and signing it."

But I don't want in your damned club!

Without waiting for her response, he turned and left the bedroom. Damián had mentioned a contract, hadn't he? What would she have to agree to do—or not to do? And why did her curiosity about this part of Damián's life pull at her so strongly?

*   *   *

Savi had no clue why she was doing this, but she signed her name and pushed the paperwork across Adam's desk again. She pulled her hands into her lap and clasped them to control the shaking. What had she done?

Adam pored over the two pages of the contract and nodded. He set it aside and looked at her. "Damián has talked with me about the security concerns for you and Marisol."

Savi had been so focused on the club's rules and what might happen tonight that she hadn't prepared herself for this line of conversation. She wondered how much he knew. "Did he tell you who we're running from?"

"I'd rather hear that from you."

Savi swallowed, then took a deep breath. "My father's business partner found me in December. He's the one who beat me. He was supposed to take me back to…" She shuddered. "Father thinks he owns me. He won't stop until he finds me, but I'm more afraid of what he'd do to Mari."

Adam's mouth drew tighter. She had to remind herself that his anger wasn't aimed at her, but still she retreated against the back of the seat, wanting to place a little more distance between them.

"I just want you to know I have you covered, just as Damián did. Nothing is going to happen to either of you under my watch."

Savi looked down at her hands and saw that she was picking at the skin around her fingernail. She clasped one hand over the other to hide what she'd been doing. She needed to stop that nervous habit. She looked up at Adam, wondering why she'd confided in him. Something told her he could be trusted to keep a confidence. The contract she'd just signed talked about the importance of confidentiality. Would he honor that outside the club, as well? Hadn't the agreement she'd just signed made her promise not to "out" anyone she might meet in the club if she knew or saw them outside this world?

But, more likely, it was Adam's eyes that had instilled that level of trust.

She took a deep breath. "My father is an abusive, controlling man."

"We can't choose our parents. Lord knows I'd have chosen a different father if I'd been given the chance."

Savi relaxed a bit. Perhaps he understood. "I escaped from his house when I was nineteen, soon after I met Damián. But how do I put him behind me and move on?" She thought she'd done that, but all of the flashbacks and memories that had come flooding back recently told her she'd only hidden that pain away. She hadn't dealt with it, not at all.

"I'm not the best example of someone putting bad memories behind them, hon. I basically blocked out my own past, until recently. Now I'm trying to come to terms with where I came from."

"I can relate to blocking things out. The memories keep bubbling up when I least expect them. I don't know how to process them."

"As I'm sure you know in your line of work, our brain is a pretty amazing thing. When it senses we're ready to deal with things, it gives us the flash of memory or reveals some part of our life we couldn't handle mentally or emotionally before. In my case, I think my subconscious knew I had Karla there to help me deal with the past. Maybe your mind is trying to tell you Damián can be there for you, making it safe to reveal those things to you now."

The flashbacks *had* started after she'd returned to Damián. Did he have that kind of effect on her? Did her subconscious mind trust him, even though her body and conscious mind still couldn't?

"But more important than the past is where you go in your life from here, the choices you *do* make about your present and future."

Savi's eyes burned at his words, but she blinked away the discomfort. "I've made lots of mistakes…"

"We all do, especially when we aren't taught any better or we're fighting for survival. If we have sins to atone for, and I've certainly had my share, then we do that. We try to make life better than the way we found it for those we love and those who need us. From what I can tell, you've done that in spades. You've raised a daughter who is smart, respectful, and who loves you, and now her daddy, very much." He smiled. "Seeing them together does this beat-up old heart a lot of good. Don't you apologize about what you've done. You're a survivor and you've raised a strong daughter who will be even better equipped than you were to face whatever life throws her way."

Savi squirmed in her seat, not comfortable with his words of praise. "I had lots of help in those early days from a friend and the priest at a local church. Otherwise, I'd have been clueless and would have messed up every…"

He leaned forward. "You were smart enough to seek help. That's not the easiest thing for a lot of us survivors to do. We sometimes think we have to do it all ourselves, all the time. Believe me, I know." He sat back in his chair.

Why did he keep trying to convince her she was so good? That she'd done the right things? Why didn't he see what she really was? She cast her gaze into her lap. *I'm not good enough for your son.*

"Define good enough."

Oh dear Lord. Savi looked up at him again. Had she spoken the words out loud? Her face grew hot. She'd rather the floor open up and swallow her than to have to respond to Adam's directive. She looked down at her hands and saw blood pooling at the base of her middle fingernail. She'd picked the skin until it bled. Embarrassed, wanting to hide the evidence of her distress before he noticed, she fisted her hand.

"Let's just say I'm not the wholesome person you and Damián think I am."

"Somehow I doubt you're as bad as all that. But Damián's no saint, either. This doesn't mean you can't commit to a relationship with each other that'll bring out the best in both of you."

Savi shook her head. "There can never be anything more. I'd only hurt him."

"Maybe if the two of you would stop hurting yourselves," he glanced at her hands then back at her, "you'd see you're perfect for each other."

Savi squeezed her hands even tighter, embarrassed that he'd noticed she was mutilating herself. But what was he saying about Damián hurting himself, too? She'd seen no evidence of that.

"Would you trust Damián enough to let him help you redirect some of the negative messages that are messing with your head by using some of the techniques he's learned for his role at the club?"

Savi shook her head. "No. I don't think I could trust anyone that much. I'm sorry."

"Hon, you don't have anything to apologize for. But if you're still worried Damián might do something to hurt you, well, you can put those thoughts to rest. He's one of the most controlled Doms I've ever known. He never takes a sub further than she's ready and willing to go. He never does a play scene in anger. I've gotten no complaints from anyone, and the Dungeon Monitors have never—"

Savi looked up. "*Dungeon* Monitors? Damián told me there were monitors, but he didn't say anything about a dungeon."

Adam grinned. "You don't have to worry about the dungeon, little one. Most members never venture down there, and those who do go with full knowledge of what they'll be doing and seeing. There's actually a waiting list for that area of the club most nights. But Damián wouldn't take you there unless you were ready—and, believe me, you aren't. In the broader kink community, some people refer to entire clubs as a dungeon, though. Dungeon Monitor is just the term the community came up with for those members who have been trained to monitor scenes at clubs or play parties to make sure everything is safe, sane, and consensual, or at least fall within the boundaries set for a particular club or party."

Savi grinned. "This world needs a glossary or cheat sheet for newbies to be able to make sense of it all."

Adam laughed out loud. "I have some books in my room, if you're interested in exploring it further. But you'll learn more by just going to the club tonight, talking with others, and observing what goes on in some of the play scenes and interactions."

"Will Damián be there?"

"Might be."

Oh, Lord. Could she face him again after what had happened last week in his apartment?

Adam leaned forward. "If it helps, Damián also knows I'll kick his ass if he ever did anything to hurt you or anyone else. I have a responsibility, especially to the subs in this club."

Subs? But she wasn't a sub.

"Hon, you have my word that no harm will come to you here."

Savi glanced at the contract she'd just signed. She had no idea what tonight would bring, but curiosity got the better of her. Adam and Damián weren't monsters. They didn't seem to let their emotions and…male appetites…rule them. There were also Dungeon Monitors to keep an eye on things. What did she have to worry about?

Chapter Ten

Damián thanked Grant and carried the drinks back to the table where Savi waited for him. He had no clue what Adam had said to get her in here, but he wasn't about to complain. He knew from his experience with some of the other abused subs in the club that parts of this lifestyle could help her deal with some of her past trauma and abuse, but he didn't want to be the one to inflict that pain on her. Realistically, there wasn't anyone here who could give her what she'd probably respond to best. The thought of watching any other Dom work with her just twisted his gut.

Get a grip, man. Savi wasn't here to experience sadomasochism tonight. More than likely, she just wanted to satisfy her curiosity about this lifestyle he'd told her about—see how it differed from what she'd experienced in the past.

Dios, he'd missed them. Damián had been floundering like a ship bobbing in a hurricane since Savi and Marisol moved out last week. He couldn't believe how quickly they'd become his rudder. He'd barely been able to sleep, even though he'd finally returned to his own bed for the first time in months to disastrous results.

"Here you go."

He placed the tall "Sex on the Beach" in front of her. Figuring out why this drink was the first thing that popped into his head wasn't hard. But he certainly was, remembering that time with Savi.

Her eyes grew large when she looked at the drink. "That's huge! I'm not much of a drinker."

"You asked for fruity. I told Grant to go easy on the vodka. No worries."

Savi picked up the curvy-shaped glass and took a sip. "Mmmm. That is good. What is it?"

Damián squirmed a minute trying to figure out how to answer without showing her where his mind was. "Peach Schnapps, O.J., cranberry juice, and a little vodka."

She took another draw. "If she'd gone heavier on the vodka, these could be dangerous. Tastes too good."

"You don't have to worry about getting drunk. We limit people to one or two drinks for the most part—someone with your tiny frame only gets one. Just enough to be social. Drinking and BDSM don't mix."

Savi's gaze became fixated on some of the implements hanging on the wall. Most were just for show; Dominants all had their own toy bags filled with their favorite playthings. Judging by the queasy look on her face, though, Savi expected someone to grab something off the wall and beat her with it at any moment. He needed to focus her mind on safer ground.

"What did Marisol do in school this week?"

Fuck. Here he was sitting in the club with Savi and all he could think to talk about was Marisol's school life. But, as he listened to her response, he realized how much he'd missed hearing about his daughter's escapades. *Dios*, he'd missed them both so much.

When Dad had come over this afternoon to talk with him, Damián was more anxious to hear about Marisol's playing in the snow. News of his daughter's happy, relatively normal day helped calm Damián's nerves and lift him out of the downer he usually felt after a post-traumatic stress episode. Still, he wanted to be the one playing with her in the snow.

Damián realized Savi had stopped talking. He took a long swig of his beer. More silence ensued. Why was he so fucking nervous around her? He felt like a teenager on a date. Only he didn't know of any teens who took their dates to a kink club.

"So what do you think of the place so far?"

Savi looked around again. Damián was glad that the only members present, so far, were dressed casually, probably having stopped by right after work. Some would venture to the theme rooms or dungeon later. Adam had announced earlier, and posted signs on the door leading upstairs and to the kitchen, that the bedrooms were off-limits while his granddaughter was here. Damián grinned. The man would become a grandfather and a father in the same year. He seemed to be embracing both new roles.

But Damián appreciated him doing that, and he knew it helped put some of Savi's worries to rest, too. He and Karla continued to look for a place to move to before the baby arrived but hadn't found anything yet. The baby probably would be here in four months.

"Other than the...décor," again her gaze went to the whips and chains on the wall, "it's not much different than a bar. Maybe even a little quieter, nicer."

Her compliment made him smile. He wasn't sure what people expected in clubs like this—and maybe there were some that were a lot wilder. "Most of the people who come in here just want to get away from the rat race and hang out with people who share a common interest."

"Whips and chains?"

He grinned. "Some do. But those are just play implements. That's not what this is about."

She leaned forward. "Tell me what you get out of all this, Damián. You seemed very...turned off by those sadists back at the hotel all those years ago."

His mind returned in a flash to the hotel where he'd worked as a busboy. When he'd found Savannah in that bed, bound and splayed open, he'd wanted to string those men up by their balls. In retrospect, he'd probably inflicted much worse pain on women since then—but the difference was they'd always consented. Most of the bottoms he worked with needed that level of pain in order to reconnect and feel something, or to get past some emotional block.

Nineteen-year-old Savannah had been begging the two men to stop, had probably screamed her safeword, and they'd ignored her. When he'd entered the room, they were using a violet wand. From what he'd learned about wands later at the club, the mushroom head they'd been using on her shouldn't have caused such an extreme pain response from her. A red demon's tongue or smaller head would have been much more intense. Yet she'd been terrified of it.

Damián had no idea what they'd done to elicit that much fear in her. Maybe it was an accumulation of things. They'd beaten the soles of her feet bastinado style until she could barely walk on them. The insides of her thighs had been bloodied with a quirt.

Damián remembered how he'd panicked at first, wanting to get her out of the fucking ropes, but not having a knife handy to cut her loose. When he'd finally freed her, she'd escaped across the bed, terrified of him, as well. Afterward, she'd fallen into an exhausted sleep, mentally escaping from it all. He'd watched over her, careful not to touch or disturb her. Damián had been nineteen, too. He'd had no fucking clue what to do with her, just knew he couldn't leave her there alone, even if it did cost him his job. What if one of those bastards had come back to hurt her again?

"What they were doing to you wasn't consensual, Savi. Your handler coerced you into that scene. Those men were torturing you. When I heard you screaming—not because you liked it either—and saw what they'd done to you, I had to interfere."

"How did you go from that sensitive, gentle man to owning a club where people beat on each other like this?"

Damián took another draw on the bottle, as he formulated his response. How much did he want to reveal about where he'd come from to get here? He took a deep breath and released it. "When I left the Marines, I was fucked up. Being in the Scene has helped me regain some control over my life."

The puzzled look on her face told him she didn't understand at all, but he found himself wanting to assure her she didn't need to be afraid of him ever hurting her.

"Savi, we talked a while ago about monitors and how they keep things SSC in here—safe, sane, and consensual."

She nodded and sat back. "Dungeon Monitors?"

Damián nodded. He wondered where she'd heard the full term. Had she been reading up on BDSM? Then he realized Dad would have explained the safety measures in place to get her in here. "Marc was on duty as a Dungeon Monitor last August when he rescued Angelina from an abuser posing as a Dom in one of the rooms here."

Anger flashed in her eyes. "Was she badly hurt?"

"Bad enough. We didn't expect her to come back to the club, but Marc found her eventually and showed her how an authentic Dom treats his sub."

"Too bad it didn't work out for them. She seemed to adore him."

She still did, according to Karla, who'd kept in touch with her after she'd gone back to her house in Aspen Corners. Sounded like she was going through a really rough time since she'd left. So was Marc. Damián knew how it felt to be separated from Savi for just a few days. He didn't know what he'd do when she and Marisol left Denver, but he knew she wanted to get back to her life in California, once the threat of her father and his partner had been eliminated.

Remembering the point he'd wanted to make about Angelina, he leaned across the table, but Savi retreated against the back of her chair. *Stop flitting away from me*, savita. "There are some so-called Doms who take the gift of submission they're entrusted with and go far beyond a sub's limits or endurance, with no care for their sub's needs. They may call it BDSM, but that's nothing but abuse. Selfishness."

Savi nodded, her expression wary. With all this talk of abusive, out-of-control individuals posing as Doms, he'd scared her more than put her mind at ease. *Damn.* Why was this shit so hard to talk about with her? Why couldn't she understand they might be freaks, but they weren't abusers?

Of course, Savi's past abuse and trauma were the polar opposite of what went on at the Masters at Arms Club. *Give her time, Orlando. She just needs time.* He drained his beer and set the bottle down. "Can I freshen your drink?"

She reached for her glass of now watered-down vodka-flavored juice. "No. I'm going to make this last me most of the night, then I'll switch to soda."

Damián had a two-beer limit on nights he was scening, but even tonight, he planned to stick to that limit.

"Damo, sorry to interrupt, but Patti needs you. It's bad."

Fuck. Not tonight. He looked up at Victor, then over at Patti, kneeling on the floor beside the table where he'd seen Victor sitting earlier. He'd thought she seemed a bit withdrawn tonight, but Damián had been so focused on Savi, he really hadn't paid her much attention. From the look of her, this wouldn't be an easy session.

Fucking-A.

Patti was terrified of the dungeon because some of her abuse had taken place in a cellar. Most times, he did their scenes right here in the great room.

No way was Savi ready to see this.

He needed to get her out of here.

Now.

* * *

Savi sensed something was wrong when the tall African American, who reminded her of a bald Shemar Moore, approached their table and spoke to him. She followed Damián's gaze to a petite blonde kneeling beside a table across the room with a catatonic stare in her eyes.

What was wrong with her? And what was Damián supposed to do about it? She looked like she needed to talk with someone. Not a mechanic, but a professional therapist, like herself. Maybe she should offer to help.

"Something happened while I was at work today, Damo. Some trigger on the TV, I think, but she won't even talk to me about it. We had a session at home tonight, and I thought she was better, but I went ahead and brought her here in case someone could help. I've never been so glad to see you, man. I know you can help her."

The man looked at Savi, who suddenly wished she wasn't here. Still, Savi's heart went out to the woman kneeling across the room. "Would you like me to talk with her? I'm a therapist." *Well, I was anyway, once upon a time.*

The man stared at her as if she'd grown a second head, then turned to Damián with a silent question in his eyes.

"Sorry, Victor. She's not in the Scene. Just a guest tonight."

Now she felt unwanted by both of them. Apparently, she'd broken some protocol. Oh, yeah. Wasn't there something in the contract about subs not speaking to Doms unless invited to? How was she supposed to remember all these archaic, sexist rules? Of course, there were female Dominants here, too. But, as with most places, it seemed to be primarily a man's world within these walls and this community.

"If you'll excuse me—" She would have gotten up and left, but the man named Victor turned to her.

"Sit. Down." He spoke as if commanding a dog, but still she planted her butt in the chair before realizing and regretting her response. Satisfied, he turned to Damián and continued.

"I know you're here with someone. Patti told me not to bother you because of your lady friend, but she needs you bad. You know me. I can't get her to that level."

Level of what? Curiosity, despite the feeling she wasn't wanted here anymore, won out. Savi chose to remain.

Damián looked at her, emotions warring on his face, then turned back to the intimidating man. "I don't think I can tonight, Victor."

He was refusing to help because of her, so she leaned forward. "Help her, Damián. I'll wait here."

Karla began her opening set on the stage, an edgy tune that distracted Savi for a moment. She'd been so involved in the drama at her table, she hadn't seen Karla come downstairs. The singer wore a black leather collar with a dogtag and some other trinkets hanging on it. Savi wondered what the significance of the collar was.

Grant must be with Mari now. Savi had been unsure about Grant's ability to relate to kids at Christmas. The woman barely said two words to Mari.

Over the months since, though, Savi had gotten to know her a little better. She and Damián had a strong friendship, and Grant had been to the apartment at least once a week.

Grant had even bought Mari her first GI Joe. The woman was quiet and intense, but after seeing her teaching self-defense skills to Mari using Barbie and GI Joe as models, Savi believed the woman would be a good influence on her daughter. She'd also protect Mari as well as anyone in their surveillance team. Heaven help any man who tried to overpower Grant.

Still, old habits die hard. Savi would go up later to check on them but couldn't leave now. She needed to know what Damián was going to do for this woman. *With* this woman.

When she turned to look back at Damián, his attention was on Adam, who stood near the stage looking like a bouncer, arms folded. As if tugged by an invisible string, Adam tore his gaze from Karla and turned toward Damián who made several hand gestures toward him. What had he just conveyed? Whatever it was, it looked like he wanted her to take a hike. When he realized she'd seen him, he looked a little sheepish at being so rude, but didn't back down. He wanted her out of here.

Adam started toward their table but didn't even speak to Damián. "Savi, join me over at the stage. Karla wants you to be front and center during her show tonight."

It wasn't an invitation, but a command. Karla didn't seem the type who would demand such attention, but Savi didn't know how to refuse the man politely. She looked at Damián to see if somehow that's what he'd signaled to Adam, but he was glaring at the older man. Without waiting for a response from her, Adam pulled her chair out with her still in it, as if she were nothing more than a stuffed animal at one of Mari's Teddy-bear picnics.

He picked up her glass, still more than half full.

"How about a refill? What were you drinking?"

Savi wasn't sure and looked at Damián for the answer. He didn't make eye contact with her, but said to Adam in a voice she could barely hear, "Sex on the Beach."

Savi's face grew warm. *The rat.* Why couldn't he just forget about that day?

Adam grinned. "One 'Sex on the Beach'—coming up."

"No, Adam." She reached out and took the glass from him. "Anything diet for me. I know my limit."

Adam took Savi by the elbow. "Come with me, hon."

Savi didn't like being told what to do, nor being treated like a child, but she was a guest here and could easily be asked to leave if she didn't do as the Doms said, especially the owners. It was written in the damned rules she'd agreed to follow. That one she remembered, because it was unbelievable to her that people actually followed such dictates in this day and age. The subjugation of women was alive and well in Damián's kink club.

While Damián wanted her out of the club, Adam planned to let her stay. Good. If she could manage to remain here, she could see what Damián planned to do.

Adam led Savi to a table next to the stage, but positioned her with her back to the room. Karla made eye contact and winked, and Savi decided not to push the issue, for the moment at least.

"One diet coming up." He bent down to her ear. "Eyes on Karla. She likes the attention, but most folks here are too busy with their scenes and partners to watch the show."

Savi tuned in to Karla's beautiful voice a moment. Unfortunately, curiosity got the best of her and Savi turned her head to find that Adam wasn't at the bar at all, but back at Damián's table. Damián shook his head vehemently, and she could read the "No way" on his lips, but Adam just squeezed his shoulder in a paternal way and walked over to the bar to retrieve the soda waiting there. Her face flushed again.

When Damián turned toward her, a frisson of electricity coursed down her spine. *Busted.* She quickly turned her attention back to the stage but couldn't focus on Karla. She needed to know what was going on. Savi turned again and watched as Damián crossed the room to the woman kneeling on the floor. The blonde didn't look up or acknowledge him in any way. He bent down to her, placing his hand on the back of her head, and said something. The woman nodded without opening her mouth or looking his way, and he reached down to take her elbow to help her to her feet. She kept her gaze cast downward but let him guide her to the center post.

The woman wore a red halter dress that hugged her curves. Damián reached up, pushed her long hair over her shoulder, and undid the knot at the nape of her neck. He let the top drop to her waist, then took her hand and fastened a cuff to her wrist. Savi couldn't help but notice the scars on Patti's back. Had Damián inflicted those marks?

Victor came up beside them and did the same with the other wrist, then each fastened one of her ankles to cuffs. All four cuffs then were attached, two at a time, to chains on the post.

Oh dear Lord. He was going to beat her! The acid from Savi's stomach rose in her throat.

"Where did I tell you your eyes should be?"

Savi jumped and looked up at Adam, feeling a little guilty at having disobeyed. *Wait!* She wasn't his sub or slave or whatever it was called. She was just a visitor. A visitor who wanted answers.

"Tell me what's going on."

"Is that how you address one of the club's Doms?"

It was all Savi could do not to scream. "*Please* tell me what's going on, *Sir.*"

He smiled. "Acceptable. For a first-time visitor." He set the glass on the table in front of her. "I thought you might be curious." Adam took her chin and turned her head toward Karla again, then sat down beside her.

"Why doesn't Damián want me here?"

Out of the corner of her eye, she watched Adam lift a bottle of spring water to his lips and take a long drink, then place it on the table. "Because there are some things he doesn't want you to know about him. But I think you need to know and that you can handle that information."

Savi's heart pounded. Somehow she knew before he even had to reveal a thing. She turned to Adam to gauge his reaction before blurting out, "Damián's a sadist."

He smiled, then grew serious and nodded slightly. "In Damián's case, I prefer the term *sensual* sadist, or even better, a Service Top. He doesn't do this to get off on a woman screaming in pain or because he enjoys placing his marks on her body like many sadists would. Not that he isn't proud of his skill at marking the skin without permanently scarring her."

Savi felt a shiver course down her spine. "But there are scars on Patti's back."

"Those aren't Damián's marks. They were put there by Patti's abusive ex." Adam continued, "Damián isn't doing this for his own thrill. He does it because he needs to feel a sense of control and the feeling of accomplishment that comes from executing a well-planned mission."

"Mission?"

"In his mind, that's what an SM scene is. Normally, he'd take time to meticulously plan for such a scene, get his equipment ready, practice if he needed to." He paused, his gaze moving in the direction of where Damián and Patti were, then added, "Damián likes the control aspects of the community. When he first came to live with me, he could barely leave the house without having a PTSD attack." His gaze returned to her. "He saw everyone he met out in the world as a potential enemy. In Iraq, you never knew who would welcome you and who would blow your fucking brains out." He grinned at her. "Pardon me. Once a Marine…"

"Don't apologize. I've heard worse."

He sobered again. "Anyway, just going to the grocery store required an intense amount of planning in order to execute his objective of buying supplies. It got so bad, he could only go into the store at about zero-two-hundred—sorry, 2 a.m.—because there were fewer potential enemies he had to keep an eye on at that time."

Savi knew he must have been through hell. No one gets out of a war like he'd been through—not where he'd come so close to being killed—without some severe emotional scars. But she hadn't seen him exhibit this kind of PTSD behavior in the time they'd been living together. What had changed for him to be able to regain control of his life?

Adam went on, "Tonight, though, is an emergency situation. He didn't get to prepare for it as he might have normally."

"Damián didn't seem to want to do the scene with her tonight. Why does it have to be him? Why can't you or someone else here do it?"

He smiled in a self-deprecating way, the corners of his eyes crinkling, making him seem a little less…daunting. "I can't wield a whip worth shit without putting someone's eye out—most likely, my own. Luke Denton over there," he pointed to the man she'd met on Christmas who now was standing behind the bar, dressed in a blue-denim, long-sleeved work shirt and a Stetson, "is becoming skilled with the bullwhip, but he's no sadist."

Adam took a drink of water and sobered as he turned his gaze to her. "Damián, on the other hand, has done a lot of scenes with Patti in the past. He knows what to do to get her there the fastest."

It bothered Savi to think about Damián and Patti being together so many times. Clearly, the woman was with this man now but had she had a sexual relationship with Damián at one time? Pretty hard to do this without having sex, even though there hadn't been any talk about sex being part of the service Damián was providing for Patti.

Serviced with a whip? Whoever heard of such a thing?

Then something Adam had said struck her. "I thought everyone into BDSM was either a sadist or a masochist…that it was all about people who need to feel pain in order to get turned on sexually finding someone willing to dish out sadistic pain until they…responded." Savi's face grew hot. She'd almost said "came" in front of a man she barely knew.

Adam grinned. "Common misconception, but it's not about pain for the most part. It's about control—the taking and giving of control. Damián's not trying to turn Patti on—not sexually, at least. He's trying to break through a mental block that, while it has served her for years as a coping mechanism, is only keeping her from connecting to her body, her partner, and those around her now. Damián's goal is for her to return to being present in the moment."

Patti's responses to triggers sounded so much like Savi's. The woman may even share some of Savi's traumatic experiences. God, she didn't wish that on anyone.

"Victor has called on Damián a number of times since he joined the club to provide Patti with a level of pain that he's not comfortable delivering himself. She's a masochist, but Victor's not a sadist."

"Why doesn't she find a sadist to be with?"

Adam seemed pained as he looked up at Karla on the stage. "One thing we don't have a lot of control over is who we fall in love with."

Karla had told Savi a little bit about how hard it had been for her to convince the much older Adam she wasn't a young girl, but a woman. Okay, so Victor and Patti couldn't help that they'd fallen in love, either.

"Why are you telling me all this, but not letting me watch?"

He turned his gaze back to her. "I didn't say I wouldn't let you watch at some point. I just wanted to make sure you understood what was going on first. Patti has a dark past, not unlike your own."

Savi wondered how much Damián had told Adam about her past but didn't really want to know.

"She was nearly beaten to death any number of times by her ex, who also got off on humiliating her publicly and privately, and in caging her for long periods of time, often when he wasn't home, like some kind of animal."

Dear Lord, the woman really had survived a living nightmare.

"Sometimes when the demons are unleashed like they were today, she goes to ground. There's only one way she can reconnect to the moment and that's with intense pain."

"But it sounds like something she should be getting therapy for, not something to be beaten for."

"She's gone as far as she wants to with therapy. It hasn't helped her in this area. Sadomasochism, on the other hand, helps her stay on an even keel, functioning at her job and in her life."

"Do you mind my asking what happened to her?"

"It's never been a secret here. Victor's a fireman. He rescued her in a fire at her apartment building. Found her locked inside a cage in a room filling with smoke."

Her stomach knotted. "Oh, God. How terrifying!"

Then she remembered how Damián had rescued her, although Savi's circumstances had been a walk in the park compared to the mental torture Patti must have suffered in those moments she thought she might suffocate, if not burn alive.

"Victor kept in touch with her while she was hospitalized and in outpatient treatment afterward, while living in a battered women's shelter. One thing led to another…" Adam paused a moment and Savi's mind reeled to try and process this bombardment of information. "They started out in a D/s relationship—Dom/sub—but she feels safer being his service slave."

Slave? "Wait. What did you say?"

"Consensual slavery, not what you see on crime shows on TV. Serving Victor's needs helps her feel worthy of his love, even though she doesn't have to do a damned thing. She earned it long ago, but she just feels she needs to serve him. That also gives her a sense of accomplishment, not unlike what Damián gets from doing a scene for her."

Who knew there were varying degrees of slavery? Or that Patti could choose what kind of slave she wanted to be. "Why is it called slavery if it isn't forced on her?"

"Forced slavery is illegal, for one thing."

"But that hasn't deterred some people." Like her father.

Adam scrutinized her until she squirmed in her seat. She remembered her own experience as a sexual slave during the year before she ran away. Lyle assured the men there were few limits. They abused her body in so many disgusting ways that Savi would never be able to experience intimacy with a man without fear and revulsion. Sometimes she woke up at night screaming in pain, and it took hours to realize the pain was only in her head now.

But she'd been Father's personal sex slave for a decade before she'd been pimped out to his business clients. Sweat beaded on her upper lip. *No. I don't want to remember those years.* She'd made her escape many years ago and hadn't looked back.

"Let's be clear, Savi." Adam's words brought her back to the present, and she relaxed into the chair again. "I'm talking about consensual slavery. Before anyone goes into this kind of arrangement, there is a long discussion and negotiation phase." A cloud of regret crossed his face and he looked up at Karla again. Did he regret that Karla wouldn't be his slave? God, what did the man want? She was so devoted to him and clearly loved him.

He turned back to her and tried to regain his place. "Service slaves have a need to please, to provide all levels of service to their Dom or Master from domestic chores to—"

"Can't he just get a maid for that?"

Adam smiled. "It's more emotionally involved than that. Patti needs direction and discipline to feel wanted and loved."

"Discipline? Like a child?"

"Patti, like many other service slaves, has a need to serve and obey, but not just any orders. She needs consistent, intelligent, unambiguous rules. She needs someone who understands her needs and can have the presence of mind to provide that kind of direction and discipline."

"Angelina and Karla don't fit that description."

"Hell, no. I can only speak for Karla, but she doesn't need to be a slave to find fulfillment. And the Master/slave relationship has always been deeper into the lifestyle than I've wanted to go, although my wife wanted that at one point in our marriage."

Savi looked up at the young woman on the stage nearby, whose eyes were closed as she sang her heart out. Karla should be singing to an audience that was paying attention, not this club crowd.

Whoa. Wait a minute. Hadn't he just said she wasn't interested in being his slave? "Karla wanted that, too?"

"God, no. Not Karla." He chuckled, drawing Savi's attention to him, then he grew serious. "I put an end to that kind of relationship with Karla within a couple of days. I'm referring to my first wife. She died of cancer almost ten years ago."

"Oh, I'm sorry."

He nodded. "She was a fine woman and so fucking loyal and faithful to me, despite all my deployments. Maybe that's what made serving me so important to her when I was home." He shrugged. "I never completely understood how we got there, but for a period of time before she got sick, she was my service slave."

The expression on his face told her it wasn't something he'd enjoyed. Good thing, because the thought of Karla being a slave for him was ludicrous. The woman didn't even know how to cook, from what Savi had observed this week. Both Adam and Karla had been thrilled to turn the kitchen over to Savi, which she'd enjoyed, too. She'd needed something to do to keep busy. Although Karla wasn't bad at baking, and was very sweet to help Marisol make Damián's birthday cake—

The crack of a whip popping in the air caused Savi to jump out of her seat and release a sharp hiss. She started to turn to see what was going on behind her, but Adam's firm command stopped her.

"Eyes on me." She complied, feeling deep down that he was safer to look at than whatever was going on behind her. "Relax. He's just warming up. He hasn't even struck her with the bullwhip yet."

Bullwhip? Shouldn't he use that on a bull?

"'Til now, he and Victor have been touching her mostly, talking to her, slowly transferring power from Victor to Damián for the scene."

"He's going to use a whip on her? That's barbaric!"

Adam sighed. "I can see how you might think that, but it's what she needs. She's consented to being whipped, has even begged for it many times."

"That's not healthy."

"To get the endorphins going, to help her come to grips with whatever has a stranglehold on her now, I'm afraid it's very healthy. Damián's goal tonight will be to get her to scream—maybe even cry, if he's successful. He wants to get her to process whatever happened earlier today that shut her down."

Savi fought hard every day to achieve that—and *she* was able to cope without having the daylights beaten out of her. Well, she coped most days. Lately? Not so much. And cry? Never.

"Why is it so important that she find release this way and not some way less…painful?"

"Patti keeps her emotions bottled up until she's numb."

Numb. Like Savi.

Adam continued. "Right now, she can't feel, can't respond to any physical or emotional stimuli. If she doesn't come back into the moment, she'll be unable to function. If she went to a shrink—sorry, a mental-healthcare facility—more than likely, they'd just medicate the problem away first and talk later."

Being a therapist, not to mention a patient herself, Savi knew that was a real possibility. When she'd had a particularly bad episode after Mari had turned three—the last time she'd cut herself—she'd been hospitalized for a week until the doctor determined it wasn't a suicide attempt. She just hadn't realized how deeply she'd cut her arm. The pain of the razor blade hadn't registered at all. She'd only been seeking that endorphin rush that was getting harder and harder to find.

She shuddered. She'd never wanted to have that happen again—and it hadn't. So far. But she'd come closer than ever last week in Damián's bathroom.

"Usually, Victor can provide disciplinary maintenance to keep her from going this deep, and he's learned some techniques from Damián that are palatable to him—like administering pain through pressure points, flogging, and some mindfucks—"

"Mind whats?"

Adam grinned. "Mindfucks. Messing with the sub's mind. Making her think something much worse is going on than what's actually happening. Can be very intense for a sub—and a helluva lot of fun for a Dom."

Savi had no doubt this man enjoyed them immensely. Was Damián into those kind of mind—games, too?

"Anyway, Victor uses those kinds of play activities to help Patti stay in the moment without going beyond his own hard limits."

"Doms and Masters have limits, too?"

Adam laughed. "Hell, yeah. Lots of limits. A sub can take us to the brink of our hard limits, and even beyond them." He looked up at Karla again. "We also have to be vigilant during a scene and know when our sub has reached her limits, or if she hasn't used her safeword when she probably should have."

He seemed riveted to the stage and Savi's gaze followed. Karla was singing a softer tune Savi didn't recognize. When the singer looked down at Adam, she winked, and seemed to be serenading him alone. The love in her eyes for her man—her Dom—was evident and the same was clear on Adam's face. Savi had to look away. The intensity of their exchange made her feel uncomfortable, as if intruding on an intimate moment.

Adam cleared his throat. "Anyway, sometimes the Dom recognizes that he's gone too far, even before his sub realizes it." He lifted the plastic bottle to his lips and took a long swig. "A Dom or Master's primary objective has to be to make sure his sub's needs are met and to protect her from harm, including self-inflicted harm."

Savi shivered. Damián had protected her like that so many times, most recently when he'd found her in the bathroom. Her hand touched the place on her arms where the old scars would forever bear witness to the times she hadn't been able to take care of herself in a safe way. She forced herself to reach out and pick up her drink.

The whip slashed something soft and Savi jumped, sloshing soda onto her shirt. This time, she was certain the painful implement had made contact with Patti's skin and she pictured blood running down the woman's back. The sound and image made Savi feel sick to her stomach.

"Take a sip." Adam guided the glass up to her lips. "It sounds worse than it feels for her at this point. I doubt she feels anything yet. He'll start slowly. Maybe you should watch from the beginning, because I have a feeling the images you're conjuring up are much worse than what's going on behind you. Are you up to watching?"

Savi hesitated.

Was she ready? How did someone prepare to watch a woman being slashed to a bloody pulp with a freaking bullwhip? With a shaky hand, she took the drink from him and drained it. Maybe she gave up on alcohol too soon tonight.

"I think I'm ready."

"You'll have to do better than that."

Savi drew a deep breath. The whip slashed again and she jumped, but not as high as the last time. She nodded. "I'm ready."

Adam took her chin and forced her to look him in the eyes. "If you scream or disturb their scene in any way, I'll boot your ass out of here faster than you can blink."

She needed to see what Damián had become. She needed to understand this side of him. She had no intention of leaving this room, willingly or by force.

Movement behind him caused her to look up as Karla approached the table. So engrossed in what she imagined unfolding behind her, Savi hadn't heard her stop singing.

"Are you sure this is a good idea, Master Adam?"

Hearing Karla call him Master caught Savi off guard. Outside the club, she just called him Adam.

He looked up at her but didn't smile like he usually did when he looked at her. "That's for Savi to answer, Kitten. Personally, I think she needs to see this scene," he focused on Savi again, "or I wouldn't have let you stay in here."

Was Adam like the uber Dom here, making sure the needs of all the little subs were met? Savi shivered. She was just a guest. She'd just been curious about this part of Damián's life, but had no idea what she'd agreed to when she signed that contract.

Should she play it safe—or stay?

Chapter Eleven

Sweat rolled down between Damián's shoulder blades. He and Victor had gotten nowhere with pressure points; he'd hoped they could avoid this scene tonight. Now he fought to keep his focus on Patti and where the bullwhip would fall on her upper back, ass, and thighs, but having Savi sitting across the room was a huge distraction. Damn Dad for ignoring Damián's request and keeping her here to witness what he had become.

Don't think about Savi watching this.

Definitely the deal breaker if there ever could have been anything between him and Savi again. He hadn't told her about his sadistic tendencies. She'd see him as no better than the monsters from her past and would want nothing more to do with him after watching this. Damián wouldn't hold back, because this was just what Patti needed and his duty as the club's sadist Service Top.

Tonight wasn't about Savi.

Damián broke his stance and stepped over to the table where he'd placed his bag and gear. He laid down the whip and reached for the bottle of water, chugging half of it and forcing himself not to let his mind stray toward Savi. He needed to put her out of his mind altogether. Since embracing sadism as his coping mechanism for PTSD, he'd been able to maintain a firm grip on his body and his mind. He needed to regain that control, and soon.

Damián stared at the scratches he and other Doms had made on the floor long ago, many of them placed there in earlier scenes with Patti. It had been months since he'd served as her Top. Only he had the expertise to give her what she needed tonight.

But he could hurt her if he didn't stay focused on her needs and responses—or if he transmitted his own emotional upheaval to her through the whip. The scratches on the floor usually had a way of grounding him further but not tonight.

Picking up a towel, he wiped the sweat from his brow and took the whip in hand again. He focused on the weave of the kangaroo-leather handle, working to get his mind on the mission ahead.

Focus on the objective.

A sense of calm descended on him as, at last, he found his center and took a deep, cleansing breath. He was in his element. His controlled world.

He breathed the scent of leather deeply into his lungs.

Feel the weight and balance of the serpent's tongue in your hand.

With his mind, he heard the whistle of the fall and the popper as they displaced the air on their path to her waiting back and ass.

Listen only for the sound of Patti's response.

He imagined in slow motion throwing the whip again, watching the rolling curl of the fall make its way to stroke Patti's back with love, care.

Become one with the instrument.

He turned his complete attention to the petite blonde strapped to the center post. Her head was erect, eyes closed tightly, the muscles in her arms rigid. *Long way to go.*

He'd only laid two stripes about an inch apart just below her shoulder blades. Those thin, red lines wouldn't welt, but he'd have to give her welts before she'd get the catharsis she needed tonight.

Patti needs release, to connect with her body again.

Did Savi need to experience that level of pain in order to reconnect with her body?

Patti. Focus on Patti.

Gunnar's oft-repeated words came back to him: "If you can't control yourself, you can't control others."

I'll take you there, Patti.

Damián took a deep breath and walked over to Patti. He stroked the back of her head, confirming the tension he'd observed while trying to ground himself further with her body. How many times had he looked at Patti's blonde hair and imagined she was Savi?

Fuck that shit. He'd never done so during a scene and wouldn't start now.

Focus, man.

"How are we doing, *bebé*?"

She nodded, but her eyes remained closed as tight as a gnat's ass.

"Look at me." She opened her eyes slowly, and he waited for her to blink until she appeared to focus on him. He spent a few minutes telling her what he was about to do, how she would respond, laying out what should have been said earlier if he hadn't been so distracted. The only reaction he got was her pleading gaze, begging him to start, take her there.

"Ready for more?"

She nodded.

"Speak."

"Yes, Sir. I'm ready."

He tamped down his anger at the bastard who'd caused her so much pain in her young life, but he'd learned early on there were evil men in this world who thought nothing about abusing defenseless women. Rosa, Teresa, Patti, Savi. The fucking list seemed endless.

He couldn't help them all, but tonight, in this moment, he could help Patti. Time to give her what she needed from him.

Damián glanced back at Victor, standing well beyond strike range of the whip, in a direct line behind Patti. From past experience, he knew having Victor's voice at the start of a scene coming from the same direction Damián stood with the whip helped Patti conjure up the image of Victor being the one wielding the instrument. That imagery would make the transition of power back to Victor go more smoothly after the whipping.

"Hold on tight, Patticakes." At the sound of Victor's voice, Patti's shoulders tensed.

Damián was taking so fucking long to get this scene under way, her focus had shifted now to how hard this was for her Dom to watch. Damián needed to take care of her now, get her into subspace.

With a signal from Damián, Victor added, "Here we go, Patticakes. That's my good girl."

With those scripted words, Victor knew not to interrupt the scene again. Patti needed release. All three of them did. Damián stepped into his strike zone for the serpent's tongue, drew back his arm, and let the whip crack the air. Patti tensed. Without further delay, Damián drew back the whip again and threw it so that the lash fell an inch farther down her back. Her hands chained above her head clutched into fists.

He threw the whip several more times. Patti sighed as she relaxed into the rhythm, the pressure of the leather burning stripes into her back. No catharsis yet, but it would come when he reached the level of impact she sought.

Thwack!

He laid several more stripes across her back, noticing that the flesh across the previous lashes was now raised and growing redder. She was nowhere near her limit. Moving below the no-strike zone of the kidneys to the curve of her ass, he laid three more stripes in quick succession. After the third, he heard her moan.

Getting there. Good.

Still a long way to go to take her home, though. If the serpent's tongue hadn't done the job by now, he needed something he knew would get her there. Damián stepped over to his toy bag and pulled out the well-oiled cat. He'd spent the afternoon preparing his implements, not so much because he expected to use them, but the ritual had helped calm him down after the PTSD episode.

Patti was the only person at the club who'd ever been able to take this level of pain from him and, even then, only on rare occasions had he needed to use it. The knots on the nine tails provided an intense amount of pain over a broader range on her body. He'd take her the rest of the way with the cat.

He drew back and threw the braided tails against Patti's upper thighs. She moaned more loudly as the pain registered in her mind.

Damián's chest swelled. He was the only one here who could give Patti what she needed.

Maybe Savi needed it, too, but tonight was all about Patti. The pain had begun to take hold of her. Time to carry her the rest of the way home.

* * *

What had Damián become? Where was the gentle man she remembered from the beach cave? Or the man she'd lived with for months? She'd never seen this side of him. *Thank God.* She didn't want him anywhere near her with that menacing whip flying.

Adam hadn't said much since the scenario began to play out. Karla had curled up in his lap, her head on his shoulder and her back to the whipping scene. A glance in their direction found Adam's chin resting on the top of Karla's head, his hand idly playing with the ends of Karla's long, black curls lying against her arm. His left arm supported her back. Clearly, she wasn't able to stand the scene playing out before them. So there *was* someone here who couldn't watch the barbaric scene.

But Karla must be the only one. Savi looked around the room, now nearly silent, and saw that every gaze was glued to what was happening at the whipping post. Savi didn't understand her morbid fascination—maybe it was like a wreck on the 5—but she couldn't turn her gaze away either.

Damián stepped away, coiled the menacing-looking whip, placed it into his leather bag, and pulled out another whip.

"My God! It's a cat-o-nine tails!"

Adam growled at her. "Quiet."

Karla groaned. "Poor Patti. She must be in a really bad way this time. I can't stand that she's hurting like this."

Savi was confused, but she remembered to keep her voice low. "But Damián's the one hurting her."

Karla sat up and turned toward Savi, tearstains on her cheeks. "I know it looks like that. I used to think the same thing. I steered clear of Damián for a very long time when I first came here last summer. He scared the shit out of me. But wait 'til you see the change in Patti when this is over."

Savi wasn't sure she could last until then. Her stomach churned. "I think I'm going to be sick."

Adam reached out and touched Savi's arm. "Do you need to go upstairs?"

Did she?

Thwack!

The sound of the tails finding their marks against the blonde's skin caused Savi to jump. She turned to watch the new stripes—she supposed if she counted, there would be nine—turn red across Patti's upper thighs. Savi's focus was drawn to Victor's profile. Pain. He looked as if every lash of the whip had come down on him. The anguish on his face made it clear why Patti had to come to Damián for this.

He must have no feelings whatsoever to be able to do this to another human being, yet Victor did nothing to stop the whipping of his woman.

Victor's voice carried across the room to her. "That's it, Patticakes. Almost there. You're so brave. So strong."

Patti tensed again at his words but didn't open her eyes. Damián turned to silence Victor with a stare.

Adam sighed. "Victor probably shouldn't be here for this part."

"Why not?"

"He's anxious to get the painful part over with and move on to aftercare. This probably hurts Victor and Damián more than Patti, but his talking just pulls her away from focusing on the cat. She knows how Victor feels and is worrying more about him than herself right now. It'll take Damián longer to get her into deep subspace and achieve catharsis if Victor continues to interrupt."

Damián swung with increasing force, and Savi watched as the woman's face actually grew more relaxed the harder he whipped her. This didn't make any sense.

Even more surprising, there wasn't a drop of blood on Patti's back. When Savi had sought her endorphin release years ago by cutting, there had been bloodletting. Damián's whip and the cat had only raised red welts. Maybe he did know the limits he could go to without permanently marring her flesh.

A gentle sadist? No, Adam had called him a *sensual* sadist. A Service Top. Whoever heard of having someone train to provide a service like this? But Damián's skill with the whip wasn't something he would have picked up without many years of training.

Other than the comments he'd made a few minutes ago, Victor stayed out of the scene now. This was between Damián and Patti.

"He's continuously gauging her body language to determine where she is, how much more she needs to get where she needs to be. When she totally relaxes, he'll know she's there." Adam kept his voice low, and she strained to hear.

More welts formed on the woman's backside. Savi cringed. How much longer? What was Damián watching for? "How can anyone relax after being whipped like that? She hasn't even screamed."

"Patti's a masochist. She doesn't process pain the same way a non-masochist would."

She turned back to Adam. "Pain is pain."

"No, it's not that simple. You probably learned in physiology, or was it anatomy?—I didn't get that far in school." He shrugged. "Anyway, I've read a lot about body structure and how the body does what it does. Our body actually only feels the temperature and pressure associated with the impact instrument. It's the brain that then interprets those sensations as pain or pleasure."

The man may downplay his formal education, but his knowledge base on pain was broader than what she'd been taught in school.

"That's what makes pain so subjective—why one person has a high tolerance for pain while another is debilitated by seemingly minor hurts."

Savi had a high tolerance for pain, but she'd developed techniques to help her tamp down the pain out of necessity. She chose to be numb.

Adam continued, keeping his voice barely audible. "Patti's learned to embrace the energy the whip or other implements deliver, rather than resist it. Her brain will interpret the lashes as pain eventually. Right now, Damián's trying to get her to focus on the present rather than hide within herself where she doesn't feel anything. He's trying to get her to express the emotions she's feeling, like anger, which she can't let out otherwise."

Again, the similarity between Savi and Patti was too close for comfort. Savi faced him. Adam's gaze bore into her, and she squirmed in her seat. She wasn't speaking abstractly but directly to her.

"It takes an extreme level of pressure from the whips to get through the defenses she's built to cope over the years."

He could have been talking about Savi—and probably was. Savi turned away from his intense gaze and watched in silence as several more blows were delivered across Patti's already red butt.

"Patti's coping mechanism of making herself numb has worked for her for a long time, but until Victor and Damián, she hadn't really been living—merely existing."

Savi understood that feeling too well. Her skin usually felt anesthetized, as if she had been injected with Novocain from the top of her head to the soles of her feet. That inability to feel was normal for her now. She'd become accustomed to it. Still, she hated that she couldn't feel the sensation of Mari hugging or kissing her. Savi wanted so desperately to feel her baby's arms around her but...she felt nothing but pressure. Of course, she would go through the motions and return the affection, but she'd always been left to wonder what it would feel like to—well, *feel*.

Is that what Damián was helping this woman to do?

Savi blinked her eyes to remove the unwelcome sting of unshed tears. She remained riveted to the spectacle across the room, knowing she wouldn't be able to leave until this scene played out. Patti now seemed to be riding some kind of high, moaning, and even smiling.

Savi turned to Adam. "If I didn't know better, I'd say she was stoned."

Adam continued to stroke Karla's arm. Savi was mesmerized by the gentle way he touched her, wondering what it would feel like if a man touched her that way. She'd probably run screaming from the room, although Damián had touched her like that. She'd even enjoyed it.

Adam smiled. "Endorphins. She's getting closer now."

Endorphins. Like the ones released when Savi cut her arm all those times so long ago? She still remembered that euphoric feeling.

On the next stroke, Patti let out a cry of anguish, and her body sagged against the post. Damián only struck harder the next time. She screamed again. Seconds later, tears began to stream down the woman's face.

"That's my good girl. Let it out." Damián's words made Savi cringe, but she tamped down the emotion.

Thwack! Thwack!

Patti screamed out, "I am not your whore!"

Savi's chest tightened, and the walls began closing in on her.

"Let it go, Patticakes. That's my sweet girl." Victor's voice spoke to Patti in firm, soothing tones. She began to babble more about not being someone's whore. Savi was certain the woman wasn't referring to Victor but some abuser from her past.

"You're *my* slut. Only Sir Victor's slut. No one else's."

Savi couldn't breathe.

"You okay, Savi?"

She turned to find Karla's look of concern aimed at her. Savi nodded automatically. It occurred to her that Patti was the one in pain, yet Savi was receiving Karla's sympathy. This place was seriously fucked up.

She was seriously fucked up, because Savi found herself wishing Damián had called *her* his good girl. But she'd hated those words her entire life.

Damián had become silent since he'd spoken, except for the swish and crack of the cat. Why didn't he stop? Couldn't he see Patti had zoned out? She didn't need any more pain—or whatever they wanted to call it.

No way would Savi ever let anyone abuse her like that.

But she had. Many times. And she'd enjoyed it, too.

Filthy whore. Dirty slut.

Only Patti didn't act as if she was being abused. Her face was at peace. Bliss-filled. She had the look of a woman who'd surrendered herself totally into the hands of another. And not gentle hands, either. Patti had turned over the decisions about how hard to whip her to Damián, trusting him to give her what she needed rather than self-medicating and keeping herself numb.

How did what Patti experienced now compare to the rush Savi had gotten from cutting herself? They seemed unrelated. When Savi had cut herself years ago, she'd remained in control of how long, how deep.

No, she'd only had the *illusion* of control.

Cutting herself with a razor blade, she could have caused serious damage and not realized it until it was too late. Would she have cut herself if Damián hadn't found her last week? No, she'd already laid the blade down, hadn't she? No matter, she'd stopped in time.

But having someone else in charge of delivering the relief she craved would be safer if she could trust him. She remembered what Damián had said soon after finding her on the bathroom floor.

"Would you like to find other ways to get that rush without cutting yourself?"

As she watched the cat slap against Patti's back again, Savi tamped down a momentary jealousy. *Oh dear Lord.* Was she a masochist, too? Did she need what Patti was going through in order to feel something again? Had the sadists in her past conditioned her to crave severe pain in order to feel anything, sexual or otherwise?

Victor came over and placed a hand on Damián's shoulder and, without a word, the two of them walked to the post. A woman came over from the bar and offered Damián a wet towel and, while Victor stroked Patti's head, Damián pressed the towel against her burning skin. Luke brought over a tube of some kind of ointment and a pair of gloves, and Damián began to administer first aid to the stripes he'd placed on her back.

Victor bent down and unstrapped Patti's ankles, while Damián freed her wrists. The gentle way they ministered to her made Savi's eyes burn and she blinked until the discomfort receded. Patti collapsed into Victor's arms, and the linebacker of a man carried her to a loveseat where he wrapped her gently in a blanket and softly stroked her arm. Patti's eyes remained closed, tears flowing freely down her cheeks. Her blonde head lay against his brown chest, her face serene. Calm.

"They haven't spoken a word."

Adam said in a low voice, "Victor handles aftercare a lot better than the actual whipping. He knows she's still in catharsis. Talking now would pull her out too soon. She does need to know Victor is there for her, so he'll touch her, but he won't intrude until she's finished processing the emotions she's just released."

Savi continued to watch, mesmerized. This might not be therapy, but for Patti it certainly was therapeutic. Damián had given her what she needed. A Service Top.

Savi had been a pawn of Lyle's and her father's many times, passed around to service whichever clients were on the agenda. But none of those men had cared about her needs or taken care of her the way Damián and Victor were taking care of Patti. These two men weren't doing this to meet their own sexual or sadistic needs. The scene had been all about meeting Patti's emotional needs.

After what seemed like an eternity to Savi, Patti's eyelids fluttered open and she looked up at Victor. Something he said brought a smile to her face. When he kissed her, Savi turned away, realizing she'd been intruding on a private moment.

In an instant, Savi had a flash of clarity. *She* wanted to be the one chained to that post. *She* wanted Damián to use the cat—well, no, maybe just a whip—on her. Like Patti.

She glanced across the room and watched as Damián finished cleaning his whip. He must have taken care of the cat while she was mesmerized with Patti and Victor's decompression—no, Adam had called it aftercare. Damián applied some kind of lotion to the leather, coiled it, and tucked it into his leather bag. He zipped the bag, picked it up, and turned toward her. Something knotted in the pit of her stomach.

Damián, I want to feel *again.*

Savi blinked rapidly, but her eyes continued to sting with unshed tears. A look of regret crossed Damián's face. He turned away from her and walked toward the door.

Thank God. What on earth was she thinking? She'd never be able to experience what Patti had tonight. She'd never even be able to get beyond being restrained again, much less take that level of pain.

She was beyond hope. Savi wished she could shed the tears stinging the backs of her eyelids.

"Breathe, Savi. Now." She blinked and found Adam face-to-face with her. "Damián can help you, too."

She shook her head, briefly wondering how he'd known what she'd been thinking. "No one can help me."

"Bullshit. Trust him."

"I can't trust anyone that much."

"What are you most afraid of?"

Savi drew another deep breath, prepared to give her pat answer that she wasn't afraid of anything. But she was. She couldn't lie to herself any longer. "Too many things to name."

"Name one."

"Restraints. I can't let anyone restrain me."

* * *

Savi had no clue how she'd wound up back in the club again the next morning, soon after dropping Mari off at school. Nor how she was about to let Adam do the very thing she'd sworn no one would do to her ever again.

"Which is your dominant hand, Savi?"

Savi swallowed, looking up at Adam who held a menacing bundle of olive-green rope in his hand. "My right."

"Okay, I'm going to restrain your left hand and arm first. You'll still have use of your right one for a while, until you get used to the restraints—and me."

She could inflict a lot more damage with her feet and legs than with her hands anyway, but she couldn't keep from pointing out the obvious. "Like fighting with one hand tied behind my back?"

Adam grinned. "One hand tied at your side, actually." He tweaked her nose as if she were a kid, similar to what Damián had done last week. "Trust me, little one. You aren't going to need to fight me off. Remember what we talked about? I'm just going to work on decreasing your fear threshold. Starting now. Deep breath."

She forced herself to draw a slow, deep breath. No point trying to deny it. He had to know she was scared to death.

So why was she even considering letting him do this to her?

Because she needed to get past her fear of being restrained before she'd ever be able to experience what Patti had with Damián last night. Damián had told her once that being restrained actually would make her feel freer. Dear Lord, she hoped so.

"Okay, I'm ready." Sweat broke out on her upper lip. Savi steeled herself for the terror to come.

Adam chuckled. "No, you aren't. I think you need reinforcements. Wait here."

Where would she go? Her legs had turned to mush. Maybe she wouldn't be able to protect herself, after all. A knot formed in the pit of her stomach. She watched Adam walk toward the hallway leading to the kitchen, remembering back to Christmas Day when she'd nearly opened the other door to this room with Mari in tow. Thank God they had kept the doors to the club locked. She didn't blame Karla and Adam for house hunting. This was no place to raise a child. Savi appreciated how carefully they had shielded Mari from the club and its members last night, though.

As she waited, Savi wondered what kind of reinforcements he had in mind. She really just wanted to get this over with before she worked herself into a full-blown panic attack. Adam came back into the great room with Damián and Karla following close behind him. Seeing Damián, the duffel bag carrying the whip and cat-o-nine he'd used on Patti last night slung over his shoulder, caused the knot in her stomach to flip-flop to life. He wore his black leathers and a black Harley Davidson leather vest. No shirt. The tail of the dragon tattoo snaked down his bicep and arm, and she remembered how he'd made the dragon's mouth move when he flexed his pec.

Her face grew warm. Damián didn't approach her. Instead, he came to a standstill a few feet away. Surprisingly, she wished he would take her in his arms again. She'd missed him so much.

Now where had *that* impossible wish come from?

He grinned at her and set the bag on the floor beside him, but she sensed he also was a bit nervous by the way he clenched and unclenched his jaw. "Dad tells me you might need a little encouragement."

There was no censure in his voice for not letting him be the one to introduce restraints to her. She wasn't sure how much Damián could help, but his presence did relax her a bit. She trusted Damián to make doubly sure nothing happened against her will. Karla, too.

But was he disappointed that she hadn't asked him to do this? He'd left the club almost immediately after the scene with Patti. In her need to find out whether she could be restrained, Savi had turned last night to Adam and Karla for help, but it had gotten late. She needed to get back upstairs to Mari. Savi had tossed in bed all night, worrying about what she'd agreed to let Adam do.

Karla stepped up to her side and whispered in her ear, "Remember what I told you last night about my first time in rope bondage?" Savi nodded. "Good. Just relax and give in to the rope. It's an incredible feeling."

"I feel silly needing so many people to do a simple arm restraint."

Karla stroked her upper arm. "Oh, Savi, for my first time, I had Adam, Marc, Angelina, and Luke all there with me."

Adam's large hand reached out and stroked Karla's expanding tummy. "I was the one who was scared shitless that time. Either you or Angelina roped me into that scene. I still haven't figured out who the guilty party was."

Karla looked up at Adam and smiled innocently, the love on her face so apparent. Savi's gaze went again to his hand on her belly. *Lucky woman.* Karla would have Adam by her side when she gave birth. Savi wished... She glanced at Damián.

No. Don't even go there.

Savi might not have had Mari's daddy at her birth, but she'd done fine without him. Anita had been an excellent coach. The woman had four kids of her own.

Adam kissed Karla on the lips. With obvious regret, Karla broke off the kiss and turned her attention back to Savi. "Sorry." She blushed. "Where were we? Oh, yeah. Well, I trusted Adam to never do anything to hurt me when I let him tie me up that first time. But we'd known each other for nine years by then." Karla touched Savi's forearm. "You can trust him, too. He's a master at Shibari and a completely honorable man."

Intellectually, Savi thought she could trust them all, but connecting what her mind thought with what her body felt wasn't going to be easy. The fears of the past prohibited her from trusting anyone emotionally, but she was tired of living in fear all the time. Holding her chin up, Savi took a deep breath and released it slowly. "I'm ready."

Damián took up a spot an arm's length in front of her, and Karla stood beside Adam, who began to unwrap the bundle of rope.

"Eyes on me, *savita.*"

Savi's gaze was drawn to Damián's face. He smiled and took a step closer, invading her personal space. Her heartbeat tripped, then kicked up a notch, beating wildly. Damián's hands reached out, and he stroked her shoulders and upper arms, having a surprisingly calming effect on her. Adam lifted her left elbow and positioned her hand in the air at a ninety-degree angle, as if she were waving to someone in the distance. Quickly, he looped three knots around her three fingers, leaving only the thumb and pinkie free.

Here we go.

"Breathe, *querida.*"

Perhaps because she didn't respond quickly enough, Damián took a breath, and Savi mimicked him by drawing in a deep one of her own. Adam drew her hand back, nearer to her shoulder joint.

Damián's hand stroked the underside of her arm. "You have such soft, beautiful skin."

The touch of his warm fingers set forth an outbreak of gooseflesh, followed by warning bells. When her nipples hardened, she reached with her free hand to cover her chest, but he entwined his fingers in hers and returned her hand to her side.

"Breathe, *savita*."

She squirmed in discomfort, doing as he'd reminded her. At least he didn't point out her body's traitorous betrayal—or take advantage of her.

Adam's voice brought her back into the scene. "This technique is called the claw." He wrapped the rope close to her armpit, pulling her wrist closer to her upper arm. Her fingers curled into a claw-like pose. "Let me know immediately if the ropes get too tight or you feel any tingling or coldness anywhere."

Well, her skin was tingling but not from the rope. Adam's concern for her comfort helped her relax a bit more. She nodded.

Karla whispered in her ear, "It's best that you give him verbal responses and address him as Sir. Good practice for when you come back to play in the club."

Savi certainly didn't feel comfortable calling Adam "Sir," so she just said, "Yes, I understand."

Adam grinned at her blatant omission but went to work. One end of the rope began to fly as Adam looped it under and around her forearm and upper arm more quickly. Savi flexed her fingers and tried to move her hand to see how much mobility she had left.

"Are you in any discomfort?"

Adam's question stilled her movements. He seemed so attuned to her. "No. I'm fine." She continued to resist calling him Sir. The gentle tug of the rope began to relax her. She still had a free hand and two unrestrained legs, and they had done a very good job of making her feel calm rather than threatened. At this moment, she wasn't worried about fighting them off. Karla's presence helped, too.

Adam continued to tie the rope, then pulled the end through once more and gave it a tug. He dropped his hands to his sides and came to stand beside Damián, but his gaze remained on her. "How are you doing, hon?"

"Okay…Sir." Now where had that come from? The man somehow just commanded respect.

"Good girl."

The beginnings of panic clawed at her throat. Hearing the words from

Adam didn't have the same effect as when Damián had said them to Patti.

Damián seemed to be aware of her distress and stepped even closer. His body brushed against hers, and he locked gazes with her, grounding her. "Deep breath, Savi." He wrapped his arms around her and stroked her back through her T-shirt as he turned to explain to Adam that those words were a trigger.

Damián seemed a little upset, but she quickly realized he wasn't angry with her. Being held so securely, she was surprised to find her body relaxing against him.

"Fuck. I'm sorry, hon. Damián told me about your triggers, but I'm just so used to saying that to Karla and the other subs, I forgot."

Savi didn't want to upset Adam. "It's okay."

"No, it's not. A Dom needs to consider everything that might go down in a scene before he starts—and definitely needs to remember a sub's known triggers. You have my sincerest apology."

Damián pulled back and glowered at Adam. She didn't want to come between these two, although she had the distinct feeling that's where she was.

"It's not Adam's fault. It's just two silly words, really. I shouldn't let them bother me."

Damián turned his focus back to her and brushed a loose strand of hair from her forehead. "Anything that has that kind of effect on you isn't silly. Don't negate your feelings. If you feel something, own it."

Validate your feelings. How many textbooks had preached that homily, yet she'd spent a lifetime tamping down her feelings. Of course, she wasn't going to change that mindset in one evening. Damián seemed to sense that and just took her in his arms again. Her eyes began to burn. She'd never had any man other than maybe Father Martine consider her feelings to be all that important. It was comforting and made her want to cry for some reason. Not that she could. She never cried.

Savi resisted the urge to lay her head against his shoulder. She let him continue to stroke her back. So gentle. Memories of how he'd touched her in the beach cave flitted around the edges of her brain, but she pushed them away. Those images were too painful, knowing she could never have that with him again.

For now, though, she was content to just feel safe in Damián's arms.

An amazingly safe place to be.

Chapter Twelve

Damián could kick Dad for not being more careful about Savi's triggers after Damián had shared them with him once he heard what Savi wanted to do. The man had never been careless like that in a scene with a sub.

Adam cleared his throat. "Son, I think Savi might be more comfortable having you bind her other arm."

Damián pulled away from Savi, took a step back, and looked at Dad, who winked at him. *Fuck it all.* He should have known the man's mind was like a steel trap. No way would he have forgotten something as important as that trigger. Clearly, this was a set up to get Damián into the scene with Savi.

Dad had called him to come to the house a couple of hours ago. Damián had no idea what was up until he'd gotten here. Learning what Savi wanted to do and what the plan was—at least what he *thought* it was—Damián had informed Dad about Savi's triggers, the ones he knew about anyway. When Dad had come into the kitchen to get him and Karla, Damián had walked into the great room to find Savi waiting at the Shibari station. All rational thought left his head.

Damián couldn't get enough of the sight of her. Touching her again sure wasn't enough. He wanted more. So much more than he could ever hope to have.

The thought of binding her with the ropes about brought him to his knees. But had they established the needed level of trust? What had changed from last night when she'd had tears in her eyes after seeing what he'd done to Patti? Yet today she'd let Dad restrain her arm—and they were relative strangers. What the fuck had changed?

Damián cupped her chin and turned her face toward him. She didn't flinch or pull away. *Progress.* "Would you let me bind your other arm, Savi?"

Her body stiffened, and he hid his disappointment as he prepared himself to hear her say "no." When she lifted her free hand, he expected her to push him away, but she turned her hand palm upward and offered herself to him in the sweetest gesture he'd ever seen.

Damián didn't want to waste time analyzing what had made her ready and willing, but he hoped he would be able to get through this scene without losing it. His emotions were too close to the surface right now after so many sleepless nights without having her in his apartment.

If only she'd asked him to do something he was better trained to do. Shibari had always been a little too…tame for him, so he hadn't spent a lot of time working on learning the skill. He'd watched Dad and Marc enough times. Even Luke had started showing off some of his growing skill sets lately. Hell, if Baby Dom could do it, how hard could it be? Luckily, the claw was a technique Dad had worked on with him before.

Besides, Dad stood by and would walk him through it if he started to make a mess of things.

"Karla needs to get off her feet. If you'll excuse us, we're going to sit over here and watch."

"I'm fine, Adam…oh!" Dad scooped a squealing Karla into his arms and carried her about six feet away from Damián and Savi, then set her on her feet while he sat down on the loveseat. With a smile, she curled into his lap.

Damn the man. Dad probably had orchestrated this entire scene right from the beginning. Damián shook his head and turned his attention back to Savi. Her smile wavered. He needed to act soon or she'd withdraw her hand. Bending down, he picked up a bundle of dyed silk rope and began untwisting it.

Shaking it loose, he took the seven-meter length in both hands and doubled it, then brought it up and over Savi's head and around her neck. He let the ends fall over her breasts and wished she wasn't wearing the long-sleeved T-shirt, but he wasn't going to let a little fabric deter him from enjoying the hell out of this scene.

Damián took the rope and massaged it against her neck and shoulders. She grew even more stiff. "What are you doing?"

"Preparing you for the rope."

"I'm already half roped. Besides, Adam didn't do that." She bit her lower lip and glanced over at Dad and Karla.

"Eyes on me, *savita*." The pulse point in her neck throbbed against his fingertips. "Every Dom has his own technique." He didn't want to tell her

Adam had been treating her as if she was a demonstration model, not a lover. Not that Damián could exactly call himself her lover, either. Hearing him say that would, sure as hell, freak her out. Of course, she hadn't seen Dad and Karla in one of their incredibly sensual scenes yet. She probably wouldn't until after the baby came.

Damián worked the rope up the column of her neck until the pads of his thumbs rested on the pulse points just below her jaw. Her pulse pounded against his thumbs like a frightened rabbit's. With the rope entwined in his hands, he let the tips of his fingers move into the hair at the back of her neck. As he massaged her scalp, she closed her eyes and released a sigh. Her eyes bolted open again. Was she surprised at her response or worried she'd disobeyed by not keeping her eyes on him?

He reached out and placed his thumbs over her eyelids and closed them, holding them down until he was reasonably certain she would keep them closed. Seeing her get into the scene like that was a great turn-on. She furrowed her eyebrows, but she kept her eyes closed as he continued to massage the rope into her scalp. She emitted another soft moan. "That's it, *bebé*. Just relax. Feel. Become one with the rope."

Savi's head lolled back. So soft. Malleable steel in his hands. He hadn't expected her to be so responsive given how tightly she'd held the reins on her body to this point. He wished he could continue like this for hours, but he didn't have that long before Savi's brain would kick in and she'd probably knock him away, so he slowly withdrew his hands.

Her eyes flickered open, and she held her head erect again. Her pupils were dilated. Was it from arousal or just that she'd had her eyes closed? Before the relaxed mood was gone, he reached for one end of the rope and fashioned a double-coin knot, then took Savi's hand in his.

Her fingers were held rigid, but she didn't pull away. She lifted her gaze to his face, and he stared into the blue depths of her eyes. He took the knot and slipped the center over her middle finger, then eased the other two fingers into the other holes before sliding it down her fingers to her knuckles. He didn't want to think about how similar it was to slipping a wedding ring on a woman's finger, because he'd never experience that with any woman. Even so, it sure felt like something he wanted to experience—with Savi.

Damián walked around behind her and drew her hand back to her shoulder. When he encountered resistance, he massaged the tension from her upper arm. "Don't fight it, Savi."

Don't fight me, either.

Damián leaned forward and breathed in the heady scent of her hair, then regained mastery of himself as he placed a kiss on the side of her neck. She moaned again, and his dick throbbed in response. He went to work completing the claw tie, glancing over at the one Dad had done on the other hand a couple of times to make sure his was as good. Not half bad, but Dad's looked neater. He straightened out one of the double lines of rope that had crisscrossed each other and stood back.

He looked over at Dad who smiled slightly and nodded. Karla looked a bit mesmerized by the whole scene. Unfortunately for her, Dad barely did more than hair corsets with her these days, worried he might hurt the baby. How either of them was going to survive the next few months was beyond Damián's comprehension.

Regaining focus, he walked around to face Savi. Her pose with her hands in that position reminded him of when Teresa and José had played cops and robbers and one of them would be held at gunpoint. Yeah, memories of his niece and nephew might keep him from getting too turned on by Savi.

So not working. The T-shirt now strained against her breasts, which were pulled higher. Damián wasn't sure what he might have done if they were alone. Not that either of them was ready to find out. Good thing they had chaperones.

He stood closer. "How are you feeling?"

She blinked. "Fine."

"Describe *fine* to me."

"Maybe fine isn't the right word." She nibbled on her lower lip before answering. "I feel…very vulnerable."

"I appreciate your honesty. What are you afraid I might do?"

"Tou…" She cleared the frog from her throat. "Touch me."

"You know how much I'd love to touch you, Savi, but I won't take advantage of your vulnerability. Can you trust me?"

"I'm t-trying."

"Thank you, *mi sueño*." Damián glanced down at her breasts, her nipples protruding against her shirt. His balls tightened. *Fuck.* Maybe this wasn't a good idea after all. Like it or not, her body was responding. He needed to end this scene before he scared her away.

"Son, this might be a good time to explore some of the things we talked about earlier."

Damián blinked. Dad hadn't needed to coach Damián in a scene in years, but he really had lost his train of thought any number of times since this one had begun. He was acting like a fucking rank amateur. Of course, this wasn't his usual type of scene, but Savi certainly wasn't ready to engage in an impact session. Not after the one she'd witnessed last night. She probably thought he'd start out that hard on her, too, although he and Patti had worked up to that level of pain over dozens of sessions in several years.

He still hadn't completely forgiven Dad for letting her watch the scene with Patti. He'd never be able to get Savi to see him as anything but a monster for what he'd had to do.

Then again, that probably was for the best. Nothing could ever come of the two of them. He wouldn't allow it.

But she wasn't cringing away from him now. Maybe just this once. He stepped closer, and she didn't pull away. "What kind of pain do you need, Savi?"

A flash of fear crossed her face. "I don't feel I need any pain."

"What do you feel right now?"

She paused a moment, then whispered, "Exposed."

"In what way?"

"Emotionally. I don't like feeling like this."

"Why not?"

"Emotions are…messy."

"Messy in what way?"

She drew a deep breath. "They give you way too much power over me."

"Yet you've let me…" he nodded toward Dad, "…*us* restrain you."

"That's different."

"How so?"

"My body may be easily dominated, but I've never relinquished my mind and don't plan to start now."

Had she really thought she'd been able to remain in control mentally in the past? From what he'd seen in that hotel room, he didn't think so. But the illusion seemed to be important to her.

What was she afraid would happen if she released that hold? Would he ever get her to submit her mind to him?

"Well, then, we'll start with you giving me dominion over your body."

Savi drew a ragged breath before she stood taller. "I can still knock you on your ass, Damián."

Damián grinned at her sweet, albeit false, bravado. "Is that so?"

Fire burned in her eyes a flash of a second before her right leg wrapped around the back of his left knee. He was lying flat on his ass looking up at her before he knew what had hit him. *Mierda.* His little dream was a fucking powerhouse.

Then a look of horror crossed her face. "Oh my God, did I hurt you?"

Only my ego, chiquita.

"I forgot about your foot. I just went on instinct, and you were so smug, and—"

"You what?"

She stared blankly. "What...what?"

She'd forgotten he was a cripple? *Fuck, yeah.* Damián grinned, never so happy at having been knocked on his ass by a girl before. Dad chuckled as Damián got up off the floor. For a brief moment, Damián had forgotten he and Savi weren't alone.

"Where'd you get that kind of strength in your legs? You jump hurdles or something?"

"No. I haven't done it in forever. I had no idea I still had that kind of strength." Savi looked away. "It was in self-defense training and..." She paused.

"And what?"

"Nothing."

"Answer me, Savi."

She pierced him with momentary anger before backing down again, biting her lip.

Damián invaded her personal space and tilted her face up to his. "Answer. Me."

"All right. From pole dancing."

Damián opened his eyes wide. "I'm the last person to judge anyone's lifestyle choices, but no way in hell can I picture you in a strip club."

Savi gave him an exasperated look. "No, you ass. I'm in...I *was* in classes at the gym. Exercising with dancer poles is all the craze now in Southern California. My therapist thought it would be good...exercise for me."

Damián stared at her, but images of her wearing a low-cut tank top and short-shorts while dancing with a stripper pole obliterated her face before him at the moment. *Mierda.*

He could hear the laughter in Dad's voice when he spoke. "Damián and I would be happy to install a pole here at the club if you'd like to be able to work out again, Savi."

Damián looked over at the man and grinned. Dad had just redeemed himself for last night. Damián planned to work on Savi's stripper pole at the shop this week during his free nights. It would give him something to do while Savi and Marisol were staying here. He'd given up trying to sleep anymore.

"Okay, you can get me out of these ropes now. I think I'm over my fear of being restrained."

Was she really now?

Maybe it was time to work a bit on that galvanized-steel mind of hers.

* * *

Damián leaned closer, and Savi's breath caught in her throat. She swallowed and took a step back.

"If you're really over your fear, you wouldn't keep running from me. What are you afraid I'm going to do? Will you let me touch you?"

With her arms splayed open like this, she couldn't control how close he got or where he touched her. Yeah, she could send him sprawling again if she needed to, but did she want to?

No.

Still, knowing she could—and had, despite having her arms restrained—empowered her. She didn't fear that he'd hurt her. Adam—and probably Karla—would intervene if Savi couldn't handle him herself, but the thought of Damián hurting her seemed farfetched. So what was she afraid of?

Feeling again.

She didn't mean physically but emotionally. How could she protect herself from the onslaught of emotions she always tried so hard to control? Her tight rein had been slipping bit by bit until, now, she wasn't sure she even wanted to keep fighting.

But she had to. She'd never be able to turn off the triggers, and everything seemed to trigger something deep inside her.

"Judging by that move you just put on me, I don't think you need Dad and Karla as bodyguards anymore. Do you agree?"

"Bodyguards? What do you mean?"

The twinkle of humor left his eyes, and he grew more serious. "Don't change the subject. I asked if you trust them enough to let them go on about their day and leave you here with me—in restraints."

Her heart hammered. She turned to Adam.

"Hon, I'm not going anywhere unless you say so. We've got nothing on the agenda today for hours, except to be here with you, so don't let him talk you into something you aren't ready for."

Knowing she wouldn't be abandoned by them made it easier to reply. She had a choice. Control. She could continue to play it safe with Adam and Karla here as buffers—bodyguards—or she could take a chance and trust that Damián wouldn't do anything to harm her. He'd never stepped over the line before. He'd cared for her when she was at her most vulnerable—at her father's hotel all those years ago—and hadn't taken advantage of her. She could trust him more than any man she knew.

Savi turned to Damián and quickly put out of her mind what she'd witnessed last night in this room. That wasn't between Damián and her—that was what he'd negotiated earlier with Patti. She'd watched as Damián had taken Patti to the edge, helped her find emotional release, and then transferred her back into the arms of Victor who had provided the nurturing and care the woman had needed.

Savi still couldn't believe the change that had taken place in Patti later last night when she'd fully recovered from whatever state she'd been in after what Adam called her aftercare on the loveseat with Victor. The man had held her a long time as the two of them talked quietly and seemed to process what had happened to put her into such a dark place. She'd been animated and lively. Later in the evening, Patti had even let Luke and Victor restrain and suspend her from the ceiling.

Savi had lain awake half the night trying to visualize herself in Patti's place, but Damián and Patti were on a whole different level. She wasn't about to try and compete with them, but she did want to explore endorphin release under Damián's hand, as opposed to her own. Adam had told her last night Damián wouldn't take her beyond her limits. He wouldn't even take her to what they called their dungeon. Would she ever be able to work up to being able to tolerate the whip? What other implements could he use to deliver pain—and catharsis?

She wasn't going to run away anymore. Swiveling her upper body, she addressed Adam and Karla. "I'm okay to stay with Damián now. Thank you."

"You're sure this is your decision? No one is going to coerce you in here."

His protectiveness was touching, but she needed to do this. "Yes, it's what I want." *I think.*

"Then Kitten and I are going to go rustle up some chow. You'll probably be hungry later."

Adam went over and whispered something to Damián, who nodded and thanked him. After they'd left, Savi drew a deep breath. "Okay. What did you have in mind?"

"First, I think we'll get you out of these ropes."

"Don't you want me restrained?"

"Oh, I plan to restrain you, but ropes are Dad's thing—not my restraint of choice."

Something fluttered in her stomach, but she tamped it down. *Trust him.* Savi glanced over at the center post briefly wondering if he'd chain her there the way he'd restrained Patti.

After he removed the ropes on her left arm, he massaged the muscles and checked her range of motion, restoring the blood flow. She groaned as her joints and muscles protested being moved again. He released the other arm and repeated the process, then walked behind her and kneaded her shoulders and arms. She melted.

The man's hands were magic—until he pressed a particularly sensitive area. "Ow!"

"Why didn't you tell us your arms were uncomfortable?"

"I didn't notice any tingling; numb is normal for me."

Damián's thumb pressed into a tight knot and she groaned. "Sorry, *bebé.*" He placed a kiss on the spot.

Savi moved away from him. "I think it's better now. Thanks."

He chuckled and bent to pick up his duffel bag. "Come. We're going down the hall."

He took her elbow and guided her across the room. As they passed the bar, he reached behind it and grabbed two bottles of water. He handed one to her. "Here. Drink this. You'll need to stay hydrated."

She drank half the bottle, not realizing how thirsty she was. He led her down the hallway toward the kitchen but didn't go as far as that. He stopped, opened a door, and motioned for her to precede him. When he switched on the light, she found herself staring at an X-shaped cross. The cherry wood had a line of eyebolts along the sides from top to bottom and a platform at the base.

"What on earth is that?"

"Something Luke made for us. It's used to restrain someone you don't want to move even minutely." He led her into the room and they stopped in front of the cross. "Before we start, we need to talk about limits."

He planned to push her limits? Or honor them?

"Dad shared the checklist you filled out as part of the membership contract. No needles. No sex, including oral. No touching your pussy. No anal. No restraints. Obviously, we can amend the list for that last one now. Are there any new restrictions you need to place on restraints?"

"Keep my legs free."

He grinned. "So you can take me down again?"

Her biggest fear was being splayed open and him discovering her mark of shame, but she couldn't convey that to him or he'd just push her into letting him do it. Wouldn't he? She forced a smile to her lips. "If I have to."

"Unfortunately, in the scene I have in mind, I can't have you moving around even a bit or you could get hurt. I'll need to restrain your legs, too."

Her heart rate doubled. He stroked her upper arms.

"What scares you most about having your legs restrained?"

She blinked several times, waging a losing battle over whether she should explain. Maybe a half-truth. "I don't want you to touch my pussy."

"Fair enough. That's already on your list of hard limits. I won't need to touch your pussy in this scene. Anything else?"

Wait. Had she just agreed to having her legs restrained? Was she ready for this?

"I don't know enough to know what I don't like."

"Limits aren't about not liking something but about not being able to tolerate it, physically or emotionally. If you choose to go deeper into the lifestyle, you might find yourself wanting to explore some of the things that are hard limits now. My job is to make sure you keep an open mind and that you trust me not to disregard any hard limits, at least until we've had time to blur the lines a little bit." He grinned.

She nodded. A frisson of fear bubbled up inside her.

"Breathe, *querida*. We haven't even started yet."

"Will you tell me what you're planning to do first?"

"No. Just trust me not to go beyond any of your hard limits."

"What if I have limits I don't even know about yet? What if surprises are a limit?"

"You have a safeword for that. Say 'tamale' and everything stops. We'll talk about the issue at that point."

Every time he mentioned her safeword, she pictured him stretched out on the bed, half naked, his dragon tat taunting her. Her face grew flushed.

"Yes, *mamacita*, remember that '*hot* tamale' means something totally different than 'tamale.'"

"I am *not* thinking of you as a hot tamale, Damián."

He nipped her earlobe and whispered, "Liar."

"Egomaniac."

He laughed and stepped behind her. The heat of his body warmed her, even though their bodies didn't touch. She tried not to think the words "hot tamale," but suddenly she could think of nothing else.

"Now, your body also will be communicating to me." His hands brushed against her nipples. Her very erect nipples. "Right now, you're thinking about something—or some*one*—that has your body very excited. Since I happen to be the only other person in the room, I believe you're thinking about me. That pleases me very much."

"It's just cold in here." Savi's face grew warm. "Can we get started?"

"Ah, the lady is anxious to feel the bite."

Her body grew stiff. "The bite of what?"

He chuckled. "Wait here."

She did as he told her and watched him set his duffel bag on the floor in front of her and bend down. He pulled out a pair of leather cuffs not unlike the ones he'd used on Patti last night. After fastening them to her wrists, he stuck his finger inside. "Too tight?"

She shook her head.

"I want verbal responses, followed by Sir."

"What?"

"Yes, Sir. No, Sir. Don't just nod or shake your head."

"Why?"

He gave her a stern look.

"Why, *Sir*?"

"First, because I need to learn to judge your reactions by the tone of your voice along with the visual cues. I also might not have my eyes on you at the moment and could miss something important. Lastly, you say 'Sir' to show respect for the person you're submitting to."

She'd submitted? Well, what else would you call it? "Thank you for explaining it, Sir."

Damián kissed her cheek, making her feel cherished. "Having you in restraints is a dream come true for the Dom in me, *mi sueño*."

Her heart fluttered at his nearness, but she reminded herself this wasn't sexual or romantic. She was only trying to learn to process her feelings better.

"Before I restrain you, I'm going to remove your clothing."

"Wait! I'm not sure…"

"I am. I can't do this scene with you if you're clothed, and you said nothing about nakedness being a hard limit."

"Not the panties."

"Why not?"

"Because I don't want you to touch me there."

His hand went to the curve of her ass, warming her through her jeans. "As much as I want to see and touch your pussy, you have made it abundantly clear that area is off-limits. You need to learn to trust me if this is going to work. I will not be touching your pussy, however I will be touching you here." He patted her ass but that didn't set off any warning bells.

"I trust you not to touch my…pussy." She couldn't believe she was calling her privates such a provocative name, but she didn't want to use a clinical term, which would embarrass her even more.

"Thank you, *savita*. Now, strip."

Her stomach dropped, but the sooner she got this over, the better. With trembling hands, she pulled the T-shirt over her head. The necklace he'd given her for Christmas lay warm in the cleft of her breasts. Before she could reach back and unhook the bra clasp, he brushed her fingers aside and released it for her. He pushed the scraps of fabric away and ran his fingernails along the center of her back and up to her shoulder blades. Numb.

"Your skin is so soft." His lips kissed her shoulder, near her neck, and she shivered.

"I don't think I like being kissed like that, Sir."

"Hard limit?"

She shook her head, then remembered to say, "No, Sir. Just makes me uncomfortable."

"We'll be working on that comfort zone of yours today, Savi." He massaged her shoulders and upper arms, and she emitted a moan. He chuckled. "Now, the jeans…and panties."

"Damián…"

"Now, Savi."

Her fingers shook so badly, he reached out to undo the button of her jeans for her. She brushed his hands aside and slid the zipper down herself. Too close. Face flushing, she shimmied the tight jeans down her legs, taking the panties with them, not wanting to do a strip tease for him or prolong her embarrassment. She realized she hadn't removed her shoes yet and looked to him to make sure she had his permission. He nodded and held out his hand so she could steady herself as she pulled them off one foot, and then she shifted hands to remove the other. The jeans and panties soon followed.

"So fucking beautiful."

Savi closed her eyes, too mortified to make eye contact with him. She closed her legs, hoping to shield herself, but he was intent on her wrists at the moment and didn't seem to care that she was totally naked. But she certainly was aware. Intensely so.

He guided her until the intersecting boards of the cross pressed against her bare back and then took her left wrist, stretching her arm toward the top of one side of the cross. He fastened a clip on the cuff to one of the eyebolts. Soon the other hand was clipped to another bolt on the opposite side, stretching her out like a Y. She pulled at the restraints, but wasn't going anywhere. Tension coiled inside her. Fear? Anticipation? What did he plan to do to her?

Damián stood in front of her. "Tell me what you're feeling now, Savi."

Why did he insist on talking about her feelings all the time? Why didn't he just do…whatever he planned to do?

"Answer out loud, Savi."

"Sir, I feel like I've been stripped bare."

He smiled. "You have, *mi sueño*." His hand stroked over her bare butt, and she tensed.

Blood roared through her ears. *I can't do this.*

"Yes, you can."

She'd shared her thought out loud? She hadn't meant to.

"Stay with me, Savi. Focus totally on me."

Trust Damián. He wants to help you. She needed this. She wanted him to make her feel again. She needed the pain. Damián knew what she needed. *Trust him.*

The litany continued in her mind.

"Inhale." His gentle but firm voice soothed some of her anxiety. She breathed in deeply, and a bit of the tension released from her body. "Exhale." She imagined breathing the negativity out of her body as she exhaled. "Again."

In…out.

Pressure on her back. Damián's hands. Strong, warm, tender. His hands stroked down her sides to her butt, and she clenched her butt cheeks as if to escape him. His hands moved up her back again to her shoulders, then downward in a circular motion. She tensed each time his hand neared her butt, but he honored her limit. She wasn't ready for him to touch her privates. She never would be.

"Inhale, *savita*."

His hands massaged her behind. *Smack*. She jumped when his hand impacted with her butt. "I said *inhale*."

"Yes, Sir."

She did as she was told. Her lungs burned before she filled them, proof that she'd been holding her breath. *Focus on your breathing*.

In…out. In…out.

"That's it, *bebé*."

Savi released the tension that had held her rigid. Damián's hands brushed her breasts, pinching the sides of them both. Numb. His hands moved constantly now along her sides, pinching her at regular intervals. Once she felt a slight sting, but mostly…nothing.

He reached around her and something cold pressed against her belly. She looked down to see a two-inch wide leather belt that he buckled into place, holding her snuggly against the cross.

"Spread your legs."

I can't do this.

"Now, Savi."

Trust him.

She spread her legs for him.

"Wider."

She spread them farther apart.

"Even wider."

Feeling like a wishbone, she spread them as far as she could go without dislocating her hip.

"Perfect." He patted her on the butt. She tried to jerk away, but could go nowhere. He chuckled and spanked her again playfully but followed by rubbing her ass cheek to take away the sting. "You can't evade my touch, Savi. Know that I will honor your limits and not touch your pussy, but anywhere else I wish to touch you or look at you, I will. *¿Comprendes?*"

"Y-yes, Sir."

He took two more black leather cuffs from his bag. Kneeling on one knee, he fastened the cuff to her left ankle and attached it to a bolt on the cross. He scooted over and did the same with the other. His head was so near her mons, she clenched, but she could do nothing to hide herself from him. Her chest constricted as she fought in vain to shield herself, but his face remained focused on her ankles, as far as she could tell.

Another trip to the bag produced two smaller belts. He wrapped one around her thigh and attached her even more tightly to the cross, then repeated on the other side.

"Breathe, Savi."

She did so, but the fear didn't recede this time. Why couldn't she just trust him? He'd kept all of his promises so far.

He reached up and stroked her abdomen above and below the belt. "Beautiful." He placed a kiss on her belly, and she wondered what he found beautiful about her curveless body with its many stretch marks.

He stood again. "Now, I'm going to test your threshold for pain—establish some benchmarks."

Savi remembered the welts he'd placed on Patti's back, and the fear threatened to overtake her again, but she forced it away. He wouldn't hurt her like that. Not yet, anyway. She shuddered at the thought.

Damián left her side and returned a moment later holding a sleep mask in front of her. "I think this might help you to focus without being distracted." He stretched the elasticized band over her hair and adjusted it over her eyes and nose. "How's that?"

Dark. "Fine, Sir." *Too dark.* Her voice quivered.

His hands brushed the sides of her breasts, and a jolt of electricity coursed through her. She gasped, so not expecting that.

"Are you okay?"

No. I'm afraid of the dark. "Y-yes, Sir." Her voice sounded high-pitched, like a child's.

"Where are you, *savita?*"

Unable to speak, she shook her head.

"Tell me. We can't continue if you keep anything from me. What are you

213

feeling?"

"Afraid."

His hand stroked her sides. "Afraid of what?"

He would think she was a baby. Weak. Pathetic. How could she tell him? But the main thing he demanded from her was honesty. He wanted to know what she was feeling. For this little experiment to work, she must be honest.

"Savi." His prompting told her he wasn't happy with her delay in responding. She didn't want him to become angry.

"I'm afraid of the dark, Sir." Her voice sounded even more childlike than Mari's. *Oh dear Lord.* She wanted to disappear into the floor. A slight tug of the mask against the back of her head and he pushed it onto her forehead. She blinked to let her eyes grow accustomed to the welcome light. Much better than being in total darkness.

"Better?"

Overcome by an inexplicable emotion, she only nodded. He was going to let her do this without being blindfolded.

"Tell me what scares you about the dark."

The fear clawed up into her throat just thinking about it, and she shook her head. "I can't talk about that."

His gaze intensified. He didn't release her from his stare. "Yes, you can, *savita*. Who or what made you fear the dark?"

His hand continued stroking her sides, gently but firmly. Her skin remained numb, her mind registering only the pressure of his hand, nothing more. No gooseflesh. No tingle. Totally numb.

She closed her eyes.

"Look at me."

I can't do this.

"Now, Savi. Tell me where you are."

She opened her eyes and stared back at him.

Numb. In hell.

Tell him. You don't have to go back there ever again. Just tell him. It's not about you anyway. It's about Savannah. Savannah's dead. No one can hurt her ever again.

"He took away her night light the night Maman went away." The words came out in a rush, almost as if she were vomiting them from her mind.

His hand stroked her, soothing her. "What did she do?"

"She cried. She always cried. About everything."

"Lots of kids would cry in that situation. Lots of kids are afraid of the dark."

She swallowed and closed her eyes.

"Look. At. Me."

"I can't."

"You can, and you will. Open your eyes. You're with me now. You're safe."

She did as he instructed but couldn't meet his gaze.

"Savi."

She complied, breathing in shallow, rapid bursts.

"Now, tell me what happened in the dark."

Damián's eyes were warm and caring. Trying to keep the memories inside the box was becoming too daunting. "She'd hide from him...under the bed." The words poured out, her voice high. "It was so dark under there. Scary. But so much safer than when he found her. The princess hid with her so she wouldn't be as scared."

"Deep breath, *bebé*."

It took several attempts to execute his command. Her heart pounded in her ears. He didn't speak again until her breathing became relatively normal. His hands moved up to stroke the undersides of her arms.

"Who is the princess?"

Images of her Christmas Barbie filled her mind's eye. "Savannah's beautiful doll. She had blond hair like me, but dark eyes like Maman. The princess made Savannah feel as if Maman hadn't left her after all."

His hand reached up to her face and his thumb brushed against her cheek. "Then what happened?"

Wingtip shoes and dress pants. She watched the feet and legs, backlit by the hallway light, enter the oh-so-dark room.

An ironic thought strayed across her mind. Her father came from the light while Savannah cowered in the dark, but he was the evil one. She was safe in the dark until he came after her.

No, that was Savannah. A bubble of anger boiled up inside, but she managed to tamp it back down.

"Stop doing that. Don't cage your emotions, Savi. You need to let them out."

Numb. She wanted to remain numb.

She felt a slight pressure against her arms and sides as he continued to stroke her, calming her.

Damián waited, but her anger was gone. "It's too late. I'll try to do better next time."

"That's all I ask, *bebé*, that you try. It's not easy to change coping mechanisms that have worked for us for so long."

"You sound like a therapist."

He laughed. "Just life experience. No degree, like yours. But this way, I get to dispense lots of free advice." He grew serious again. "Now, tell me more about the dark."

The man wasn't easily distracted.

"Savannah tried to make herself invisible in the dark. But he always found her."

Damián's hand slid up the underside of her arm, stroking her firmly, gently until her breathing became regular again.

"He can't hurt you now, Savi. That's in the past."

"He didn't hurt me. He hurt Savannah. She's dead."

At least she hoped Savannah and the monster that spawned her really were relegated to the past, although Savi's healed rib made it clear her father might never truly stop being a threat to her until...*he* was dead, too.

"You don't have to be afraid of the dark now. You're with me. I would never take advantage of you like he did."

Not intentionally.

"I don't think I can do this anymore, Sir."

"Do what? All you have to do is stand here, talk to me, and feel—experience. I'll be doing the physical work, but I get the impression you aren't going to reveal anything more to me about the dark right now, so let's move on in the scene."

Savi looked at a row of impact implements hanging on the wall—crops, whips, canes. She shuddered, remembering having some of those things used on her in the past. How could the use of those implements break down the barrier between her mind and her body? She'd prefer to leave those memories buried.

"Which one will you use?"

"That's not anything you need to be concerned with. You just need to focus on your breathing, on where I touch your body, on what I'm saying to you, and on what you're feeling. *¿Comprendes?*"

Was he freaking serious? Why had she agreed to try this? "I don't think..."

"I don't want you to think. I want you to focus on me. Submit to me."

"I can't surrender."

"I haven't asked you to surrender, Savi."

She definitely heard the unspoken "yet." How long before he would demand more than she could give?

Chapter Thirteen

Savi was tired of letting the past control her. She needed to try this. Maybe Damián could help.

"The session I have in mind, Savi, will help you reconnect with your body. Today, I want you merely to submit that iron will to me. Accept what I am going to do to your body, knowing I will push you up to your limits without going beyond them. If you do reach a limit before I recognize it, you have your safeword."

She nodded. "Okay."

"Is that how you speak to your Top?"

"I'm sorry, Sir." The protocols he had explained and that she'd read in the contract still seemed silly to her, but if she was going to get into this kind of thing, she might as well try to follow the script.

"The complete surrender of your mind isn't required at first, but you will need to let go of that tight leash you place on your feelings."

"I'll try to, Sir."

"Thank you, *bebé*." His hand stroked her sides. "What's your safeword, Savi?"

Her lungs constricted. *Here we go.* "Tamale, Sir."

"You understand that I'll be the only one here with you. No one else is going to touch or hurt you without coming through me first. *¿Comprendes?*"

"*Sí, Señor.*"

He slapped the side of her butt again, but his smile told her he wasn't upset with her smartass response, although her ass did smart a little bit from his slap. He did seem pleased that her mood had lightened. His had, too, but he quickly became serious again.

"Do you trust me enough to proceed with this scene?"

"Yes, Sir."

"I'd like to try the blindfold once more, but if you can't take it, you have your safeword."

Her heart pounded. "Do I have to be blindfolded?"

He nodded. "I think it will help with the scene. Would you allow me to blindfold you?"

Only Damián. She was safe.

She took a deep breath. "Yes, Sir. I think so."

He held up the mask again. "Ready?"

The last thing she saw before he placed the mask over her eyes again was his smile, which gave her strength. She could do this with Damián here beside her.

He pressed a kiss on her cheek and whispered, "I'm proud of you, *savita.*" His praise caused an odd sense of warmth to spread throughout her chest.

Darkness.

"Breathe, Savi."

She did.

"That's my brave girl."

Damián. Only Damián. No one else. He will never hurt me.

His hand stroked her arms and sides in long, tender touches and the fear receded a bit more.

Damián won't let anything harm me. Damián will protect me.

He reached up and removed the mask again. She blinked and met his gaze, confused. He smiled at her.

"You did well, *savita*. I wanted to test you to see if you would let me blindfold you again, even though you were afraid. You're very brave."

She'd pleased him, which made her very content within herself. She could do this, with Damián's patient guidance. Savi met his smoldering gaze and something unfamiliar stirred inside her. She glanced down. "Thank you, Sir."

"I'm putting blindfolds on your list of hard limits for now, though, until we can work on it more."

"Thank you, Sir."

"It actually will be helpful to me to see your eyes. They're the most expressive part of your body and can help me gauge where you are. So you'll keep them open and you'll keep your eyes—your focus—on me. *¿Comprendes?*"

"Yes, Sir."

After another foray into his bag, he held a tall, leather collar in front of her with D-rings and studs on either side as well as in the front. "This is a posture collar, an alternative to using a blindfold in this scene. With this, you will keep your focus straight ahead and on me, and it will minimize any reflexive responses."

Reflexes? What was he planning to do?

After placing the sheepskin-lined collar around her neck, a kinky neck brace of sorts, he hooked the rings on either side of her neck to chains already attached to the cross. Her chin rested on a tiny shelf in front, her head locked firmly in place. She tried to bend and turn her head but couldn't move anything except her eyes. She could see straight in front of her but couldn't see below her nose and the tops of her cheeks.

Damián picked up his duffel bag and moved it behind her. She heard the clatter of lightweight pieces of wood. He came back around to stand in front of her and molded his warm body against her. She felt his erection press against her belly, sending a wave of panic clawing at her chest. He said this wouldn't be about sex. She tried to move her hips away from him but couldn't budge in the restraints. *Breathe.*

"Shhhh. I'm a man, Savi. Touching a beautiful woman excites me, but I'm not going to act on those urges. You're safe with me."

Odd as it seemed, with her in restraints and totally helpless, she did feel safe with him. He'd never done anything to betray her trust. As she relaxed again, his warm, gentle hand stroked the bare skin above and below the waist belt in long circles, calming her after a time.

Still so numb, which frustrated her. She didn't want to be numb anymore.

Anxious to get the scene started, she willed herself to relax. Warm lips pressed against her cheek. His goatee should have tickled her, but—nothing.

Numb.

Savi groaned.

"Breathe, *savita*. You're doing great." His warm breath on her ear caused her to open her eyes. Inhaling deeply, she felt something small and hard in his hand pressing against her abdomen. She tried to look down to see what it was, but remembered the collar wouldn't give her that much leeway. Then he removed all doubt as he raised it above her breasts, and she saw he held a wooden spring clothespin. Images of him using it to clamp what would be very sensitive parts on the bodies of most people crossed her mind, but would she even feel it? He'd promised not to play with her genitals, but she hadn't put other sensitive places off-limits, like her nipples. She'd heard the clattering of more than one clothespin in his bag of toys. What did he plan to do with all of them?

With his other hand, he gathered a pinch of skin at her side, near her breast, and squeezed the flesh.

Pinch.

She gasped. While still numb, the clothespin had surprised her. She didn't like surprises.

"Here comes another little pinch." She didn't know where he would attach the next clothespin until he pinched the skin on the opposite side, in about the same place. He fastened the wooden pin to her skin. Again, pressure, but no real pain. She felt her skin warming where the clothespins pinched her. He stepped away, and she grew cold in the absence of the body heat that had provided so much warmth.

"How are you doing, *mi sueño*?"

"Fine...Sir."

He shook his head and chuckled.

"Now, I am going to continue more rapidly so we can move further into the scene. All you need to do is breathe. In...and out." She heard the rattle of more clothespins and supposed he was stocking up.

For the next several minutes, he continued to pinch the clothespins at regular intervals down her sides, alternating from one side to the other, and restocking again when he ran out. He must have applied a couple dozen of them by the time he stopped above each of her hips, but he wasn't finished yet. The next one was attached to the underside of her arm. She hissed. That one broke through the numbness a little bit, probably because she'd expected him to continue working down her body. He did the same on the other side, but she anticipated that one and shut down her pain reflex.

"Savi. Stay with me. You don't have permission to zone out."

She remembered the goal here was for her to *feel* something, but her old habit had helped her survive for so long that the response was automatic now.

"Focus only on your breathing, *savita*."

Easy for him to say. He wasn't under attack from so many fronts at once. Again, she forced her attention back to the task at hand.

In...out.

Damián left her side again, and she almost gave in to the fear. As she made herself breathe in a very regulated manner, the way she'd been taught to work through the contractions as she'd prepared for Mari's birth, she regained her discipline. Focusing her mind on each individual breath she drew and released helped calm her.

In…out.

Damián stood behind the cross and pressed his hands into the clothespins on her sides. They must be digging into her flesh, but she still felt nothing too terribly uncomfortable. Numbness and pressure.

"Savi, when it's time, I'm going to remove the clothespins one at a time. Immediately after each one is removed, I want you to attach a memory associated with a negative emotion—fear, anger, rage. You can scream, cry, swear, or do whatever it takes to release that memory and feel that emotion, but you need to do it aloud and immediately."

Savi's mouth grew dry. She shook her head. "No, I don't want to think about those things, much less speak them."

Damián came around her and stood before her, demanding that she meet his gaze without saying a word. "You need to let those memories go, so they'll no longer control or hurt you. As long as you hold them back, they hold *you* back. Even though you aren't consciously thinking about them now, they have held you hostage your entire adult life, possibly most of your childhood, too."

"I've repressed much of my childhood."

"Then those will be some of the last memories you'll recall during this scene. It will take them longer to surface. But you will release even the most painful of them."

She groaned. He seemed so certain. She didn't think she could remember them, not after all these years.

"Can I just think them? Don't make me say those horrible things out loud, Sir."

Savi didn't want him to know who she was, what she had been. She'd fought hard to hide that part of herself for years.

He reached out and stroked her cheek. "Speaking them is the best way to lessen their power over you. Otherwise, this will just be an exercise in pain for pain's sake. No value. No learning. No healing."

"But I don't feel pain. I don't feel anything."

Damián chuckled and patted her cheek before withdrawing his hand, leaving her face cold. "Oh, you'll definitely feel something before I'm finished, especially as the last pins are removed. The longer they pinch off the blood supply to your skin, the more you'll feel."

He truly expected her to feel something. He would be terribly unhappy with her when she didn't react at all. For some reason, the thought of disappointing him bothered her almost as much as remembering those events from her past.

"Be my brave girl?"

"I'm not brave. I'm afraid of everything."

"Bullshit. You aren't afraid of me, are you?"

"You haven't hurt me, Sir. Not yet. Please don't ask this of me."

He placed a kiss on her numb cheek and whispered in her ear, "Savi, do you trust me to know what you need? To know what's best to help you?"

I think so.

Yes.

No!

She groaned again in frustration. How could he demand so much so soon? She'd expected him to start slowly, not force her to remember those horrors, much less speak of them. She'd relegated the most traumatic of those memories to the recesses of her mind long ago, right where she wanted them to stay.

"Trust me, Savi?"

If she didn't try this, she'd always wonder if it might have helped. She *needed* to try this. She nodded.

"I need to hear you say the words."

"I…trust you, Damián…Sir."

"That's my girl."

He pressed his lips against hers briefly. Her eyes stung. She wanted to feel his lips, but…nothing.

His girl. She wasn't his girl, his dream, his anything. Why was it that, when he spoke of her like that, some broken, damaged piece of her wished she could be his? Realizing a relationship with Damián could never happen left her feeling surprisingly sad.

"I have restrained your arms, head, waist, and legs, *savita*, so that you won't be able to move. It's critical that you remain as still as possible so that I don't miss."

Miss what? What had *she* missed?

"You don't have to worry about doing anything but attaching a memory to each pin as I remove it. *¿Comprendes?*"

"Yes, Sir."

Her heart pounded, but he brushed his lips across her ear. "I'm so proud of you."

That unfamiliar warmth spread through her again.

"Now, breathe for me, *savita*."

In…out.

He stepped away, moving behind her. As the time stretched out without contact, she felt her body craving his touch again. More time passed. Silence. Fear surged to the surface. Where had he gone? Her eyes burned, and she blinked them to ease away the sting.

He'd left her once before. Memories of his abandoning her at her father's house surfaced, but she tamped them down. He hadn't known what he'd delivered her to, what was happening in that perfect-looking mansion.

He wouldn't abandon her here. He'd stayed with her all night long in that hotel room, while she'd slept and recovered from her ordeal with the sadists.

Silence.

As the walls began to close in, Savi drew a ragged breath. "Sir? Are you still there?"

Seconds later, he stood in front of her and she stared into his warm brown eyes. He placed his hands on the sides of her face, and she nearly hyperventilated as she refilled her lungs in relief.

"Slow, deep breaths, Savi."

She smiled, almost giddy. "Yes, Sir." She'd been ridiculous to think he'd leave her alone again. Why had she assumed the worst about him?

Because people in the past often had let her down.

He brushed his thumbs across her cheeks. "I will never leave a sub or bottom alone and in restraints. We might negotiate a mindfuck—a scene where you have the illusion something is happening that isn't quite what's happening—where I might make you *think* you're alone." He placed yet another soft kiss on her cheek, then pulled back. "Look at me, Savi." She raised her gaze, staring into his deep, fathomless brown eyes.

"There will be times when I want you to spend time in your head, like now. I want you to be thinking about some of the scenes you will release for me soon. Don't think for a second that I might leave you alone, though. Okay?"

Part of her wished he meant he'd stay with her forever, but she pushed that impossible dream aside. No one could ever love someone so broken. He just meant he wouldn't leave her during a scene.

"Thank you, Sir."

His lips brushed her forehead. Tingling. She'd actually felt something! Perhaps because she hadn't anticipated it. Maybe if she let her guard down more, gave herself permission to feel something, this scene actually could do some good.

He stepped away from her and turned to give her the once over. Savi pictured herself as Damián must see her, naked, arms and legs spread wide, exposed. She hadn't placed herself in such a vulnerable position with a man since she'd regained control of her life and body after escaping her father and Lyle.

He uncoiled his bullwhip from his beltloop. *His bullwhip?* When had he put that on?

Her heart beat rapidly.

Crack!

Savi jumped, much as she'd done when she'd first heard him crack the whip last night. Well, given how tightly he'd restrained her, she barely moved. But her heart pounded in her ears. The sound of the whip popping in the air brought her senses to full alert.

Damián came to stand in front of her and threaded the whip between the skin of her back and the cross. He warmed her with his body's heat and pulled the whip from side to side against her back, heating her skin with the friction of the warm leather.

"The whip is going to free you, Savi. I don't want you to fear it. I want you to embrace it as it is embracing you right now."

He made this implement of pain and torture sound like a lover. The slow, gentle movement of the whip in Damián's hands, the texture of the leather against her skin brought back memories of their time in their cave. The leather continued to caress her skin, back and forth. No pain. Just a steady pressure as a fire was stoked beneath her skin. Her knees grew weak. She'd have been lying in a puddle at his feet if not for the arm and waist restraints.

He pressed his body against hers and placed a kiss behind her ear. What would it have felt like if she weren't so numb? She didn't really want to know. The whip continued to slide against her skin in slow, sensual motions, then slipped away silently as he stepped back. Damián's body heat receded as well.

His expression grew even more serious. He wasn't angry or punitive, like her father had been when he'd used a whip on her. He just appeared to be concentrating, getting in the zone. He looked down at the whip, checking the handle much like a tennis player adjusts the webbing in a racket, then simply stared at the braided handle as he took several deep breaths. He planted his feet apart, stared up at her again, and nailed her with his gaze.

"Prepare yourself, Savi." His voice dropped a full octave, his words clipped, precise.

Prepare? How was she supposed to prepare herself for a whip?

"Have your first negative memory ready to speak and release immediately after the whip removes the clothespin. I want you to let go of that memory before the tail recedes."

He was going to remove them with the whip? "No, wait!" Her body grew tense. He'd cut her to ribbons.

Crack!

She jumped again as the sound of the whip split the air, but he hadn't struck her. The man was messing with her head.

"Collect the first memories you want to release. The faster you spit them out, the quicker the pins will be removed."

Well, it was good to know she controlled that aspect of the scene at least. If it hurt too much to release another memory, she'd just stop or slow down.

"The longer they continue to pinch your skin, the more intense the pain will be when they are removed, regardless of whether they're removed with the whip, or by my hand if you safeword."

Oh dear Lord. She needed to do this quickly then, regardless. But she wasn't going to safeword. She hoped not, anyway. She didn't want to disappoint Damián. She tried to think of some of the memories she could share, so she could rattle them off quickly.

"Just as the sting increases in intensity with each one, I want your memories to escalate in the level of power they hold over you. With the release of each one, you'll break another of the shackles that have held your mind and body captive for so long."

"Sir, I don't think I can rank them in order of their power."

He didn't get angry or upset, which relieved her. "Fair enough. Do your best, but releasing the less traumatic ones first will help you build up to the more debilitating ones. It is to your benefit to speak the memories as quickly as possible, release them, and then move on to the next one. Don't let the emotion of the event you're releasing overwhelm you and don't place yourself back in that dark place. Just get the memory out and move on. We'll talk about them more in aftercare."

Savi remembered Patti's aftercare with Victor. She wanted that closeness with someone, but the intimacy she'd witnessed between the other couple scared her spitless.

What had she gotten herself into? She now knew that the longer she waited, the worse it was going to get.

"Ready, Savi?"

Was she? She nodded automatically, then tried to focus on which memory to reveal. She didn't want to remember.

"Speak."

"Yes, Sir. I'm ready."

"Excellent. Prepare to release your first memory, Savi."

Would the whip hurt her? He wasn't going to strike her skin, just the clothespins. She wouldn't feel anything. So what was the point of this exercise again?

Pop!

The sound registered in her brain a second or two before she identified the pressure, followed by heat, just above her right hip. The clothespin snapped shut and clattered to the floor. The last pin he'd attached to her side became the first to be removed.

"Speak, Savi. Now."

In her surprise, her mind had gone blank. Quick! Which memory should she reveal? She thought of a safe one she'd shared with Damián before, on Christmas morning. "Father let Whiskers go outside. He knew my indoor cat would be killed or die, but he didn't care."

By the time the heat from the pinching of her skin had faded away, she immediately tried to think of the next memory. He told her not to dwell on each one.

Even though she hadn't felt pain, she knew it would be difficult for her to use her pain-coping mechanisms with so many unpredictable sensations and memories bombarding her.

"Prepare yourself."

Pop!

He didn't give her much time to think. The next pin came from the opposite side. She had to speak quickly. "My feet. The sadists in the penthouse beat the soles of my feet so badly. No one had ever done that to me before." Again, a safe memory. Damián had seen what had happened to her there.

Pop!

Without a verbal warning, the next pin was removed. He was alternating sides, moving up her body in the order those pins had been attached. Knowing the pattern helped her to prepare for the next one, but she liked it better when he gave her a verbal warning.

"Speak."

Think! "Those bastards took pictures of me when I was…spread open. I don't like to have anyone touch or look at me there, much less photograph me."

For the next few pins, she revealed more of the abuse that had occurred in her father's hotel. How many more pins were there? How long could she continue to spoon feed Damián more memories of that day, without revealing the ones that held more of an emotional hold over her?

"Let's move to an earlier memory. Tell me about an abusive scene with your father or your handler from the hotel."

God, he was on to her.

Pop!

Savi hissed, feeling the bite this time. He had changed from a predictable pattern, because this was one of the clothespins he'd attached under her arm. Anger boiled up inside her. *No!* She would not give in to that emotion, knowing it would only lead to a beating. It always did. She took several deep breaths and suppressed her anger, hoping this session would end soon. She couldn't reveal those darker memories. She heard footsteps and Damián moved to the left. Beads of sweat sprang up along her hairline.

Thwack!

The whip struck again, only this time the tail wrapped around the back of the cross and thudded against her right hip. A half-second later, she felt a stinging pain bloom in the side of her left butt cheek where the tip of the whip had struck her skin. "Ow! There weren't even any pins there!"

"You didn't give up a memory fast enough with that last one. There are consequences to keeping those memories inside, *savita*—and I'm not talking about the sting of the whip on your hot little ass, either. Don't hesitate the next time."

He returned to his original position, and she watched him draw the whip back and let it sail toward her. Think!

Pop!

Another pin was released, this one near her left breast, stinging more than the one on the other side had earlier. He was right. The longer the clothespins remained, the more pain she felt.

Hurry. Think.
Filthy whore.
No!
You wanted it!
Nooo! I didn't!
Thwack!

Another sting to her butt cheek. The raw emotion made her throat burn, closing off her words, but she fought to get them out. "Maman left me alone with him! She didn't want me anymore!" Earlier, she'd revealed to Damián that her mother had left her; she hadn't shared her feelings of rejection.

She tried not to think about that time in her life. The one person she should have been able to trust above all others—her mother—had walked away without a backward glance. No goodbye. No communication to explain why she'd left. The feeling of abandonment remained with Savi to this day.

Pop!

Damián continued to pick off the pins in random order. He removed two more pins as she spoke of lesser hurts from the past and fought to regain control quickly in between. She needed to pull back from those more horrific memories no one could discover—those memories that hurt as badly after she spoke them as they had before the pin was removed. This wasn't going to work at all.

Savi lost her train of thought, but she must have babbled something as the next pin was removed. Her attempts to suppress the darkest memories became harder and harder. The lesser memories would no longer come to the surface at her command, obliterated by the ones she didn't want to speak.

Thwack!

The whip thudded against her left hip, snaking across the crease at the juncture of her upper thigh and hip. The wrapping of the whip around her just made it sting all the more when the tip struck. She opened her eyes and realized he'd stepped closer to the cross, but to the side. She could only see him in her peripheral vision; she could no longer see the whip. Moisture wet her cheeks, whether from sweat or tears, she didn't know.

Savannah, stop being such a cry baby. It's very distracting.

A sob tore from her throat before she could stop it. "You're hurting me, Father! Get off me!" She struggled with her bonds, but she couldn't push her father off of her. She felt paralyzed.

"Savi, where are you?"

"My b-b-bed."

"Savi, this is Damián. Tell me where you are."

Firm, gentle hands stroked up and down her sides, and a warm body pressed against her chest. She opened her eyes. *Not Father. Damián*—and he wasn't on top of her at all. The touch of Damián's hands pulled her back to him.

She took a deep, cleansing breath and exhaled the negativity from the flashback. "I'm with you, Sir. In your club."

"That's my girl.

From the stroke of his hands, she knew the clothespins were gone from her sides. He soothed the skin where she'd been pinched by the last ones he'd removed. All that were left were the ones remaining on the undersides of her arms. His hands brushed against them, making the flesh burn and bringing her even more into the moment.

"I feel that. It hurts."

"Good."

He wiped the tears—yes, they were tears—away from her cheeks. "I'm so proud of you, *savita*."

Damián was proud of her. Her chest swelled with his praise.

He kissed her cheek. "Ready to continue?"

She nodded.

"Remember, answer verbally."

"Yes, Sir. I'm ready."

"What's your safeword?"

"Tamale, Sir."

He pressed a kiss against her cheek, then stepped back to where he had delivered the last blow. With the heat of his body gone, her nipples grew erect. She felt that, too, and willed her body not to respond to him in a sexual way.

Pop!

The sting of the pin being removed from the underside of her right arm registered as sharp, but not as sharp as his gaze on her erect nipples. He could see her body's blatant sexual response.

Filthy whore.

Thwack!

The tip of the whip came down again on her butt cheek, and she jerked against the restraints that held her tight. She needed to give up another memory.

"I'm a filthy whore!" *Oh, God, no!* It was too late to call back the words once they'd been spoken. She hadn't meant to reveal that to him, but the words had been at the forefront of her mind. Damián wouldn't want to touch her now that he knew what she was. A sob tore from her throat. She didn't want the whip to strike her skin again. That hurt much worse than removing the pins.

Then she realized she had felt the pain. She wasn't numb any longer!

Pop!

The pin pinching the underside of her right arm was removed, and pain shot through her body as if the whip had lashed her skin again.

"Lyle chained me to my father's desk, face down."

Pop!

"My father pressed his weight on my back. I couldn't move. I couldn't get away. I couldn't breathe. Oh, God, no!"

Burning. Intense, searing pain.

Wracking sobs tore from her throat as she screamed, "Tamale! No more! Stop!"

"Shhh. I have you, *savita*."

She felt the heat from Damián's body. In quick succession, he removed the last two pins, and she screamed at the pain as his hands rubbed the sore spots. "I'm just helping to get the blood back to those spots. It'll help the pain recede faster."

She'd almost made it. Only two more to go. She'd failed him.

"I'm sorry, Sir." She gasped for a breath on another sob.

"I'm so proud of you for allowing yourself to feel something again, Savi. I can tell you felt the sting of some of those—and you released some long pent-up memories."

Damián stood in front of her but her eyesight was blurry from her tears—the first ones she'd let fall in so many years.

She tried to turn away, to hide them, but the collar wouldn't allow her to hide from him. Confused, she blinked them away and focused on his warm, chocolate-brown eyes.

He smiled. "You were so strong for me. So brave." He removed the chains holding the collar to the cross and removed it from her.

A sob caught in her throat. She needed to stop crying. She didn't want to make him angry. Father beat her harder if she cried.

He held her face and she focused on his eyes. "Let it out, *bebé*. Don't cage your tears. I think it's beautiful that you've let out some of those emotions this way."

Damián really wanted her to cry? Good thing, because she was unable to contain the sobs any longer.

He unbuckled the waist belt before he knelt to release her ankles from the cuffs and the belts from her thighs. He stood and tears continued to stream down her cheeks as he released the wrist cuffs. Damián swept her into his arms with a grunt and carried her to the leather loveseat in the corner of the room. He returned her to her feet and quickly wrapped her in a soft blanket. Once he sat down, he gazed up at her.

Damián held his hand up to her. "Come. Sit on my lap, *mi sueño*."

Memories bubbled up of being forced to sit in her father's lap and endure his hands in places she didn't like being touched. She needed to get out of here.

No. This is Damián. He won't hurt me.

Chapter Fourteen

Damián saw the hesitation. He had hoped they'd progressed past her fear of him a bit, but apparently not.

He reached up and pulled her hand until she plopped into his lap, then wrapped his arms around her, holding her tightly against him.

"Don't touch me. Promise you won't touch me there."

"I'm not going to touch your pussy, if that's what you mean, Savi. You need to be specific, though. I can't read your mind."

He heard her sniffle—sweetest sound he'd heard in a long time. They'd made some progress there, at least. Long way to go, though. He'd worked with a lot of subs with abuse issues but never one as disconnected from her body as Savi.

Savannah.

Would she ever be able to reclaim Savannah? He hoped so. He'd never been able to forget that sweet girl. He didn't get the impression she had a split personality, just that she wanted to keep the painful Savannah memories buried and to try and make a life for her and Marisol that wasn't touched by the horrors of the past.

A sob tore from her and he held her even tighter. "Shhh. I'm here, *bebé*. Just let it out. You're safe."

She hiccupped and released more tears. He'd done that for her. A feeling of accomplishment swept over him, like the rush he got hitting his target as a sniper or completing a long, hard mission in which he'd had to struggle. She'd kept so many things locked inside for years, maybe even decades. He was pissed that any *one* of the memories she'd released to him had happened to her, much less all of them. Maybe they could make more progress today in releasing some of the emotional blocks shutting her down.

Time to work through more healing. He handed her a bottle of water. "Drink this—slowly." He waited about ten minutes, until she'd finished the bottle, and set it on the seat beside him.

"Now, what are you feeling, Savi?"

"Fine, Sir."

Maybe he needed to work on her listening skills first. "I didn't ask *how*, but *what*. Let's start by you describing what you're feeling—and if you say fine again, I'll turn you over my knee until you stop feeling fine."

Her hand touched his Harley vest. "Okay, um, maybe fine isn't quite the right word, Sir."

When she didn't elaborate, he prompted, "What *is* the right word, Savi?"

She paused a long time before giving him in a near whisper the response he sought. "Raw. Vulnerable."

"Ah, two words, actually—and just what I would expect you to be feeling right now."

She shivered, and he stroked her arm through the blanket.

"Damián, I don't know how to stop the memories or the tears now that they've started."

"You kept the lid on that bottle for a long time. A lot of pressure built up over the years. No way can you put the lid back on, especially not while it's exploding and spewing out those memories."

His words unleashed more tears. "That's my girl. Don't hold anything back." She sobbed against his chest, and he tightened his hold on her. After the tears had slowed again, she sat up and pulled a couple of tissues from the box next to them to wipe her eyes. She yanked another tissue from the box to blow her nose. No sooner had she returned her head to his chest than the tears began again.

"Oh, God, Sir. Why won't they stop bombarding me like this?" She hiccoughed between her next words. "I feel like…the tears…the flood of memories…will never end."

Damián knew what she was going through. When he had finally let the memories of the grenade explosion on the rooftop in Fallujah invade his waking thoughts, he hadn't been able to process the feelings of failure and loss. In a flash, mere seconds, Miller had bled out on top of him. Damián had been dismembered. Marc had been injured trying to save Damián's life. If Dad hadn't found Marc in time, no telling if another life would have been lost. Even Grant, who hadn't been injured physically, had been wounded psychologically by what she'd witnessed up there.

Damián had kept a lid on those memories as long as he could. They'd only seeped out in nightmares, soon dismissed after he awoke. But he'd merely put them out of his mind in the months before being forced to talk with Dad and the shrinks about them. No slow buildup over years like Savi's repressed memories but equally painful to deal with when they came out.

How could he help her the way his friends, Marc and Dad, had helped him?

"Savi, sometimes life bites us in the ass. It's not our fault. There's probably nothing either of us could have done to alter what happened in the past." That had been the hardest thing for Damián to accept. The helplessness. The lack of control. Something small but powerful had changed his life—and the lives of several Marines and their families—forever.

Small but powerful. Not unlike the woman sitting on his lap right now. She brought out his protective instincts.

"It does my heart good to hold you like this, *bebé*." He rested his chin on the top of her head. "Now, if the memories are still surfacing, tell me about another one you need to release. Or would you rather we talk first about some of the ones you already released?"

"Have I really released them just by saying them out loud? I still can't get them out of my head."

"The goal isn't to erase them from your memory, but you fought long and hard to keep some of those things buried so no one else could see or hear them. When they were secrets, they had a lot more power than they do now that they're out in the open."

Her body grew rigid. She shook her head. "Can you just keep holding me like this? Do we have to talk about it?"

I'll hold you like this forever if you'll let me, mi sueño. He couldn't let her off the hook that easily, though. He might not be as blunt as Dad was, but he couldn't back down now.

"Talking about them is the next step to removing their hold over you. Tell me why you think you're a filthy whore."

She pushed away from him and, if his arms weren't holding her so tightly, she'd probably have escaped from his lap before he could stop her.

"Let me go! I don't want to talk about this anymore." She drew a shaky breath. "It's embarrassing enough already. I can't believe I've admitted those things to someone…to you."

He caged her chin and turned her head to face him. Her tears had stopped, leaving her eyes red rimmed and puffy. He wished he had a cool, wet cloth to soothe them, but he wasn't ready to turn her loose yet. She needed to face this if she would ever be able to let it go. "Savi, I need to understand why you think you're those things so we can work on redirecting those negative messages."

A pained expression passed over her eyes, and she whispered, "I'm not who you think I am."

"Tell me who you think you are, Savi."

She pulled away from his hand and avoided his gaze. "The therapist who tried to help wounded children but got fired anyway. The woman who tried to be a good mother to her daughter but brought evil into their lives. The woman who normally keeps it all together but is failing miserably lately." She turned toward him again. "In truth, I never held anything together—I just masked it well or buried it. I'm a total fake."

He knew all about that fear of being discovered a fake or less than what people expected him to be, but she was all he'd ever wanted in a partner. She'd always been fucking perfection to him.

"Let's take those self-perceptions one at a time, Savi. First, I've seen you with Teresa. You're a professional, and you're good at what you do. You helped Teresa function again after the rape. You may not be her therapist now, through no fault of your own, but I'm grateful you were there when she needed you most."

Tears filled her eyes again. "I abandoned her and the others."

"You had to. Your highest priority had to be to protect Marisol and yourself from danger, which is how I know you're a damned great mother, too. You gave up everything to protect our daughter."

"I didn't do very well at that, either. I just ran to you for help."

"Asking for help doesn't make you weak or some kind of failure." He brushed a tear away from her cheek and pulled her against his chest again. "In the Marines, we learn to depend on every person in our unit. Each one has a skill he—and sometimes she—brings to the unit that can make or break a mission. We fight as a team, and we leave no one behind." *Not if we can help it, anyway.*

"Savi, you sought out someone you knew had expertise at combat because you thought you might have to fight the bastards off. That's fucking smart, if you ask me. You wound up getting a whole unit when you came to me. I'm glad you did."

"I guess I did make the right decision that time." She paused before admitting, "I don't always make such good choices."

"Like when?"

"Cutting myself, for one."

"You haven't done that in a long time. You were trying to stop the pain the only way you knew how." Tears splashed onto the blanket.

"But I came so close last week to reverting to my self-injurious behavior."

"Close, but you didn't injure yourself. You stopped even before I came in and found you, Savi. And you've since taken a big step to allow me to show you some new coping mechanisms to help in the future when you're being bombarded by a lot of confusing emotions."

"Why can't I make you see what I truly am—a screwed-up fraud? No matter how you spin it, I'm bad news for anyone who comes near me. I'm not Mother Teresa or Super Woman or perfect at anything—except maybe being a magnet for sadists."

He chuckled. "*Chica*, I know one sadist who sure is happy you're his magnet."

She slapped his vest playfully and giggled. How long had it been since she'd giggled? *Score*. "Well, Sir, in your case, I think you were the magnet."

"And you the steel. You're one tough lady." He still needed to have her hear some more truths about herself. Of course, she wasn't going to take his word for them. Maybe over time, she'd come to see herself the way others did. He lowered his arm until she was lying back in its crook staring up at him. With the tip of his finger, he traced an invisible line along her cheek and jaw.

"Marisol and I think you're the perfect *mamá*. Hell, you had to be the daddy, too, for almost her first eight years. There's nothing easy about that. It took a lot of work and sacrifice, but you did it."

"I'm sorry I didn't try harder to find you when she was little. I just couldn't trust anyone around her. Now it seems I'm turning her over to people all the time to watch her."

"Trust takes a long time to build, but you have good instincts. I've known these guys longer than you have, and I'd trust them with my life."

"She seems so happy here. I think maybe I was smothering her."

"You were protecting her the only way you knew how. But you've come a long way toward letting her become more independent since you've been here."

"It's not easy."

"Nobody ever said being a parent would be."

They sat in silence a few moments, letting the words sink, he hoped. "I know a lot of people who would disagree with the view you have of yourself. I just want you to stop hiding behind those thoughts and see yourself the way I see you."

"I've hidden my true self from you and Mari."

"I doubt that." If only she knew how much Marisol adored her mommy, as did he.

"Now, tell me about Lyle." She'd mentioned Lyle when he'd removed one of the clothespins.

She drew a shaky breath and snuggled closer to him. He wrapped her tighter in his arms. "He was the man you saw with me in the hotel restaurant. My father's business partner, although I think his main job was to be my handler."

He had to ask. "What did Lyle do to you?"

Her entire body tensed.

"Breathe, Savi."

She took her own sweet time drawing another breath. "He did whatever my father told him to do. He enjoyed hurting me, hearing me scream. I tried not to…but most of the time, he succeeded."

"It's pretty common for someone being abused to fight to keep from giving the abuser what they want. Withholding screams as long as you could gave you a measure of control. Your inability to express tears or to cry are probably remnants of a similar coping mechanism."

He gave her a moment to think about that. "Tell me why you think you're a whore." Her chin quivered against his chest. He pulled her tightly against him again, brushing her hair with his fingers. "Talk to me, *bebé*. Let it out."

"I heard it over and over."

"Why are you letting some *malditos bastardos* determine who you are?"

Her hand played idly with his leather vest. "Because those fucking bastards were right. I did whatever they wanted me to do, including meeting with clients and letting them use me like a…whore. You saw what I did in the penthouse."

He had to admit there was a brief time in the hotel restaurant when he'd assumed she was getting paid for her services, a willing participant. The thought was ludicrous, he discovered, once he'd found her being tortured in the penthouse suite when he'd made the rounds to collect room-service trays. By the time he'd untied her and realized how much control Lyle had over her, he knew there was nothing consensual about that scene. Apparently, her father controlled both Savi and Lyle—but Lyle could have walked away. Savi couldn't. Big difference.

"That was against your will, not a choice."

"But sometimes I even enjoyed it."

"Define enjoyed."

She paused so long he didn't think she'd respond. After a few minutes, when he wondered if she'd fallen asleep or zoned out, she said in a small voice, "I got...excited. I...even came sometimes. The sadists you ran from my room probably would have made me come, as well, if you hadn't intervened. Other clients called me the best pain slut they'd ever had. I got off on the pain."

Damn all those fucking bastards to hell for what they'd done to her. Her father and Lyle were the biggest shitheads. If not for them, she wouldn't have been put through any of this. He anticipated the day he came into contact with them again, so he could rip their fucking heads off and shit down their necks. He wasn't going to wait for them to come to him. He wanted to exact revenge—no, justice—for Savi.

Savi tensed and would have pulled away, but he held her tighter. He needed to reassure her.

"*Savita*, they controlled your body and forced you to respond sexually. Hell, anyone can force an orgasm on someone. Big fucking, macho deal. Coming doesn't mean you asked for it or even wanted it. It's a physical response. A natural release. Nothing more. Coming doesn't make you a whore, *bebé*."

"But I *am* a pain slut. I never came without severe pain being inflicted first."

"Just how many times have you tried to come since then?"

She shook her head, whether to evade the question or to give her answer, he wasn't sure.

"Savi, in my community, it's considered a good thing to be someone's slut."

She sat up and pulled away, letting the blanket slip down off her shoulders. She stared at him as if he'd just arrived from Mars. "You've got to be kidding. How could any woman want to be called a slut?"

"It's a term of endearment—and a pain slut is just another term we use for masochist." He grinned. "Sounds a lot sexier and less psycho-babble." He remembered he was talking to a shrink when she scowled at him for the dig at her profession. "Nothing wrong with needing pain to get off. You'll make some sadist very happy someday." He tapped her nose but regretted that she could never be his pain slut.

Damián knew he wasn't the right man for her. He wasn't a natural-born sadist. He might be able to deliver what she needed, but he didn't get off sexually watching her in pain. At one point during the scene with the clothespins, his body had shut down sexually. He never got turned-on during a scene with Patti or any of the other bottoms at the club. Oh, he'd had sex with some of them, but that had more to do with an attraction to their bodies. A physical release.

But he had to admit to getting a hard-on at one point in today's scene. Not because of the pain he was delivering, as far as he knew. Hell, it was pretty mild compared to what he could dish out, but she wasn't ready to take anything harder yet. Besides, what man wouldn't get turned-on seeing such a beautiful woman naked and restrained for him to touch? Hell, even without the restraints—

"Sluts are dirty."

She pulled him from where his thoughts had strayed. *Focus, man.*

"I'll never be anyone's slut ever again. Not even yours, Damián."

"No, not mine, *bebé*. On that we can agree." She deserved someone much better.

Before this conversation took a turn in a direction he wasn't prepared to go, he thought it might be best to continue to explore her negative connotation of the word slut. "Were there consequences if you disobeyed the men?"

"God, yes. I would be severely beaten, at the very least." She drew a ragged breath, but her tears seemed to have stopped.

Suddenly, he needed to know something he'd wondered about ever since he'd learned what her father did to her. "What happened that night I left you at your house in Rancho Santa Fe?"

He waited, but she didn't speak. Her stillness worried him.

"Breathe, Savi."

She did but remained silent.

"Tell me, Savi. This scene with me isn't going to be over until you tell me that."

She sighed. "They chained me to the desk and beat me."

She said the words as if recounting something mundane, ordinary. Damián felt as if his gut had just been ripped from his body. The thought of her being tortured and beaten after he'd delivered her into the hands of the bastards made him sick.

"I'm so sorry, *savita*. If I'd known…"

She pulled away and looked him in the eyes. "None of what they did was your fault. You didn't know. I couldn't tell you. They threatened to sell me to a street pimp if I ever told anyone."

Fucking bastards.

She buried her face in his chest, and he continued to stroke her hair. "Shhhh, *bebé*. They can't hurt you anymore."

"I used to think being a street whore was so much worse than being a penthouse one, but it really didn't make any difference. A whore is a whore."

"Most of those street whores are controlled by their pimps and uncontrollable circumstances, just as you were by your father and Lyle. Add drug addiction to the mix, too. I doubt very many would choose that lifestyle willingly, if they had any other options."

"But I did."

"Why do you say that?"

She drew in a sharp breath, clearly hit with another incoming memory. He continued to hold her and stroke her silky hair, giving her a minute to process it before demanding that she tell him. He wanted to give her a chance to volunteer the information.

Finally, in a whisper, she said, "When I turned eighteen…" she paused and took a deep breath. "…Father promised to stop having sex with me if I would submit to his clients' fetishes in scenes like the one you interrupted in the hotel. He didn't allow them to have sex with me; other than that they had full use of my body without penetration. I chose to surrender to them because I didn't want my father to do that to me ever again."

Fucking asshole.

"It's weird, Sir. Until just now, I thought he'd stopped having sex with me because he didn't want me for…that, anymore. But he actually gave me the choice to make."

Some fucking choice. The pedophile probably didn't get off on having sex with someone of legal age. He'd have probably stopped having sex with her soon anyway. Instead, he needed to further degrade her by coercing her into becoming a sex slave.

"*Savita*, what if you'd chosen neither of those options?"

"That wasn't an option. Him or them. That was it."

"Exactly. You were coerced. You knew the consequence of refusing would be being turned over to a street pimp. You also didn't want your father raping you again." She stiffened at the mention of rape. "You *had* no choice." He brushed a strand of hair over her ear, and she shivered. "The bastard was fucking with your head, *bebé*. Trying to make you think you willingly chose to be either his whore or a pain sl…a *masochist* for his clients." He wouldn't sully the word slut to describe what they had done to her.

"I didn't have a choice." It wasn't a question. Good for her.

"Hell, no, you didn't."

This time she did pull away, and the defiance in her expression was a welcome sign. *That's right, Savi. Fight back.*

"I didn't choose to be a sex slave. My life wasn't anything like Patti being Victor's willing service slave."

"Far from it. There was no loving, nurturing relationship with those men in your past. Nothing like what Patti and Victor share consensually. You were a brutalized victim."

The flash of anger in her eyes took him by surprise. "Don't call me a victim. I'm a survivor."

Score two.

He grinned. "That you are, *savita*. You're the strongest person I've ever known. To go through what you did, find a way out, protect our daughter, and make a life for both of you—I agree you most definitely are a survivor."

Savi smiled. Maybe there was going to be healing for her—at last.

* * *

The expression on Damián's face was priceless—surprise first, then pride. He was proud of her.

Savi didn't want this moment to end, and she laid her cheek against his chest again, wanting to prolong this time together. She loved aftercare. Watching Victor and Patti together, she'd found herself jealous of that special bond that they'd formed after such a painful, cathartic experience.

Something melted inside her heart when Damián pulled her closer. Safe. She hadn't felt treasured and protected like this for such a long time—almost forever. Maman used to hold her this way when she'd been sick or upset about school or something that scared her at night. That had been a very long time ago.

"I could get used to this."

"So could I, *bebé*."

She didn't realize she'd spoken out loud and wondered if she should even think about getting used to this kind of thing. But she wasn't going to worry about the future. She was just going to enjoy the moment. With Damián.

All too soon, the doubts assailed her once more. Nothing could ever come of a relationship with Damián, or any man for that matter. He'd eventually want a sexual relationship with her and that was out of the question. She could never let any man touch her that way again.

Adam had said BDSM was about discipline, not sex. Maybe Damián would be willing to be her Top—and her friend. She'd like both. They would always share the raising of—

Mari! "Oh, my God! What time is it?"

"About 1430. Er, two-thirty. Why?"

She pushed herself upright and tried to get off his lap. She'd never forgotten her daughter before. What kind of mother was she? "I need to go pick up Mari at school."

"No, you don't. Karla and Dad are picking her up today." With him working at the shop and Savi in classes to prepare for whenever she'd be able to take the social-work licensing exam, Savi had agreed to add Karla and Adam to the emergency card at school, so they could fill in when Savi or Damián weren't available.

"Stop worrying. Marisol's wanted to ride in the Hummer forever. She thinks it'll be like what I rode in while in the Marines." He grinned. "Close enough for a civilian, anyway."

Savi blinked a couple of times. "When you plan a scene, you think of everything, don't you? Even childcare."

He grinned. "I'll admit to not doing most of the planning for this one. Other bottoms I've worked with have found this scene useful in the beginning, so I could just fall back on past history. Dad planned the childcare detail. He told me before he left us for lunch not to worry about it. He and Karla would get her."

The panic receded some but not the guilt. She'd never gone this many hours before without a thought about fulfilling her daughter's needs. Damián had totally taken over her mind, as well as her body. How could she have allowed that to happen?

He leaned over to the coffee table and picked up another bottle of water and handed it to her. She knew the drill. Stay hydrated. He'd been pushing water at her to help her adjust to the altitude since December but had told her BDSM scenes also led to dehydration. Double whammy. She drank it slowly, trying to think back over the scene and how he'd managed it.

"What are you thinking about, *bebé*?"

"Nothing."

"Savi." The warning tone in his voice told her she wasn't going to get away with evading the question.

"How did you do it?"

"Do what?"

"How did you take over my mind like that? You pushed everything out of my head, including the person most precious to me in all the world."

"Ah, that." He chuckled. "I didn't hypnotize or brainwash you or anything, if that's what you're thinking. I just got you to focus, made you think more about connecting to your body and the memories than to thoughts about other things. It's part of the discipline a sub learns. You have incredible focus, by the way. You'd make a great submissive."

She shook her head. "I can't submit to anyone—well, not long-term, anyway." Clearly, she'd submitted to him, though, much more of herself than she'd intended.

"Well, it's good practice for being a bottom, too. We'll keep working on it."

"No. I think I've had enough."

He grasped her upper arms and pushed her away from him. She looked down and realized the blanket had nearly fallen to her waist. When she reached to pull it up again, he took her chin and forced her to look into his eyes.

His mood changed quickly. Not angry, just very determined and serious. "Savi, we aren't finished yet. There is much more you need to deal with, if you'd only let down some of those barriers that keep you so closed off."

"Those *barriers*, as you call them, are my main line of defense. They've kept me from emotional turmoil for a very long time."

"How's that working for you?"

Ouch. He was right. Some of the walls she'd erected had affected her ability to feel when Mari hugged or kissed her. Tears stung her eyes. Closing herself off from her daughter wasn't what she wanted in her life.

If she had a choice anymore. The emotions and memories kept bubbling up, and it was getting harder and harder to tamp them back down into her box of secrets.

Today, Damián had forced her to face some memories that hadn't even attempted to come to the surface in a very long time, but what if she accidentally let something slip about her deepest shame? What if he…?

"I would never take advantage of you. You know that."

She nodded and pulled the blanket up to wrap herself in it again. "I…trust you."

"What are you hiding from me, Savi? What is it you're most afraid I will discover about you?"

Involuntarily, she clamped her legs tighter together, and his gaze went to her lap.

"Ah, the hardest limit of them all. Don't touch your pussy."

Her face grew flushed as he continued to stare at her down there. She squirmed on his lap and tried to get away, but he placed his hand at the back of her neck and held her still.

"Define pussy."

"My vagina."

"Anything else?"

She grew uncomfortable, but answered. "The labia." Most definitely the inside of her labia, where her father's brand had scarred her for life.

"How do you feel about my touching your mons, your clit?"

If he was expecting to elicit some kind of sexual response from her, he'd be disappointed.

"No, I don't want you to touch me there, either."

He grinned, which puzzled her. She'd just told him the whole area was off limits.

"Now, tell me what it is you're afraid will happen if I touch your pussy."

She couldn't speak but shook her head. The blood pounding in her ears made it difficult to hear his next words.

"I asked if you would trust me enough to remove that boulder from your path to healing."

"I trust you, Sir…but not that far."

He chuckled again. She thought he'd be angry at her for telling him no.

"You're a stubborn one. Whatever the secret is, it must be deep-seated. We'll work on it later."

His confidence that she would eventually let him touch her there made her all the more resolute that he wouldn't.

"Thank you for sharing some of your secrets with me today. I'll wait for another session to explore the depths of this one."

She should have known he wouldn't take no for an answer, even though she was confident he wouldn't force her to go beyond her limits against her will. She still had control of her hard limit.

But he had a way of turning her mind to mush. What if he broke down the barriers and got her to remove this hard limit from her list?

Savi shuddered.

No, she'd never be able to reveal her deepest shame to Damián. Never.

Chapter Fifteen

A week later, on a busy Friday night at the club, Damián led her into a new theme room—the medical room. She despised her annual gynecological checkups and didn't expect this exam or test or whatever he had in mind to be any more comfortable for her.

Breathe.

She tried to coach herself now when the panic started to claw at her throat.

"That's my girl." He stroked her bare back, and she relaxed even more. Damián seemed so completely tuned in to her every breath, her every mood, and many of her thoughts, whether they were in a formal scene or simply sitting together.

Savi couldn't take her gaze away from the sterile-looking exam table, complete with its paper covering. There was a cabinet and stand nearby displaying latex glove dispensers with three sizes of gloves, a container of cotton swabs, a new tube of lubricant, and a sink. The Doms at Masters at Arms had certainly made the room seem authentic. But she was relieved to see neither stirrups on the gyno table nor a speculum on the cabinet. She didn't want to be splayed open for Damián to see her shame.

Earlier, in the great room, Damián had told her to remove her blouse, but she still wore her jeans. She remembered the stares of several other Doms as she'd complied. Damián clearly was testing her level of trust, obedience, and discipline, all things he'd worked on in her training this past week. Apparently, she'd passed, with very little hesitation.

Showing her boobs didn't bother her. She'd breast-fed her daughter in public, not that she had totally revealed them then, but she'd probably flashed people a few times. No big deal with their insignificant size; no one would get excited looking at them.

But Damián's hot gaze had zeroed in on her bare chest with a look of appreciation—and lust. Her nipples grew erect again remembering the intensity of his gaze. He'd seen her body's response to his interest, but he hadn't commented on it or touched her, for which she was grateful.

Too late, she'd remembered the cuts on her arm and looked around hoping no one had noticed. Adam had seen them; his pity had mortified her. She didn't want anyone to feel sorry for her.

"Do you trust me, *savita*?"

Her focus returned to Damián and the medical room. She did trust him, more and more each day. He hadn't taken her beyond her hard limits, although he'd certainly discovered things that probably would have been high on her limit list if she'd known they existed.

Like exposing her body in public. Who would have thought he'd ask her to do that? He took great joy, it seemed, in shattering her inhibitions before she'd even had a chance to formulate in her head that they *were* inhibitions. Over the last week, he'd had a session with her every day, some in private and some, like today, a mix of public and private.

At least she hoped this part would be private. She looked toward the door and saw a curtained window. Would he open the curtains and allow club members to watch? She shuddered.

Some of the scenes this past week had been more silly than intense, like when he had restrained her on a St. Andrew's cross and fed her. The man seriously had an obsession about getting her to gain weight. But that scene and all of the others only served to deepen the level of trust growing toward him.

Not to mention that he made her melt a little more after each scene when he'd hold her in his lap, secure within his arms, and just make her feel cherished and safe. Sometimes they talked about the scene, but more often than not, they just cuddled.

She liked aftercare best of all.

"I asked you a direct question. Do you trust me?"

Why did he keep asking? What test did he plan to put her through next?

"Yes, Sir…I trust you more than any man I've known."

He patted her butt, which he did often now, as if claiming his territory, even when they weren't in a scene. "I'll take the qualifier, for now."

She smiled, feeling warmth spread throughout her body despite her nakedness. She'd discovered a source of strength inside herself since she'd been training with Damián. But whenever she told him she was afraid of everything, he always reminded her about her core strength and courage and how it had come to the fore many times over the years as she'd faced so many frightening and daunting situations.

Yes, she realized she'd been building on that strength all her life. She just hadn't acknowledged it or unleashed its maximum potential. But, as Damián continued to stretch her boundaries and encourage her to draw from that source deep within, he made her believe she was strong, that she could face anything.

She looked at the gynecological table again as he bent down and pulled out the step stool from inside the foot of the table. He stood and faced her.

"Give me your right hand."

When she hesitated, he scowled. With reluctance, she placed her smaller hand in his strong, warm one. When he squeezed reassuringly, she relaxed.

Damián ran two fingers inside each of the wrist cuffs he'd placed on her earlier. He'd already checked the fit. Maybe he was distracted. Or nervous. His nervousness made her a little more so, as well.

She'd become a bundle of nerves when he'd taken command of her in the great room. She'd barely gotten through half of what was becoming her drink—"Sex on the Beach." With each sip, their special day at the beach played out in great carnal detail in her head.

Occasionally, in brief snaps of time, she got the feeling she was Savannah, experiencing what Damián had done as he'd made love to her many times that day. She remembered his hands on her body, his tongue on her…

"How does that feel?"

She blinked, eventually realizing he was talking about the cuffs, not her… *Focus, Savi.*

"Still good, Sir."

"Maintain your focus. You will remain in the moment during this scene."

"Yes, Sir."

Damián was so serious. The air sizzled between them, alerting her that he had planned a play scene beyond the baby-step ones they'd done this past week. Until tonight, they'd only played in private, mostly because they'd had to make sure someone could watch Mari. Everyone they knew who could babysit was connected to the club's activities. But Angelina was back in town visiting Karla this weekend—avoiding Marc and the club, of course—so Angelina and Mari had gone over to Damián's apartment to "play in the kitchen," as they put it.

"Now, strip off the jeans."

Savi blinked. Once again, she'd strayed from the scene. So much for great focus. As she unbuttoned and unzipped the jeans, she recalled how Damián had explained discipline to her the other day. He'd drilled her about training her mind to stay in the moment but also wanted to keep her mind on the play scene at hand. Twice in the past few minutes she'd let herself stray from focusing on Damián. She needed to work harder at keeping discipline, keeping focus.

Savi wriggled out of the jeans. She'd noticed lately that her jeans were getting tighter. Damián and Adam both insisted that she eat more. At this rate, she'd need to move up to a bigger size if she wanted to be able to breathe and bend over.

She placed her hand on the table, crinkling the paper as she pulled one pants leg off, then the other. She hadn't worn panties. Damián had instructed her not to when he'd told her how to dress for this evening. Thank God he hadn't made her strip totally in the great room. But she hadn't noticed anyone else totally naked there, either. A few had worn skimpy fetish…

Focus.

"That's my girl."

He smiled and reached into the small duffel bag where he kept his "toys," as he called them. He pulled out several lengths of chain and two cuffs, longer and more narrow than wrist cuffs. They were too big for her arms. He motioned for her to get up on the table and she did so, turning to face him before she sat. He placed one of her hands in his and wrapped his other around her back, guiding her into the desired position on the table. The paper-covered vinyl was cold against her back, and her nipples puckered even more.

Without hesitation, he took one of the chains, pulled her arms above her head, and restrained her wrists to a point somewhere at that end of the table. She tried to move her hands but couldn't budge. Walking to the side of the table, he took one of the larger cuffs, unbuckled it, and wrapped it around her left thigh like a miniature belt. Taking another length of chain, he looped one end through the thigh cuff's D-ring and doubled the chain. He tugged on it until her leg raised into the air, bent at the knee; her foot dangled freely.

The cool air assaulted her privates as he threaded the chain through something metallic on the side of the gyno table. Savi's heart pounded as adrenaline pumped into her system.

Breathe.

Her lungs constricted, making it impossible to follow her own instruction. He walked around the table and strapped the other cuff onto her right thigh, applying a separate chain. When he began to raise her leg in a similar fashion, full-blown panic set in.

"Sir, permission to speak!" The words came out in a rush, without thought.

Damián's hand movements stopped, and he turned toward her face. He leaned closer, his hand firmly stroking her head from her temple to around the curl of her ear. "What is it, *savita*? Does something hurt, feel numb?"

She shook her head and cleared her throat. "You remember my hard limit, right?"

"I never forget a bottom's limits. Why do you ask?"

"Well, you're about to open my…open me up, and I wasn't sure if you remembered."

"I remember." He smiled. "Trust me, *querida*. I do not plan to touch your pussy…until you give me permission."

Until? That would never happen, but she didn't want this, either.

Savi's heart pounded. If he splayed her open like this, he'd be able to see what she'd hidden—what she wanted to remain hidden.

"Sir, I have a new limit!"

He frowned. "What limit would that be?"

"You can't look."

"I can't look at what?"

"My…" He insisted she call it by its vulgar name, but she was in enough trouble already for interrupting his scene, so she would just say it. "My…pussy."

He smiled. "I see. Well, this might present some challenges to the scene I have planned for you, *savita*." He thought a moment, as if solving a math problem, then grinned. "But a Top needs to be resourceful. Very well. I will not look, but that requires that I chain you to the table a little differently. Are you ready to proceed?"

She couldn't form the words and merely nodded.

Without further delay, he moved back to the head of the table and unchained her arms. After he released her right hand and laid it across her abdomen, he rechained the other above her head. Returning to the duffel bag, she heard more chains rattle as he pulled them free of the bag. He also took a bundle of soft-looking rope out and laid it on her chest.

When he didn't do anything further with her thigh, she relaxed a bit. Instead, he went back to the toy bag and pulled out more rope, as thin as macramé cord but softer than the scratchy rope holding up her planters.

"Normally, on this table, I would restrain you with the leather belt across your belly, but I want to minimize the amount of metal coming into contact with your body. I'm going to lace you instead."

"Lace?"

His glower told her she'd spoken when she wasn't supposed to. Still, what difference could it make if he used rope or something metallic? Unless...

Electricity!

No. Damián wouldn't use that vile wand-like thing on her. He'd have to know how terrifying it would be, the way the sadists had used it in the hotel penthouse. Something terrified her about that sound...

Sweat broke out on her forehead, but Damián didn't seem to notice her distress. He knotted the rope to several anchor points up and down each side of the table and soon he had the rope crisscrossed between her breasts and another rope across her abdomen. She tried to raise her torso and hips up but couldn't move.

"Deep breath, *querida*. I want to make sure it's not too tight."

When she didn't respond fast enough, he tweaked her nipple. She drew a shaky breath, and he smiled.

"That's my girl."

Her nipple engorged, causing heat to diffuse into her face. When he pulled her left thigh up and outward, spreading her open even farther, she tried to fight him by pushing her leg down.

He stopped, but her leg remained in the air, cradled by his hand behind her thigh, just above the knee. "What is it? Have I hurt you?"

Savi shook her head.

"What's going on then?"

That's what she wanted to know. "Please, Sir. Tell me what you're going to do."

"You need to trust me, *savita*."

She gave him a feeble nod. "I'm trying."

"Have I ever gone beyond your hard limits?"

"No. Thank you, Sir. But—why do I have to be on this kind of table?"

The only reason she could think of was to be splayed open. She shuddered.

"It's not for you to ask, but because I want you to remain calm at this point, I'll explain. I'm going to bring back some of those bad memories you released last week—from the time you were tortured in the penthouse."

She remembered having her legs raised, spread open, and restrained to the headboard—*ropes, quirt, electricity*. As much as she hated those things, the implements weren't the reason for her distress at all.

He smiled and reached out with his free hand to stroke her cheek. "You've come a long way in a short time, Savi. Don't bail on me now. This is an important test of your trust in me."

"I do trust you." *Mostly.* "I just don't like being restrained like this."

"I thought we were beyond your fear of restraints."

He'd restrained her in other ways many times, but he'd never splayed her open. How to explain the actual problem? "I mean with my legs spread open like this. Promise you won't touch or look at my…pussy?" She still blushed when she referred to her private area that way.

He sighed. "Will you trust me to remember your limits, *savita*, and fully submit your body to me?"

Submission.

"I trust you, Sir. I'll try, but…"

Damián bent his head to her face and pressed his lips hard against hers in another show of possession. She thought he might cover her mouth and steal her breath away again, but he kissed her briefly, stood, and reached down to tweak her nipple. Harder this time.

The sadists had used Shibari rope-tying techniques on her breasts, coiling the bindings tightly at the base of each. The exposed tips of her breasts had become swollen and hypersensitive, which she noticed whenever one of them reached out to twist her nipple.

Savi blinked back to the present. She wasn't in the penthouse. She was with Damián. She wished he would stop touching her like that, though.

As if he'd read her thought, he frowned. "Whose nipple, Savi?"

She sighed. "Yours, Sir."

Trust him completely. Submit.

Drawn into his warm, chocolate-colored eyes, she relaxed her leg into his hand. "My body is yours, Sir."

"Thank you, *querida*, for your most precious submission."

Not waiting for her to change her mind, he lifted her thigh higher in the air and outward, then grabbed the chain dangling from the D-ring on the thigh cuff and clamped it to the side of the table. He had fully exposed her pussy and ass to his view. All he had to do was move to the end of the table. How could he not look?

How could he not see her shame?

He stroked her hair. "Relax, *bebé*. Trust me. I'm restraining you like this so I can make sure you can't move and won't get hurt."

How could she relax when he was so close to discovering—?

Hurt?

"Now, for a little improvisation." Damián glanced up at her and smiled. "Give me your hand, Savi."

She lifted her unrestrained hand off her belly and extended it to him. He picked up the bundle of rope he'd laid between her breasts earlier, warm from her body heat, and shook it loose. Similar to the claw design Adam had used, he entwined the rope just above her wrist and ran it down and in between each of her fingers. With the end, he fashioned a thick knot and carefully positioned it over the palm pad between her middle and index fingers. He released her hand. What did he have in mind?

She didn't have long to wonder.

"Touch your breasts."

"Wha—?" Remembering that he hadn't asked her a direct question, she quirked her head, leaving the question unfinished but clear.

"I. Said. Touch your breasts. I want you to pull on your nipples, pleasure yourself as you do when you're alone."

She'd never touched herself like that.

When she remained frozen, Damián went to the bag and pulled out the quirt. "Savi. Are you willfully ignoring an order from your Top?"

Memories of how the quirt had made her inner thighs raw all those years ago made her insides quiver. She tentatively slid her hand up her abdomen to her left breast and took the nipple between her thumb and index finger. She squeezed and rolled it the way Damián sometimes did, not sure exactly how she was supposed to do this.

"Pull your nipple away from your body."

Her gaze remained riveted on Damián. She pulled the nipple taut, stretching her breast upward.

"Release it."

She let go, and her breast regained its natural shape.

"Again."

Savi licked her suddenly dry lips, and Damián's gaze zeroed in on her mouth. She pulled at her nipple again and released it, imagining he was the one pulling on it with his fingers—or teeth. She grew warmer but still didn't truly feel anything. What did he want her to feel? Damián's breathing quickened, became shallower. The knowledge that he was getting turned on by watching her sent a tremor through her body. No one had ever asked her to pleasure herself before, much less watched her do so.

"Breathe, *savita*." Damián's stern command reminded her to take a breath, but her heart pounded so loudly in her ears she couldn't keep her mind on her breathing. She needed to calm herself down. If he gave another command, she wouldn't be able to hear it.

I can't do this.

Damián set the quirt across her belly and stood between her legs. Her hand froze before she realized he was standing too close to see the thing she most wanted to hide.

"Look at me, Savi."

She locked gazes with him.

"What do you feel?"

"Nothing, Sir. I feel numb."

He nodded and roughly scraped his blunt fingernails against the skin on the backs of her legs, raising gooseflesh wherever he touched. Her skin tingled.

"Roll your nipple."

She complied.

"Harder."

When she applied more pressure, his fingertips rounded her hips and scraped her butt cheeks. A jolt of electricity shot through her breast to her privates. Her eyes opened wider. She'd felt that! Damián's gaze drifted from her face to the nipple she wasn't even touching, which was becoming erect. He smiled and looked into her eyes but remained true to his word. He didn't look at or touch her pussy.

Damián's fingernails continued to abrade the skin on her thighs and butt. She held her breath, but he always drew away before touching her pussy.

She relaxed.

Reaching for the loose end of the rope tied to her wrist and hand, Damián tugged slowly and drew her hand down toward him. She released her nipple when she couldn't stand for it to stretch any farther. Slowly, her hand crossed her abdomen, skimming over the ropes he'd used to lace her to the table. She provided some resistance as he drew her hand over her mons, but the displeasure on his face caused her to relent.

Seconds later, the palm of her hand lay splayed over her mons. He made adjustments to the rope on her hand until the knot on her palm pressed firmly against her pussy lips, just over her clit. Savi tried to pull her hand away once more, but he answered her movement by tying the rope more tautly at the lower end of the table. She had nowhere to go.

Damián stepped away, and she panicked before realizing her fingers and hand covered her shame from his sight. His improvised scene left her just barely within her hard limit, but within it, nonetheless. The man had a devious mind.

He folded his arms across his chest and leaned his back against the door, his gaze on the hand between her legs. "Take your fingers, and open your pussy lips."

Heat crept up her neck. Other than washing herself in the shower, she'd never touched herself there in a sexual way when alone, much less while a man watched her. When she remained still, he pierced her with his gaze.

"Masturbate for me, Savi. Now."

Her face grew hot as her embarrassment spread. "I…I don't know how."

He raised an eyebrow in surprise. "You mean you've never even—?"

"No! And I don't want to now either!" She struggled to pull her hand away but only managed to stroke herself with each movement.

Damián chuckled, the rat bastard. "Relax. Take a deep breath." Maybe he was going to release her. Instead, he stepped away and went over to his toy bag. "Do. Not. Move. I don't want to miss anything."

She tried not to hyperventilate as he rummaged around. When he turned toward her again, he had retrieved a phallic-shaped, light-blue vibrator and held it up to her.

"Do you know what this is?"

She hadn't just crawled out from under a rock, but wasn't about to admit to him that she'd never seen one in person. "Yes. Of course I do."

He smiled. "Good." He turned a switch on a small blue box he held in his other hand, and she heard the vibrations before he clicked it off again.

"You're not putting that thing inside me!"

He shot daggers at her. "Savi, remember your place and who is in control of this scene." He glanced at the quirt resting on her abdomen. "We've been through this enough times tonight. Another outburst and I'll use the quirt to work on teaching you how to better discipline your mind—and your mouth."

"I'm sorry, Sir." She wasn't really afraid of the pain of the quirt; she just didn't want to displease him. The vibrator, however, was another story. That scared her. If he wasn't going to insert it into her vagina, what exactly did he have in mind?

Before she had much time to ponder his intentions, he set the remote on the cabinet and picked up a bundle of thin rope from the cabinet beside him. With a few twists and pulls, he had the vibrator strapped to the back of her hand, looking like a rocket about to launch between her legs.

Savi closed her eyes. *Oh, dear Lord.* With the click of the remote, the vibrator roared to life again. Her entire hand began to pulse against her mons, her clit, and the middle finger tingled as it pressed against the opening of her vagina.

"Look at me."

With reluctance, she opened her eyelids and stared into his piercing eyes.

"Please my body, *savita*." His voice was low, just above a whisper. "Please *me*."

Mesmerized by his eyes, she begged him silently to tell her how. She wanted to please him. "Spread the lips of your pussy and place your middle finger inside that tight hole."

How did he know if it was still tight? Probably not, after having a baby. But he kept his gaze on her, so she took her fingers and pushed the labia aside, keeping her finger where the brand could remain hidden. She never took her gaze off Damián as she pushed the tip of her finger against her opening. She paused at the resistance there.

"Harder. Push it inside."

The vibrations slowed to a lower frequency, and she actually felt the sensation more intensely than when it was vibrating faster. She pressed her middle finger against her hole and pushed past the snug opening until her finger was inserted to the first knuckle. The muscles clenched around her as the vibrating knot in the rope pressed harder against her clit.

Zing!

Savi's eyes opened wider. Damián's smile confirmed he knew what had happened. *Oh, God. I can't do this.*

"Deeper. Push it in."

Obey him. She pressed her finger to the next knuckle; the vibrations spread throughout her pelvis and into her thighs.

"Two fingers inside. Now."

She pressed her index finger against the opening to her pussy and pushed it inside. Damián's eyes remained locked on her face, rather than what her fingers were doing. Somehow that made it easier for her to free her inhibitions more. She pushed her fingers in as far as she could at this angle.

"Finger-fuck yourself, Savi."

His dirty words startled her. The electrical pulses between her clit and pussy fired even faster. She withdrew her fingers, relieving the pressure of the knot against her clit, before plunging her fingers back inside her wet pussy.

"Again, Savi. Don't stop. Faster."

Savi increased the rhythm, feeling a pressure building up inside her. She wished it were Damián's hands on her again.

"Close your eyes, *bebé*. Give in to the sensations."

Savi's clit throbbed. *Please, touch me again. She'd never asked a man for what she wanted; she wouldn't start now.*

Savi blinked herself back into the moment. She wouldn't zone out. Why did her mind keep returning to that beach cave?

"I said, close your eyes." She'd displeased him. She closed her eyes again.

"Good. Now breathe through your mouth. Take your wet finger and move it to your clit, Savi. Imagine it's my tongue on your clit—stroking the sides of your swollen hood."

"Please, let me taste you."

Savannah's face grew hotter. He was begging? How could she deny him? No one had ever asked before. It was dark in here. He wouldn't be able to see. She nodded her head and watched as he smiled before lowering himself to her again. When his tongue flitted against her swollen clit, all thought receded. Her pelvis surged toward his mouth.

"Ohh!"

"That's it, *bebé*. Give it to me."

Empowered, he took his finger and wet it against the opening of her vagina, then plunged inside her in one strong stroke. "Yes, Damián! Oh, Lord, yes!" *The combination of his tongue and finger was delicious. When another finger joined the first, and he moved them in a "come here" motion, it was her undoing. An odd pressure built inside her making her feel she could fly. She bucked against his hand and mouth, simulating intercourse. No, more like lovemaking. There was a difference...*

"Faster, Savi. Stroke it faster. Come for me, *bebé*."

She did as he instructed, wanting more, needing release. "Ohh, yes!"

Savi stroked herself faster, harder. Pressure built until her insides felt as if they'd explode. She couldn't stop now if she wanted to. She didn't want to stop. No way.

The vibrations increased again; she screamed. "I can't stop it!"

"That's my girl. So fucking hot. Fuck my pussy, Savi."

She plunged two fingers inside her pussy as the knot rubbed hard against her clit.

"Come for me. Now."

Almost there. Just a little more—

"I'm coming! Oh, my Lord! Oh! Ohh, Sir!"

She screamed her release, feeling as if her body had just levitated off the table despite the restraints. Her body convulsed several times, completely out of her control.

Damián stroked her thighs, her butt cheeks. "I've got you, *bebé*. Ride the wave for all it's worth."

She rode the euphoric high of the orgasm for as long as she could, never wanting this magic carpet to touch the earth again.

Little mewling sounds invaded her consciousness; they were coming from her. Not quite the sounds of someone in pain, but close.

She wished it really had been Damián's tongue on her again, his fingers plunging inside her.

But she could never let him. Never again.

Chapter Sixteen

Watching Savi's face as the orgasm built and exploded was the most beautiful thing he'd seen in a long time. Surprise, excitement, and discovery all warred with each other in her expressions.

But Damián was the one who reigned supreme. He'd given her that orgasm, just as surely as if he'd touched her clit and pussy himself. A sense of accomplishment washed over him, threatening to overwhelm him more than her orgasm had. How long had it been for her? He didn't know when he'd thrown out his intentions for the scene he'd planned originally but was glad he had.

Seeing Savi pleasure herself was hotter than anything he could have done with her. Realizing the vibrator was still on full blast, he reached over to turn off the remote and stepped around the table to her side. A sheen of sweat covered her body. Her eyes remained closed, mouth open, as she panted for air. A tear spilled from the corner of one eye down her face and into her hair.

He leaned close to her ear, draping his arm over her breasts, and turned her head toward him until his forehead touched hers. "Shhhh, baby. You did great."

A sob tore from her.

"What's wrong, *savita?*"

She shook her head.

"I asked you a direct question."

She drew a ragged breath. "I…that was…I'm sorry, Sir. I don't have words. I just wish it could have been with…I mean, better for you."

He laughed out loud and leaned away so he could look at her face. "Don't worry about me, Savi. From the first look of surprise on your face until you screamed your release, that scene was smoking hot to watch, even if it was not what I had originally planned for us tonight."

She opened her eyes, worry visible in them. "I'm sorry if I messed up—"

He placed his finger against her lips. "Stop apologizing for everything. It doesn't get any better for a Dom or Top than to watch his girl come like that."

She smiled. "Thank you, Sir, for doing that for me." She glanced at her knees in the air above the table and nibbled her lower lip. His dick throbbed against his leathers. "I guess we're finished for tonight."

Did he notice a pang of regret in her words?

"How are your legs? Any numbness?" He reached up and stroked her silky calves.

"No. A little less numb than usual, actually." She smiled at him.

"Good, then we'll continue with what I had planned for tonight."

He heard the catch in her breath—anticipation, a little excitement, and just enough fear to please him.

"First, we're going to work on making you more aware of your pain level."

On Tuesday, he'd taught her to rate her pain on a scale from one to ten, with ten being the worst she'd experienced. In that session, he'd managed to get her to admit to a four, although he'd have expected most bottoms to have rated it higher than that. With Savi's mental block on pain and ability to zone out, he had to be careful how far he went. She could get hurt, if he underestimated her limits. Hearing her say it was a four when most subs would have rated it a six or seven let him know where to set the limits.

"Ready?"

Fear filled her eyes. She swallowed hard and looked at the box on the counter. "Electricity?"

The pulse in her throat pounded visibly. Instinctively, he knew that would be what they needed to work up to tonight. She had a real aversion to it, and he wanted to help her overcome that.

"Not yet, *savita*. We'll play with the violet wand later. Let me remove the necklace now, though. I don't want to forget you're wearing that when we play with the wand."

But I don't want to play with that thing!

Why hadn't she put it on her hard limits list? She still had her safewords, if necessary.

He removed the necklace and placed it on the cabinet. Returning to her, he stroked her ass, claimed his body, calmed her fears. "You've submitted your body to my care tonight. You know I am going to take very good care of you and give you what you need. You will offer both your pain and pleasure to me."

She swallowed hard. "Yes, Sir."

"We're also going to work more on attention and staying in the moment. Anytime I think you've zoned out on me, I am going to bring you back to the scene very forcefully."

He'd made an evil stick at the shop this week, just for this session. Nothing would bring her back to the present quicker than a thump of the wooden, heart-shaped head when he pulled the titanium rod back and let it go. The sting, not to mention the red heart each kiss of the evil stick would leave on her pale skin, would keep her in the moment.

"Are you ready to begin the next phase of your training, *querida?*"

She nodded then remembered herself. "Yes, Sir. I'm ready, if you are."

He reached out and pinched her nipple. *Dios,* he loved watching them swell before his eyes. Lucky for him they weren't off-limits. "Oh, I've been ready a very long time, little Savi."

He picked up the quirt, which had grown warm from lying against her skin.

"Don't think about what anyone else did to your body using a quirt. This scene is just between you and me. *¿Comprendes?*"

"Yes, Sir." Her gaze went from the quirt to the hand still restrained against her pussy. "May I ask a question?"

"Speak."

"Are you going to restrain my right hand above my head like the other?"

He grinned. If his instincts were right and she was a masochist, he had her hand right where he wanted it to give her another orgasm. If he couldn't touch her there himself, he wanted her to enjoy this scene to the fullest, even if it was with her own hand. "Having your hand covering my pussy will remind me it's a no-strike zone." As if he needed a fucking reminder.

She nodded, and he watched her body relax. She still didn't trust him to honor her pussy limit. He understood it being a hard limit, even respected it, as he should, but he really would like for her to face the emotions surrounding the limit. Maybe this scene could help her sort the reasons out. He'd push her a little, and they'd discuss it during aftercare, but he had no intention of badgering her into letting him touch her. She'd let him, eventually. He was certain of it.

He could guess why it was a hard limit given her early life, but this scene wasn't about revealing some shocking news to him. He wanted to get her to face down her own fear and revulsion about her body so she'd realize the problem wasn't with her but with the *cabrones* who used and abused her body.

After all, she was fucking perfect.

* * *

The afterglow of her orgasm faded quickly at the mention of the violet wand. The sadists in the penthouse had used the frightening thing during her last scene there. The instrument made her scream like she'd screamed only once before. The sadists hadn't even gotten close enough to touch her with the wand before her screams brought Damián to the rescue. He'd broken down the door, carrying a...

Thump!

Pain exploded at the back of her thigh near her ass from some unfamiliar source, like the thumping of a middle finger times one hundred in intensity. The pain bloomed in a tiny area but quickly spread throughout her thigh.

"Do I have your attention now, *savita*?"

She'd zoned out on him, already? She couldn't see what he'd used to bring her back, because he was standing at the end of the table. He kept his hand at his side, hidden by her raised thigh.

He picked up the quirt he'd laid on her belly again. How long had she tuned him out? Whatever he'd struck her with didn't feel anything like a quirt. She'd experienced *that* sting before but this was different.

"I'm sorry, Sir. I'll do better."

He grinned. "I know you will."

She didn't want him to do that to her again. She'd keep her eyes on him for the rest of the scene. She wanted to please him. She could do this...for Damián.

He set whatever he'd used behind the violet-wand box on the cabinet and raised the quirt in his left hand. Rather than hit her with the implement, as the sadists in the penthouse had done, Damián stroked the back of her thigh with it, taking away the sting that had lingered. "You have a lovely little heart right—here." He bent and kissed the spot where the sting had been the worst.

A heart? A quirt wouldn't leave the mark of a heart.

His free hand and the quirt continued to stroke her thighs, moving down to the globes of her butt. She spread her fingers over her mons and pussy, hoping to shield herself from any stray glances, but when she looked up, his gaze was on her face.

"You have the silkiest skin. So pale. I'm looking forward to changing that color now. First to a dark, dark pink. Then red."

Her heart thumped loudly as he sidestepped a couple of feet and raised his left hand as if holding a tennis racket for a backhand swing. With her thighs raised high in the air, and restrained at the sides of the gyno table, her entire backside was exposed to him, except for where her hand hid her pussy. She wondered where he would strike.

The quirt whooshed toward her, displacing air as it moved. Oddly enough, the movement appeared to be in slow motion. Flashes of what the men in the penthouse had done in that final scene as a sex slave tried to pull her attention away from Damián, but she pushed those memories away.

This was for Damián.

Slap!

The leather tip came down hard against the back of her thigh, where he'd stung her before. Savi jumped but didn't scream. She would never scream.

Slap!

The next blow landed on her other thigh, stinging just as much as the first, but she maintained her composure.

Slap!

Pause.

Slap! Slap! Slap!

Oh dear Lord. The quirt rained down in random, unpredictable blows; the pain registered as she was catapulted back to the penthouse suite at her father's hotel all those years ago.

Don't scream.

Slap!

Sadists get off on your screams Savannah. Don't give them the satisfaction.

Thump!

"Where are you, Savi?"

The localized stinging sensation bloomed in her butt cheek this time. She opened her eyes to find Damián's face inches from her own, as he stroked her breasts with the tip of the quirt, like the caress of his fingers. Her nipple raised to meet the quirt and her finger spasmed against her mons. She forced her hand to remain still as her vision cleared. She looked into his warm eyes, which comforted and grounded her. His dark eyelashes fanned against his lower eyelids when he blinked, fascinating her.

"I'm here with you, Sir."

He smiled. "That's my girl."

He stood and returned to the position below and at the right of her, delivering several more backhanded blows between her knees and her hip joint. Her thighs burned. How much longer would he focus on the same area? Why didn't he smack her butt instead?

"What's your level of pain, Savi?"

Of course, he wasn't going to accept "fine" as a response. He'd taught her to number her pain level.

"Two, Sir."

The quirk of his eyebrow led her to amend that. "Okay, maybe a three. It's starting to burn longer after each blow now, and those places where you stung me hurt like hell."

He grinned. "But you're doing much better at maintaining your focus. Good job, *savita*."

"Thank you, Sir."

He nodded and moved to stand between her legs and, once again, she shielded herself. If he looked at her, he'd be able to see the brand.

The quirt stroked her arm from her elbow to the webbed rope on the backs of her hand leaving a path of raised flesh. She shuddered. She wasn't used to feeling anything, yet suddenly she did. She couldn't describe the sensation, but it wasn't numbness.

He kicked something at one leg of the table and again on the other and repositioned the table more toward the center of the room. She looked at the windows, but they remained curtained. Relieved, she watched him move to stand with the cabinet behind him.

The quirt whistled toward her with all the forward momentum he seemed capable of—quite a lot—and slapped against her butt cheek so close to her pussy that her hand jumped. Her middle finger entered her vagina and the knot of the rope jolted against her clit. A zing bolted through her.

Again and again, he delivered harder and harder blows onto both of her ass cheeks with no indication he would stop anytime soon.

...the Asians had opted to spread her knees wide, exposing her pussy more fully. The quirt burned against her inner thighs.

Get into your zone. Go to your safe place, Savannah.

Thump!

She blinked and zeroed in on Damián's face. Why couldn't she keep her focus on this scene? She wanted to please him but was doing a poor job of it.

"Stay with me, *savita*. I don't want you thinking about any sadist but me. *¿Comprendes?*"

She nodded.

Something flashed in his eyes, and he raised the quirt at a new angle. She watched it descend, knowing where it would land before it came down hard on the top of her hand. She jerked. The blow sent another jolt to her clit. She fought against the restraints and only created more friction there.

"When I ask a direct question, you answer verbally to make sure I hear you, Savi."

The sting of tears burned her eyes, not from the pain as much as from disappointing him. "Y-y-yes, Sir. I understand."

Slap!

The quirt struck her inner thigh. "What's your pain level, Savi?"

"Four, Sir." *One very strong, motherfucking four.*

"I want to hear you scream for me now, Savi. We're going for a six."

Six? How could she get there from a four? Not that it mattered what level he took her to. She would not scream.

For what seemed like an eternity, the quirt landed time after time on her already raw thighs and ass, stinging more with each blow. After the particularly strong strike of the quirt, a scream nearly ripped from her throat before she could capture it.

As he began again, she became aware that she'd been stroking herself. *Oh, dear Lord.* The quirt hurt less when she fingered herself. She moved her hand against her clit, letting the knot excite the bundle of nerves there. Pressure similar to what had built up when she'd masturbated earlier began to build again.

The quirt landed on her ass, just above her anus, for five hard blows. Her finger and hand moved faster. The scream that surged up couldn't be contained. "Please don't! Stop!"

"Where are you, Savi?"

"With a sadistic bastard!"

Thump!

She opened her eyes, letting her hand still. "Why did you sting me? I was talking to you, Sir."

He grinned. "Thank you, *savita*. My apologies. I thought you were screaming at someone from your past." His grin widened with smug satisfaction. "What's your pain level?"

Her eyes opened wider. "Oh, God, Sir. I feel a six!"

He chuckled and bent to place another kiss on her burning ass cheek, then the other. She closed her eyes at the pain.

"I'm *your* sadistic bastard, Savi. Don't you ever forget that."

The calm way he delivered that statement at first made her want to rake her nails down his face to wipe the smugness away, but he distracted her by tapping the handle of the quirt against her hand. Embarrassed at what she'd been doing before he stopped, she tried to escape from his touch, but the restraints kept her firmly in place.

"Are you ready for me to take you home, *savita*?"

They were finished? She frowned. He couldn't leave her like this. *Wait.* She didn't want to feel a pleasurable response to pain from her traitorous body.

"If that's what you wish to do, Sir. I had a good time tonight."

Damián tilted his head in puzzlement and laid the quirt on her belly. "I didn't mean take you home to the apartment. I meant are you ready to come for me again?"

Oh! Why didn't he just say so?

"Yes, Sir! I'd like that very much!"

He chuckled. "Yes, you will."

He walked over to the cabinet and opened the box. A shudder coursed down her body. *No! Not with that!* After removing the wand and attaching a mushroom-shaped tip on it—like the one the sadists had used at the penthouse—he plugged the cord into the wall. He used his foot to roll a stool on squeaky wheels toward the juncture of her legs.

She knew what was coming. She had to stop him. "Sir, you promised you wouldn't touch me there!"

She withered under the expression on his face. "Savi. Have I ever broken a promise to you?" She took short, rapid breaths, fighting to regain control. "*Have* I?"

She shook her head.

"Verbal answer." He reached for the quirt.

She rushed to respond. "No, Sir! You haven't, but—"

"Then why don't you trust me?"

Deep breath. Her chin quivered. "I don't know, Sir. I'm trying." Her voice sounded shaky and pathetic in her own ears. It wasn't a lack of trust really.

Damián sat down facing her. He placed the cool purple globe against her burning skin and she fought to get away but couldn't move. Her mind registered that it somehow soothed the sting of the quirt and the unseen stinging from the thing he'd used to bring her back into the scene.

He rubbed the uncharged globe against her hand, which stimulated her clit even without electricity flowing. *Zing! Oh, dear Lord. So close.*

"Tell me what it feels like when you touch my clit, my pussy."

She refused to open her eyes to watch him. "Nice, Sir." *But dirty.*

"What was that thought?"

Would she never learn to school her expressions when she thought something negative? Even with her eyes closed, he could read her. But the thoughts just flitted in when she least expected.

"Answer me."

She drew a deep breath and let it out slowly. "I…it just seems a little dirty."

"There's nothing dirty about touching yourself, Savi, about loving yourself, giving yourself pleasure. If *I* can't touch my pussy, *you're* the only other person I want to see touching it."

The sound of electricity crackled in the air.

"Nooooo!" She fought the restraints as hard as she could, hoping she might actually break them. She needed to escape. Memories bombarded her senses. Fear clawed at her chest, leaving a burning pain behind. "Please, Sir. Don't hurt me like that. I can't do that again. Please, Damián!" She was babbling, but she needed to get through to him before he did something that would make her hate him.

"Focus on your breathing, Savi. Inhale."

"I can't breathe." She tried to drag air into her constricted chest. "Please don't do this!"

Thump!

Damián held a thin stick with a heart-shaped piece near the top. "I. Said. Inhale. Now, Savi."

She'd displeased him. Still, he didn't seem angry. Concern was evident in his eyes. He cared. But how could he think she was ready for this? It was too soon.

"In…hale."

She wanted to please him. She tried once more to draw a breath, but it sounded more like a gasp.

"Again."

She tried again. A little better.

"Do you trust me to know what is best for you, *savita*?"

No. Yes. No.

"I don't know, Sir." Tears spilled down her cheeks. "Please don't expect me to like that…that thing."

"Savi, all I'm asking is that you trust me. You've only experienced the violet wand in a torture scene, but the sensation can be quite incredible if you'll let yourself experience it in a different way."

She shook her head. "I can't. Please don't ask that of me, Damián." A sob broke from her throat, already raw from her screams.

"I didn't ask you to experience it, Savi. I don't need to ask. Unless you use your safeword, you will accept whatever I decide you need. You know I will respect your hard limits, but this wasn't one of them. Your body belongs to me. You are mine to pleasure any way I wish. Isn't that so?"

She'd enjoyed some of what he'd done. Damián wasn't a born sadist. He hadn't hurt her for the sake of hurting her or to get himself off. She wouldn't have been able to stand having him jacking off to her screams, like some of the sadists in her past had done. Why couldn't she place herself into his hands to do this? She wanted him to be pleased with her.

Her body began to quiver. She wanted to curl herself into the fetal position and cower in a corner somewhere. She wanted him to release her and just hold her. "Not this. Please, Sir."

"Please is not your safeword. What is?"

Her safeword. "Tamale, Sir." She could stop him if he went too far. He'd stopped before when she'd spoken her safeword. She trusted Damián to stop, unlike those sadists in the hotel penthouse.

Damián won't harm you.

Savi closed her eyes and breathed in and out several times, filling her lungs more deeply with each breath. After a moment, she opened her eyes again and looked into Damián's warm, brown ones.

This was the final test. If she failed it, he might not want to be her Top anymore. He would stop if she used her safeword. She was certain of it.

Perhaps she should see what he meant about it being enjoyable, rather than painful. She took one more deep breath, never breaking the connection she had with Damián's eyes, and felt some of the fear recede.

"I trust you, Sir." Her heart pounded, as if not quite as convinced as her voice, but she would trust him to take care of her. Always.

Damián smiled, and she forgot everything else. "I'm so proud of you, my brave girl."

She'd pleased him. Some of the crushing weight on her chest lifted, and she gave him a tremulous smile. He placed a kiss on her inner thigh and stroked her ass cheek before lifting the purple mushroom globe again.

"Remember, this isn't a punishment scene, Savi," he began. "I want to show you that the implements used against you earlier don't have to have such negative connotations. Every implement can be used for good or bad pain, but we're going to explore where the levels are for you to gain enjoyable, erotic pain from them."

"But I don't feel…" She'd started to say she didn't feel erotic responses, but she had while touching herself. Heat rose through her body, frissons of excitement coursed through her as she remembered her orgasm from earlier tonight. "Yes, Sir."

"If the pain goes beyond your tolerance level, I want you to use the word guacamole."

The man certainly seemed fixated on food during his scenes.

"That's not the same as your safeword. If you say tamale, the scene will stop entirely. But guacamole will let me know you need to stop, regroup, cool down, discuss what's going on. Then we'll determine when you're ready to continue."

Using a safeword seemed so much more final when sometimes she only wanted to slow things down. Damián was doing everything he could to make her feel at ease.

"Thank you, Sir, for giving me that choice."

He reached out with both hands and stroked her inner thighs. She gasped. They were sore from the quirt, but as his hands continued to touch her, she felt another zing to her clit as the circuits started firing again, albeit intermittently.

He smiled. He knew.

"Remember. You're in control, *savita*. You determine how far we go, whether we stop or continue." His hands barely brushed the skin, sending goose bumps to the surface. She shivered.

"Yes, Sir." His hands began to make her thighs tingle. Suddenly, she needed more.

Smack.

Damián hand-slapped her ass, still raised off the gyno table, and she squealed in surprise. Her skin felt raw, burning from her ass to her inner thighs.

Smack.

When he struck her other butt cheek, she began to feel something, but she needed so much more. He smacked her thighs several more times; her skin began to burn more intensely.

Damián scooted the squeaky stool back and lifted the purple globe again. She braced herself but closed her eyes, not wanting to see it coming at her.

"Look at me, Savi."

Don't make me connect on that level, Sir.

He'd already laid her bare. Why did he insist she look at him? She'd drown in the intensity of his smoldering gaze. He'd exposed so many of her secrets.

Vulnerable.

Yet she couldn't refuse him. She opened her eyes but, rather than stare directly into his, her gaze zeroed in on the vile implement in his hand. He moved it to his right hand and picked up the quirt off her belly with his left.

He brought it down several times against her thighs.

Sonuvabitch. The blood lying so near the surface intensified the pain. Why didn't he just use the violet wand and get it over with? It couldn't hurt any more than this.

The quirt whooshed through the air again and again, impacting against her thigh close to the earlier strike. *Yes.* The sting of the quirt burned.

More. Savi moaned. She wanted more.

As if her moans fueled him, he sped up the strikes, never hitting the same place twice, but always so very close. He began to smack the inside of her other thigh. Over and over, the blows rained down. Savi grew lightheaded, afraid she'd pass out. No, not faint, exactly. Different. Like…

Floating.

Belonging.

I am his.

As the feeling washed over her, she surrendered. Damián continued to strike her as she floated free of the bindings, free of the pain. She no longer felt anything but this intense sense of belonging to Damián.

Her fingers plunged inside her pussy again. Memories of Damián's penis filling her left her weak, needy, wanting.

Wanting only Damián.

Her finger and hand moved against her pussy hole and clit. Faster. So close.

The buzzing of the violet wand pulled her out of her euphoric state. Her fingers stopped moving. She tensed. *Not that!*

"Inhale, Savi."

She did as he told her and forced herself to relax again. *Trust him.*

"Exhale."

Again she followed his orders. He helped her find her center of focus again. She heard the buzzing, but fought hard to keep it from pulling her away from focusing on her breathing.

"We're going to start with a mushroom head, just like the one they used on you in the penthouse, but I'll be using a lower setting to begin. You'll feel the electricity like a warm current, a tingling sensation."

She watched him turn a knob; the buzzing grew louder. Her body shriveled up inside. *Escape! Become invisible.*

The wand drew closer to her thigh. Sweat popped out at her temples.

Crackle!

The sensation of the violet wand touching her inner thigh tingled. It didn't hurt but wasn't enjoyable either.

Crackle!

The globe sent a charge through her thigh. She shook her head. "Stop! I mean, guacamole!"

Damián turned off the instrument and soon filled her vision as he stood over her. He brushed the beads of sweat off her skin and into her hair. "Shhh. Deep breaths." He gently stroked her hair.

"Tell me where you are, Savi."

She shook her head. Too confusing. The past scene in the penthouse faded as a flash of memory bombarded her. Desk. Pressure. Pain. Crackling sounds.

Her heart beat faster. The crackling of electricity filled the air. Had Damián turned it on again?

"Savi, answer me."

No, he was standing over her; the wand had been turned off.

She'd never seen one before the clients in the penthouse pulled it out.

She didn't even know what it was called until…but that sound!

Desk. Face down on the desk. Pressure.

"It hurts. The buzzing sound…hurts my ears." She detested that thing. Before she remembered any more details of the scene, she needed to tamp that memory down again.

He frowned. "Has anyone else used a wand on you?"

She shook her head with vehemence. But had they? Dread seeped into her psyche.

Damián paused, waiting. "Let's continue then."

No, I can't! Savi drew a breath and nodded instead. "Let's finish this, Sir." She braced herself, fighting to keep the memories at bay. Damián returned to sit between her legs and picked up the wand.

Zap!

The wand touched her hand, and a jolt of electricity went through her mons and into her pussy hole. She tried to pull her hand away, tried to bolt out of her restraints, but could go nowhere. She was totally and completely at Damián's mercy.

The feeling of the electricity wasn't painful at all. No, the pain came from the sound emitted by the wand.

Father's weight crushed her breasts against the desk. Whatever Lyle used sent a searing, white-hot pain through her labia…

"Fire!" *Oh, dear Lord, they were burning her!*

No. That's not Damián. She trusted him to take care of her. Don't give in to these memories. Stay in the moment. Focus.

Zap!

Father's office. Face down on the desk, arms and legs restrained. Unbearable weight on her back. No escape. The buzzing noise filled the air. What was that sound? She'd never heard it before.

Searing pain. Burning. Her flesh was burning.

"Nooooooooo!"

Damián ignored her. Had she screamed out only in her head? Wait. "No" wasn't her safeword, or even her slow-down word. She tried to squirm away from his touch, but there was no escaping him or his wand.

Her mind. She could escape into her mind. Into her cave.

Savi ran over the sand toward the arch to the cave, but the cave never got any closer. Gasping for breath, she finally stopped and fell to her knees. The crackling grew louder. She looked up.

Father.

She froze. He'd found her safe place.

Thwack!

A sting against her thigh jolted her back to the present. The crackling sound had stopped.

"Where are you, Savi?"

She looked up at him. *In hell. My own living hell.*

Fear clawed at her again. Savi fought against the restraints, thrashing her head side to side. "Please, Damián. Let me go!"

He placed his hands on her cheeks to hold her head still. She begged him silently to release her from this hell, but he ignored her. "Look at me, Savi. Tell me where you are."

Savi shook her head. She couldn't voice her thoughts. She just needed him to stop.

Filthy whore...Dirty slut...You deserved it.

"What was that thought?"

Savi opened her eyes and looked into Damián's, just mere inches away. A flush of warmth spread up her neck and into her cheeks. She shook her head. Never would she tell him. Her secret shame.

"Savi." His stern tone of voice made her stomach muscles turn to jelly. "What were you thinking?"

"I'm dirty."

"Bullshit. You just had a shower, if you did as I instructed before coming downstairs to the club."

She nodded. She'd obeyed, part of her learning discipline. She wanted to be able to have control of herself again. That was the whole point of this exercise.

"Then tell me what else you were you thinking."

Anger boiled up quickly; she couldn't stop it. "Do I have to tell you every fucking thing I think now?"

He grinned. "You do if you want me to be your Top. You do if you want to continue this scene."

"What if I don't want that anymore?"

He squinted his eyes and the grin faded. She'd hurt him. "Then you use your safeword, and it's over."

Why couldn't she let go of her fear and trust him? Damián had never done anything but care for her, to try to help her put the past behind her and move on. She owed him more than to keep running in the opposite direction.

"Safeword or continue, Savi? But, if we continue, you *will* answer my questions."

She took a deep breath. "Continue." God help her, she wanted to continue.

"Thank you, *bebé*. Now tell me why you think you're dirty."

"I can't." She could never tell him about the brand.

Damián pulled away as if she'd slapped him in the face. "Maybe you need more time to think about what it is you *do* want, *savita*. If not me, there are other Doms and Tops I could suggest who'd work with you here at the club. Or maybe you just don't want to have anything more to do with dealing with your past in this way."

Damián unfastened the chains that bound her left arm and went to the foot of the table to release her other arm. He pulled the extension out at the end of the table and released the chains holding her right thigh, lowering her leg to the table. He methodically unchained her other leg, massaging both to relieve the ache from her muscles. Next he released the thigh and wrist cuffs.

Was he also releasing her from their Top/bottom agreement? Tears stung her eyes.

He held out one hand, then wrapped another behind her shoulders to help her sit up.

"Sit a minute and let your head and legs get steady again."

He placed the cuffs in the duffel bag and began putting away the other equipment. He was ending the scene. Could he do that? Well, if she wasn't cooperating with him, what choice did he have?

"Wait!"

Don't leave me!

Savi wasn't sure where that thought had come from. All she knew was that she didn't want Damián to give up on her. She didn't want to spend the rest of her life paralyzed by fear.

She blinked rapidly to fight off the tears and whispered, "It's hard for me to say the words."

He sighed and turned to face her, still standing a few feet away. "You know you can say anything to me. I'm not going to judge you. Those things happened to you against your will."

Why wouldn't he listen to what she was trying to tell him? Why couldn't she find the words to make him understand? "I'm not what you think I am."

"You shouldn't presume to know what your Top thinks. So tell me what are you, then?"

She needed to tell him. Maybe he'd stop picking at this scab afterward. But deep down, she didn't want him to know what she was. "I can't say it."

He closed the gap and spread her legs until his hips were wedged between them. She wanted to close her legs, but couldn't. Just inches from his crotch, she felt some of the old fear rise up.

"How can I know what to avoid, what your triggers are, or what to work on if you won't talk to me, *querida*?"

Savi nibbled at her lower lip until Damián zeroed in on the motion with a smoldering gaze.

Her stomach churned. "Don't look at me like that, Sir."

"Like what?"

She paused long and hard, but his intense gaze told her he wouldn't let up. She forced the words past the lump in her throat. "Like I'm your whore."

Damián flinched and pulled away. "Why do you think that's what I think when I'm looking at you?"

She looked down, staring at the tail of the dragon tattoo that slithered down his arm. "How can you help it?"

He sighed. "Savi, we've been over this before. I don't see you that way."

Savi withdrew inside herself. "Please, stop." He didn't understand at all. How could she make him see? "Sometimes I responded, even enjoyed those things."

"Involuntarily. It's natural for your body to respond to that kind of direct stimulus. I could make you come now, whether you wanted to or not."

She turned her head away, unable to meet his gaze, and added in a whisper, "I can't feel anything like that anymore."

"You sure felt it a couple times tonight. You even came once—maybe twice."

"I mean, I can't...with a man. I'll never feel anything when a man touches me there."

Damián chuckled. "You sure know how to throw down a fucking gauntlet, *bebé*."

She scowled at him. How could he joke about something so serious? Why couldn't he see? "I'm not what you think. I'm a filthy whore. *His* whore."

Damián took her chin and tilted her head back, but she refused to meet his gaze.

He frowned. "Whose?"

She closed her eyes.

"Look. At. Me. Do not withdraw your attention from me again, Savi." His stern voice told her he was angry with her. "Whose whore?"

Surely he could guess, but he must want her to speak the words. "Lots of men, including Lyle, but mostly my father's," she mumbled.

Damián leaned closer. "Yes, well, I wouldn't take the word of two *cabrones* that are worse than dog shit on the bottom of my boot. Why are you giving them that much power over you?"

Because they've always had power over me. They'd continued to control her, even after she'd gotten away. The fear and shame had sunk into her bones and mind, their words replaying over and over in her head. She'd never really escaped them.

"When I look at you, Savi, I see a beautiful, sexy woman. The mother of my daughter, who…"

She tried to turn away, but he kept a firm hand on her chin. "How is it you see something so different than what I see, Sir?"

He brushed his thumb across her cheek. "Because I see the real you. They fucked with your mind to distort how you would see yourself. They wanted you to see what *they* saw, what *they* wanted to make you. But they didn't succeed, *querida*."

She frowned. "They didn't?"

"Savi, you submit to me, but your submission is a cherished gift. You aren't bartering your body for anything. You're trying to find healing, peace. I meant it when I said your body is sexy, beautiful."

She wished she could believe him, but years of seeing herself one way couldn't be erased no matter how much she wanted them to be.

"When you decide the time and the person are right, you're going to make some man very happy by submitting to him. I'm honored you have entrusted your body and your healing to me. For now, though, we'll keep working on those negative messages in your head. But you still haven't answered my original question. Who else used the violet wand on you?"

The man was tenacious. She might as well answer him. Maybe this would be the thing that repulsed him to the point he would finally see her as she was.

Before she could get the words past her lips, Savi began shaking. Damián lifted her into his arms and carried her to a cushioned bench in the corner. He placed her on her feet, and then he sat and pulled her onto his lap. He wrapped a soft blanket around her and handed her a bottle of water.

She drank slowly. Maybe she just wanted to postpone the inevitable, but she liked their time together after a scene more than the actual scene—well, most of the scene. Parts of them were nice, like when Damián had coached her to her first orgasm in a very long time.

When she finished the bottle, he took it from her. He leaned back against the wall and pulled her to his chest and stroked her hair. "What did they do to my precious *savita* with the violet wand?"

Precious? She wished he'd always think that of her, but he wouldn't after she told him the truth. Okay, maybe this was the part where he would give up on her and leave. Savi had known it would happen eventually; she just hadn't wanted it to happen so soon. But it was inevitable. Nice, honorable men like Damián didn't fall in love with a slut like her.

"You know I would never judge you for anything they did to you. You weren't in control."

"It's not that." Nothing about the branding scene had led to a pleasurable response from her body.

"What did the head on the violet wand they used look like? Maybe if you describe it, I'll know more what they used."

"I don't know. I couldn't see it. I could only hear the sound."

"What did it feel like?"

"Please, Sir. Don't make me think about that anymore." She snuggled against his chest, hoping he would just hold her, comfort her.

He didn't say anything but curled himself to her body, his head in the crook of her neck. "I'm not going anywhere. I can wait here all night if that's what it takes."

She wished he'd leave it alone. Why did he want to keep bringing it up if she said she didn't want to talk about it?

Tell him. Get it out. You can trust him.

Suddenly needing to get it over with, she blurted out the words.

"It's what they used to…" Even so, her voice still hitched before she could reveal the truth.

"To what, Savi?"

"…to brand me."

His body stiffened. His hand stilled. His breathing stopped. "They did what?" The barely leashed shock and outrage in his voice frightened her.

She struggled to get out of his embrace, but he applied pressure to her neck to hold her still. Tears welled up in her eyes; her chin shook. "Please, Sir. Don't make me say it again."

Chapter Seventeen

Madre de Dios.

Damián's guts twisted. Had he heard her correctly? He could easily guess where they'd branded her, given her hard limit. *Puta madre.* If he ever got ahold of those *cabrones*...

Not now. Later.

He held her closer, as much to calm himself down as to console her.

"Who did it?" He wanted to be sure he got the name right before he tore the fucking man's balls off with his bare hands.

"My father gave the orders."

The man would pay as surely as Damián knew he'd take another breath tonight.

"*Querida*, I don't know where you found the strength to survive all they did to you, but you are a survivor. You're one of the strongest people I've ever met, stronger than some of the Marines I served with."

"I wasn't strong. I was terrified. After they did that, I just wanted to die."

"Being scared doesn't make you any less strong. You should have seen how terrified I was in Fallujah and after..."

Slipping her hand outside the blanket, she reached up and stroked his cheek. "Oh, Damián. I'm so glad you came home safely."

Safely, maybe, but far from whole. But this was Savi's aftercare, not a time to talk about his past. "Tell me about the branding."

Her hand lowered, and she gripped his vest as if it were her lifeline.

"Breathe, *savita*."

She took a deep breath, continuing to hold onto his vest. "It happened just a month before I met you. It was the final degradation." A sob caught in her throat, and he held her tighter. "I wanted to die."

"I've got you. You're safe. That's far in the past." As if something like that could ever completely be eradicated.

"I can't erase it."

"No, you can't. But we're going to keep working on redirecting those memories so they don't have the same power over you. We've already made good progress in a short time, but this process can take many months, even years, to complete."

After a moment, she took another deep breath. "I planned to end my life the night you first saw me in the restaurant at the hotel. That was going to be my last time to be abused by Father's clients."

Jesús. They'd both come so close to ending their young lives when they'd thought there was no hope for a future.

She choked on her sobs. He'd help her find a way to shed the tears she'd kept inside so long.

"That's it, *bebé*. Let it out." If he could cry, he'd have done so now himself—for his sweet, tortured Savannah.

Realization dawned. He'd thought before that Marisol had come close to not knowing her daddy, but she'd almost not been born at all. The world would have been a much bleaker place without Savi and Marisol in it.

After a while, her body stopped convulsing from the sobs. "I changed my mind."

Dad and Marc had changed Damián's plans, when he'd come within a day of putting his sidearm into his mouth and pulling the trigger. "What changed?"

She played with the edge of his vest, her cool fingers touching his chest. He willed his dick to behave but wasn't sure he could with her in his lap like this. He wasn't about to let her go anywhere, though.

"Well, I'll admit that I didn't figure out right away why I couldn't go through with it. That day with you was so beautiful that I had a glimpse of something better out there. But that first night…I…was too weak from the beating I got for running away that day."

Damián raged inside at the thought of her being punished because he'd run off with her—and brought her right back to the monsters who had done such horrific things to her. But if he hadn't come into her life in that penthouse, would she have followed through and killed herself?

"Then I thought maybe I could find you and you could take me away." She'd looked for him?

"Did you get any of the messages I left at your gate? I gave you my phone number and address."

She pulled away from him, blinking away her beautiful tears. "You came back?"

Fuck. She hadn't turned her back on him; she just hadn't gotten his messages. "*Dios*, Savi. I came back almost every day for weeks. I even staked out the hotel in La Jolla, hoping to catch a glimpse of you, but security told me to beat it or they'd have me arrested for trespassing."

She smiled. "You came back for me." The awe in her voice ate away a piece of his heart. "I didn't think anyone wanted…" A new wave of tears filled her eyes.

He brushed the tears away from her cheek as they spilled. "Savi, I'd never met anyone as special as you. After I took you home that night, you were all I could think about for months." Years, to tell the truth, but he couldn't admit that to her, because she'd wonder why he'd given up looking for her.

Now he wondered that himself. Pride. Dad had said pride goes before the fall—and man, had it ever. He'd never thought a girl like Savannah would want to have anything to do with a jobless, wounded Marine like him. But that was later. Being a jobless Chicano hadn't kept him away until one of the Gentry household's cleaning staff had found him at the gate when she came to work one morning. The woman had told him he needed to leave immediately; Savannah wanted nothing to do with him.

Soon after that, when he'd lost his Harley and was close to being evicted, he'd joined the Marine Corps. In the back of his mind, he thought maybe if he were a war hero, she might give him a second glance. Then he'd gotten his fucking foot blown off. A wounded Marine wasn't worth anything to a rich girl like Savannah. Pride, pure and simple, had kept him from her. He wouldn't pursue her as half a man. He was too busy plotting his own demise and feeling sorry for himself to go after her.

As a result of his foolish pride, he'd missed out on being a part of Marisol's life from when she was a baby. He should have been there to take some of the burden of parenthood off Savi.

Realistically, even if he'd wanted to pursue her, he'd never have found her. She'd changed her name when she'd moved away from home.

She reached up and stroked his cheek. "Just think how different both our lives would have been if we'd run away that night after the beach." The sadness in her eyes probably mirrored his own, but they both knew it was too late to go back.

"Everything happens for a reason." *Oh, yeah.* Tell someone who'd been tortured a good portion of her life shit like that. Dad would know the right words, but he wasn't here. Still, one thing he knew for certain. "We are who we are because of all those circumstances—good and bad."

Savi's gaze lowered to his mouth, and he wondered if she was waiting him to continue. Hell, that was about as philosophical as he ever got.

Then she surprised him by letting her fingertip trace one side of his mustache, sending electric jolts to his groin. *Not now, Chico.* With her on his lap, there would be no hiding a hard-on.

Savi smiled and surprised him by sliding her hand around to the nape of his neck and pulling his face toward her to meet her lips. *What the fuck?* He held himself still, waiting to see what she intended. She was in aftercare, vulnerable; he wouldn't take advantage of her but his body's involuntary responses might make her think the wrong thing.

Gently, she brushed his lips with hers, igniting a flame that was totally wrong in this moment. His balls tightened as if they hadn't figured that out yet—or maybe they'd gone OFP on him.

He should stop her. She wasn't thinking clearly. She was still coming down off the endorphin high. She didn't know enough about a man's libido to know what kind of signal she was sending out.

Besides, he'd waited this long to kiss her again. He could wait a little longer, until she was ready.

Aw, fuck that *shit.* He was a Dom. He could stop once she came to her senses. Just a matter of showing some self-discipline himself. He *had* control; he was *in* control. No question. He also had limits, and this was pushing him close, entirely too close to the line he should not, *would not* cross.

But he'd already lost control of the lower half of his body as his tongue traced along her closed lips. When she didn't pull away, he slipped the tip of his tongue inside her mouth, testing her.

She moaned and brought her other hand out of the blanket to grab onto his neck—or maybe just to hold on. Needing no further invitation, he grasped the sides of her head to hold her steady. His tongue delved farther inside, prodding her teeth to part for him. They did, with no resistance. His tongue pressed against hers, waiting to see if she wanted more. When hers sparred playfully with his, he had his answer. He tucked a finger under her chin and tilted her head back, opening her mouth wider for his tongue to explore. She held on more tightly to his neck as he pulled her body close enough to make her feel secure. His hand slid down to cup her breast expecting it to be covered by the blanket, which had fallen when she'd moved her hand. *Mierda.* He pinched her nipple, not too hard but enough to get her cute little ass to squirm against him.

She grew still.

Aw, fuck. Don't stop now, bebé. *We were just getting to the good stuff.*

She pulled away and looked at him. "I'm sorry. I don't know what got…"

"I'm not sorry in the least. I've dreamed about kissing you again for years."

"I think I'd better go."

"You live here."

"Oh, yeah. Then I think you'd better go."

She was adorable, all flustered from their first kiss in fucking forever. Damián reached up and brushed a strand of hair from her eyes. He missed her being a blonde. He missed having her and Marisol living with him.

"You know, we can remedy this confusion about where you live. You can come back home to my place tonight."

She swallowed hard and blinked a couple of times, but she didn't say "no" outright.

"*Bebé*, it's just not the same there without you and Marisol. I'll still sleep on the couch and give you two the bedroom."

Still no response, but she seemed to be sorting something out in her mind. When she looked down at her lap, he figured she'd tell him to "take a hike."

Better to beat her to it. "Never mind." He nudged her to indicate it was time for her to get up off his lap and helped her sit up. "Why don't you get dressed? I'll take you over to pick up Marisol. I want to see how she's doing. You can ride back over here with Angelina."

She reached up and brushed the tip of her index finger over his lips, which were still wet from their kiss. His dick sprang to life as if she'd touched him there.

Her eyes grew round. She'd definitely felt that, too.

He kissed her finger, and she pulled it back. Oh, well. One step forward. Two steps back.

"Damián, I think that's a good idea."

She'd just short-circuited his brain so badly he didn't even know which particular idea she was talking about. He'd had a lot of ideas in the past couple of minutes she probably wouldn't think were all that good.

"Mari wants to live in your apartment. She asks me every night when we're going back. She's missing Boots…and you."

He grinned. He'd take second billing to a kitten if it got Savi back under his roof again. *Fuck, yeah.* It was a start.

"What about you?"

She nodded. "Adam and Karla have been wonderful hosts, and there's lots of room here, but…I think Mari and I both felt more at home at your place."

He hoped he wasn't making a mistake. He'd already involved himself more emotionally with her than with any other bottom he'd ever worked with. He should man up and do the right thing; tell her she needed to stay here—for her own good.

Hell, who was he kidding? *He* wanted her to come home to him, too. All he'd wanted since she'd left for Dad's was to have her back. He hoped he wouldn't start wanting more than she could—or should—give him. She wasn't ready for sex, that's for damned sure. Maybe he wasn't either, although he had let her see his stump. That was a huge step for him; it made him fucking vulnerable to her, but she hadn't been repulsed by him.

Savi had her own body-image issues. She was as hung up on her brand as he had been about revealing his maimed body. *Madre de Dios,* if she only knew how much he wanted her, just the way she was.

He could continue to live without sex; he hadn't been with a woman in more than a year now. The objective with Savi wasn't sex but intimacy. He needed to let her know how fucking sexy and desirable she was. To change the way she interpreted those messages rattling around in her head. And to let him inside those incredible walls she'd erected to protect herself from pain and emotion.

Time to plan another scene.

"Let's go pack your things. We're going to see if Angelina can watch Marisol again tomorrow, because we have a boulder to shove out of the way." He paused. "It's time for you to let me see the brand, Savi."

She grew tense. "No, Damián, I don't think…"

"I do."

She pulled at the skin around her thumbnail, and he placed a hand over hers to still them. She often drew blood when she picked at her hands nervously. They were worse than ever today. After several moments, she looked up at him, blinking rapidly to fight back the tears. *Damn.* She was shutting down again.

"I'm scared."

He held her quivering chin. "Savi, you've hidden that damned thing so long that you've let it rule your life."

She pulled away from his hand.

"*Bebé*, that brand doesn't define you or anything about you. How can I make you see that what makes you special to me and a lot of other people isn't your body? It's what you think and feel that counts, and that's what we're going to continue to work on getting you to see, even if it takes us months. You've made a big difference in a lot of people's lives—especially Marisol's and mine. That's why I…" *Fuck.* He'd almost said he loved her. He wasn't ready for that any more than she was. "It's what I find so damned attractive about you."

The frown on her face told him she didn't buy any of his speech—and she wouldn't until she let go of the hold that fucking brand had over her. He probably should strap her down on the gyno table again now and get this behind them, but she hadn't relinquished her tight hold on that hard limit yet. If he forced the issue, he'd be no better than the men who had abused her in the past.

"Just think about it, Savi." He helped her stand and rose from the bench himself. Pulling the blanket up around her shoulders, he looked around for her clothes. "I think we left your blouse in the great room. Why don't you get your jeans on while I go get it? Don't forget your necklace on the—"

She grabbed his hand before he could start cleaning up after the scene. "No, wait." She took several deep breaths.

You can do it. Be brave, mi savita.

"Okay." Her voice was so low he wasn't sure he'd heard right. Had she agreed to push the limit?

"Come again?"

She looked at him. "I said, okay. I mean, okay, I'll think about it tonight, and I'll let you know in the morning what I decide."

He wasn't sure if she'd backtracked to the discussion on moving home with him, so he wanted to be sure he knew what they were talking about.

"Think about what, Savi?"

She swallowed. "About letting you see the brand."

That's my girl. He stroked her soft cheek. "Thank you, *savita*, for being so brave." He bent to brush her lips.

She pulled back. "I haven't agreed to anything yet."

"No, but even considering it is a big step forward. I'm very proud of you."

She blinked slowly, but he let her get away with hiding her emotions this time. Tomorrow would be time enough for her to really let go. He was going to go ahead and plan the scene, regardless. If not tomorrow, he hoped he'd be able to get her to reveal it to him someday soon.

* * *

I can do this.

"Breathe, *savita*."

Damián stroked her arm and placed his other hand against the small of her back as he led her into yet another theme room. How many were there in a kink club like this? He seemed to take her to a different one for every scene.

She couldn't believe she'd agreed to do this particular scene at all, but after tossing and turning in bed last night, her battered defenses were worn thin.

The way Damián responded to the news that she'd been branded went a long way toward crumbling those walls, too. He'd comforted her, told her how strong she had been, and hadn't been repulsed by the idea of her having been branded at all.

He'd even kissed her. Well, she'd started it. What had gotten into her? Having his lips on hers—when he wasn't stealing her breath away—had been delicious. She'd enjoyed his kisses before but knowing him so much better now just made it that much nicer.

But kissing was the farthest thing from the plan tonight. Would letting him see the ugly mark really release the hold it had over her? *Dear Lord, please let it be so.*

She looked around the room, trying to figure out the theme for this one, but it seemed rather eclectic. There was some kind of leather sling hanging from chains in the corner. In the opposite corner was a stockade like ones she'd seen in books about witches in the eighteenth century. There was a low bench nearby it for someone to sit on and…

Oh! She realized what they could do in that position and looked over at the sling again and saw a similar bench she hadn't noticed before.

Was he going to strap her to one of those in order to look at the brand? Before she could speculate further, Damián walked over to a hinged, horizontal cross. "Come, Savi."

The cross had a padded seat covered with a hand towel. There was a hinge near the seat, and the wooden "legs" were in the lowered position. She walked over to the contraption and stared. As with the other equipment in this room, there was a small step stool at the juncture of the legs of the cross. Her face grew warm at the thought of the view someone would have while sitting on that stool.

Damián took her hand and guided her up onto the step. Well, sometimes a step stool was just a step stool. She relaxed a bit, reining in the demons.

"Turn around."

She turned to face him. He'd already told her to strip, again in the great room amongst the Saturday night crowd. It was becoming easier for her to do that now, although he'd made her strip nude this time. While Damián had seen her naked body many times, it was the first time she'd been totally nude in front of the other club members.

Tonight, though, she would reveal something making her much more vulnerable. How he hadn't seen the brand at the beach, she didn't understand. Maybe because the cave was dark and he was more focused on…other parts of her body.

After today, she'd have no more secrets from him.

Damián stepped closer. "Now, I'm going to teach you how to present yourself upon my command."

He took her arms and placed them at her sides, then took her left hand and bent it at the elbow until the back of her hand was pressed into her lower back. He did the same with her right elbow, overlapping her hands behind her. "Clasp your elbows with your hands."

She did as instructed, noticing that her chest now jutted out even more than before. Warmth suffused her face. *I can't do this.*

He came back around and his gaze drew hers like a magnet.

"Very pretty."

He smiled and she felt the warmth pool in her abdomen. She wanted him to think her pretty, even if she wasn't.

He wedged his prosthetic foot between her legs and tapped her ankles. "Spread your legs to shoulder width." Savi complied, careful not to place her feet too wide for the stool. She felt as if she was standing at attention for inspection, as she'd seen the troops do in the movies and on TV.

"Beautiful."

If he got off on military fantasies, why didn't he go after Grant or someone who was much more adept at being what he wanted? Why try and make her into…

"What was that thought?"

She shook her head. "I haven't submitted my mind, Sir. Only my body."

He smiled. "Oh, but I think you've submitted both, Savi." He caged her chin. "Now tell me what you were just thinking."

She tried to withdraw emotionally by glancing away, but he gripped her chin even harder. "Look. At. Me." He bit out the words and waited.

Uncomfortable with the silence, Savi complied. "If you're into military fantasies, why don't you find a female Marine to fulfill them." Maybe she *had* submitted her mind; it certainly seemed intent on doing whatever he told her to do.

He raised his brow. "Who said anything about a military fantasy?"

She would have looked down or away, but he wouldn't let her move her head. "The way you've…posed me. I feel like a soldier at attention."

He laughed and tweaked her nipples. "You're definitely standing at attention, but I'm not into soldier fantasies. Nor Marine ones. You're presenting yourself to me, your Top, as a show of respect for my authority over your body—and mind."

His mouth latched onto her right breast and, without thinking, she released her elbows to push him away.

He growled. "You forget yourself, *chica*. Whose body is this?"

Why had she done that? He'd touched her there before. She resumed the position. "Yours, Sir. I'm sorry. I don't know what came over me."

But she did know. The reason she was on edge had to be very clear to both of them. The thought of him seeing her brand petrified her.

"Before I continue, I want you to tell me once again about any places on your body that are still hard limits and not to be touched or looked at."

Savi took a deep breath. "None, Sir. I have no more limits. My entire body is yours to touch—and look at." Surely he could hear the wobble in her voice, but when he smiled at her, she felt a calm come over her.

Damián won't judge me. Damián won't harm me.

"That's my girl."

His hand rested on the back of her neck, and her entire body relaxed.

Remembering herself, she straightened her presentation stance.

I can do this...for Damián.

"Now, how do you feel about penetration?"

Her next heartbeat jumped into her throat. "Of what, Sir?"

He reached between her legs and laid his middle finger along her cleft, claiming his territory. "Of my pussy for this scene."

"W-with what? I don't want to have sex."

"Not with my dick then. What about toys, my fingers, my tongue? We haven't negotiated those yet because your pussy was a hard limit until tonight. Now that you've allowed me access to it, I want to clarify how much consent you're giving me."

Sex was still off-limits. Good. But was penetration of other objects a hard limit for her? No clue. Memories of his tongue on her clit at the beach cave sent a flush into her cheeks. She'd thought he was just going to look at the brand and be done with it. "I'm not sure."

He took his hand away. "Fair enough. You have your safewords—tamale for stop and guacamole for slow down—if you need them."

"Yes, Sir. I remember." She held her chin a little higher. "And you know I'm not afraid to use them, either." She didn't know where that defiance came from. Would she never learn to discipline her tongue?

He grinned rather than scolding her, easing some of the tension in the room. "No, that you aren't, which actually makes my job easier. Thank you. Sometimes bottoms are so afraid of disappointing their Dom or Top that they don't use their safeword when they should." He reached up and tweaked her nipple, causing it to engorge. "All right, then. We'll continue."

She took a deep breath. Only he knew the plan. Apparently sex hadn't been part of it, if he was continuing without a change.

She looked around the room. Unlike some of the dark theme rooms, there was a lot of light in here. He would see everything.

"Ready?"

"Y-yes, Sir." *No.* She'd never really be ready for this. Once he saw her brand, he'd be so repulsed by her.

When he lowered his mouth to her nipple, she steeled herself but didn't pull away. She didn't understand what pleasure he got from sucking it; *she* felt nothing. Her breasts had been desensitized long ago.

He bit her nipple, and she jumped. *Whoa!*

He flicked his tongue over the tip and something coiled deep inside her, much like the pressure that had built last night as she'd stroked herself to an orgasm.

Her breathing grew shallow, hitching a couple of times, and she fought the urge to push him away again. She closed her eyes and hoped he would finish soon.

When he pulled away, she relaxed, but he soon descended upon the other breast. His hand gently cupped her breast as his mouth devoured her again. He continued to bombard her senses, stirring long-buried memories. He let go and blew on her wet nipple. The peak grew larger under this assault on her senses.

When Damián stepped back, she shivered, missing his body heat. She kept her eyes closed, embarrassed to look at him, but she heard his leathers creak as he moved.

"I made these nooses just for you."

Nooses? She was afraid to look, but curiosity led her to open her eyes. In his hand, he held a pair of what looked like red-and-black, seed-beaded earrings. However, instead of the hooks to place them into her earlobes, there was a small plastic loop like the thin string she and Mari used to make beaded bracelets.

He slid the beads down the doubled string and the loop—no, the noose—grew larger. He placed it around her engorged left nipple, and pushed the beads toward the nipple to tighten it just to the edge of pain.

As he attached the other, he said, "I want to keep these babies at attention throughout the scene. They'll be a good indicator for me of your state of arousal."

His expectations were too high. "I don't want to disappoint you. What if I can't get aroused again, Sir?"

He chuckled and pulled on the beaded part of the first noose. Her nipple grew even more swollen, and she gasped at the pain as it was squeezed by the already tight noose. *Oh, dear Lord, it hurt!* Her clit zinged. *She'd felt that!*

He tightened the other noose and tugged on it with the same results.

"At ease."

It took her a moment to realize he wasn't giving the order to her nipples. She stifled a giggle at her silliness. What had come over her? She regained her composure and drew her legs together as she lowered her arms to her sides.

"Sit."

She sat on the towel-covered seat at the center of the horizontal cross, and Damián spread her legs and stepped between them, standing just beyond her hips. He lifted the lower half of the cross and locked it in place and stretched out her left leg. He didn't restrain her, just laid it on the cross and then did the same with the right. Her legs were now jutting out in front of her, with Damián standing in the juncture of her thighs. She wanted to draw her legs together to hide her pussy, but she'd committed to this and would see it through.

Trust him.

She drew a deep breath. Damián placed his hands on her right thigh and began massaging it. She tensed. The skin was still red from the quirt last night.

"Relax."

Easy for him to say. Next, he rubbed the muscles of her left thigh and placed one hand on each leg to stroke her, beginning at her knee and working his way toward her hips.

"Mine."

She looked up at him as he continued to lay claim to her body. "Yes, Sir. Yours."

As his hands drew closer to her pussy, she involuntarily moved her legs even though she couldn't close them with Damián wedged between them.

Damián slapped her thigh, and the sting, which she definitely felt, made her wince. "I'm sorry, Sir."

"I thought we might try this without restraints, but I think you'll do better if you don't have control over your arms and legs. Now scoot your ass right to the edge, just like on the gyno table." Using her legs for leverage and balancing on her hands behind her, she scooted her hips closer to him. He made a come-here motion with his fingers. "Closer."

He sounded like her gynecologist. Savi never could get close enough to the edge to please her, either. When it felt like her butt cheeks would go over the edge, he motioned for her to stop.

"Perfect. Lift your hips." He adjusted the towel beneath her. "Down."

She felt like an obedient dog as she followed his orders.

He stepped away from the vee of her legs and walked over to the now-familiar duffel bag. Within minutes, he'd applied Velcro cuffs to her wrists and ankles and had clamped them to the cross securing her in a spread-eagle position.

He smiled and nodded. "Very pretty."

Savi's face grew flushed as he continued to stare at her. He reached up to tighten the nipple nooses around her deflated nipples. Dear Lord, if she got aroused, those nooses were going to hurt like hell. She'd just have to hope he wouldn't be able to get a rise out of them again. When he'd finished testing her comfort with each of the cuffs, he gave each nip a pinch, and she watched them become engorged before her eyes.

"Too tight!" God, they *hurt*.

Damián just chuckled. "Remember what I told you about involuntary responses your body might make?"

She closed her eyes, willing the pain to recede—the emotional pain more so than the physical.

"Answer me, Savi."

The stern tone in his voice caused her a moment of panic, but one look at him and she knew Damián wasn't really angry at her.

"Yes, Sir. I remember."

He smiled. "I know you still think you can control your body's responses, but before we're done today, *querida*, you'll be screaming from any number of involuntary responses."

She looked at the implements hanging on the wall. Which did he plan to use on her? She hadn't expected this to be a pain session; she thought he just wanted to see the brand. Well, not that he *wanted* to see it but that he wanted her to *let* him see it. In such a vulnerable position, she hoped it wouldn't be anything too awful.

Why didn't he just look and get it over with? Lying here exposed like this made her want to crawl into a corner. But she knew not to ask what he had planned. He wanted her to anticipate it—whatever *it* might be. She'd wait quietly, if not patiently.

Damián pulled the step stool out a foot and sat down just inches away from her privates. Well, not so private anymore. Her heartbeat soared to a rate it usually took a strenuous session with the dancer pole to achieve. She couldn't breathe.

"Thank you for preparing yourself for me, *querida*."

His words of praise calmed her somewhat. At his instructions, she'd shaved herself for him—*everywhere*. Going outside with a freshly shaven pussy had been an interesting revelation. The cold had penetrated her clothing causing unexpected sensations over her pussy. Maybe if she was in California and not Colorado it wouldn't have been as much of a shocker.

Damián pressed his face closer and spread her folds. She squeezed her eyes shut, steeling her muscles and dreading his reaction to the brand.

"Open your eyes, Savi."

She blinked a few times and looked down to stare into Damián's eyes. "You tense up when you close your eyes tightly like that. I want you to relax."

Yeah, right.

"Let me continue."

She watched his face get closer and closer. How could he possibly see the brand with his face so…*Oh, God!* Surely he isn't going to…*oh, yes he is.*

"No! Not that!"

Damián stopped. "Whose body is this, Savi?"

She groaned in frustration. "Yours, Sir."

"You are not to speak unless asked a direct question or you need to use one of your safewords. *¿Comprendes?*"

She nodded and belatedly realized he'd asked a question. "I mean, yes, Sir. But may I just say one thing?"

He sighed with impatience. "What is it?"

"You won't be disappointed in me if, well, if I can't…you know."

He grinned. "I assure you that you will not disappoint me, Savi. Your responses to this point make that very clear."

Her body *had* responded to him involuntarily, just as he'd said it would. She'd also responded to his mouth and tongue in their beach cave so long ago.

"Relax—and do not speak unless you need to safeword or answer a direct question. You may scream if you feel the need." *I need to hear you scream for me again, Savi, as you come.*

Without waiting for a response, Damián lowered his face again. Nothing was going to get her to interrupt him again. That part of her body belonged to him at the moment. She needed to submit to him completely.

Discipline.

Focus.

Her one job was to focus.

On feeling. On Damián. On what Damián was doing to her…

When his breath blew against her exposed clit and pussy, she closed her eyes for a second, but opened them again, hopefully before he'd noticed. How was she supposed to take this kind of torture? His tongue traced the cleft between her pussy hole to her clit hood, and her hips bucked up as if to welcome him home. She hadn't intended to move at all.

Involuntary response.

She willed herself to lie still as his tongue traced around the hood, but something strange was happening. She opened her mouth to take in more air as her breathing became rapid and shallow. What was he doing to her?

Again he traced a path to her pussy hole, and she realized she'd become wet. *Oh, my!* He focused once again on her clit, flicking the sides of the hood with his tongue. She squirmed, sometimes to evade him but other times because she wanted to feel more.

So intense.

She'd remembered when Damián had done this to her in the beach cave, as if she watched from above. The sensory memory of what it felt like—long repressed—came crashing back like waves on the shore.

Her mouth became dry from panting. She hadn't even realized she'd been doing it, so focused was she on what Damián was doing with his…tongue. Her breathing grew even more rapid.

Damián's hands reached up to tweak the nipple nooses, sending a twinge to her clit.

"No! Oh!"

"Silence, Savi. Remember your discipline."

How could she think about discipline and focus when he tormented her this way? His finger stroked the tiny nubbin, and she nearly came up off the cross. Dark memories threatened like storm clouds on the horizon, but Damián pulled her back into the scene.

"You're so fucking hard for me, little one. Thank you for giving me that sign of your arousal."

Memories of their time in the beach cave sent her body jerking against his finger. Why hadn't he restrained her waist so that her hips would remain still?

"More!"

He bit her tender inner thigh, and the pain shot into her pussy. "Did I ask you a direct question?"

Shit. She wasn't supposed to talk.

His hand moved from her breast to her shaven mound, and he parted her lower folds, sliding his finger inside her slickened hole. Another finger followed. His thumb stroked her clit, and she fought her restraints, trying to break free of these intense sensations. Her enlarged nipples felt as if they were being strangled by the nooses.

"Too tight."

"No, *bebé*. Just right."

"No, no! Guacamole! The nooses are too tight!"

Damián stood up and released first one, then the other. *Oh, God!* As the blood rushed back into her nipples, she screamed in pain. Immediately, Damián's hand went to work on her clit and pussy again. He was killing her. She needed him to stop before...

"Come for me, *savita*."

She felt as if she was hanging on the edge but couldn't make it over. Savi groaned in frustration. "I can't! Please, Sir. Don't ask me to do that." She hated the thought of disappointing him but she'd be even more disappointed in herself if she didn't relax that final tether holding her back.

He worked his thumb on her clit. She groaned. Her pussy became even fuller when he added a third finger. Pain. Too tight.

Let go!

His finger movements sped up. Suddenly a dam burst inside her.

"Don't stop! Oh, Sir, please don't stop!"

A scream echoed through her mind, and she realized it was her own scream echoing throughout the room. Her pelvis bucked between his thumb and fingers.

"Give it all to me, *querida*. Don't hold anything back."

"I won't. I can't. Oh, God. Damián!"

"Come, Savannah. Now."

She convulsed against the restraints, her hips pivoting up and down as she rode Damián's hand. "Damián! Don't stop! Oh, my God! I'm coming!"

She exploded for him. *Oh, dear Lord.* There really were stars bursting in her head!

* * *

Damián came close to exploding with her—emotionally, if not physically. *Jesús*, he'd never wanted a woman to come for him as badly as he'd wanted this from Savi. Experiencing Dom space with her was better than reaching his own release.

Her pussy walls clenched around his fingers, squeezing him like a vise. He wished he'd been able to bury his dick inside her, and he hoped that someday she would let him inside her once more.

Her moans as he continued to stroke her overly sensitive clit told him she'd had enough. Before she'd completely come back to earth, he needed to look at the mark that had defined her sexually for so many years. Damián parted her folds and looked at the brand.

GG. Two letters. Two fucking letters had made her feel as if she was dirty, some man's filthy whore.

If he'd been alone, he'd have pounded his fist through a wall, but a Dom or Top never lost control of his emotions in a scene. When he met up with the bastard who had done this to his own daughter—and Damián knew that day would come sooner rather than later—Damián would unleash his beast.

In this moment, though, Damián remained in control of himself and this scene. He needed to help Savi put this trauma behind her. He lowered his face to her pussy once more and pressed his lips on the ugly brand. GG. He didn't know what the letters stood for—the second maybe for Gentry, her last name. Had the arrogant bastard branded her as his property with his initials?

From this day forward, they would stand for something good. When Damián heard a sob tear from her throat, he pulled his fingers out of her pussy hole and met Savi's gaze.

"*Savita*, I'm claiming this brand, too. From now on, this is *my* brand on you. You are *my* good girl. Just like the brand, those words won't hold any negative connotation from the past for you." He bent and kissed the brand again. "This is now *my* marking on *my* good girl's pussy. *¿Comprendes?*"

She choked on another sob but nodded her head, keeping her focus on him despite her distress. "Good girl." Damián stood on shaky legs and released both of the ankle cuffs; he walked around her legs and leaned over her face.

"Mine, *savita*."

Tears fell from her eyes, but she nodded and gave a tremulous smile. He bent to kiss her lips. His lips moved to the side of her face to kiss away the tears. "Close your eyes a minute, *savita*, and rest."

He walked to the upper portion of the horizontal cross and unlatched the wrist cuffs, and began massaging her arms. The scene had progressed faster than he'd expected. He needed to get her into aftercare as quickly as possible, to process it.

Her muscles began to relax, and he moved her arms down to cross over her belly. He massaged her calves and thighs, careful to avoid the welts he'd placed there last night. When she sighed, he walked up to her head and stroked her face from her cheek to her chin.

"Can you stand?"

She nodded, and Damián helped her to sit up before lowering the hinge on the cross. When she stood, Savi teetered a bit. He scooped her tiny body into his arms, ignoring the strain on his leg, and carried her to the overstuffed loveseat in the corner. He set her on her feet first, steadying her when she began to shake and reaching for a blanket from the nearby basket. Once he'd wrapped her shivering body, he grabbed one of the two bottles of water he'd placed on the coffee table earlier and sat down.

Placing the bottle beside him, he patted the top of his thigh. "Come, *savita*."

She crawled into his lap and he held her head against his shoulder as she continued to sob quietly.

"Shhh. You are so perfect, *bebé*. Thank you for giving your body and your orgasm to me. They are precious gifts I'll honor and cherish always." He knew this relationship wasn't about forever, but he wished it could be.

She choked and pulled away, sitting up and searching deep into his eyes. Her tear-stained cheeks tore at his gut. Did she regret what had happened? Was she crying because of her intense release or because he'd seen the brand?

She cupped his cheek and brushed the pad of her thumb across his lips. "I should be the one saying thank you, but any words I might come up with would sound really lame right now. That was so…incredibly moving." She smiled. "And I don't mean the earth-moving part. Thank you for accepting me as I am."

Damián relaxed as her words fed something that had been starving deep inside him for a very long time.

"Savi, when I showed you my stump, you didn't hesitate to accept that as a part of me. Your kissing it was no different than my kissing and accepting you and your wound. We're both wounded warriors. You just engaged your enemy on the home front." Hell, she'd battled a traitor within her own fucking home.

Something Dad and Damián's contacts at a wounded-warriors organization he'd joined had been trying to drum into his head for years suddenly became clear. When he looked at Savi, he saw a strong warrior. She may have been wounded by what she'd been through, but she hadn't given up the fight to survive.

He reached up and stroked her cheek. He'd never call Savi broken. Why did he think it was acceptable to think of himself that way?

"Savi, we may be wounded, but we're not broken."

A sadness came over her. "Where do we go from here?"

Madre de Dios, he had no fucking clue. How about a change of subject until he had time to formulate a new plan?

"Let's talk about that orgasm. It's been a while since a man has given you one, rather than taking one, hasn't it?" *Oh, yeah. Fucking idiot.* This wasn't about him claiming bragging rights.

She nodded and smiled, making him feel less of a moron.

"First time since a handsome young man rescued me from a tower in an evil man's castle and took me away on his Harley to a secluded beach cave."

She grinned and rolled her eyes. "Damián, deep down I never wanted anyone else to touch me. You were special and set the bar too high for anyone else. Then, by the time I found you again, I'd been shut down for so long that it was easier to just keep the lid closed tight on that part of me."

Damián felt something break around his heart, as surely as if a hammer and chisel had been taken to the layers of concrete he'd placed around it to protect himself from the pain of so much suffering.

"You honor me, *querida*, by allowing me to be the one to help you rediscover that part of yourself, both last night when you pleasured yourself and tonight when you allowed me to bring you pleasure. The gratitude is all mine. Thank you for entrusting me with your body."

A tremor ran through her, and he pulled her against his chest. He tucked the blanket over her shoulders and for a moment became afraid he might wake up any minute and she would disappear from him once more.

He opened the second bottle and handed her the water. "Drink this." Like his good girl, she did as he'd instructed before laying her head on his shoulder.

"You just rest now, little one." Holding her in his arms like this, he felt like Victor must feel when he held Patti after an intense session. Damián had only served as a Top to others in the community; never as a Dom to a sub. Starting today, he wanted to be much more than a Top to Savi, but she wasn't ready for that. Baby steps, like the ones Dad had taken with Damián as he'd helped him cope with his PTSD and other issues after Fallujah.

Savi had let down her defenses in the most personal way today, though. He wished he was half as brave as she was. She'd come to him fragile and wounded but had allowed him to break down so many walls that had held her a prisoner all these years.

Maybe it was time he broke down a few of his own. Savi had placed her trust in him, and he'd earned it by never going beyond her hard limits. She'd repaid him by allowing him to remove those limits, one by one, faster than any bottom he'd ever worked with. She'd faced her fears head on.

He wanted to be with her—forever. How could he do that if he kept a part of himself hidden from her? He needed to trust her not to hurt or reject him.

So what the fuck was he going to do to fix that?

"Damián?"

He'd thought she was sleeping. "Yes, *querida?*"

"I feel strange."

I'll bet.

"Strange how?" He hoped she wasn't dropping. For her, having someone gift her with an orgasm had to be as intense as any impact session.

"I don't know. Just different."

"Different good or different bad?" He smiled. This sounded like a conversation he might have with Marisol or with Rosa's kids when they were younger. Twenty Questions.

She paused, as if to assess the situation on the ground. "Different good. Very good."

He wanted her to analyze the feeling a bit more, especially since she seemed to want to talk about it. "What can you compare it to? What does it feel like?"

She placed her hand on his forearm. "It feels...*I* feel...safe. In your arms, I feel protected, no longer afraid of everything. I haven't felt like that in a very long time."

Damián's heart swelled at her words, and he hugged her closer. "Thank you, *mi sueño*. I'm going to do all I can to make sure you never feel frightened again."

Savi curled against him and soon her breathing became slower, her weight heavier. She slept.

No fucking way could he let her go. *Mierda.* What the fuck was he going to do if he couldn't protect her and his baby girl? Those *cabrones* were still looking for them. How could he eliminate the threat and keep his girls safe?

Damián hadn't felt this helpless in a very long time.

Chapter Eighteen

The next day, Savi found herself back in the same theme room as the night before. He had placed her in the sling this time. When she hadn't been able to come for him a few minutes ago, he'd given up.

Her arms were at ninety-degrees to one another, hands about the height of her head and restrained at the wrists. The sling was bolted to the ceiling and hung on chains. Her hands held onto two large rings attached to the chains. Her nipples were in the beaded nooses again.

Black leather slings encased her thighs and were attached to the same rings that held her hands and wrists. Her legs were spread as wide as they could go without making her into a wishbone. That he'd wanted to splay her open again surprised her. She'd have thought he'd seen enough.

"What was that thought?"

She sighed. It seemed she couldn't even think without him battering down her fortress walls. Damián got into her face and made her wish she could pull away, but there was nowhere to go.

"Answer me, Savi. Now."

"I just thought you'd seen enough of it already."

"Enough of what?"

"My brand."

He grasped her chin. "Whose brand, *chica*?"

She sighed. "Yours, Sir. But I still don't understand why you would want to claim something so awful."

He sighed. "Remember what I said. From now on, it stands for Good Girl."

Those words would forever make her cringe.

He slapped her ass, which was bared to him in the sling. She jumped and sent the contraption swaying.

"If you don't start *being* my good girl, I'm going to have to plan your first punishment session."

Punish her? She'd upset him. Savi began to shake, enough to make the sling continue to move. Her gaze returned to the row of crops and canes on the wall. Her father beat her when she wasn't a good girl. She blinked, trying to fight back the tears, but they were so much closer to the surface these days. Holding them back was becoming impossible.

"Where are you, Savi?"

He stood in front of her and pulled the nooses again, and she hissed at the pain as her nipples became more engorged, but he had brought her back from the abyss.

"With you, Sir."

He tugged on them again and the edges of darkness faded. "Are these too tight?"

"No, they're fine." After last night, she knew enough to postpone their removal as long as she could.

His grin told her he knew exactly what she was doing.

"Well, since we didn't get you there this time with my tongue, I think we're going to have to try some toys."

Why didn't Damián just give up? She couldn't relax her mind enough to allow herself to just feel tonight.

"Maybe even a little impact play. I know how much you enjoy the endorphin release."

Enjoy? She dreaded when he went to the toy bag, but mostly because she didn't know what he'd pull out. She hated surprises. Once again, he'd placed the bag out of sight behind her.

He stepped around the sling that suspended her from the ceiling, and soon she heard a vibrator buzz on and off. She smelled a whiff of strawberries and heard him move a stool up behind her and sit. He placed his face against her lower back and wrapped his arms around her waist.

She looked down and saw the vibe from the other night in his hand. It looked wet.

"We're going to see if we can overpower that mind of yours so you can get off tonight. I don't want to leave you frustrated."

"I'm not frustrated." Her words sounded breathless when she spoke.

"Well, I am. I need to hear you scream for me again, Savi, as you come."

The vibrator buzzed to life, and he lowered it between her legs. How could he even see what he was doing from behind her? The vibe seemed to be disembodied, floating. Having him behind her gave the feeling she was alone, pleasuring herself.

The head of the vibrator touched the hood of her clit. Surprisingly, he hadn't fumbled around at all, homing right in on her core. He reached up with his free hand and tugged at one of the nooses at the same time as he bobbed the vibe against the hood of her clit, as if knocking on a door.

Pressure built and the next time the vibe touched her, she nearly came out of the sling. "I think your clit wants to come out and play tonight, after all."

The overload of sensations made her jump; whether to get closer to or farther away from the vibe, she wasn't sure. She would have set the sling in motion if he hadn't anchored her with his body.

"Someday, it will be my dick knocking, wanting to play with your clit and pussy again."

The image of his penis touching her there sent an inexplicable ache through her.

"First, Chico would dip his head inside your sweet pussy." He pushed the tip of the vibe inside her. *He'd named the vibrator?*

Oh, no! He wasn't talking about the vibe anymore. Her face grew warm as she imagined his penis where the vibe was, just inside her vagina.

She tried to clamp her legs together but couldn't move.

"Then he'd pull out and stroke your clit some more." The vibe played along the edges of her hood, not touching the most sensitive place on her clit. He left her panting, wanting more.

He bobbed the vibrator against her clit, and her head fell back. She closed her eyes, and her mind's eye pictured Damián standing in front of her, his erect penis in his hand, bobbing the tip against her clit. A moan escaped. Her eyes flew open.

"I'd bring you to the edge, just like that." And he did.

"Oh, Damián."

"What did you call me?"

"I'm sorry. I mean, Sir."

"Although Chico would like to hear you call out his name."

No effing way was she talking to a vibrator—or Damián's penis. So ridiculous; she almost giggled.

"Come on, tell Chico what you want. Be my good girl now."

As if he'd thrown a cold, wet towel over her, he'd spoken two of the words she'd hated to hear her entire life. No, Savannah's life. *Savannah* had been Father's good girl. *She* had done whatever Father wanted, hoping he wouldn't hurt her for disobeying.

She cringed. Despite Damián's attempts to desensitize the words, Savi wanted nothing to do with that name.

"That's a good girl, Savannah. You make Father so happy when you touch him that way."

No! She wasn't touching him. Not willingly, anyway. He gripped her much smaller hand, trapping her, forcing her to touch him. Wet. She hated to touch his wet pee-pee. She wished he'd hurry and explode so this would be over—for tonight, at least…

"Where are you, Savi?"

She opened her eyes and gasped. Her hands were restrained in leather cuffs above her head. She wasn't Savannah. She wasn't touching Father's penis at all.

"I'm hanging from the ceiling in a theme room at your club, Sir."

"Good girl."

She tensed.

"It's going to take you hearing that phrase a lot from me to redirect the old messages in your head."

"I *hate* them." Her voice sounded like a scared little child's. *Savannah's.*

He stroked her face. "I know, *bebé*. I'm really not doing this to be sadistic, but those words are used a lot in my community. I don't want you to be triggered every time you hear someone say them at the club."

That made sense. Adam had said it was a compliment to be called that by a Dom, although she hadn't heard him call Karla that. Maybe he just didn't say it to her while Savi was around. He definitely hadn't called Savi that either, not since the first time.

Had he really forgotten that time? Savi suspected he had been trying to get her and Damián together. She was grateful Adam had brought Damián into the room, because Savi had come close to bolting from the club at the sound of those words. Damián had protected and comforted her.

"You're right, Sir. I'll try to hear them as something different when you say them, or if I hear them in the great room."

"Good girl." He tugged at one of her nipple nooses and sent an electrical zing to her pussy.

The sound of the vibe invaded her focus again, stroking the cleft between her pussy and the edge of her clit, back and forth. Wetter and wetter.

The pressure began to build again.

She licked her lips, which had gone suddenly dry. She fought the urge to fight the restraints, wanting to take the vibe and place it directly against her clit. Chiquita wanted release.

Chiquita? Oh, dear Lord, now she'd named her pussy. What next?

"When he knew you were just about to come, Chico would thrust inside Sir's tight pussy." Damián rammed the vibrator far inside her.

"Oh, God!"

He pulled out and thrust inside her again. He reached up and released the tension on one of the nooses, and she waited for the pain. *Oh, dear Lord!* Her freed nipple began burning and the heat quickly spread throughout her breast. He released the other. The nooses hung on her engorged nipples, and he reached down to stroke her swollen, sensitive clit as he continued to thrust Chico in and out of her pussy.

"Come for Chico, *savita*."

"I'm coming!"

"I know you are, *bebé*. Don't hold anything back."

She bucked against his finger. When he pulled Chico out, she whimpered.

"Tell me what you need, *bebé*."

"I need you…I mean, Chico…inside me…now."

He rammed the vibe inside her, and she felt the vibration all the way to her cervix as his finger stroked her clit until she felt her insides explode.

"Yes! Harder!"

Damián's teeth sank into the flesh at the top of her butt and sent her over the edge. "Oh, Chico! Yes! There!"

She sobbed her release, never expecting to get there today after their false start. Her emotions rode a wild roller coaster. She didn't know if she wanted to laugh or cry. As she came down from the high and felt Damián's arms around her—his lips kissing her lower back and ass—she choked back a sob at how badly she wished she could have let Damián inside her; wished it was Damián making her come, not a plastic vibrator.

"That's my good girl. Chico's pretty proud of his slut for coming like that."

Dirty slut.

Savi tensed.

Damián sighed. "Where are you, *savita*?"

She didn't respond.

He released her, stood, and came around the sling to stand in front of her. Cupping her chin, he raised her face toward his to bring her focus back to him. "What triggered you? Your response seemed more intense even than when I called you 'good girl' earlier."

She shook her head. "Don't make me say it."

"I'm not going to continue playing these games. It couldn't have been Chico. Hell, you were screaming his name before you came."

She flushed with embarrassment. She had?

"Tell me what sent you into a tailspin?"

Several minutes of silence ensued, the tension building until she had to respond. "I'm a dirty slut."

Her words must have been too soft because he leaned closer. His eyes opened wider. "That must have been buried deep. It didn't even surface in our clothespin scene."

He stroked her cheek. "You know, *bebé*, there's nothing dirty about being a slut. It's used by a lot of Doms for their subs. Some subs even call each other slut."

"How could anyone want to be called something so degrading?" She couldn't let him call her that and enjoy it. Maybe he would want to stop being her Top now.

Damián smiled. "We have much more work to do, *querida*."

Savi looked into his eyes. "More work?" He still wanted to work with her?

"Make arrangements for Angelina or Karla to keep Marisol tomorrow night. You and I are going on a date."

"A date?" She sounded like a frigging parrot but couldn't help herself.

"Yes, a date." He tweaked her nose.

"I don't think—"

"Exactly. You are not to think. That's my job. I will plan everything right down to what you're going to wear—and not wear. Because we'll be starting and ending at the club, I'll have a new outfit laid out in the bedroom you used here at Dad's. What size?"

"I've gained weight. I don't think I'm the same size anymore." Most of her clothes had gotten tight, but she hadn't wanted to ask to go shopping. She'd been enough of a financial burden on him already.

"What size were you before?"

"Zero."

"Zero? What the fuck kind of size is zero?"

Already on edge from being called a slut, she lost control and allowed her temper to boil over. "I was a size zero so men like you wouldn't leer at me, okay? Men pay no attention to women without curves."

He seemed surprised by her outburst, then grinned. "*Mamacita*, I assure you I noticed—and you have beautiful curves in all the right places." He reached up to tweak her nipple. "In fact, one of the first things I noticed were your breasts. You didn't lose weight there."

She didn't want him to think she'd done anything unnatural to enlarge her breasts. "I breast-fed."

He continued to tug on both nipples now, making them engorge again, but there was sadness in his eyes. "I wish I could have been there to watch."

Her body heated when he gave her a smoldering once-over, lingering a little longer before and after on her breasts. He met her gaze again.

She reminded herself to breathe. Time to get this conversation away from her boobs. "I don't think I'm a size zero anymore, the way you guys keep making me eat." Would he lose interest in her if she got fat?

"And we'll keep feeding you, too. I want my girl to have a little flesh on her—otherwise I'll be afraid I'll break you too easily."

The image of Damián having sex with her in their cave flashed across her mind, and she stiffened.

"Okay, for starters, I'll bring over clothes in Size Two. When you've grown into those, we'll move up to a four. What's your bra size?"

She blushed. Boobs again. "I have plenty of bras."

"What. Is. Your. Bra size?"

She sighed. "Thirty-two B."

"Done."

"Damián, I'm not a child. I can dress myself."

"Whose body is this?"

She glanced down. "Yours, Sir."

"Good girl. Now, breathe."

She found that calling her a good girl didn't bother her nearly as much as when he called her a slut.

He reached up and released her hands by undoing the Velcro on her cuffs. She started to pull her arms down, and groaned. So stiff. Damián stopped and massaged her shoulders and upper arms, helping to release the tension until the blood flowed into them again.

"There, *bebé*. How does that feel?"

She moaned. "Wonderful."

Her eyes flew open, and she frowned. How was she supposed to take him? He was a sadist, but he never gave her pain beyond her limits. He wasn't repulsed by her background, her body, her shame. He took such good care of her.

Damián reached out and cupped her chin, forcing her to stare into his warm, confident brown eyes. "I know it's not easy to let go of the crap muddying up your thinking. It's going to take what I think you call adjustment therapy."

"Behavioral modification."

He grinned. "Call it whatever you want. We're going to do some modifications and make some attitude adjustments."

"So you're in the business of psychotherapy now?" At least he could practice his without a license. She was in limbo, unable to start the licensing process here in Colorado for fear of bringing the hounds of hell after her and Mari.

* * *

Damián thought the timing couldn't be worse, but he'd made a promise years ago to never miss a Colorado funeral with the Patriot Guard Riders if he was home. Fallen heroes deserved nothing less. He ran his finger under his leather wristband. He hoped Sergeant Miller had received a hero's welcome on his final trip home.

If Damián had been keeping up with the email alerts, he wouldn't have been blindsided by this one early this morning. Afghanistan. Ambush. Another Marine dead.

To keep his mind off the funeral and what lay ahead, he had gone to the mall and purchased the outfit he wanted Savi to wear for their date tonight. They might have to go out a little later than planned, but she'd understand. He should make it back in time for their date. He had a scene in mind to work on redirecting some of the negative messages that continued to clutter up her head. He'd sure as hell have to work on slut, because she'd hear that a lot if she spent much more time around the club's great room or any public scenes there.

"Sure you don't want me to get you some lunch before you leave?"

He looked up to find Savi standing in the doorway to the kitchen dressed in her tight jeans and a long-sleeved shirt. Tonight, he'd get rid of those damned sleeves in public, too.

He took another sip of coffee. "Nope. I need to get going." He walked across the room and gave her a peck on the cheek. She didn't pull away. *Progress.* Slow and steady wins the race. He just hoped he could hold out to the finish line, which sometimes seemed to be a receding target.

In the living room, he picked up his helmet and opened the door. "Keep the door locked. Remember you guys are always under surveillance, at my apartment or Marisol's school, so no one can get to you. I should be home by 1800."

"Yes, Sir." She grinned.

"Six, I mean."

"I know." The smile left her face. "Just be careful and take care of yourself. I know today has to be hard for you."

He nodded.

"Don't worry about us, Damián. We'll be fine. Karla's coming over in the Hummer. You're right, Mari loves it. We'll go together to pick her up after school."

"Sounds like a plan." Damián lingered a moment, wishing he could be here with her, but duty called. The Patriot Guard had given him a purpose in life—honoring the remains of fallen heroes while protecting their families from protestors and any dirtbags who wanted to make a political or pseudo-religious statement or to seek media attention at the expense of heroes and their grieving loved ones.

"It's a good thing you're doing, Damián. I'm proud of you. Now, go. You don't want to be late."

He nodded, too choked by emotion to speak. He walked out the door and closed it behind him. A quick survey of the parking lot revealed Victor's SUV in the corner. Someone equally trustworthy would be at Marisol's school. If those bastards came anywhere near his girls, they'd have to go through the Marines to do so.

Damián strapped on his helmet as he walked down the stairs. He climbed astride the hog, fired it up, and pulled out of the lot onto the street. His focus turned to the mission ahead. Another combat casualty. Would it ever end?

Not fucking likely.

* * *

"Damián, someone's here."

Fuck.

The urgency in Savi's hushed voice over the cell phone sent adrenaline surging through him. He was still twenty-five minutes from home. "Where are you and Marisol?"

Her whispered words shook with fear. "We're in the bedroom closet." He'd hoped to eradicate that emotion from her entirely, but he understood her fear—and the helplessness. This time, he had to admit he was afraid, too. He wished he was closer to them. He accelerated well over the residential area's speed limit.

He should have been there to protect them. What happened with Victor or whoever the hell was supposed to be watching them?

"Don't say anything else. Just listen, *bebé*. My seabag is hanging on the left side if you're facing the closet doors. Get Marisol inside there, zip it up, and then cram the hanging clothes against it to hide her. Tell her to stay quiet until she hears Daddy's voice. Tell her I'm coming." Marisol would follow instructions. He hoped the shitheads weren't too smart and would only look at the floor and miss the seabag altogether.

"Are you both wearing your necklaces?"

"Always."

"That's my girl. After you get Marisol secured in the seabag, I want you to move to the other side of the closet to divert their attention from her." He hated that he hadn't been able to convince Savi to carry a sidearm, but her fear of weapons would have just made the situation more deadly for them both.

"If they find you," and they would, if the good guys didn't get there PDQ, "tell them Marisol is with me." So fucking helpless. "I'll be there as soon as I can, *mi sueño*. Be brave for me." Not wanting her whispers to give her away any sooner than the inevitable, he said goodbye and disconnected the call.

Por favor, Madre de Dios, protect them. Don't let anything happen to them. They're my whole life.

He called Dad to report the situation. "Fuck. Victor called ten minutes ago and said something was wrong with Patti. I'm headed to your apartment now, but I've hit rush-hour traffic."

"Just get there. They're in the bedroom closet. Call in reinforcements, too." Damián ended the call and drove the last two fucking miles having to go closer to the speed limit, stuck in the same traffic situation. If he could have ignored all the traffic lights, he would have. The Harley roared into the parking lot and pulled up next to Dad's Hummer. Damián looked up to see Dad entering the apartment. The door was already ajar. *Damn.*

A Jeep screeched to a stop near the stairs. Not bothering to park in a marked spot, Grant exited with her sidearm drawn. She took the stairs two at a time with Damián right behind her, silently cursing his fucking foot for slowing him down. He needed to get inside. Fast.

They rounded the corner and entered the living room. Grant had both hands on her sidearm as she moved in front of him sweeping the room. Rage tore through him. While there was no sign of a struggle, he knew they were gone. Dad stood ready to charge into the bedroom. Damián gestured to Dad and Grant that they would go in together and provide him cover. They hugged the walls, listening. No sound.

Dad and Grant entered the bedroom first, sweeping the perimeter as Damián prepared to take the *cabrones* down. No hostiles. Grant gave the bathroom a quick check and gave the all-clear signal.

Damián's focus went to the closet from which Savi had made the call. Maybe the shitheads hadn't found them. They'd better hope they hadn't, because if those fucking bastards had touched a hair on the head of either of his precious *chicas*, he'd rip their goddamned throats out.

Damián's heart pounded as he walked over to the opening on the right side of the closet, where he'd told Savi to wait. Empty. He slid the doors to the right and his body sagged when he saw the seabag hanging there. No movement.

"Not you, too, Marisol."

A shrill whistle rent the air.

"What the fuck is that?" Dad asked.

Damián grinned. *"Mi muñequita."*

"Your what?"

"My little doll." Damián pushed the clothes aside and unzipped the seabag. Huddled inside, the Christmas necklace's steel whistle clamped between her lips, he found Marisol.

"Daddy!" The tears staining her cheeks broke his heart.

"Well, I'll be." Dad held the flaps of the seabag open so Damián could reach inside and pull his shaking doll-baby into his arms. She latched onto his neck and held on almost as tightly as he held her. He breathed in her sweet baby-shampoo scent.

Damián quickly pulled her the rest of the way out of the bag. She pulled away and stared at him. "Daddy, we have to hurry. We have to rescue Maman from the evil prince."

"Don't you worry. Daddy's going to find Maman and bring her home, but you're going to go stay with Karla."

"No! I have to help!"

"Don't argue with me." She pierced him with her angry stare but backed down. His fierce baby warrior was going to be a force to be reckoned with someday.

"Daddy, there were two of them. They smelled nasty, and Maman called one of them Lyle." She concentrated on her description. Very observant witness.

Despite his urgency to find Savi, pride swelled his chest. "You did well, my little warrior." He gave her a kiss on the cheek and set her on her feet. He turned to watch as Marc ran into the room.

"Sorry it took me so long."

The man looked as if he hadn't showered in a week and hadn't shaved in twice as long. Hiding out in the mountains again, no doubt. When was he going to admit he needed Angelina and go bring her home?

Right now, the only person Damián wanted home was his girl, Savi. After filling Marc in on what had happened, Damián hunkered down in front of Marisol.

"Uncle Marc is gonna take you over to Karla's house. I might be gone a while, but she'll take good care of you."

Marisol wrapped her arms around his neck and hugged the heart out of him. "Please let me help you find Maman, Daddy."

He hugged her right back, saying a prayer of thanks that he'd found her safe and unharmed. "No, *querida*. But you can bet we'll bring her home safe."

Breaking her tight hold on him, he extended his hand to Marc. "Take good care of her."

"You know I will. I'll rejoin you as soon as I can." Marc turned his attention to Marisol. "*Bambolina*, how would you like to take a ride in my sports car?"

Her fierce expression made her look more like a *Rambo-lina*. Marisol stuck her lower lip out, but Damián didn't have time to give in to her sulking. At least he knew she'd be safe. He needed to find Savi—before it was too late.

He watched as Marc led her out of the bedroom, her pissed-off gaze remaining on Damián until she could no longer see him, at which point, Damián turned to Dad. "Bring your laptop in so we can get a fix on her location."

"She's wired?"

"GPS in a necklace I gave her for Christmas."

"Good thinking, son."

"Yeah, if they don't get rid of it."

Grant reached out and squeezed his shoulder. "Damo, we have a good chance of finding her before…" Her voice trailed off, but she didn't need to say what was foremost in everyone's mind.

Damián just nodded.

Be brave, mi sueño. *I will find you.*

* * *

Savi fought her way back to consciousness, but her mind was numb. No, fuzzy. Her tongue felt three times bigger than the space in her mouth. She groaned.

"About time you woke up."

Bile rose in her throat. *Lyle.* Her father's puppet. She dearly wanted to make him suffer some of the pain he'd delivered to her when he'd served as her handler, but with her hands restrained, that wasn't possible right now.

Savi kept her eyes closed, hoping they would think she was still out of it and tried to block out the image of the man who had pimped her body out for over a year.

"Where's your brat, Savannah?"

Mari? Relief washed over her. They didn't have her daughter. Thank God Damián had helped hide her.

Slap!

She gasped as his hand struck her cheek, leaving a sting much worse than anything Damián had delivered with a whip or quirt. Savi's eyes blinked open, but her focus was blurry.

"I asked you a question, you filthy whore. Where is your daughter?" The vehemence in his voice told her he wasn't in control of his emotions. Not like Damián. She might use that to her advantage. People who got emotional also got careless.

"She's with her Daddy."

"That spic on the motorcycle? Is he the father of your bastard daughter?"

Savi didn't respond.

"Your father and I knew you'd whored for him that day he ran off with you."

"You can't hurt me anymore, Lyle—"

She didn't see the fist coming until it crashed against her cheek. Stars exploded in her eyes, and it took an undetermined about of time for her to regain her senses. Savi fought her way back and smiled. Very definitely, he was out of control. "You won't ever get near my daughter, not as long as Damián and I are alive."

He grinned. "As I recall, Savannah, you don't like to scream. Well, you'll be screaming before much longer." He turned to speak to someone above her head. "Max, get me the wand."

No! Savi tried to get up from the bed, but she'd been restrained in a straightjacket. Looking down, she saw she still had on her jeans, but her legs had been restrained at the ankles to some unseen tethers underneath the metal bed. At least she wasn't naked.

Her relief was short-lived. Lyle picked up a pair of scissors and began cutting the jeans from her ankle upward; the cold steel soon warmed against her leg. When he reached the juncture of her thigh, he made sure he cut her panties, as well. Savi held her breath, hoping he wouldn't cut her skin. When he couldn't cut through the thickness at the waistband, he merely started cutting up the other leg. He admired his handiwork, grinning as he yanked the panties away from her crotch.

"It's been a long time, Savannah. Still have the brand I placed here?" His hand groped her crotch.

Her stomach revolted. *Don't touch me.*

Then she remembered what Damián had told her. This was *his* pussy, *his* brand. "If you touch me again, Damián and his Marine buddies will hunt you down and make you regret you'd ever been born."

He pulled back. "I'm not afraid of them."

Oh, but you are. I see it in your eyes.

"I don't have time to play right now. Your father is waiting for you in California."

California? Did she still wear the necklace Damián had given her? She couldn't tell because of the jacket they'd wrapped her in. If not, how would

Damián find her? Where was her father waiting? At his house? At least Damián knew where that was.

"We have a long ride ahead of us. I'm sure your father will reward me and let me have my turn with you when he's finished."

She shuddered.

Lyle looked up above her head again. "Give her another dose."

Dose of what? A smelly handkerchief filled her field of vision and pressed tightly over her nose and mouth before she'd had a chance to fill her lungs with clean air. She struggled to hold her breath as long as she could, knowing the chloroform would knock her out again when she needed to remain aware. Black spots danced before her eyes.

No!

Savi closed her eyes and slumped against the bed, hoping to fool them into thinking she'd passed out, but the cloth remained tightly over her face until she had no choice.

She gasped for air.

The room went black.

Chapter Nineteen

Damián yanked off his ski mask and leaned forward until he was inches from Lyle's face. The color drained from the face of the *cabrón*, giving Damián some small measure of satisfaction.

The GPS tracker on Savi's necklace had led the team straight to her father's mansion in Rancho Santa Fe a day and a half after her abduction. Not knowing about her well-being for thirty-six hours had him ready to rip this fuckface's balls off and cram them down his throat. He'd come close to it, when a search of the man's pockets a few minutes ago had turned up her necklace.

So where the fuck was Savi?

He needed to get this bastard to talk. Damián forced himself to grin at the man who had beads of sweat popping out on his forehead. This interrogation scene wouldn't take long. Damián would get the man to talk. No doubt about it. He'd make the man do more than sweat.

His eyes never leaving *Cabrón's* face, Damián extended his left arm and waited as Dad, who had tied Lyle to the office chair earlier, placed the cordless power drill into Damián's hand. Leaning back, Damián held up the drill and revved the motor a couple times. He pressed the drill bit against the man's left kneecap. *Cabrón's* eyes nearly bulged out of his head. When he applied a little more pressure, the bastard looked like he was about to shit a brick in his three-piece suit.

"Tell me where she is."

Sweat beaded on *Cabrón's* upper lip. The bastard didn't seem to like being the one without any control.

Justice for Savi.

Lyle was in Damián's world now, and Damián had been trained to be a killing machine. He wouldn't hesitate to off the man if he'd done anything to hurt Savi, but first they needed to find her.

Where the fuck was she?

Damián revved up the drill a couple more times, the bit taking hold of the fabric of the man's pants. Without looking anywhere but into *Cabrón's* eyes, he imagined the twisting of the fabric. "Talk or you'll be walking with a limp the rest of your life, just like me."

"Look, man. I had nothing to do with planning this kidnapping. I just work for the crazy old man. He runs the show."

Damián remembered how this man—Lyle—had pimped out Savi's body. With no thought to Savi's safety, the bastard had left her restrained and alone in that penthouse with two known sadists.

Time to set things right.

Damián pressed the drill bit harder against the man's kneecap and revved it again. The scream of the motor matched *Cabrón's* screams as the bit worked its way through the man's skin.

He and Dad had anchored the chair to the desk to keep it from moving, knowing the man would twitch and squirm, which he most certainly was doing now. Lyle's movements would only become more erratic as they worked him over until he divulged the information they needed to rescue Savi.

Before Damián had even applied enough pressure to do more than break the skin covering the bone, *Cabrón's* screams drowned out the whine of the drill. *Too bad.* Damián wouldn't get his satisfaction—yet. Fucking shame.

"Stop! Jesus Christ! You're fucking insane!"

"Oh, I'm perfectly sane—just your worst fucking nightmare." He leaned closer and whispered, "Where. Is. She?"

"He took her to a cabin outside San Bernardino. In the desert, back side of Bear Mountain!"

Damián was familiar with the area, having completed a training deployment at nearby Twentynine Palms. He'd also detoured there on his return trip from California last November and ridden his Harley through that stretch of desert. It was a big fucking area.

"GPS coordinates."

Cabrón looked down at the drill pressed against his kneecap. Seeing the slow-growing bloodstain there drained any remaining color from the man's face. "In my phone!"

Dad, face still concealed by his ski mask at Damián's insistence, hurried over to the restrained man and rifled through his suit coat pockets until he found the smartphone. *Cabrón* revealed the password without any resistance and told them where to find the address without giving Damián the chance to pierce the skin of his other kneecap.

If Damián discovered they'd been lied to or, even worse, if Savi had been hurt, he'd be back to finish the job later. No time to waste now, though. Damián withdrew the bloody drill and laid it on the desk, noticing some blood spatter on his Kevlar vest.

He'd let the bastard stare at the bloody drill bit while they went after Savi. Damián grabbed his mask, and he and Dad ran for the door.

"Wait! You can't just leave me here like this!"

Damián turned toward the shithead. "The only difference between my leaving you here *like this* and what you did to Savannah in that hotel is that I haven't left you alone with two sadists."

Damián glanced at the drill, then back at *Cabrón*. "But if I have time—or Savannah's been hurt—I'll be back to show you how a sadist like me makes a piece of shit like you scream."

The man's eyes opened wider, and he shook his head. Again, Damián started for the door but turned once more as he waited for Dad to exit ahead of him. The bastard was staring in horror at the small bloodstain on his pants leg. Damián knew the wound was superficial, but *Cabrón* didn't seem to realize that. *Good.* Let him worry a while. Damián left the room.

As they rushed toward the front door, adrenaline pumping, Damián asked, "If I don't make it back, promise me you'll let him fucking rot tied to that chair."

Dad nodded as he removed his mask. "Consider it done."

They ran across the flagstones in front of the mansion, and he thought about how Savi's screams for help over many, many years of torture and abuse had gone unheeded in this fucking place. Damián's gut twisted thinking about how he'd brought Savannah home to this torture chamber that night. He'd had no idea what awaited her.

Before they'd gotten twenty feet from the house, he heard *Cabrón's* faint screams for help. That pussy could scream his fucking brains out and no one would hear him. The nearest neighbor was nowhere in sight. He'd be hoarse within an hour at this rate.

Damián and Dad raced back to where Marc and Grant stood guard near the gate to the property, Marc waiting to administer first aid to Savi, if needed, and Grant to monitor communications.

Marc glanced at the blood on Damián's vest. "Do I need to administer aid to anyone?"

"Not yet, Doc."

Without another word, they packed up Grant's gear and the four of them power-hiked back to the rented SUV parked about a block away from the gates of the estate.

With Damián behind the wheel, Dad programmed the coordinates into his GPS. He flung the phone outside the window to avoid being traced in case anyone had a tracking app connected to the number. Only *Cabrón* knew where they were headed, and he wouldn't be talking to anyone anytime soon.

Damián still couldn't believe he'd thought Savannah had lived a spoiled existence back in the exclusive Rancho house. Guess you can't judge a real home by its price tag. Damián had grown up in a tiny bungalow in the shadows of Rancho, with parents who worked for the wealthy bastards up here. He'd been loved.

Savannah hadn't had that. She'd…

Dad put a hand on Damián's shoulder, pulling him from his thoughts. "I said we'll stop outside Rimrock and change into our desert digitals."

"Roger that."

Hang on, bebé. *I'm coming for you.*

* * *

Savi's temples throbbed. How long would this scene last? She'd lost her focus. What was the goal this time? Damián hadn't told her. He sometimes wanted to teach her patience, discipline, and to get her to anticipate.

She didn't have a good feeling about this one. She went to rub the pain away from her temples, but her hands were stretched above her head and wouldn't budge. Her legs were spread open, also restrained.

Safeword, Savi.

She needed to use her safeword. She opened her dry lips to speak, but something hard obstructed her mouth, compressing her tongue. He'd never gagged her before. She'd seen subs with ball gags strapped to their faces in the great room at the club, but he'd said she wasn't ready for that, that it would serve no purpose in her training at this time.

Her eyes fluttered open. Darkness. Blindfolded.

Whatever was tied around her head dug into her eye sockets. Panic rose in her chest. Why had he restrained and gagged her? Silence. He'd promised he'd keep her safe, never to leave her alone like this, but…

Damián wouldn't lie to her. Damián hadn't done this.

Breathing.

She heard him…

"You know it excites me to watch you struggle, Savannah, especially when we both know you've escaped from me for the last time."

Needles of fear stabbed at her stomach. Not Damián! She hadn't heard that voice since she was nineteen. *Father!* How had he…?

Mari! Oh, God. Where was her baby?

Savi jerked against the arm and leg restraints and bit into the ball gag, tasting the latex, but she wasn't able to remove either.

"Your body isn't so different from when you were a teenager. I'm glad you stayed skinny for me."

No! She hadn't stayed thin for him, but to keep molesters away from her.

"Remember the pleasure only I could make you feel?"

Involuntary responses. Damián gives me pleasure. He doesn't force it.

She fought against the bindings, but her impotent struggles soon exhausted her. So weak. She had to have been drugged. How long had she been unconscious?

Where was Mari? She needed to get to her baby and hold her. Comfort her. She must be scared to death. Savi had lived that fear around her father daily from the time she was eight until she'd escaped at nineteen. She never wanted her own daughter to experience it. Tears stung the backs of her eyes.

And where was Lyle? Please, God, don't let him be with Mari. He'd been the one to inflict the most heinous of the torture on Savannah, including the branding.

Why had Savi let her guard down? How had they found her? She was supposed to protect her daughter, but she'd failed once more. What about the guards Damián and Adam had arranged for?

Damián, I need you.

"When Lyle brought you to me, the first thing I checked was to see if you still carried my brand. It pleases me that you want my mark on you, that you still understand you are *my* slut."

Her shame.

No! Her father was the one who bore the weight of all the shame. Savi would no longer own that emotion.

She *had* altered the brand. Her body, the brand, all belonged to Damián.

Her father's clammy hand squeezed her nipple, which became engorged. *Oh, God. Don't let my body respond to him again.*

Involuntary. It didn't mean anything. She relaxed and separated her mind from what he was doing to her body, not letting his touch affect her in any way.

Slap!

Her head jerked, intensifying the pounding in her temples. His palm left her cheek burning.

"Ah, I see I have your attention. Tune me out again, Savannah, if you want me to place more of my marks on you—more marks you'll wear for the rest of your life, which could be a substantial number of years, if you continue to please me."

Was this another mind game? Blame her for his perversions, then kill her when he tired of her? Could new scars be any worse than the mental anguish he'd inflicted, the pain she would always suffer?

She'd entrusted her body to Damián's care and training, and he'd accepted her as she was. She only wanted Damián's marks on her—marks of love.

Love. Yes, she knew Damián loved her. She wished she'd been able to lower her guard enough to surrender her heart to him before her father…

Failure.

Slap!

Father slapped her other cheek. She groaned.

"That's it, Savannah. Father will give you what you want now. We'll begin with the whip, then I have a special treat, one of your favorites, because I know how long you've waited for me to give you what you want."

Fear clawed at her throat. He wouldn't respect her limits as Damián would.

"You wanted me to find you and bring you home, didn't you, Savannah? Why else would you run to that spic? Once I realized it was his sister's house I'd seen you at in the news coverage, I remembered my former employee. I can't tell you how many times I'd watched that touching video of you two together until you stole my hard drive. You'll pay for depriving me of the pleasure of watching you with my clients, as well. But your Mexican must not be able to get it up if he didn't have sex with a dirty slut like you while he had the chance. You're nothing but a dirty slut—and dirty sluts have to be punished by their loving Masters."

Yes. Keep him busy with me. She prayed that God would keep Mari safe in the meantime, until she escaped or Damián freed her. Blindfolded, she had no idea in which room she was being held, but Damián knew where her father lived. He would know to track them here. Soon, she hoped. The longer they were held captive, the more chances something awful would happen to Mari.

"You'll also tell me where Lyle can find your brat. He says the Mexican has her. She's my granddaughter. I want her."

Mari wasn't here? Savi's body sagged into the mattress with relief. *Oh, God, thank you.* She remembered now that Lyle had been looking for her, too. Why was her head so fuzzy?

Suddenly, she realized she couldn't feel the necklace around her neck. Had her body gone numb again?

Even if Damián did find her, at what cost? Father would have tight security around his home. Damián might be hurt or killed in the process of attempting to rescue her. The thought of him suffering any further injury made her sick to her stomach. Mari couldn't lose both her parents.

Oh, God. Savi needed to get her father to release her in order to have any chance at escape. She struggled against the restraints. Whatever bound her wrists had scratched her skin raw. She continued to struggle, numbing herself to the pain. If she could get loose, she might be able to overpower her father long enough to get away.

"Imagine how pleased I was to see that you shaved yourself for me. You wanted to return to me all these years, didn't you, Savannah?"

No, everything is for Damián. My body will never belong to you again.

As long as the ball gag was in place, he didn't require her to respond.

"Lyle tells me the Mexican is a sadist at a club in Denver. I see you fully embraced your natural role as a pain slut. I know a dirty slut like you needs to suffer pain often. I let you enjoy some time with my clients, Savannah, but they must not have given you what you needed, if you ran away from them. I can satisfy you like no one else. I'm your first and only Master."

She heard his footsteps as he crossed the room, followed by the sound of buckles clanking as he rummaged for something. "This is a good time for us to get reacquainted, as a Master and his pain slut. Time for me to give you what you crave. You must be terribly frustrated because I'm sure that spic hasn't been able to bring you release the way I can."

Fear threatened to overcome her. Safe place. She needed to go to her safe place.

"First, why don't I reward you for helping me find you? A few dozen lashes with the bullwhip might be just the thing you need to get off. I've missed hearing you scream as you come for me. For punishment, though, we'll have to use the riveted leather flogger. Do you remember how these instruments made you feel, Savannah?"

Memories of the slashing sting of the tiny metal rivets embedded in the fingers of the flogger sent a wave of panic over her. She needed to escape before he used that implement on her. Her skin would be cut to shreds.

"Let's remove these first." The touch of his hands as he removed the gag nauseated her. "Open." She stretched her jaw as far as it would open, and he removed the slimy rubber. Her jaw wouldn't close right away, having been in this position so long.

His hands fiddled with the knot on the blindfold and soon the fabric was moved to her forehead.

Savi opened her eyes and blinked several times until the room came into focus. The demon's face before her had aged from the one in her nightmares. The sight of him sickened her, and she turned her head away. Looking around, this room was unfamiliar to her. Rustic. Dirty. Nothing like her father's house.

Oh, God, no! If this wasn't her father's house, where was she?

She looked down at her chest. The necklace was gone. Tears pricked her eyes as she lost the last bit of hope. Damián would never be able to find her.

Her body's aching need to crawl into Damián's arms for comfort surprised her. For the first time in her life—no, the second—she craved a man's touch, but the man she needed was too far away.

How could she get back to him, where she belonged?

"I was always a good Master, making sure my dirty little slut got off when she was being my good girl. Wasn't I, Savannah?"

She narrowed her eyelids, but remained silent.

"You know you need to be punished for running away from your loving Master. You will not come until I let you. Understand?"

Memories of the times her father had forced orgasms from her body flooded her mind.

He moved to where his face was inches from hers. "I asked a question, Savannah."

Fear embedded its claws so deeply inside her, she succumbed with a whimper and nodded.

"Good girl."

The fight returned to her. *Damián's good girl. Not yours.*

He stood up, but kept his evil gaze on her. "You know it is my responsibility as your Master to ensure you will never be able to run away again, you dirty slut.

Dirty slut.

No! I'm not!

"Such pretty blue eyes. Not like your whore of a mother's eyes at all."

Maman wasn't a whore any more than I am.

"Your daughter's eyes are brown, like your mother's." He sneered.

Savi's skin crawled. He'd seen Mari? When? Where? He said they hadn't captured her. Were her memories confused from the drugs she'd been given, or was he playing mind games?

"You are such a good pain slut, giving birth to an otherwise pretty little gift for your Master. Don't worry, Savannah. When I find where that spic's hiding her, I'll begin training her the way I trained you. She's just the right age now, but I won't let her turn into a filthy whore like you and your mother did."

Fear threatened to choke off her ability to breathe. Mari would turn eight in June; Savi's abuse had begun at that same age. She struggled anew against her bonds, screaming obscenities for all the sadistic things he'd done to her.

The back of Father's hand impacted her jaw, whipping her head back.

Wait. He doesn't have Mari. Whatever breakdown there had been in security, Damián would never let it happen again. Besides, if her father came anywhere near Mari, Savi would kill him with her bare hands. Despite his perverted threat, Savi felt a sense of peace come over her.

"You know, she deserved what she got. Filthy whores don't deserve to live."

An intense pain stabbed her temple. Was this a mindfuck? Had he captured Mari after all? Had he killed her? The pressure built to the point where she thought her head might explode. Her body began to shake.

No, not Mari. A blinding white flash filled the room. She found herself transported back to her father's house.

Yelling. Maman and Father were fighting again. Savannah didn't like to hear them fight. Maman always wound up screaming in pain and crying for hours. Why did Father treat her so badly?

Sometimes Savannah fantasized about running away with Maman. Today, they had been in their beach cave having a picnic, swimming, and napping. Father hadn't been there. He was always working, but that was okay. He didn't like the beach, anyway. Too smelly and dirty, he said.

Maman had asked her today if she wanted to live somewhere else. Savannah couldn't imagine living anywhere but the house she'd grown up in. Maman hadn't said where she wanted to go, but Father would never want to move. He liked living in the mansion that had once belonged to Maman's parents. When he lectured Savannah or Maman about something they'd done wrong, he called it "my" house—"You will not do that while living in my house."

Property. Sometimes, Savannah thought Father looked at her and her mother as if they were his property, too, just like this house and the hotel he owned. He didn't take care of Maman the way he should. He made her cry. Sometimes he hit her. Maman was kind and gentle; no one should ever hurt her like that.

Earlier today, in the cave, she and Maman talked about leaving their house. Late, in the afternoon, a strange man had joined them. Savannah didn't recognize him, but Maman did. She smiled at him, and he smiled back, with a twinkle in his eyes like Santa's. He helped Maman up from the beach blanket, and he kissed her. On the mouth.

Savannah was so confused.

When he'd hunkered down beside Savannah, he'd smiled at her, too. Even though his eyes were kind, she'd still wanted to shrink away and hide behind Maman. But he blocked the way to Maman. Savannah would have to get even closer to the strange man to get to Maman; she scooted away from them both instead.

"It's okay, Savannah. John is my friend. He's going to help us start a new life."

Savannah didn't want him to be in their new life. She just wanted to be with Maman. Why did Maman want to spoil their day and have him here with them?

"Give her time, Elise. It's a lot to take in. Why don't we take a walk on the beach? There are some changes in the plan I need to run by you."

Maman turned to her. "Savannah, why don't you stretch out on the blanket and take your nap."

Maman didn't want her. Savannah watched as the man took Maman by the hand and they left the cave, leaving Savannah alone. The warmth left the cave with them, and Savannah began to shiver, then cry.

When she woke later, they were just returning to the cave. The sun was setting. Somehow, Savannah knew this would be the last time she'd get to come to the beach cave just with Maman. She blinked away a tear…

Savi blinked. The cave. She was transported back to the day Savannah and Damián were there. The sunset had mesmerized her at the end of that perfect day. It had been the last time she'd gone to the cave with Damián, too.

The distant past pulled at her again, and Savi felt herself catapulted into Savannah's bedroom. Was it the same night? The night Maman had left her? She thought so, but time was all mixed up in her head. She couldn't remember most of her childhood.

"You can't stop me, George. I've put up with your abuse long enough. Savannah and I are leaving."

The sharp crack sounded like a slap. Savannah flinched. Maman screamed.

She scrambled up from the bed. Savannah needed to go help her.

"You filthy whore."

Savannah didn't know what the word whore meant, but the way her father said it, she knew it was a bad thing. Her bare feet quickly grew cold on the tiled floors of the hallway. Her parents' bedroom door wasn't closed all the way. She heard a sound she couldn't recognize.

Maman's voice sounded funny, like it was being squeezed. "Take...your hands...off...me!"

Savannah pushed open the door until she saw Father on top of Maman, sitting on her tummy. Maman's legs kicked the air, but with Father sitting on her, she couldn't kick him. Father's hands choked Maman's throat until her face turned red. Why was he hurting her?

Savannah ran across the room and rounded the bed to face Father. His eyes were scary as he focused on squeezing Maman's throat.

"Stop it, Father! She can't breathe!"

But he didn't stop. Maman's pale-pink fingernails that Savannah had polished in the cave this morning clawed at his hands and wrists as she tried to break his tight hold. Blood trickled from his hands, but he didn't let go. Savannah climbed onto the bed and pushed against her father's side, but he didn't notice her at all. She pounded on his arm with her fists. He broke his hold with one hand long enough to swat Savannah away like a pesky fly. She landed with a thump on the floor and looked up to watch Maman's legs stop moving; her hands falling to her sides. She lay very still.

Even so, Father didn't let go of her neck. Savannah stood up and looked at Maman's face. After what seemed like forever, Father let go and stood up. He staggered a bit as he got off Maman. Savannah climbed back onto the bed and rushed to Maman's side. She shook her shoulder.

"Wake up, Maman. I'm scared."

Maman's eyes were open. She wasn't asleep at all. But Maman couldn't see her anymore.

"Go to your room, Savannah."

Father's voice was even colder than usual. She should be afraid of him, but for some reason she wasn't. Maman needed her help. Savannah needed to get Dr. Morris to come. She couldn't leave her like this.

"I said go to your room. I will take care of your mother. Then I'll come tuck you in."

Father never tucked her in. Maman always did that. She didn't want him to tuck her in.

She shook Maman's shoulders as hot tears spilled down her cheeks. "Maman, please wake up!" But she didn't move.

Strong arms grabbed Savannah's skinny arms.

"No! I want my maman!"

Father turned her to face him. His eyes were different. Scarier. He shook her until her teeth banged against each other.

"You're just like her, you dirty slut. I said go to your room. You will do as I say. No more being coddled by your mother. I'll take care of you later."

Father didn't mean taking care of her the way Maman did. Afraid, she hurried out of the room and returned to the safety of her bedroom—but the room didn't feel safe anymore. Father was going to punish her. What had she done wrong? It must have been something very bad to make Father so upset with her. He frightened her.

Grabbing the princess doll off the top of her pillow, Savannah crawled under the bed. She didn't want Father to find her. Clutching the doll to her chest, she tried to imagine herself in a fairy princess's castle with brave knights and a handsome prince to protect her. It was dark under the bed, but she pictured the princess with Maman's warm brown eyes. She didn't feel so alone.

Much later, she heard the door creak open. The light from the hallway shone behind his dress pants. Father's once-shiny black shoes now were caked with mud. He never got dirty. Savannah knew her father had come to punish her. Her body shook as she watched his legs walk to the closet. They looked like they were separated from his body. Then he turned and stood in the middle of the room.

"Where are you, Savannah? I don't have time for your games."

Savannah squeezed her eyes tight and tried to picture her castle, but all that she could see was the beach cave. Maman was waiting for her there.

She needed to run away.

Escape! Now!

Chapter Twenty

The riveted flogger slashed across Savi's back. Searing, white-hot pain radiated throughout her upper body, but it paled in comparison to the pain slashing at her heart.

Maman was dead.

The lashes struck her upper thighs.

Maman was dead.

The trauma of Maman's murder washed over Savi as if it had just happened. To Savi's mind, it *had* just happened. How could she have forgotten something so abhorrent all these years? But she hadn't forgotten. Savi had never known. *Savannah* had repressed it.

Maman was dead.

Savi couldn't reconcile the loss in her mind. She couldn't blame Savannah for needing to block something so horrific from her mind. The little girl's innocent mind couldn't handle the truth and had simply surrounded that knowledge with protective barriers that kept her from remembering. Savi didn't know how to process it any better, even as an adult.

How many other things too horrible to accept had Savannah blocked out?

Savi's head hung listlessly. Father wanted to hear her scream. She tried to escape from the pain as the riveted flogger pounded against skin already torn from the whipping earlier, but each strike wrenched her away from her refuge in Damián's arms inside the beach cave.

"Scream for me, Savannah."

She had no safeword with her Father. She'd never been safe around this monster.

The pain of the flogger was excruciating, but she refused to give him the satisfaction of screaming. She wished she could zone out, but she didn't want to forget what he was doing to her. She wanted to remember everything. She wanted justice for Maman. Savi intended to prosecute him this time for everything he'd done to them.

"Damn you, Savannah. My arm's tired; I'm taking a break. We *will* continue this later, but I won't go as easy on you then."

She heard him walk out of the room and close the door.

Remembering the visualization technique her therapist had taught her, Savi found her focal point—the left leg of the ottoman she was tied to—and imagined she was with Damián. He would never inflict pain like this just to hear her scream. He took care of her; gave her only what she needed to release the pent-up emotions.

Damián loved her, protected her—

Peace descended. The pain receded as she escaped into her mind.

Escaped from the pain.

From Father.

The salt air washed over her as they rode Damián's Harley up the Pacific Coast Highway.

Escape. Freedom.

"I'll carry you." He removed her helmet—well, his helmet, since he only had the one—and secured it in the compartment with her shoes.

She laughed. "I can walk in my bare feet once we get to the beach."

His hands spanned her waist under the open jacket, and he lifted her up as if she weighed nothing. She grabbed onto his shoulders to steady herself, laughing. His muscles corded beneath his black T-shirt.

"I'll carry you again when we get to the rocks, then."

Damián couldn't carry her down those steps, over those rocks, anymore. He'd lost his foot serving in Iraq.

Damián handed her the towel, and he lifted her into his arms. "Oh!" She screamed in surprise…

How on earth could he hold her weight now? His foot…

Guilt assailed her for making him carry her. "You can put me down. I can walk."

"I'm carrying you."

His tone didn't invite disagreement, so she held on tight, hoping to ease some of her weight from his arms.

She stared at his profile. His nose had been broken at some point. Had he been an athlete in school or had he been injured fighting? He had a closed-up hole for an ear piercing. No earring. A lock of hair fell over his forehead that she itched to brush back with her fingers. His devilish appearance did strange things to her libido—like ignite it.

Strange, indeed.

Why do I feel at home in the arms of this stranger?

This man who simply made her feel. Period. She'd been numb for so long. How had he gotten past her fortress at all, much less in such a short time? A first for her with any man.

He'd broken through the numbness, not once but many times since the first time at their beach cave.

"Oh, Damián."

He pulled her hair, painfully yanking her head back. The beautiful scene disappeared as she was jerked away from the sanctuary of Damián's arms.

"Don't you ever use that spic's name around me again, Savannah." *Father.* "Now I'm going to make you scream for me, Savannah. It's been too long."

Savannah caught the glittering reflections of the overhead light winking off the tiny steel rivets imbedded in the fingers of the barbed flogger as he unfurled the wicked instrument before he stepped behind her once again.

At the fall of those fingers, searing, burning pain clawed its way through her body. Damián faded away, a sad expression on his face.

Damián, don't leave me here! I can't go through this without you!

* * *

The day's heat radiated off the sand beneath his belly and sweat poured down Damián's neck as he lifted the ski mask for some relief. Damián didn't care if he was identified, but if the others were forced to wear the masks, he should suffer with them.

He studied how they would gain access to the isolated cabin. Grant had scrambled the communication signals between the cabin and the security detail, and they'd managed to take down three of the four guards, hog-tying them and leaving them gagged in the back of the sweltering SUV. The perimeter had been much wider than expected, so they'd taken nearly an hour to low-crawl this far.

Still no sign of Savi. Knowing his girl was in danger just yards away made him constantly recheck his thinking to make sure he didn't blow the mission with his impatience.

It wasn't optimal to go in before nightfall, but the longer Savi was in the hands of that fucking bastard, the greater the risk she would be hurt. Savi had been through enough already. He didn't want her psyche marred any more than it already was by this nightmare.

Maldito bastardo.

Once Savi was safe, Damián planned a special one-on-one session with the bastard who fathered her before turning him over to the authorities. First, though, he had to get his girl out of there. No amount of screaming from the man would get Damián to back off either, not after he'd abducted Savi two days ago, to say nothing of the despicable things he'd done to her in the past.

Damián needed to hear the *bastardo* scream as he delivered pain on par with the pain and suffering the man had inflicted on his daughter. Memories of the mark burned into her most tender flesh cemented his plans. Thoughts of her having to endure the branding would forever be seared onto his mind.

A hand on his shoulder brought his focus back to the present. "Breathe, son."

Damián turned to find Dad stretched out beside him. They'd separated in their approach to the cabin. When had he joined him?

Focus on the mission, man. You can't afford to let your emotions get the better of you. Savi needs you. Don't fuck this up.

Dad's gaze returned to the cabin. "Everyone's in place, waiting for your signal. Ready?"

"Hell, yeah."

Damián hit the press-to-talk button on the radio on his shoulder to give Marc and Grant the code. After giving the agreed-upon signal, he and Dad low-crawled toward the back door. Marc would approach from the front, his rifle and sidearm with him. Marc was supposed to wait for the all-clear signal, unless something went wrong. As a Navy corpsman serving with a ground unit of Marines, Marc had been trained as a rifleman, but he hadn't kept up with practice since his medical discharge in 2005.

Damián and Dad were better shots. If a sharpshooter was needed, Damián would have the best chance of hitting the target, because he and Dad spent a morning once a month at a firing range, too. Target practice relaxed them both.

The infrared instruments hadn't shown any body heat in the front of the house, so he doubted Marc would have to fire on anyone. Most likely, their targets would be back here. There only seemed to be four or five rooms in the cabin to clear.

Grant monitored communications near the SUV with her rifle ready, too, in case anyone tried to escape. She guarded the most likely exit, unless the rich bastard had access to a helicopter or plane. Regardless, Grant would make certain the bastard didn't escape, even if something happened to Damián and the others here at the cabin. With luck, he and Dad could take the old man down before shots were fired.

He didn't want Savi endangered by a stray bullet.

Working in tandem with Dad at the back door of the cabin, they immobilized the guard who'd been more intent on his skin magazine than doing his job. Damián hoped Marc didn't encounter any resistance out front. By their intel, though, there were only four guards—pretty light security—in which case, this was the last one. He'd probably been guarding the perimeter of the cabin alone. Dad trussed him up and gave the signal to move in.

Savi's high-pitched scream ripped through his gut. Rage surfaced; this time, he found it impossible to suppress his inner beast. When Damián got his hands on the lowlife, he would pay for everything he'd ever done to Savannah, including whatever had made her scream.

Damián had everything he needed packed away in the SUV to right those wrongs.

The sound of a flogger striking skin elicited another piercing scream, letting them know in which direction they'd find her. While Damián wanted to charge in, Dad's hand on his shoulder and a motion to take it slowly stopped him between two closed doors on opposite sides of the hallway. The lash of the flogger and an exhausted moan from Savi told them which door to break down.

"He will never own your body the way I do, Savannah. Never."

Savi's strained voice made him ache. "I am Damián's. Always."

Before the man could strike another blow, Dad booted open the door and Damián charged in. The man he remembered from the entrance of the mansion—who he'd thought at one time was Savannah's sugar daddy—held a riveted leather flogger in the air high above his head. Damián aimed his sidearm at the man's hand, and the cracking report split the air as the flogger was blown out of his hand.

"What the fuck…?"

Damián stormed into the room and slammed into the man, shoving him away from Savi and against the wall.

"Who the fuck are you?"

Damián lifted the mask and waited for recognition to dawn. He wanted the bastard to have no doubt who he was dealing with—and why. A sidelong glance at Savi who appeared to be barely conscious, tied and strapped to an ottoman, her ass and back raw and bleeding from the flogger added more fuel to the fire-breathing beast raging inside him.

He turned his attention to the man he'd so easily overpowered. Damián kept his voice calm, knowing he needed to get Savi to safety before he could play with his prey. "You'll pay for every mark you've ever put on her body or mind, you fucking *bastardo*."

Impotent rage made the man's face grow splotchy. "You'll never own her the way I do. I placed *my* brand on her."

Savi moaned. "No. Not yours…Damián's good girl."

Something inside him swelled with pride. Even in the white-hot haze of pain, she remembered. His good girl. *Fucking right!* Now they needed to get her out of here and to a hospital.

Dad squeezed Damián's shoulder and motioned for him to see to Savi. He probably didn't want Damián doing prison time for killing the motherfucking bastard. Dad repeated the gesture more forcefully, and Damián took a step back. They'd keep conversation to a minimum.

Dad grabbed the bastard and threw him across the room into another wall where he slumped to a heap on the floor. With his identity hidden, Dad could get away with more than Damián might. Damián still planned to get his later, and he didn't care who knew his name.

The shithead sputtered as he stood again. "You're on *my* property." He stabbed his finger toward Savi. "*She* is my property. Leave or I'll report you to the police."

Dad pushed the man into the corner and knocked his feet out from under him. "Shut the fuck up. Now."

Well, so much for the plan of anonymity. Dad was as pissed as Damián.

Savi's father didn't defy Dad's order; he cowered in the corner like the rodent he was. No longer worried about having to defend Savi or Dad, Damián turned his attention to his girl, moaning in pain, hair soaked with sweat, eyes closed. He heard Dad radio Marc and Grant the all-clear code.

His focus on Savi, Damián couldn't bear to look at how the asshole had left her skin raw and broken. He knelt in front of her and focused on her face instead. The throbbing in Damián's stump, rubbed sore from crawling across the desert, didn't begin to compare with what Savi was experiencing. At least he knew she was alive, although the welts and cuts on her backside would leave yet more scars on her body—and mind.

He brushed the hair from her forehead, dampened by sweat. "I'm here, *bebé*. You're safe. It's all over now."

"She's dead, isn't she?" Her voice a scratchy whisper.

"No, *querida*, Marisol's fine. You protected her well."

She shook her head. "No. I remember. He killed her. Oh, God." She squeezed her eyes shut. "I watched him kill her. How could I shut it out all these years? I thought she'd left because she didn't want me." A sob tore from her throat.

Years? Who was she talking about? "Where are you, Savi? Who's dead?"

"Maman."

The goddamned lowlife killed her mother? While his daughter watched?

I'll get justice for you, mi sueño.

Savi—Savannah—*would* have justice before Damián left this cabin.

With the opening of old wounds, would Savi be able to reclaim Savannah as her own? Calling her that name could help start the process of healing—or trigger her.

"I'm so sorry you had to see that, Savannah." His eyes never left hers, gauging her reaction.

A voice from behind him said, "She's a filthy whore, just like…"

The crunch of fist on bone silenced the man. Damián glanced over to see blood trickling from the corner of the bastard's mouth. Dad flexed his fist a few times to work out the sting, but Damián knew he was probably grinning behind his mask. The man had no tolerance for abusers, murderers, or pedophiles—and Savannah's father was all three. Damián gave Dad the thumbs-up sign.

Savannah moaned, drawing his attention back to her. She lifted her head and opened her pain-glazed eyes, struggling to focus on Damián. "Where's Mari?" When he didn't answer fast enough, her eyes opened wider, and she struggled against the bonds. "I need my baby! Take me to her!"

She must be rolling in and out of the past and present. He needed to ground her, bring her back, and keep her focused. "Breathe, *savita*. Marisol is safe. They didn't get her. She's with Karla in Denver. They'll fly out here as soon as we give them the go-ahead."

Savannah slumped against the ottoman in relief, and a new spate of tears trickled from her eyes. He reached out to unbuckle the strap around her waist. The welts the strap had made showed how hard his warrior-woman had fought the restraint. Next he moved to her ankles as Dad came over to release the ropes binding her wrists to the ottoman legs.

The discharge of a weapon sent Damián hovering above Savannah's bleeding back to shield her just as Dad covered her head.

Savannah's father screamed. "Jesus Christ! I'm shot!"

Looking across the room at the whining excuse for a man, Damián saw blood trickling from the bastard's thumb. A pansy-ass .22 lay on the floor beside him. Damián's attention turned to the doorway where he recognized Marc, still wearing his ski mask. Marc entered the room and retrieved the puny sidearm.

If Marc hadn't been there, there was no telling where the bullet might have landed. "Nice shot, man."

Marc stowed the .22 in his bag. "Out of practice. I was aiming for his chest."

The chatter broke with their plan, but Damián only shook his head, glad Marc had their six. At least he'd gotten the weapon out of the asshole's hand—and hadn't spoiled Damián plans for later. The worthless piece of shit needed to suffer longer than he would have if Marc had been a better marksman.

Adam went over to the sniveling man and patted him down, and then he turned to Damián giving him the okay. "I should have patted him down earlier. Guess I've gotten rusty, too."

"No worries, Dad." Hell, they all had. It had been a long time since they'd been on a mission together. Confident there wouldn't be any other bullets flying, Damián stood taller but his calf burned like a motherfucker above the prosthesis. He'd probably irritated the stump with all this activity.

As Savannah's father sat huddled in the corner blubbering about his superficial wound, Marc's attention turned to Savannah. He hurried across the room, pulling items from his medical bag as he moved into action.

Dad came over again and gently touched Savannah on the head. "You're in good hands, hon. I'm going to take out the trash now."

"I'm bleeding!" The shithead's continued shouts made it clear he'd be a good candidate for what Damián had planned for him later. "I'm the one who needs a doctor, not that dirty…"

Again, Damián heard Dad's fist make contact with the man's jaw. This time the shithead slumped over. As Dad hauled the POS out the door, Damián returned his focus to Savannah. Marc checked her pulse and pupils. "Savi, can you hear me?"

She nodded, but her eyes remained closed.

Marc turned to Damián. "She's not in shock." Under the circumstances, tuning out her pain might be the best thing. Marc stroked her cheek. "*Cara*, tell me the truth this time. Any allergies to pain meds?"

Damián wondered why he thought she'd lie, but Savannah shook her head. "No. None."

Marc filled a syringe and injected something into Savannah's hip. Damián wondered where a civilian had scored whatever narcotics he must have given her, but he was just grateful Doc could take away some of the pain his girl was experiencing.

Marc pulled out a bottle of water that carried a medical label and opened several packets of gauze. Apparently, he'd scored all kinds of supplies for this mission. Marc poured the water over the wounds on her back, ass, and thighs, causing Savannah to wince. He used great care to gently dab away the excess blood and clean the area with the gauze.

She hissed at the touch of the gauze against her wounds, her body growing stiff as she fought against the pain.

Damián stroked her cheek and crooned to her. "Shhh. It's over now. You're safe." A glance at her back told him a couple of the lacerations were deep enough to require stitches.

Fucking bastard would pay.

Marc applied some kind of cream to the superficial cuts and bandaged the two deepest ones. Savannah hissed at the contact against her raw skin.

"Sorry, *cara*. Almost done."

Savannah nodded and Damián stroked her hair. "That's my brave girl. Don't fight it anymore. Go to your safe place now."

A sob tore from her. "I tried not to scream, but I couldn't hold it back in the end."

"Aw, *bebé*. Your screams led me to you faster, just like in the hotel. You did everything perfectly. Just hang in there. Doc…*Marc* will have you fixed up in no time, and we'll get you out of here."

"I wouldn't say the things he wanted me to. I wouldn't let him control me again."

She'd fought so hard. Such a brave warrior.

"I'm so proud of you, Savannah."

More tears flowed from her closed eyes, but she didn't tell him to stop calling her Savannah this time. "You just let it out, *querida*."

"I tried, but I couldn't stay in the moment. I wanted to escape. I wanted to be with you instead."

With him? He didn't understand what that had to do with staying in the moment, but he needed for her to stay calm. "That's only for our special times together, *bebé*." He brushed her hair behind her ear and bent over to kiss her, feeling a pain in his lower leg. "Shhh. Rest, *savita*. I'm here now."

Her body soon relaxed as the meds took effect. The sound of the SUV pulling up outside told him they would soon be able to transport her out of here to a trauma unit in Palm Springs.

Marc put some of the supplies back in the bag. "Damián, we're going to need to call for air transport. Savi's not going to be able to stand the SUV ride on those rugged back roads."

"Savannah. Her name is Savannah."

Marc nodded and patted Savannah on the calf, one of the few places she hadn't been cut to shreds. He radioed Grant to place the call. The sooner she got to a hospital, the better, even if the call brought the police out here. Her comfort and health came first.

He also wanted her checked from head to toe so they could document everything the asshole had done to her. Then he could turn his attention to that *maldito bastardo* who would get what had been coming to him since the first time he'd raped his daughter. He'd just have to work faster if the authorities would be swarming the place soon.

If Damián found out later he or that *cabrón* Lyle had raped her again, Damián would cut off their dicks and cram them down their fucking throats. Instead, he'd just make sure they didn't do it to anyone else ever again.

Later. Focus on Savannah now.

He stroked her hair and offered up a silent prayer. Jesús y Madre de Dios, *help her pull through with minimal damage.* Savannah was a fighter, a survivor. The mental and emotional trauma would have to be dealt with later, once her body healed. He hoped she'd let him help her get through this, as well.

Rage surfaced as the beast within reared its head.

Not yet. But soon. Damián would stay behind to finish this long-overdue mission. Then he'd go after Lyle.

Savannah struggled to get off the ottoman, and Damián placed his hand on the back of her head. "No, *bebé*. Lie still. Do not move."

She gave up the fight and sank down making him wonder if she'd passed out.

Damián felt a tug on his pants and boot. "You stay still, too, son. We need to pack this wound." Damián looked down at his leg as Dad cut away the desert-digital trousers, bloodied above his prosthesis.

"Fuck, son."

Marc knelt beside Dad, his medical supply bag beside him. Damián waved him away. "I'm fine, Doc. You need to work on Savannah."

"She's stable. I want to give that ointment a chance to work before I put bandages on the rest of the cuts."

Savannah gasped. "Damián, you've been shot!"

"Just a flesh wound."

"You're bleeding. Oh, God! What have I done to you?"

Damián fought the buzzing that swirled inside his head, growing louder and louder. What did she mean, what *she* had done? He knew who was responsible for this. The sonuvabitch would pay.

He opened his mouth to tell her not to worry, but glittering stars and black spots covered his field of vision as a wave of dizziness made him sway. He would *not* lose consciousness. Fuck, he wasn't finished with his mission yet.

His skin grew clammy as darkness engulfed him. Damián fought his way back, looking at Dad. "I am not leaving here until justice is done. Go back and keep an eye on him."

"Grant's with him. He's not going anywhere the way I've restrained him."

"Damián!" Savannah tried to get up from the ottoman. It was obvious by the pain glazing her eyes that the effort was causing her even more distress.

Damián pushed himself up and laid his hand on the back of her head, pushing her down. "*Savita*, don't move."

"Son, lie down before you pass out. Savi, that goes for you, too." Neither responded quickly enough for Dad. He placed his hands on his hips and assumed his master-sergeant stance. "Do. Not. Move. Either of you. I don't need both of you passing out on me."

Savannah lowered her chest to the ottoman, but she didn't take her gaze off Damián's face. He didn't take his gaze off her either, but after a few minutes, he couldn't remain upright any longer. Damián slumped to his back on the floor, gasping for breath, trying to stay alert. Memories of Doc working on him in Fallujah, trying to save his foot—no, his life—flashed across his mind. *Fuck*. Was he going to lose even more of his leg?

Knowing Savannah was in good hands, he gave himself permission to close his eyes. Just for a minute.

Damián's eyes shot open when he felt a burning sensation in his wound. Marc poured some kind of liquid over his calf. He gritted his teeth. "How bad, Doc?" The words transported him back to that scene on a rooftop in Fallujah he'd relived many times. Sweat broke out on his forehead.

He reached for the leather wristband Sergeant Miller's daughter had given him and sent up a little prayer asking for his comrade-in-arms to help them both get through this.

"Through and through wound, fleshy part of your calf." Marc injected the skin around the entry wound with something that numbed the area immediately. "Blood loss is minimal. I don't think you'll have any long-term problems. We'll fly you to the trauma center with Savannah."

Damián reached out and grabbed Doc's arm. "*My* mission…isn't…over."

Dad squeezed his shoulder. "Son, this mission just changed. It's over."

Damián glared at Dad and fought the blackness as it encroached once more. "Not leaving…until I've finished…what I came…to do."

Dad growled and looked ready to headslap him, but he backed off and looked at Marc. "Can you do something to counter the reaction to the blood loss?"

"I can hook up an IV and do a quick infusion of ringers; it's a temporary blood replacement."

"Plain English."

Marc grinned. "Yeah, I can help."

"Do it, Doc." As Marc went to work in the background, Dad met Damián's gaze. "Son, you'd better clue me in on the next phase, because you aren't going OFP."

How could it be Own Fucking Program? It *was* his program. He'd purposely left the others out of this phase, though. They'd risked enough already. This next phase of the mission could net him prison time if charges were pressed. About the only place it might be considered remotely legal would be some Third World dictatorship.

Still, he had no intention of leaving Savannah's abuse and torture unavenged.

"This is between me and the motherfucker who hurt my girl."

Dad got in his face. "You aren't completing this mission." Like hell, he wasn't. "Not without me, anyway."

Chapter Twenty-One

Disturbing images invaded Savi's mind as she drifted in and out of consciousness. Zipping Mari into the duffel bag. Lyle and another man finding Savi in the closet and pressing a smelly handkerchief over her mouth and nose. Her father. More torture.

This time, it had been different. Damián helped her through it. Until… Images of Damián lying on the floor, blood soaking his pants leg—so much blood.

Savi opened her eyes to find herself in semi-darkness. Her eyes adjusted slowly, and she saw an IV pole hanging above her bed. How long had she been here?

Where was Damián? Or…dear Lord, what if he…?

No! She wouldn't think the worst. So why wasn't he here?

Where was Mari?

Savi's mind was fuzzy from the drugs she'd been given—Lyle had been keeping her heavily drugged. *No, wait.* Lyle wasn't drugging her now.

She was in the hospital. A doctor had prescribed these drugs. Why so many? Were they keeping her sedated to postpone the grieving process or to alleviate the pain? The only pain she felt was a sharp ache around her heart.

Numb. The rest of her body felt numb. She'd worked so hard with Damián to overcome that feeling, but she was right back there again.

"I'm so proud of you, Savannah."

Savannah? Her mind's use of the name surprised her. No, Damián had called her that when he'd rescued her.

Was she coming to terms with what happened to her younger self? Could she handle the pain of that past existence?

The pain of loss?

Something niggled at her mind. Too painful. She tamped it down again.

Mari and Damián. She needed them. Where were they? Had she lost them, too? She moaned as tears burned her eyes, and she let them flow without caging them. Her throat burned. She wanted to crawl into her cave.

Escape.

No, she couldn't go there. The images of those two very different days in the beach cave—first with Maman and then with Damián—were too painful to remember now.

Sleep. Her only escape now was to give in to the drugs and float…

When she awoke again, she heard a voice over a speaker in the hallway paging someone to ICU. Still in the hospital. How long had she been here?

"Here, sweetie. Have some ice chips."

Savi blinked, confused but calmed by the familiar voice of her friend Anita. As her eyes adjusted, she saw the woman who had nurtured her back to life after she'd escaped from her father's house all those years ago standing beside her bed again. She held a Styrofoam cup in one hand and a plastic spoon in the other.

As Savi's eyes adjusted further, she surveyed the room. Private. There was a loveseat and two chairs that didn't look very comfortable. She glanced at Anita again. The woman had been like a mother to Savi all these years. Anita had a lot more gray hairs since the last time she'd seen her in December. What, three months ago? She must have been worried sick, knowing what Savi's father and Lyle were capable of.

Savi's lips were cracked and her throat dry, so she opened her mouth like a little bird to accept the soothing ice. When a piece of ice landed on the side of her mouth, she reached up to wipe it away and saw her wrist was bandaged. Ropes.

After the small pieces melted and she swallowed several spoonsful, she decided it was time to get answers to the questions foremost in her mind.

"Mari? Is she okay?" Her voice sounded raw, hoarse, and her throat felt as if it was on fire.

"Yes. She's fine, sweetie."

"Damián? Where is he?"

"I'm sorry. He's gone, dear."

Gone? Pain stabbed her chest. "No!" Tears welled in her eyes. Not Damián, too! What would she and Mari do without him? Savi owed him her life. If not for all the work he'd done with her, she wouldn't have been able to survive her father's latest abuse—physically or mentally. Her mind and body would have completely split apart, with no hope of reintegration.

Savi hadn't told him how much he meant to her. She didn't want to go on without Damián in her life. And what would Mari do without her Daddy?

Savi's chin quivered and tears spilled from the corners of her eyes. She admitted how much she'd come to care for him these past few months. Her father had taken him away from her.

"He won, Anita."

Anita brushed the hair away from her forehead. "Who won, honey?"

Savi closed her eyes, unable to speak. The pain was too intense, and there was no creative visualization powerful enough to numb her or remove that hurt from her this time. She stopped fighting the drugs and tried to fade back into oblivion.

Sleep. Escape.

"How is she?"

Savi dreamt she heard Damián's voice.

"No change. She asked about you. Got upset when I told her you weren't here. Glad you're back. They gave her another shot of pain meds a few minutes ago. When she wakes again, see if you can get some more ice chips in her. Her lips are so dry. I'll go down to the gift shop and get some lip balm for her."

Footsteps. A chair scooted on the floor. "*Mi sueño*, come back to us. Marisol and I need you." There it was again, the whispering voice of her angel, Damián.

Perhaps she was dying, too, and Damián was there to cross her over. With a groan, she opened her eyes, wanting to see him, to go to him. Damián hovered over her, a Styrofoam cup in his hand. He smiled. A sense of peace enveloped her, and she felt her soul merge with his, just for a moment.

"Take me home, Damián."

He grinned. "Well, the doctors might not let me do that for a little while yet."

Doctors?

She blinked and looked around, adjusting to the darkened room. The Styrofoam cup floating before her gaze tipped her off. "This isn't heaven, is it?"

A shadow crossed his face. "I'm not sure they'd let someone like me in there." His callused fingers stroked her temple. "But it sure feels like heaven to me, looking into your beautiful blue eyes again, *bebé*."

More tears sprang forth, trickling down the sides of her face and into her hair. "I thought you were dead. You were shot. Bleeding."

"*No es nada.* I've been through much worse. Just slowed me down a little."

"And Mari? She's okay?"

"Yeah, Karla and Marisol flew out late last night. They and Adam are staying with Rosa and the kids. Marisol's been getting acquainted with her aunt and cousins. Teresa loves having another girl around."

Savi hadn't thought about how Mari had a whole new extended family, in addition to Damián's friends in Denver.

Emotion overwhelmed her again. She sniffled. "Oh, God. Damián, I thought I'd lost you."

He brushed the tears into her hair. "Shhhh, *bebé*. You've been through a lot. Just rest now."

She sniffled. "I'm sorry for the waterworks."

She saw his teeth gleaming against his brown skin as he smiled. "Hey, remember how hard it was for you to cry the first time?" Memories of their exhaustive first SM session, where he'd demanded nothing less than full-on tears brought a smile to her as well.

"Anytime you feel like crying is fine by me, *savita*, because it means you're feeling something again. Your tears—your emotions—are the most beautiful gifts you can give me. The rest will follow."

"Oh, Damián. You've done so much for me. When my father was beating me…" Savi winced at the memory and Damián shushed her again, but she didn't want to be silenced. She needed for him to know what he meant to her. "The pain was so awful. I imagined myself with you and I didn't even feel most of the blows he delivered. You were there with me. You carried me away from the pain, to our special place."

A puzzled look flashed across his face. He bent to kiss her lips.

Numb again. She couldn't feel him. Frustrated, she squeezed her eyes shut. "It's no use."

He pulled away to look at her, remaining close to her face. "What's no use?" He stroked her hair.

"I want to feel again, but I can't. I'm numb."

Damián took his thumb and middle finger and thumped her arm. "Ouch! Why did you—" Her eyes opened wide. "I felt that!"

He grinned. "Thought you might."

"Why didn't I feel your kiss just now?"

The tip of his finger traced the area around her mouth, not touching her lips, and she shivered as a tingle of awareness coursed through her.

"I felt that, too."

"Of course, you did. Your lips are numb because they're chapped. You got dehydrated in the desert. They're loading you up with fluids, though." She looked up and saw the IV bag.

Savi felt giddy. She hadn't shut down again. A mixture of dehydration and pain medication had probably left her feeling numb.

She wanted to touch him, too, if for no other reason than to feel closer to him. Memories of how he'd made love to her all those years ago left her craving his touch.

"What's going on in that pretty little head, *chica*?"

She smiled. "Take me back to the beach cave."

A pained looked crossed his face, and he pulled away. "You just concentrate on getting well so we can get you out of here."

What had come over her? She hadn't thought before she spoke; her defenses were gone. He couldn't possibly want that. She could never be Savannah for him again.

Savannah was a part of her and always would be. But that girl who believed her body was only good for sex no longer existed. Damián wasn't looking for a woman only for sex, but he'd at least need to have sex every now and then. She couldn't be that woman for him.

"My father? Lyle? They can't…"

He shook his head. "They won't be coming anywhere near you again, or Marisol, either. When they get discharged from the hospitals they're in, they're going straight to jail on murder, kidnapping, assault, and a bunch of other charges."

Savi wondered for about a millisecond what had happened to land them in the hospital. She didn't really care, though. They deserved whatever they'd gotten. As long as they were under guard and couldn't get to Mari or her, she could pretend they didn't exist anymore.

Their depravity hadn't touched her daughter. That's all that counted.

"Father didn't want Mari because she has your brown eyes…and Maman's. Oh, God!"

Damián set the cup on the tray table and framed her face, a worried frown on his face. "What is it? Are you in pain?"

She shook her head, but truly she was. The worst pain. She couldn't breathe.

"Where are you, *savita*?"

"He killed Maman!" Her voice sounded high-pitched in her ears.

"Where are you, Savannah?"

"Hiding. I don't want him to find me. He'll hurt me, too."

"Where are you, Savannah?"

She blinked, focusing on Damián's face. She took a deep breath. "I'm with you, Sir. Oh, God. He killed her. I always thought she'd left me because she wanted a new life and a new family with that man. She didn't. I watched Father…" she gasped for air, "…strangle her."

"I'm so sorry, *bebé*. You shouldn't have had to witness that. I don't know how you've survived all that bastard put you through. So strong."

She didn't feel strong at all. "I tried to make him stop, but I couldn't help her." A sob tore from her throat.

He brushed a thumb over her cheek. "You were just a baby. How could you fight off a grown man?"

True. Though she'd relived the scene with the eyes of a grown-up, Savannah had only been eight when her mother was murdered. She couldn't have stopped him any more than Mari could have. Savannah shouldn't feel guilty about that.

She needed to let that go. It wasn't her fault.

"I need to find Maman's body. She needs a proper burial."

"Any idea what he might have done with her body?"

"I don't know how long he was gone. I just remember bits and pieces of my childhood, especially that night. When he came into Savannah's bedroom that night…my room."

Savannah and Savi no longer felt like two separate people. A shudder passed through her as she remembered what her father had done to her for the first of many times that night. Everything was foggy, even though the memories were coming back in pieces.

"Father made me take big, nasty-tasting pills. They made me so sleepy all the time."

Savannah. Me.

"I tried to tell the maid what had happened to Maman, but the woman told me it wasn't right to tell horrible lies about my father." The woman told Savannah her Maman was a whore who had run off with another man. Left her.

The maid had helped instill the thoughts in her head that her mother had deserted her.

Savannah squeezed her eyes shut. She couldn't think about Maman's murder anymore. Father couldn't hurt either of them ever again.

She drew a ragged breath. "His shoes were muddy. She's probably buried right on the estate somewhere."

Damián nodded. "Makes sense. I'll hire someone with ground-penetrating-radar equipment. We'll find her."

Accepting the fact that Maman was gone forever was the hardest thing she'd ever done. Savi had held onto the fantasy of one day finding her, letting her meet her granddaughter, finding out why she'd abandoned Savannah.

But Maman hadn't done that at all. She'd been murdered. Right before Savannah's eyes.

Sadness and exhaustion lay heavily on her chest, and her eyelids drooped. *Escape. Sleep.*

"Oh, Savannah." The anguish in Damián's voice brought her back. "I promised you I'd never let him touch either of you. I let you down. It took me so long to find you. I'm sorry that you had to suffer at his hands again."

She opened her heavy eyelids and raised a hand to his cheek. "You were there with me, Damián. You helped me escape the pain this time."

He looked puzzled, but Savi could stay awake no longer. With Damián by her side, it was finally okay to close her eyes.

Safe.

* * *

Seeing Savannah's battered, bloodied body in that cabin had made him question whether he'd ever be able to protect her from the shitheads of the world. If he hadn't found her when he had, how much more would she have suffered at her father's hands?

Dad had talked with Victor to find out what the fuck had gone wrong. Apparently, Patti had called him in a state of panic after someone had left a threatening message on their answering machine. Victor had asked Dad to relieve him thinking everything would be okay for the few minutes the apartment would be without surveillance. More than likely, *Cabrón* had been behind the phone call. They must have been watching the apartment, too.

Dad said Victor was beating himself up over being so careless, but that *cabrón*, Lyle, apparently had spooked Patti, knowing Victor would run. How long had he been watching them to have that kind of intel?

Damián and Dad had made sure they'd exacted justice for Savannah. After the piece-of-shit old man had screamed out he wasn't the one who performed the actual branding, well, they'd finished that part of the mission anyway. Afterward, they returned to Rancho to take care of *Cabrón* in the same manner. Both had paid for what they'd done to Savannah. Justice—Marine style. Probably a good thing Dad had been there with him. He'd kept Damián from killing both the bastards.

Among those who participated in the raids—Dad, Grant, Marc, and him—only Damián could be identified visibly. They'd borrowed some equipment and supplies from friends at Pendleton, refusing to tell any of them what they were going to do with it. If they'd involved any active-duty Marines and those guys had gotten caught, it would have ruined their military careers—and possibly gotten them court-martialed.

Damián made sure the bastards who had abused Savannah knew he was the one doling out justice to them. He wanted them to wake up screaming at night seeing *his* face.

Neither man would press charges—not after Damián had made it clear he had "friends" in the California prison system, some of them being the very kids Damián had served with in juvie who'd never managed to stay out of the system.

Gentry and Lyle would be serving time—probably for the rest of their lives—after the police got the full story from Savannah. Damián knew firsthand being locked up was a helluva lot worse punishment than having a bullet between the eyes.

He watched Savannah sleeping peacefully for the first time since she'd awakened in the wee hours of the morning. She'd been in here almost two full days. The nurses said she was doing remarkably well considering all she'd been through.

Knowing she was on the mend gave him a sense of relief, although his anxiety returned when he remembered she wanted to go back to Thousand Steps Beach. He couldn't carry her down those fucking steps, not without them both winding up in a heap at the bottom of the stairway. How fucking romantic would that be?

Maybe there was another beach cave somewhere that was more accessible—but she'd called Thousand Steps at Laguna "our special place." *Damn.*

Savannah groaned in her sleep, grimacing—whether from physical or emotional pain, he wasn't sure. Damián reached out to stroke her upper arm, tracing the scars where a younger Savannah had tried to make one kind of pain go away by inflicting another, one she could control herself.

He wondered what she'd meant about him being with her to help her get through the pain her father had inflicted this time. When he'd seen how deep the cuts were to her backside, he'd been hard-pressed not to castrate the old man after he'd wrapped the coat hanger around the bastard's sac and equipment. Lyle had gotten the same treatment, for delivering Savannah to that bastard. At least now both shitheads knew what it had felt like to be branded.

Justice for Savannah. Sitting in a cushy jail cell waiting for a trial wasn't going to deliver that kind of message to them, that's for damned sure.

Damián had left *Cabrón's* kneecaps intact. All he'd wanted was eye-for-an-eye justice. Neither man would get an erection without pain now. Both would wear Damián's brand and would probably become bitches to their fellow inmates once the guys on the inside learned these two were abusers—one a pedophile who raped his own daughter. With so many inmates having been victims of sexual abuse as kids, he knew the likes of Gentry and *Cabrón* wouldn't have an easy time of it in prison.

Damián smiled.

Righteous retribution.

Of course, Damián had added two more sins to the list for which he would have to seek absolution. He hoped Mamá and Papá hadn't been watching, but he'd learned long ago it was better to ask for forgiveness than to let bastards like those walk away unpunished. He'd have a talk with Father Martine about what he might do for penance, but he'd never feel remorse or regret for the justice he'd exacted from either man. He just wished he could have done the job without involving Dad. He hoped the man wouldn't have any lingering nightmares or guilt about what they'd done.

Savannah shuddered in her sleep, and he reached down to pull a sheet over her arms.

Footsteps approaching the doorway sent him on alert. He turned to see Dad and relaxed. Not wanting to disturb her rest, he motioned that he'd be right there and brushed his lips lightly against the top of her head. "Sleep well, *mi sueño*."

She smiled in her sleep, and he turned, crossing the darkened room and heading toward the hallway.

Dad kept his voice low and shoved a sack from a burger place at him. "How's she doing?"

"Better. She thought I'd been killed. I had no idea she'd think that, or I'd have gotten here sooner."

"Not sure we could have taken care of those shitheads any faster." Dad glanced into the room where Savannah slept. "After what she's been through, it's amazing she even knows who she is anymore."

Damián nodded.

Adam gave him a sharp look. "How about you?"

Damián glanced away. "The ER docs checked out the leg. Marc did a good job, they said."

"I'm not talking about your leg, but it's good to hear it's all right. I'm talking about how the mission ended. What we did after the raid."

"I'm fine. It needed doing."

Adam placed a firm hand on Damián's shoulder and squeezed it. "I'm just glad you didn't have to go it alone. What we did was fucking justified, after all they've put her through." Dad glanced at the door to Savannah's room. "Christ, I had no idea…she's been through fucking hell. She's one of the strongest people I've ever met. Would have made one helluva Marine. You two have a lot in common."

"I haven't been through nearly as much as she has."

"Bullshit. This isn't a pissing match. You've just been through a different kind of pain, that's all."

Damián looked down at the floor.

Dad squeezed Damián's shoulder again, demanding that he look at him once more. "Karla and I are going to have to get back to Denver soon. You gonna be all right?"

"Yeah."

"Any idea what you're going to do when she gets released from here?"

No fucking clue.

"Not really. A lot is still up in the air concerning us." No sense talking about making Savannah his. He hadn't broken down that wall yet, if he hadn't gotten her to surrender her heart to him.

"You two are perfect for each other. I started to see it at your birthday party. When I talked with her in the club that night you had to top Patti, I knew it. Trust your instincts." He patted Damián on the back. "You'll do the right thing. You always do. Now, I'm heading back over to Rosa's. Marisol and Karla have challenged José and me to a game of Risk. What do you think our chances are?"

Damián chuckled. "Be afraid, man. Be *very* afraid." He gave Dad a bear hug before watching him walk down the hallway toward the elevator.

He sat on a bench in the hallway and opened the bag to find a burger, fries, and a cherry pie. As he ate, he thought about what Dad had said. Dad would want him to marry her. Hell, Damián wanted that, too, more than anything in the world. He wanted the three of them to be a real family with a commitment in the eyes of God and the law. Not that a marriage certificate would make a difference as far as his love for her and the pledge he'd already made—albeit one-sided—to protect and cherish her and Marisol forever. He realized he'd only told Marisol he loved her. The thought of losing either of his girls without letting them know how he felt ripped a gash in his gut. He needed to tell Savannah—

Fuck that shit.

Savannah wasn't ready to hear that kind of declaration yet. He'd let her heal first, at least physically. Her father had gouged opened a lot of old scars. While she seemed to have weathered the ordeal better than he'd expected by pulling from her deep well of strength, she'd been kept pretty doped up. Most of this would hit her later.

He'd be with her for the long haul. He wanted her to fully reclaim Savannah, the sweet girl he'd met so long ago. Not that he didn't love Savi, too, but having her as one whole person again would help her heal even faster. He'd talked with her therapist earlier, and the woman had given him general advice on warning signs that would indicate he might be in deeper than he could handle without professional assistance.

Damián hoped she'd let him help her by continuing to top her. They'd been making a lot of progress, before all this shit happened.

He tossed the empty bag in a nearby trash bin and stood up to go back inside to Savannah when he noticed Anita Gonzales coming down the hall holding what looked like a photo album.

"How's our patient?"

"Sleeping. Probably the best thing for her now."

Anita nodded and looked down at the album, then extended it to him. "Damián, I wanted you to have this. Father Martine brought it to me. He's down in the chapel and will look in on her in a while before heading back to Solana Beach."

Damián accepted the thick album, unsure if she wanted him to open it here or what he should say.

"There are photos there to help you fill in some of the gaps in Savi and Marisol's lives." She grinned sheepishly. "I'm a bit of a shutterbug."

"Thanks, ma'am. I'll take a look when I go back inside, while Savannah's sleeping." He knew instinctively that he needed to be alone when he looked at these photos.

She smiled. "I understand. Listen, why don't you go get something to eat? Food's not too bad in the cafeteria. I'll sit with her until you get back."

"No, ma'am, that's okay. My dad just brought me some. I just want to get back to her."

Anita's smile grew wider. "You know, she told me about how you rescued her at that hotel and watched over her while she slept, not taking advantage of her the way so many men would have. I tried to locate you after Marisol was born but couldn't get past the dead end at your old apartment address."

"I appreciate you trying, but I don't know if I would have been any good to either of them back then. I had some sh…stuff to get through myself, ma'am." Damián looked away and cleared his throat before returning his gaze to the woman who had been more of a parent to Savannah than her own mother'd had a chance to be. "I don't know of anyone whose blessing I would like more than yours, ma'am. You've been like a mother to her. When the time is right, I'd very much like to ask her to marry me."

Tears filled the woman's eyes, but she smiled. "I think Savi would be the luckiest woman in the world to have a fine young man like you, someone with so much integrity and honor."

Damián swallowed against the lump in his throat. If she knew what he'd done in the past couple days alone she might not describe him that way, however, what she didn't know about him was best kept that way. "Ma'am, don't say anything to her yet. I want to wait until the time is right, for her to heal up some more."

"My lips are sealed."

They said their goodbyes and, as she walked away, Damián looked down at the photo album in his hands. His heart pounded like a slapper on a steel fender as he turned and walked back into Savannah's room. She still slept, her breathing shallow and regular.

Taking a spot on the loveseat, he flipped on a reading light and looked at

Savi to make sure he hadn't disturbed her before he opened the album. The first page had a few photos of a very pregnant Savannah. Seeing his tiny little butterfly with *his* baby filling her belly raised bumps on his arms. Unbelievable.

In most of the pictures, she wore a smile on her face that didn't reach her sad, blue eyes. Her face was fuller than it was now. Despite what she'd been through, the young woman in the photo still held an innocence and a vulnerability about her that made him want to step into the picture and wrap his arms around her.

Next, a photo of her singing in the choir with Father Martine in jeans and a T-shirt, directing what must be a practice. Savannah was singing her heart out, belly still large with Marisol.

Damián flipped the page and tunnel vision blocked everything but the photo of Savannah holding a wet and naked Marisol, umbilical cord still attached. Marisol didn't look too happy. The squalling baby was laying skin-to-skin on her bare breasts as Savannah seemed to shush her, a supportive hand against the back of Marisol's head. A rush of unexpected tears flooded his eyes, and he looked up to make sure Savannah wasn't awake. He dashed them away, only to have many more follow. What the fuck was the matter with him?

Aw, hell. Who was he kidding? Himself. If he'd been there to watch Marisol enter the world, he'd probably have cried his eyes out then, too. He looked at the photo again. This had to be Marisol's very first photo. He should have been there taking the pictures and holding his two beautiful girls close. His chest ached at all he'd missed.

There were a number of other images taken in the delivery room, after Marisol had been cleaned up and bundled into a yellow blanket. Later ones showed Savannah in a nightgown with the snaps undone, holding Marisol's tiny rosebud mouth to her dark nipple as she nursed their tiny daughter. Something coiled deep in his gut. She'd told him she'd nursed their baby, but seeing the picture pointed out one more thing he'd missed out on.

He turned more pages in the album, savoring each glimpse into the past he hadn't shared with them. He watched his daughter being baptized, celebrating her first birthday, dressed as a princess for Halloween, carrying an Ariel-mermaid backpack on what might have been her first day of school, holding up a tooth and a dollar and wearing a big toothless grin. More tears flooded his eyes. He didn't even bother to hide them anymore.

Damián had never known a woman stronger than she was. Savannah had been forced to do everything on her own, including raising *their* daughter. He hadn't been there for either of them. Alone, she'd devoted her entire being to making a safe, happy childhood for her daughter, despite the sacrifices to her own freedom.

Now that he had his girls in his life, what could *he* offer them? He'd probably just lost his job again for going after Savannah and missing work. There was always the possibility the two *cabrones* in custody right now would squeal, sending Damián to jail himself for using Third World torture tactics on them.

How could he offer his girls a stable life? He didn't even know where Savannah would want to live. She'd probably want to get her old job back at the clinic and return to Southern California. Of course, he also had family ties here. While he'd chosen to make his home in Denver—well, initially, he'd had little choice. When Adam had visited him in the hospital and told him in no uncertain terms he *was* going to move in with him and join him in opening the club, like it or lump it, the choice had been taken from him.

However, he didn't need Dad now the way he had back then. Still, he liked having the man nearby. Damián could talk about the demons with Dad more than he could anyone else. He wouldn't burden Savannah with stories about Fallujah. Yeah, there were telephones, and it was a short drive and shorter flight between the two places. Bottom line was that he'd give up everything to be close to his daughter—and Savannah, too, if she'd have him.

No fucking way could he let either of his girls out of his life this time.

"What are you looking at?"

Savannah's voice was husky from her medicated nap and sounded sexy as sin. His dick stirred as Damián looked up to find Savannah with a worried look on her face. Embarrassed, more by his tears than his hard-on, he stood and turned away, surreptitiously wiping his tears away as he laid the photo album on the loveseat and walked over to sit in the chair by her bed.

"Anita brought me a photo album of you and Marisol."

Savannah smiled weakly, still looking a little doped up. "She was always taking pictures. I'm glad she did, though." Her voice grew even huskier. "My life started just before that album began, just like Marisol's did. We love looking at the pictures in the album she gave me. I guess she kept some prints for herself, too."

Damián bent down and kissed Savannah lightly on the lips, before leaning away to look into her eyes. "Thank you for keeping our baby. Thank you for taking such good care of her and yourself."

Tears filled Savannah's eyes. *Jesús*, they sparkled like sapphires when she teared up.

"I made so many mistakes…"

To still her negative words, Damián placed a finger on her lips and also calmed her quavering chin. "You survived, and you made a good life for the two of you. Don't let me ever hear you put down what you did. Nobody's perfect, *mi sueño*, but you're about as close to perfection as I've ever known." Would he ever be able to get her to see herself the way he did?

His eyes burned. He leaned his forehead against hers, hoping to hide his tears, but one escaped from his eye and splashed onto her face. *Busted.*

"If you tell anyone Damián Orlando cried, I'll do a zipper line on you with plastic clothespins that will hurt like hell—and I'll spare nothing but your most tender parts."

Savannah's laugh bubbled up and out. He smiled. God, he could live on nothing but her laugh for the rest of his life and never need anything more. Well, except maybe a bit of Marisol's giggle for dessert.

If only Savannah would say yes to a messed-up man like him, but he couldn't ask until he found a way to support his family. He needed to call the shop.

But what if she wanted to stay here in California? Well, he could find a new place to work out here. Maybe he'd line up jobs in both places. Hedge his bets.

He wouldn't risk having Savannah and Marisol out of his life ever again.

Chapter Twenty-Two

"I've waited over a month for tonight's date, *mi sueño*."

Savannah shivered as Damián placed a kiss on her cheek. Memories of all that had happened in the last month flashed through her mind. They almost hadn't gotten to go on this date at all.

She still couldn't believe Maman was dead. As he'd promised, Damián had hired someone to search her father's secluded, overgrown three-acre estate in Rancho Santa Fe. It had taken a couple of days, but they'd found two skeletons, not one. The two had been buried in the long-neglected rose garden just yards from the house, one of Maman's favorite places to be. Not that her father would have chosen it for that reason. The soil would have been easier to dig into there. Except for when he was beating Savannah—and probably Maman before her—the man did very little to exert himself physically.

The forensics results revealed that her Maman was truly dead, as was John Grainger, the man who had tried to take them away from her father. John had been shot in the head, the bullet found among the remains. After a search of dental records turned up a positive match with a missing-person's report, his sister had been notified. He must have come to the house that night or soon after looking for Maman—and for Savannah. They both had wanted her; Maman would never have deserted her.

Two weeks ago, Father Martine had conducted a beautiful funeral Mass and graveside service in Oceanside. John's sister had said the two presumed lovers had been together in death this long, so she and Savannah had agreed they should remain together.

Her father had confessed to both murders. He'd pled guilty by reason of insanity, probably hoping the courts would be lenient. She planned to return to California to attend his competency hearing and sentencing to make sure he got the maximum prison term possible.

Lyle maintained his innocence until Savannah produced the hard drive she'd stolen from her father's computer when she ran away, clearly showing Lyle's involvement as her handler during her sexual slavery period. He'd backed down some, but still refused to plea bargain. *Fine.* He'd get more prison time if a jury heard—or saw—what he'd done to her body. If it helped get him convicted, she'd even let the authorities take photos of the brand.

Still, she'd keep track of his trial dates. The DA assured her she would be notified whenever anything moved on either case, but Anita also promised to keep close tabs on their cases. Savannah wouldn't let anything fall through the cracks. She'd do whatever she could to make them pay for the rest of their lives, especially if that is what it took to give her closure and peace of mind. She wanted to move forward and not look back.

Maman's former attorney had produced the will her mother had drawn up a month before she'd been murdered. Maman had left nothing to her father and everything to Savannah. She'd learned that the French-style hotel in La Jolla her father prized—and had used as the setting to debase his daughter the year before she'd escaped—had actually belonged to Maman's parents until her grandmother died and Maman inherited it. But Maman had allowed Father to control all of her financial matters.

Savannah also had learned that Maman's attorney tried to have her declared deceased even before Savannah had escaped her father. Might her last years under Father's control have changed if someone had given her that freedom? A moot point, because Father had foiled the attempt by producing a postcard supposedly written by Maman a year earlier and mailed from Paris. Father seemed to have thought of every contingency to perpetuate the ruse that Maman had deserted her family. The judge, probably on Father's payroll, had denied the attorney's request.

The mansion that had been her private prison and torture chamber for so many years had been listed with a real-estate firm at a price Savannah hoped would get someone to jump at it quickly. Unfortunately, the media coverage had only brought out the curiosity seekers wanting to see the place they'd heard about in the news recently. The salacious details of what her father and Lyle had done to her and her mother had made the news channels regularly for weeks.

She had also put the hotel up for sale. The sooner she could sever all ties with the settings of her past, the better. She never wanted to return to either of those places again.

She hated the flood of repressed memories that had nearly overwhelmed her when she'd first accepted that Savannah wasn't dead. Now she embraced again the name Maman had chosen for her, inspired by a visit she'd made to the old southern city on her first trip to America as a child.

Of course, money wasn't going to be an issue for her and Mari from now on. However, Savannah didn't want to be saddled with the responsibility for handling much money, especially money her father had been managing for almost two decades. She often reminded herself that she needed to be practical. The money wasn't really her father's, but Maman's, and Mari deserved better than for her mother to have to scrape together money to buy new shoes or jeans, the way she'd had to all these years.

On the plus side, she could do a lot of good with her newfound millions. She wouldn't spend it on an extravagant house. She wanted to keep her and Mari's lives stable and normal, whatever that was.

"Sure you're up to this tonight, *bebé*? The scene I have planned for when we get back to the club will be emotionally intense, although not physically demanding."

If it would take her mind off the traumas of the past month, then bring it.

"I'm ready to move on, Damián. And I've been looking forward to our date, too."

In recent weeks, she'd healed physically from the kidnapping and beating. Knowing her father and Lyle could never touch her again also helped heal her fearful, battered spirit. Before leaving California, Savannah had spoken with the new District Attorney for the county—one who didn't seem to be on her father's payroll—and gave her a complete accounting of what these two monsters had been responsible for doing over the years, including last month's kidnapping and well-documented abuse.

Damián stroked her arm, bringing her back to the bedroom at Adam and Karla's. "Strip everything off. I only want you wearing the clothes in this bag. I was going to lay everything out, but, well, I didn't get that far."

He handed her a pink-and-silver striped shopping bag from the popular mall lingerie store. She was supposed to wear lingerie in public?

"Meet me in the kitchen. You have ten minutes."

Without waiting for her response, he walked out of the room and down the hall. Savannah opened the bag and pulled out the first article of clothing she found inside.

"Holy shit." Short shorts? *Very* short, neon-pink hot pants. Was he serious? Next, she pulled out a matching hot-pink tank top with spaghetti-straps. Neither article left anything to the imagination. She laid them on the bed, still not believing he expected her to wear this outfit on a date, and looked back inside the bag. No panties. He preferred her to go without panties in a scene where he was topping her, but on a date? No bra, either. She realized the tank had built-in cups, which must have been why he'd asked for her size.

Even with the bit of support in the top, no way could she dress like this in public. Her scarred arm would be exposed for everyone to see, along with just about everything else. Damián knew about her history of cutting, and so did anyone who'd seen her strip in the great room downstairs, but who else would see her when they went out wherever he planned to take her?

She picked up the short shorts and knew they would barely cover her butt cheeks. No effing way. How could he make pink cotton clothes look so…slutty?

Dirty little slut.

Is that what he wanted her to look like? What he wanted her to dress like when he took her out?

Savannah's heart pounded. "I can't do this."

Trust him.

Surely Damián wouldn't intentionally degrade or humiliate her. He was always so protective and caring. There must be a very good reason why he wanted her to dress like a slut.

Trust him.

Savannah reached up and unbuttoned her blouse. When she laid the sedate, navy-blue, long-sleeved blouse next to the hot-pink tank, she had another bout of nerves.

She never wore clothes that would attract attention to her body.

Where could he possibly take her dressed like this? Well, there was one saving grace. They were in Denver, and it was still early spring. She'd at least get to wear her coat. Surely.

Trust him.

Savannah removed her bra and picked up the pink tank, slipping it over her head. She tried to push her boobs into the tank's bra, but they spilled over. Hadn't he heard her tell him her bra size? Or had he undersized it intentionally?

That rat bastard.

The top didn't cover much of her belly. Even after tugging it down, she couldn't cover her stretch marks. She didn't need to put on the hip-hugging shorts to know they wouldn't reach that far, adding to her embarrassment.

But the clock was ticking and she'd dallied long enough. She shimmied out of her jeans and panties, pulled on the shorts, and walked to the dresser mirror.

He'd made a point of calling her Savannah since she'd come back to Denver. He'd also reminded her she didn't have to remain a redhead. This morning, she'd dyed her hair as close to its original blonde as she could guess until it grew out. Now, when she looked in the mirror, she saw Savannah Gentry, not Savi Baker.

Savannah's gaze lowered to her chest. Her nipples jutted against the thin fabric. *Oh dear Lord.* Thank God Mari was with Angelina at Damián's apartment. She hoped Karla and Adam wouldn't see her before they left the house.

You're a dirty slut, Savannah.

She squeezed her eyes closed. "I can't do this."

"Yes, you can."

Savannah jumped and turned to find Damián standing in the doorway, leaning against the jamb. She hadn't even heard the door open. She raised her hands, one to cover her breasts and the other her belly.

"Hands at your sides. Don't ever hide your beautiful body from me, Savannah."

Her nipples grew enlarged under his slow scrutiny of her body. The urge to continue to cover herself was off the charts, but his stare forced her hands to her sides. She clenched her fists as he stared at her.

Dirty slut.

Bile rose in her throat. She began shaking and cast a furtive glance at the bathroom door, wondering if she could make it there before she got sick.

"Savannah. I asked you a question."

Her gaze returned to his. "I'm sorry," she whispered. "I didn't hear you, Sir."

"I asked if you were ready."

"Ready for what, Sir?"

He walked across the room to stand in front of her and said, "Ready to submit to me tonight?"

She swallowed hard. How much would he demand of her? Something major was going to happen, she just didn't know how far he'd push her. "How much of myself do I need to submit?"

He reached out to tweak her hard nipple. "Definitely your body." She sucked in air and tried to step away but found her pink clad butt pressed against the dresser.

He raised his hand to the side of her face, and his finger grazed her temple. "Your mind." Her mind was mush at the moment; he could have it.

"It's yours, Sir."

Then his finger blazed a trail down her cheek, her neck, over the exposed swell of her protruding mound, until it rested in the cleft between her breasts, which seemed even more exposed. He didn't state the obvious, only looked into her eyes searching for her response.

Savannah shook her head as her heart thumped against his finger. Falling in love would mean he would want to have sex. "I can't go that far."

He grinned, but his eyes held a hint of sadness. "We'll start with your body and mind, then. The other will follow when the time is right and you feel secure enough."

He placed his hands on her upper arms, one thumb covering some of the old razor scars, and pulled her toward him. Her gaze lowered to his lips, and she expected him to kiss her. Too intimate. Before she had a chance to pull away, he bent down to kiss her on the cheek.

He took a step back. "Present yourself."

That order always made her think he was on some kind of military-fantasy trip, however one look at her outfit would dispel those thoughts quickly. No soldier would wear a hot-pink tank top and short-shorts as part of her uniform.

She clasped her elbows behind her back, and her boobs threatened to spill out of the tank. Her face heated.

He cupped each of her breasts, bending to place a kiss on the top of each mound. His mustache tickled her skin and goose bumps rose on her chest and arms. He stood again and stared at her face. "Very pretty."

His praise sent a pool of warmth to settle in her abdomen. She wanted him to think she was pretty.

He stepped back from her. "Two steps forward." She took one normal step and realized another would plaster her flat against his broad chest. She took a smaller one.

He grinned and walked in a circle around her, inspecting her. When he was behind her, he patted her on the butt, his hand caressing her bare cheeks hanging out below the shorts.

I can't do this.

"Beautiful."

Damián bent to whisper in her ear. "At ease, *mamacita*." The words sent a shiver down her spine into her pelvis.

As if she would ever feel at ease around him, especially dressed like this.

"Time to go."

For comfort, she asked if she could wear the silver cross necklace she'd found in Maman's jewelry box. He nodded. She slipped into her brown flats. They didn't go with the outfit, but she shrugged. They were all she had and he hadn't provided anything else.

A few minutes later, Savi preceded him down the stairs and into the kitchen. Someone whistled a cat-call, making her cringe inside. She looked up to find Adam with a huge grin on his face. "You look beautiful tonight, Savannah."

Damián had everyone calling her Savannah now, probably trying to get her to think of herself as Savannah, too. She came to a halt as realization dawned.

Oh, dear Lord. Other men would be noticing her body tonight, too. "Damián, I don't think…"

"No, you won't be thinking tonight. This date and evening are all about changing perceptions and misconceptions. Now, lose those shoes. You didn't ask permission to wear them."

"But you didn't include any shoes in the bag." Surely he didn't expect her to go barefoot in freezing temperatures. He wasn't *that* sadistic.

He pointed to the floor near the table where she found a pair of matching neon-pink, platform stiletto mules. She looked back at him to see if he was kidding. The man did have a serious teasing streak in him.

He grinned, but didn't back down. "I didn't want you to break your neck wearing them down the stairs."

"What's to keep me from falling in them now?"

"Me, *querida*." He reached out and stroked her bare arm. "I get to grab your sweet body to keep you from falling anytime you stumble."

Is that what men found so attractive about these kinds of shoes—all the free grabs in the name of being chivalrous? Without arguing, she slipped off the brown shoes and slid into the mules.

Adam picked up Savannah's coat from the hook by the door. "You kids have a good time tonight." Adam helped Savannah into the sleeves. She'd never welcomed a coat more than now, because it covered her nearly naked body. Damián held the back door, and they walked out into the cold night air.

Damián drove her Nissan across the downtown area to a Mexican cantina that reminded her a little bit of the one they'd stopped at on the way home from the beach cave. He'd insisted that she give him her coat at the door and forced her to walk through the restaurant in the revealing outfit. Even though there were few other patrons, she'd lost much of her appetite by the time they'd reached their table.

After ordering two huge plates of enchiladas and Spanish rice, she kept her gaze on her plate as they began to eat in silence. Her mind had been bombarded over the last month to the point she barely could focus on anything anymore. No wonder he hadn't tried a scene at the club before tonight. She wasn't even sure she could stay focused in one tonight.

Damián brushed his thumb over her cheek and wiped away the telltale dampness. She hadn't realized she'd shed a tear.

"Thank you, Damián."

"*De nada.*"

She smiled. "Not for wiping away my tears. For being such a wonderful daddy to Mari."

"I'm just grateful to be a part of her life, even if—"

She held up her hand. "Don't say it." She looked down at her plate; she'd totally lost her appetite now. They'd gone round and round about his wanting to be something more permanent in Savannah's life, but she wasn't ready yet. For now, her plan was to find a house near Damián's place and fairly close to Mari's school.

She trusted Damián. Really, she did. She wanted him to continue to be her Service Top, but lately when she looked at him, she knew he wanted something more—something she couldn't give. Spending this afternoon with Karla trying to find alternatives to actually having intercourse made it abundantly clear Savannah wasn't cut out for sex—normal or kinky. Most of the online videos squicked her out.

Damián had told her he understood why her body betrayed her at those times. Still, the words kept rolling around in her head.

Dirty slut.

Damián said tonight would be a chance to redirect those messages, but could they ever be erased? Hearing her father and Lyle speak them again last month, she'd found that the word *whore* held less power over her than when she was younger. Damián had helped her with that. She knew from her clinicals how hard it was for her patients to erase those negative mental tapes. Savannah had allowed hers to become so deep-seated, because she'd avoided tackling them for so long. She'd even tried to hide that part of herself from Damián, but he'd discovered her secrets, her shame. Would she ever be able to fully heal?

Memories of the scene at the beach cave with Damián that she'd visualized while her father was beating her flashed in her mind. Would they ever make love there or anywhere else again?

She looked up from her plate. Damián stared at her, concern on his face. He'd been taking care of her ever since she'd come out of the hospital. She needed to stand on her own two feet and stop sending mixed messages.

She smiled. "The real-estate agent called this morning, and she's found another house for us to look at. Just went on the market. A few blocks from Mari's school. Do you want to go with us? You'll probably be able to check things out better than I can to make sure there aren't any structural problems."

"You know I'll do anything I can to help you get settled here."

Mari had been quiet and subdued since the three of them had come back to Colorado last week. Packing up their things at the house in Solana Beach and saying goodbye to their friends at San Miguel's had been emotional for them both, but Savannah knew Denver was going to be a healthy change. A chance to start over fresh and put the past behind them.

However, Savannah couldn't see how a romantic relationship would work with Damián. As much as she wanted to have him near her, living together and pretending to be a healthy couple wasn't fair to anyone.

Savannah looked down at her plate and pushed several pieces of rice to the side. They'd been discussing living arrangements the past few days. Damián wanted marriage and happily ever after—the impossible dream. But in time he'd come to resent her for her inability—her unwillingness—to be a full partner in a marriage. He deserved someone whole.

"I know my place is too small, Savannah, but I still wish you'd reconsider keeping us together. We can live together in the new place."

"I can't. It would confuse Mari." *And me.*

The light in his eyes grew dim, a clear indication she'd disappointed him. Better now than later because that disappointment would only get worse with time if she wasn't honest.

"Savannah, your talk about moving away from me is what's confusing her. Hell, we *are* a family, even if we aren't married yet."

Tears stung her eyes, and she blinked them back. His "yet" implied they *would* marry someday. "That fairy-tale life wouldn't be fair to either you or Mari. I'm not the marrying type." Lately, though, she wished she could be that type of woman. Thoughts of having Damián beside her, to hold her when she needed comforting, to help her deal with the demons that still bombarded her when she least expected…

But that was selfish on her part and wasn't enough for a virile man like Damián. Marriage meant romantic love that included sex, which was impossible for her at this point, and probably forever. Better to set the boundaries now than to get his hopes up that she'd ever be more than the mother of his daughter and a bottom he helped at his club.

Damián's hand stroked hers. "You seem a million miles away, *bebé*."

Savannah glanced up at Damián and blinked. Why couldn't she let the past go and enjoy her time with Damián? She cleared her throat and looked away. "Sorry. I still can't believe all that's happened."

"Quit apologizing. Things will get better. Your life's been turned upside down these past few months." He squeezed her hand, enveloping hers in his warmer one. His thumb stroked her wrist, and she felt a spark jolt up her arm.

She pulled her hand away with the pretense of adjusting the napkin on her lap. "Dr. McKenzie hired me to work in his clinic, just as soon as I can get licensed. Until then, I'll be a Spanish translator there and help him hire some other therapists, as well." Thank God the good doctor couldn't see her tonight. Mac, as he asked her to call him, had patched her up last December, no questions asked, and won a soft spot in her heart.

"He's a good man." Damián smiled. "You'll be great there. I still remember what a help you were to Teresa last year."

It hadn't taken long for Savannah to realize she could do a lot of good with Maman's money. She'd instructed her attorney to meet with Dr. McKenzie to set up a fund to make much-needed improvements to the clinic, hire additional staff, and purchase the up-to-date equipment necessary to give his low-income patients the care they deserved, without regard to their ability to pay.

She also would give money to the children's program at San Miguel's and the clinic where Anita worked—where Savannah had been on staff until her firing last year at her father's instigation. Maybe with fewer ties to state finances, they would never have to let another employee go because someone higher up the political food chain dictated how they should run their clinic.

"I'm proud of you, *savita*. You've been to hell and back, but all you do is think about how you can improve the lives of others."

She cast her gaze away, uncomfortable with his praise. "It doesn't take any great courage to give away money you didn't really work for in the first place."

His hand cupped her chin and raised her face to meet his gaze. "You have more courage in your pinky than most people do in their entire bodies."

Savannah blinked away a sting in her eyes. "Please don't think I'm some kind of hero. If you only knew how scared I am of everyth—"

The pad of his thumb brushed over her lower lip and caused it to tingle. She pulled away, leaning back in her chair.

"Retreat, if you must. Just promise me we'll continue to date and that you'll let me be your Top whenever you need one."

She'd never known anyone to be so patient—and persistent. "I'd like that. You've helped me so much, Damián. I'd still like to try and put more of these issues behind me."

He grinned. "Good. I have the perfect scene planned for later to help you do just that."

Her heart fluttered as she wondered what it included, but she knew from experience no amount of questioning would result in him revealing what was to come. Anticipation was good for her, he often repeated. Whether true or not, she knew it was part of the discipline he talked so much about teaching her.

"You haven't finished your dinner."

"I don't think I can eat another bite—especially if you have something strenuous planned."

"Eat. It's your mind that will be getting the workout tonight, not your body."

He *would* have to keep dropping hints that made her even more curious, though. She wouldn't ask; he wouldn't tell.

She finished the cheese enchilada but left the rice. He nodded, satisfied that she'd eaten enough, and settled the check. Then he stood and came around the table to pull out her chair. She looked around to notice that the cantina was packed with patrons now.

Oh, great.

She'd have to walk past every one of them dressed like a slut, until Damián could retrieve her coat from the rack near the entrance. He placed his hand on the upper curve of her butt.

His butt.

She held her head high and preceded him toward the door. Oddly enough, the few people at the tables she forced herself to look at had no interest in her whatsoever. The women were all looking at Damián, some with blatant sexual interest, which made Savannah feel an odd sense of pride.

Mine.

As she continued toward the coat rack, it was the men who surprised her. Despite her obviously slutty-looking clothing, they didn't leer at her at all. Some nodded at Damián as a show of respect or greeting, but none of them so much as looked at her.

It was almost as if Damián had put out some kind of pheromone to alert them that she was *his* and that they'd better not even *think* about looking at his woman.

She smiled.

As always, Damián protected her. He made her feel safe.

Damián helped her into her coat. "I think you're ready to play in the dungeon tonight."

Blood rushed through her ears blocking out anything else he might have said. She turned to stare at him and make sure she'd heard him correctly. He grinned at her obvious discomfort.

Sadist. Oh, yes. No doubt about it.

Sensual sadist.

She shivered in anticipation.

Somehow, the words *play* and *dungeon* didn't go together in her mind. The very word *dungeon* sent a quiver through her; whether it was one of fear or excitement, she wasn't sure.

Just what did he have planned for the rest of this date?

Chapter Twenty-Three

Damián placed a firm hand on the back of Savannah's neck, and she nearly crumpled to the floor. With that simple gesture, he took control of her and led her across the great room to a closed door near the stage. When he opened the door, she found herself staring at two familiar-looking brick staircases.

She recognized the one that led upstairs. The door behind her was the one she'd tried to open on Christmas Day, expecting to find a Victorian living room or parlor beyond the doors. If she'd seen the way the room was decorated—like something in a film about the Marquis de Sade—she'd have run so fast Damián would never have caught her.

Keeping his firm hand at the back of her neck, he guided her toward the stairway leading down.

The dungeon lay beyond that door.

"Breathe, *querida*." His breath was warm against her ear.

Easy for you to say.

She drew in a deep breath, having become so used to obeying his commands when she was in the mindset of a bottom. When they reached the landing, he opened a door in front of them. The room ahead of her was dark, and she balked. He reached out for a wall switch, and the area became awash in bright light. She noticed the equipment along the walls on either side of the long, narrow room. It was nothing but what one would find in a weight-training room.

"It *is* a weight-training room, *bebé*."

Surprised at his words, she turned to him. Had she spoken aloud?

"This way, *querida*, before you faint from holding your breath."

He grinned. Placing a finger under her chin, he turned her head to face forward as he led her past the benches and bar bells to another closed door at the opposite end of the room. The door creaked when he opened it. A little lube would take care of that, but she'd definitely felt her stomach drop a few inches when the door screeched. They probably left it unoiled on purpose, just to freak out the bottoms and submissives brought down here to play. The eerie sound certainly had done a number on her psyche. She'd seen too many movies.

I can do this.

"After you, *bebé*."

Savannah looked through the open door into yet another darkened room. Going from the light to the darkness seemed both symbolic, yet terrifying. She took another deep breath.

Placing one foot in front of the other, she stumbled in the damned stilettos. Damián wrapped his arm around her waist, pulling her against his hard body. His hand grabbed her breast and squeezed.

"I was beginning to think you weren't going to miss a step all evening." He chuckled and just as suddenly, he pulled away and let her go with a pat to her butt. He took her by the elbow as she stepped over the threshold. She felt a bit like Alice must have after falling down the rabbit hole. She'd entered a world just as foreign and strange. The question was, how would she be changed when she left this place?

Until the wall sconces blazed to life as he adjusted a dimmer switch, her eyes couldn't make out anything. Soon a warm glow emanated from what looked like undulating flames above torches. She was mesmerized for a moment by the illusion of real flames.

Slowly, as the room came into focus better, she began to notice more details. The walls here were brick, and the floor was made of rough-hewn boards. It looked like an old cellar. The effect it had on those brought here to "play" must be daunting. She certainly felt a frisson of fear rising in her stomach.

Even more disturbing were the implements she found hanging along one wall. A pair of rusty-looking metal restraints and chains reminded her of the castle dungeons she'd seen in old movies. Were they merely here for effect or did anyone actually get chained to the wall? Hanging near the center of the wall was an iron mask. Maybe they were used as part of castle-dungeon fantasy play, if there was such a fetish.

Who was she kidding? After a number of nights at the club, she'd learned there was a fetish for everything.

She saw modern-looking leather wrist cuffs and chains on the walls as well. *Ah*. That's probably what he'd use if he were going to restrain her here. But Damián seemed to have other plans. He led her past the shackles and up to a wooden St. Andrew's cross. Why had he brought her down here rather than use one of the crosses upstairs?

Clearly, he was messing with her mind. This room was on the creepy side, for sure. Was he planning to use the whip and clothespins again? She certainly had enough bare skin to clamp the pins onto.

"Are you ready to submit to me, body and mind, Savannah? Totally and completely?"

I already have.

"Yes, Sir."

Without another word, he took her left wrist and buckled a leather cuff on her. He did the same with the other. Sliding two fingers inside each, he tested the tightness. "How does that feel?"

"Perfect, Sir."

"Like you, *querida*."

She turned away, not knowing how to respond to a comment so ridiculous.

"Look at me."

She did and shrunk back at seeing his probing expression. Sometimes she wondered if he read her thoughts. She needed to stop disagreeing with him, even in her mind.

"As always, if your fingers start to tingle or you feel cramping anywhere, I want you to tell me immediately. *¿Comprendes?*"

"Yes, Sir, but…" *Wait!* She didn't have permission to speak.

"Is there a problem or a question?"

She nodded. "Yes, Sir. Wouldn't it be easier for me to undress before you put the restraints on?"

"If I'd wanted you to strip, I'd have ordered you to do so already."

"Oh. Yes, of course, Sir." Oddly enough, this would be her first BDSM scene with Damián where he let her wear clothes. In this setting, she was grateful to be able to cover as much of herself as this skimpy outfit could.

"What is your safeword?"

"Tamale, Sir."

"If you need to stop, just say that word and all play will end. *¿Comprendes?*"

"Yes, Sir."

"Your slow-down word?"

"Guacamole, Sir."

"Good girl."

He'd lifted the first cuffed hand and attached it to the cross before she realized she hadn't reacted negatively to being called a good girl.

I'm Damián's good girl.

Within seconds, she was clamped onto the frame in a Y shape.

The familiar posture collar came out and he chained her to the cross the way he had done in their first scene so long ago. He finger-combed her hair, massaging her scalp until her knees grew weak, then pulled her hair into a scrunchee and attached the ponytail to the cross. Although it seemed like overkill, something about the act of having her hair pulled and bound made her body respond in ways she didn't expect. How primitive. Heat pooled in her lower abdomen and she almost felt the stirrings of desire.

Almost. She soon regained her composure.

Lastly, he drew a leather strap from behind her and cinched her tightly at the waist.

"Take a deep breath." He placed fingers between the strap and her belly. "Perfect."

After cuffing and chaining her ankles together, he anchored them to chains at the legs of the cross. Damián walked around behind her and brushed his hands over her breasts and abdomen as he pulled her body against the cross. Savannah's knees buckled, but the many restraints kept her from falling. She submitted to his touch, the restraints, the total loss of control.

Total submission.

He could do whatever he wished because she had absolutely no intention of stopping him anytime soon. "I've missed submitting to you."

He smiled. "I've missed topping you, too." He kissed her cheek and she leaned into his face, rather than pull away. "That's my good girl."

His good girl.

"You're doing great, *savita*."

She'd always liked hearing him call her that, knowing now it was more an endearment than her name. She wouldn't be Savita Diaz any longer, either. She smiled at him.

"Tonight I'm going to mark you as mine, my beauty."

Her breath caught in her throat, and the smile vanished. Mark her how?

God, she hoped he wasn't going to bring out the violet wand again. She wasn't nearly over her fear of that instrument of torture, despite him assuring her there were ways in which the sensation could be enjoyable.

Damián stroked her underarms and sides in long, sweeping movements, then tweaked both nipples until she felt them press against the fabric of the tank. She moaned, and caught herself. What was he doing to her body? Even though he'd touched her many times in the past month, especially as he ministered to the stripes on her back, she'd missed having him touch her in more sexual ways—no, *sensual*.

Foreplay was just the nice part about sex. She even enjoyed aftercare. It was just the part in between she didn't want.

He stepped away and soon she smelled the strong scents of magic marker and…*cherries?* He pressed the tip against her right breast and began to write, saying each letter aloud as he wrote.

"F-I-L-T-H-Y."

Filthy?

He continued to write on her left breast, again spelling out loud. Because of the collar and the way her hair had been restrained, she couldn't see the letters he wrote, but they were soon seared onto her mind's eye.

"W-H-O-R-E."

Filthy whore.

"No, Damián!" By the time her mind registered what he was writing, she tried to jerk her body away from the cherry-scented marker. No use. He'd bound her so tightly to the cross, she couldn't move an inch.

The look in his eyes told her she'd disobeyed. He wasn't happy with her, but each letter of the detestable words felt like a brand to her heart. Her throat closed as she pictured the words he'd written on her.

Filthy whore.

"Close your eyes and keep them closed."

She swallowed hard and did as he'd told her. When he pressed the marker against her forehead, she started to open her eyes, but he placed his other hand over her eyelids. She fought the restraints. If her legs hadn't been chained, she'd have knocked him on his ass again to stop him.

"Not there!" The tank top could be thrown away, but how could she remove permanent marker from her face? "Damián, please don't write anything else on me!"

"How do you address me?"

"Sir, I'm sorry, but…guacamole!" She'd never wanted to be a disappointment to him, but she had to stop a moment. More tears sprang to her eyes, but she blinked them back. "Please don't do this. I have an interview in two days to discuss my licensing exam. It would take me forever to get the ink off. Please don't disgrace me this way."

He stroked her cheek. "Do you trust me, Savannah?"

"Of course, Sir." But he'd never humiliated her like this before. Even making her dress like a street whore tonight hadn't gone this far, and he'd been there to protect her from anyone taking advantage of her for what she was dressed like. Damián wouldn't be with her when she talked with the licensing board representative.

"Have you not entrusted yourself, body and mind, to my will this evening?"

Tears filled her eyes. "Y-y-yes, Sir."

I will *not cry.*

"Take a deep breath, Savannah." She did. "What's keeping you from submitting fully to me tonight, *bebé*?"

"I don't know. I…you…I'm confused. Why are you doing this?"

"Savannah." The tone of his voice put her in her place.

"I'm sorry, Sir. I'm trying to trust you. I just wish you could explain…"

"That will be revealed when the time is right. Telling you now wouldn't achieve the goal of the scene. Are you ready to continue?"

She didn't think she could continue. Panic immobilized her.

"Deep breath, Savannah."

She tried to do as he'd ordered, hoping if she was good, he'd stop. She drew a ragged breath.

"That's my good girl."

She remembered all the vile things Lyle and her father had done to her body over the years. This didn't even make it into those monsters' top one-hundred list of humiliating, degrading acts. She could do this. She needed to trust that Damián knew what was best for her. During aftercare, he always explained things she was confused about and often told her what his goal had been for the scene, if she hadn't figured it out for herself.

Trust him.

I will do this.

If she could move her head, she'd have lifted her chin. Instead, she took a steadying breath. "I'm ready to continue, Sir."

"I'm very proud of you, *savita*. You're so brave for me."

Then he took the marker again and wrote on her forehead, again spelling out the letters.

"D-I-R-T-Y S-L-U-T."

Silent, wracking sobs tore through her. Her stomach revolted, and she was afraid she'd lose her dinner.

Trust him, Savannah.

He brushed his lips across hers, and then he kissed away the tears that had left wet tracks down her cheeks.

"Thank you for expressing your emotions through your tears, *mi sueño*, rather than keeping them pent up inside. I'm so proud of you."

She sniffled.

Damián had just marked her in despicable ways that her daughter and everyone else would see for days, if not weeks. How could she leave the house before the letters on her forehead wore off? Was there enough makeup in the world to hide the disgusting words he'd written on her face?

He stroked the undersides of her arms and down her sides, motions that would normally calm her fears. Now she only wanted to withdraw from him. "Savannah, I think one of the reasons you believe you can't be my girl is that you believe you're a slut—or was one in the past—and that I deserve better."

She'd tried to keep that inside, despite talking about this with him once before very briefly. But she hadn't thought he'd heard her because he hadn't said anything then. Ah, but that's when he first proposed this date. He'd intended to do this scene originally on the night she'd been abducted. She was surprised he'd hung onto the plan for the scene all this time.

Still, her admission had been made in private, between the two of them. How could he want to emblazon it across her face like this? She didn't want the world to know what she had been, especially not Mari.

Her shame was complete. Unlike the private shame, when she'd carried her father's mark of ownership for so many years, she would now be publicly branded, albeit temporarily.

"Why, Sir?" She choked as another sob erupted.

"Savannah, I want you to know that I love you no matter what labels you brand yourself with."

Love? How could he love her?

"I think I loved you, Savannah, from the first time I saw you in that restaurant. But I thought you were too perfect for the likes of me."

Perfect? "But you had to know why I was there. What I was."

"I saw how scared you were. I didn't have a clue what was going on when I found you in that hotel room. I just knew they were hurting you and that you didn't deserve to be treated that way."

"But I was a pain slut."

"We'll talk about that in a minute." His voice felt like a soft caress. "I fell in love with that sweet girl, even though we only spent one beautiful day together at our beach cave."

He loved her even back then? Knowing what she'd been?

When she remembered that time, the happiness she'd felt that day was what she hung onto for so long, her reason for moving forward. Knowing their encounter had also had such a profound effect on Damián made her realize how incredibly lucky they were to have found each other that day. Both of their lives had veered off into dramatic new directions—in some ways for the better, some worse.

"I never forgot you, Savannah. Not for a single day." His warm hands cupped her cheeks and he brushed his lips against hers. "When I met you again as Savi, I figured you could never love someone like me, especially not after what happened in Fallujah. But even though I was certain I couldn't have you, I still loved you. I dreamt about you almost every night."

His words made her ache. "Sir, please stop. You don't know the real me." His kind words made her feel uncomfortable.

He ignored her and placed his hand over her belly. "I love you because you carried my baby for nine months and gave birth to my beautiful little girl, the most precious act anyone has ever done for me. She's a gift to the world, not just to us."

He kissed her lips again. "I love both Savannah and Savi. It doesn't matter to me what name you use—or any of the pet names I've given you—you are the same person."

She liked when he called her special pet names.

"As we've discussed before, there is one word you insist on using to refer to yourself that I personally find offensive."

She'd always tried to keep that thought from him, had only let it slip once that she could remember.

Slut.

"You're not a whore, Savannah. You never were."

Whore? *That* was the word that offended him? Both words were equally disgusting to her, and he'd written both of them on her tonight. Did that mean…?

"If I hear you call yourself a whore again, you will receive your first punishment in your training from me, and I will make sure you never say—or think—the word again. I would begin that punishment by squirting dish soap in your mouth and making you hold it there until you can assure me with a pre-arranged signal that the word will never dirty your mouth—or your mind—again."

Wash her mouth out with soap? *Liquid* soap? Was he serious? She wasn't a child.

"I've stopped using that word. We worked on this before. I understand, but why…"

He put his finger against her lips. *Damn.* He hadn't asked a direct question—and she hadn't asked permission to speak. If he wanted her to stop using whore and slut to describe herself, why had he written them on her? "I think I see what you're trying to do here. I'll also try to stop calling myself a slut."

"Don't put words in my mouth, *savita*. You are a slut."

She cringed. Hearing Damián label her a slut was like a slap in the face. She didn't even like sex. She tried to shake her head but couldn't move because of the restraints.

Damián unclamped the collar from the cross, but didn't take it off her neck. He released her ponytail and wrists, but she remained bound to the cross from the waist down. He wasn't taking any chances on releasing her legs probably because he knew she could land him on his ass.

"I've marked you as *my* slut." He pulled a sleep mask from his leathers. "I need to blindfold you for this next part. It should only be for a minute or two. Will you be able to take the mask for me for that short period of time?"

Being in the dark was the least of her concerns now. Damián had called her a slut. Her mind couldn't wrap itself around that.

"Answer me."

She nodded, too numb to speak. He frowned. "Y-yes, Sir. I can be blindfolded." She welcomed not having to look at him. She wanted to hide.

"Good girl." He slid the mask over her head, not touching her forehead, and tucked it into place. The room went dark, and tears flooded her eyes. She didn't try to fight them anymore, and the mask was soon soaked. His hands gently stroked her arms at her sides, and she tried to stay in the moment. The past encroached again.

Dirty slut.

"Now I'm going to show you off to my friends as the Masters at Arms Club's newest slut."

Fear clawed at her throat. What did he mean show her off? To whom?

His body heat left her, and she heard him step away, crossing the room. Mortified, she wished she could curl herself into a ball and disappear into the floor.

"You can come in now."

The dungeon door squeaked, and another sob tore from Savannah's raw throat. "No, Sir! Please don't do this to me!" Maybe this was a mindfuck and no one really was there.

Footsteps. Lots of footsteps. *No!* Who had he invited into the dungeon? Who was witnessing her shame; her dirty secrets revealed? She felt stripped bare and dirty.

"I want you to meet my slut, Savannah—the first girl I've ever wanted to honor with that title." From his voice, she could tell Damián stood in front of her again.

"Oh, my God." Karla's voice. "You're so lucky, Master Damián."

Savannah shook her head, but the collar limited her range of motion. She'd thought Karla was *her* friend, too. How could the woman agree with him about something so degrading? Or had it been obvious to Karla that she was nothing but a dirty slut? After what she'd asked Karla to spend the afternoon doing…

"I'm glad you finally found your slut, son." Adam. He was okay with his adopted son wanting to be with a slut? "She's a perfect addition to our family."

"I'm damned lucky, and I know it." Damián's hands stroked her arms and shoulders, infusing some of his warmth into her chilled body. Still, she shuddered. She hadn't wanted him to make her feel anything again, and yet he'd done just that. She couldn't escape to her safe place.

"*Cara*, you've been marked by the best." Not Marc, too. Who else was in the room there? Angelina? No, she should be with Mari.

Warm hands rubbed her numb arms, cupped her breasts, and stroked her belly. She knew those hands. Damián's. He wouldn't let the others touch her. Would he? She didn't want to be touched right now.

"You're very lucky, Savannah." She didn't recognize the woman's small, almost childlike voice. "Sir has needed someone like you for a very long time."

A man spoke next, his voice deep and oddly familiar, but she couldn't place it. "I'm just hoping not to have to borrow your Top too often to help me with Patticakes." Victor, the Dom who asked for Damián's help with Patti on Savannah's first night in the club. She realized now that the unknown woman's voice must be Patti's. She hadn't heard her say much before. "And, little one, I hope you'll forgive me for not doing my job of protecting you last month. I could shoot myself for falling for such an obvious decoy maneuver."

Savannah choked on a sob. Even if these people knew she was a slut, they accepted her and cared about her.

"You're *my* slut, Savannah. I hope you'll always be my slut, even if you never consent to becoming anything else with me." He released the strap from around her waist and removed each of the ankle cuffs.

"Come, *mi sueño*. Let me hold you."

"No, Damián. I just want to leave. Please take me home."

"Not yet. We aren't finished. Unless you safeword."

What more could he want to do to her? Hadn't he done enough already?

When he began removing the blindfold, she placed her hands over his to stay them. "Please. Ask everyone to go first. I don't want to see anyone right now."

"Savannah, I will not hide my slut from my family. You will let them see you anytime I want them to while you're my bottom in a scene here at the club. They will stay."

If he hadn't left the posture collar around her neck, she would have hung her head in shame. He removed the blindfold, but she kept her eyes closed. Tears slid down her cheeks.

"I think we can remove this now, too." He lifted her chin and unbuckled the posture collar, removing it. "Open your eyes."

With the collar gone, she shook her head.

"I. Said. Open. Your. Eyes."

She blinked her eyes open, but her tears obscured her sight. Suddenly she needed to see what Damián had done to her; she wiped the tears away with the backs of her hands. She had to look.

She glanced down at her chest and did a double take. Then she pulled the tank top away from her body and read each letter to make sure what she was reading upside down was correct. It didn't say "filthy whore" at all.

M-Y P-R-I-N-C-E-S-S.

Princess?

Puzzled, she looked up at Damián, who smiled at her. "Marisol told me once you'd forgotten you were a princess. I just wanted to make sure you never forget again. You're *my* princess, *savita*. I'll never let anything happen to you. I'll slay your dragons. I'll chase away the demons that invade your sleep—and, trust me, I know they will come—but they're no match for me, *mi amor*. I'll be there for you no matter what—if you'll let me be."

But what about…she took her hand and touched her forehead. Her fingers slid in something greasy, and she pulled her hand down to find a red substance on her fingertips and the strong scent of cherries. The word on her tank top had been written in black marker. Damián grinned, reached into the pocket of his leathers, and held up a tube of red lipstick.

"What did you…?" If he hadn't written dirty slut, what had he written there?

Karla extended to her a hand mirror, and Savannah focused the reflecting glass on her forehead. Again, it took a moment to decipher the words that were backward in the mirror—and even longer to grasp their meaning.

"DAMO'S SLUT." She lowered the mirror and met his gaze.

"That's right, *mi sueño*. Mine. Damián's. I knew you were too smart for my mindfuck if I spelled out my whole name when I was telling you I was writing 'dirty.' But in my community, which you're a part of now, there's nothing dirty or wrong about the word slut—or about you, for that matter. We're going to keep working on changing those negative internal messages into positive ones—as long as you'll let me."

Savannah's face burned as she felt the eyes of the others in the room on her. Finally, she forced herself to look over at Adam and Karla. He held his arms around her, his hands possessively on her growing belly. She also wore a tank, a red one, and on it was emblazoned in black marker "Adam's slut." When Savannah could tear her eyes away from the words, she looked up to find a dreamy look on Karla's face.

Patti wore a green tank top with "Victor's slut" written on it. Victor's black arms were wrapped around her waist. Patti smiled at Savannah before looking up at Victor who bent and gave her a sweet kiss.

After a bit, Savannah turned back to Karla, who had tears in her eyes. "Savannah, it's usually considered a compliment for a submissive to be called a slut by her Dom. A very high honor, in fact. I know it doesn't seem like it would be because of how the word is used in general society, but…" She shrugged and smiled. "Who gives a fuck what they think? We're freaks."

Adam swatted her butt. "Watch your language, slut." The grin on his face and the love in his eyes spoke volumes, though.

Slut was a *good* thing? How could a term that had caused shame to her for most of her life be something she'd ever want to be called by a man she cared about? And she did care about Damián. When Lyle and her father used that term, they had made her feel so dirty.

She realized that was their intention. Their minds were so depraved, they only saw filth and smut in everyone around them. They created that and made her believe it was reality. But that was true only in their minds.

Slut was just a word. Just like the way her body and Patti's interpreted pain differently than others, the importance and meaning of the word slut was subjective depending on who used it.

She turned back to Damián, who seemed to be waiting for her to respond or react. She walked into his personal space, lifted his vest, and placed a kiss on his chest. Then she wrapped her arms around his waist and looked up. His eyes opened wider.

Still, he recovered quickly and smiled. "That's the first time you've come into my arms without being told to do so."

Surely not. She'd been in his arms lots of times. But maybe he was right. Never initiated by her.

She felt safe in his arms.

He placed his hand on her butt and pulled her hips against him. "Mine."

She wasn't sure how much territory he was claiming—her butt or all of her—but she wanted to give him more of herself than ever before.

"Yes, Sir. All of me."

Chapter Twenty-Four

Damián squeezed her ass again, surprised she'd come into his arms so willingly. *Good timing, chica, because we're about to get a whole lot closer.* "Time for some aftercare."

She looked around the dungeon. "There's no loveseat."

He let her ponder that a moment while he watched Dad steer Karla out of the dungeon with a hand to her back, followed by Victor and Patti, and then Marc, who turned to let Damián know he'd come back in to clean up the dungeon later. They'd been a big help to him in convincing Savannah to see that being a willing slut in a consensual relationship was nothing close to what had happened to her in the past.

He wished he could have found some way to get through to her other than a humiliation mindfuck. He didn't get off on degrading women and knew it wasn't a turn-on for Savannah either. Sometimes the end justified the means. She sure seemed to understand better, but he'd know more after they talked.

"Come, *bebé*. We're going upstairs to one of the bedrooms for aftercare and intimacy."

Savannah's body stiffened. She tried to pull away, and he held her tighter. "No, *querida*, this kind of intimacy isn't about sex. That's still on your list of hard limits and I respect that, but I need to hold you. All night. That was an intense scene, and I'm not letting you out of my sight until I know you're going to be okay. You don't need to be alone tonight. And sleeping with Marisol doesn't count. No need to upset her if the dragons do come back tonight."

She frowned. "But who's staying with her?"

"Angelina. Karla will call her to confirm you'll be staying here. I'd hoped for a breakthrough like this tonight, so I made all the necessary arrangements."

"But I didn't bring anything to wear." She was going to drum up a lot of excuses to get out of this, he could see.

"You won't need anything to wear."

"Damián…" The fear in her eyes made it clear they still had a long way to go as far as intimacy went, but he was patient. He'd waited almost nine years for her. He'd wait as long as it took.

"Savannah, you know I'm not going to molest you. All I'm going to do tonight is hold you, talk with you, and sleep with you—by sleep, I mean *sleep*. There's more to intimacy than sex."

Being with her like this would be hard for him, too—hard being the operative word. But after all he'd asked of her, it was time he overcame his aversion to being completely naked in her presence. He'd never let himself be this vulnerable to a woman before, revealing his scarred and dismembered body, but it was only fair that he be willing to step out of his comfort zone, too. He also wanted to test Dad's theory on the PTSD nightmares that might come while he was sleeping with Savannah. *Dios*, he hoped *his* fucking demons would give him a break tonight. He wanted—no *needed*—for this night to be perfect.

"I do plan to touch you, Savannah, but your slow-down and safewords remain in effect, if you need them.

She swallowed hard but didn't run, physically or emotionally. *Progress*.

He bent down and brushed a kiss against her cheek, then whispered, "So proud of you, *savita*."

"Thank you, Sir."

He bent to pick up his toy bag and slung the strap over his shoulder. With an arm around her waist, he led her out of the dungeon and through the weight-training room. At the base of the stairs, he stopped. "Lose the shoes. I don't want you to trip or fall."

"Not even to cop a feel?"

"Lose. The. Shoes. And the smart mouth, too."

She grinned, which helped him relax, and slipped off her shoes. He took them from her in one hand, then took her hand and they walked up to the second floor.

He'd chosen the room she'd napped in on Christmas Day, the same one he'd taken refuge in when he'd first come to Denver.

He opened the door for her. "After you, *bebé*."

When she just stared at the bed without moving forward, he placed a hand on the curve above her ass and propelled her forward. Her clothes were still on the bed from when she'd changed into her slut outfit, so he gathered them up and put them on a chair.

"You go do whatever you need to in the bathroom."

"Should I...take my clothes off?"

"Not yet." He grinned and wiggled his eyebrows. "I want to watch. But you can lose the lipstick on your forehead, *querida*. It's served its purpose."

Her face turned a pretty shade of pink, and she nearly ran into the bathroom. He was going to have fun tonight—not as much fun as he'd like to have maybe, but just being able to hold Savannah in his arms and break down some more of those intimacy barriers would be enough. It had been too long.

Savannah had made a lot of progress despite the kidnapping that had brought much more crap to the surface. She continued to amaze him. There would be aftereffects that would arise from time to time—hell, he still had nightmares and flashbacks from Fallujah—but this warrior-woman was going to be okay.

He sure hoped Dad was right about him not hurting Savannah while they slept.

Damián went to the bed and pulled down the quilt and top sheet. He'd made sure everything was ready for them tonight. Dad and Karla would give them the privacy they needed. Dad had reserved the honeymoon suite for them at the hotel where they'd spent their wedding night. Tomorrow morning, they planned to drive down to Aspen Corners to visit with Karla's friend, Cassie. They'd be sure Angelina got home to her place, too.

So tonight they had the place all to themselves. Damián sat on the bed and removed his boots and socks. When the bathroom door opened, he turned to find his beautiful princess slut standing with the light silhouetting her sexy body. Yeah, definite curves. Good thing he'd hand-picked every man in the cantina tonight. They were guys he knew from the VA Hospital, customers at the shop, fellow Patriot Guard Riders—all safe. They also knew of his reputation as a sadist. If he'd left that to chance, she'd probably have been ogled by every stud in the place earlier tonight and maybe even hit on by a few of them if he'd had to go to the men's room.

She hesitated before him, and he stood. "Come here."

Savannah took a deep breath and blew it out, then walked across the room. When she stopped two feet away, he reached out and pulled her into his arms, feeling the slight tremor in her body. She rested her cheek against his chest, and every protective bone in his body reached out to her.

After a moment, Savannah looked up at him. She lifted her hand and stroked his cheek. Naturally, his dick interpreted the innocent touch all wrong.

Not now, Chico.

She stiffened against him and must have felt his dick against her. Damián's hand made long, sweeping motions on her arm. "Relax. I'm just going to hold you, touch you tonight. Nothing is going to happen that you don't consent to."

She swallowed hard. "I trust you, Sir."

"Thank you, *bebé*. Now, tell me about your feelings from tonight's scene."

"I'm not sure."

"Tell me what you are unsure about."

"I've had these negative messages replaying in my head forever, saying I'm a whore, a slut. I've never imagined being able to turn them off, even for a short time. I'm still not sure I can completely."

"Sometimes we try to erase them, but more often the best we can hope for is to redirect the negatives to something more positive, like we did when I claimed your brand as my own or tonight trying to show you being a slut can be a good thing.

She took a deep breath. "But last month, when we worked on erasing 'whore' from my mind, it really seemed to help. The word had so little effect on me when my fa…well, I don't want to think about that anymore, either, but it helped keep me from sinking down to what they wanted me to be."

She sighed. "My entire life, I've associated the word slut with something dirty. I want to please you, Damián, but I'm not sure I can just turn off that tape. What happens if I backslide?"

He continued stroking her arm, allowing himself a moment of pride when the texture of her skin changed as gooseflesh rose. The reaction of her body to his touch empowered him.

"It's a matter of discipline, Savannah. With practice, you can rewind the tapes and replace them with positive messages. Remember how you had Teresa journal when she first started treatment for the rape?" She nodded. "And you have Marisol journal every day still, telling what she's grateful for. Have you thought about starting a journal for yourself?"

"I already do—my own gratitude journal."

"Good. But I'd like you to start a new one. A submissive's journal."

She pulled away and met his gaze. "What's that?"

"Every morning and any other time you feel the need, I'd like for you to record your experience, your feelings, as you journey deeper into submission."

"But I'm not a submissive. I'm a bottom."

"A bottom submits, too. How would you feel about renegotiating our relationship and becoming my submissive?"

"Are you serious?"

"Never more serious about anything in my life. Savannah, I think I can help you overcome some of the things you fear, some of the things that have kept you paralyzed and unable to consider being in a committed relationship with me or anyone else."

Dios, he hoped he was making sense. He wanted this badly, provided she was ready. "Like our Top/bottom agreement, we will be very clear about what you are willing to try and what is off-limits. Not that I won't test your limits as time goes on, if I think you need it. But you'll be able to stop or slow down at any point by using your safewords."

"You want to dominate me." She tried to pull away, but he held her more tightly against him.

"*Bebé*, I've already been dominating you. What I want, even if we aren't living together, is to have a relationship where it doesn't stop at the end of a date or a scene's aftercare. I want more. I want to be able to hold you all night long after a scene—like we're going to do tonight."

Tears filled her eyes, and Damián pressed her head against his chest. "Shhh. You don't have to decide tonight. I just wanted you to know how I feel. Whether I'm your Top or your Dom, we're going to tackle those messages every time one of them tries to derail your progress."

She pulled away once more and looked up at him. "I need to say this, Damián, almost as much as you need to hear it."

This didn't sound good.

"Thank you for taking the time to plan that scene for us tonight."

Damián felt a lump growing in his throat.

"You and the others have me convinced that I need to work on embracing my inner slut." She gave him a dubious grin. "This word might take a little longer to put behind me. I've always felt like a slut because I responded sexually to what they did to me. You've helped me see that I wasn't a willing slut. I understand now that to them I was nothing more than property. I had no rights. No choice."

"Our scene tonight was a long time in the making. Ever since you mentioned you had trouble with the word slut, I knew we'd have to deal with it head on. Encouraging you to accept yourself as my slut will permit you to embrace your sexuality as something good, not dirty." He tweaked her nipple and loved the little hissing sound she made.

"Trust me, *savita*, you're going to hear the words slut and whore often in the club. Some use them in consensual humiliation scenes, others just use them as endearments, the way I use slut. Whore isn't a word I will ever use when referring to you. You're the mother of my child. I can't go there."

He bent to kiss her cheek. "But both terms are used to denote ownership for some and can be used to humiliate, if that's a particular kink shared by the participants. I'm usually in attendance at every collaring ceremony at the club, and I don't want you to get triggered every time one of the Doms calls his sub a slut."

"Collaring?"

"When a Dom and a sub are at a point in their relationship where they want to make a deeper commitment to each other or take it to another level, the Dom presents his sub with a collar. Same for triads and polyamorous relationships, not just for couples."

He could see he was overloading her with more jargon. "You know the leather collar Karla wears at the club, the one with the dogtag on it?"

She nodded.

"That's her collar for the club or whenever Dad wants her to wear it. But she also has one she wears in public that's more subtle—looks like a necklace to the vanilla crowd."

Her eyes opened wider. "The one she was wearing when we stopped by to visit after their honeymoon?"

He nodded. "Dad collared her privately on their honeymoon. At some point, he'll probably have a public collaring ceremony, too."

"He'd do that in public?"

"Well, public to the club members, probably in the great room. It's like a wedding ceremony in a sense, but the commitment they're making is to the relationship as a Dom and his sub."

"I think I understand. I still think I need a cheat sheet to keep up, but now it makes sense why you and Grant congratulated her on getting a necklace as a Christmas gift. Grant even called it a collar, but that just confused me more."

"Yeah, well, I wasn't ready to tell you about this part of my life back then. You might have run from me, not that I'd have let you get away." He brushed his thumb against her cheek.

"I'm glad you shared your club with me. Well, actually, I guess Adam was the one who got me in there first."

He remembered how angry he'd been that night when Dad wouldn't get Savannah out of the club before Patti's cathartic whipping had begun. That night had been a turning point for both Savannah and for Damián. They needed each other. He wondered if Dad had seen that all along or if it was just dumb luck. Knowing Dad, it was part of a bigger plan.

He cleared his throat. "I never stopped thinking about you, *mi sueño*. You were always in my dreams."

"I dreamt about you off and on, too, but at first I just tried to figure out if you were real or my longtime Orlando Bloom fantasy come to life."

"Bloom, huh?"

"You look a lot like him."

"Yeah? Great." That's all his ego needed to hear, that she fantasized about some unattainable Hollywood actor.

"Damián, that brief time we had together seemed like a dream from the start. Not reality. Yet Mari always was my beautiful proof that our time together had been very real."

Savannah blinked and, without warning, reached up to take the lapels of his Harley vest in each hand and slid the leather back over his shoulders and down his arms. *What the...?* She tossed the vest onto the bed and lowered her gaze to the ink on his bare chest as she nearly gasped for breath. She stared at the dragon's head so long he flexed his pec to get her to snap back into the moment.

She startled, then giggled. "Sorry. I don't know how to seduce someone, so just bear with me."

What the fuck did she mean by seduce? *Whose aftercare was this, anyway?*

"Savannah, tonight isn't about me..."

She placed a finger against his lips and lowered her mouth to his chest. When the tip of her sweet tongue flicked tentatively against his nip, his balls tightened. *Mierda*.

Savannah pulled back and looked up at him in wonder. "I didn't know a man's nipples could get hard like that, too."

His nip wasn't the only thing getting hard.

The aftercare/intimacy scene he'd planned included touching and cuddling but no sex. If she kept up this attack on his body, he'd be the one needing aftercare tonight, because sex was out of the question. She was practically a virgin experience-wise. He was sure she'd only known actual lovemaking once, their time in the beach cave. He had no intention of rushing her into anything that might leave her feeling more ashamed later. She'd had enough of that from men who had abused her in the past. His job was to protect and nurture, not take advantage of her.

No la molestes.

Time to get on with the third act of tonight's scene. Damián bent down and kissed her on the forehead. "Let's get into bed, *bebé*." He sat on the edge of the bed and looked up, but the pained expression on her face surprised him.

"Please don't reject me, Sir. I'm trying…"

Clearly, she needed to do this. As her Service Top and trainer, it was his responsibility to guide her. *Madre de Dios*, help him.

"Strip for me."

Her eyes opened wide and, when a smile broke out on her face, he relaxed. This was what she needed. Still, she hesitated, despite the fact she'd stripped for him many times. Maybe he needed to take it to another level. He remembered coaching her as she'd pleasured herself for the first time.

"This time, as you strip, I want you to touch your—no, *my* breasts, *my* pussy. Play it to the hilt. Show off my sexy little body, those gorgeous curves. Turn me on."

She gazed at the bulge in his pants and back at his face. "I still can't have sex, Sir. I'm sor…"

"Savannah, I've been hard for you more times than I can count. Have I forced myself on you before?"

"No, but you haven't shared a bed with me all night before, either."

"Once upon a time, I watched over you while you slept in a hotel penthouse in La Jolla. Another time I made a bed for you with my leather jacket in a beach cave."

Her pupils dilated, and her breathing became shallow, which surprised the hell out of him. She hadn't forgotten how good it was for them both that day.

"If I'd intended to force myself on you, *bebé*, I wouldn't have needed a bed. You're safe to explore your sensuality with me—to embrace your inner slut, as you put it."

He looked down at her tank top, emblazoned with "PRINCESS." Savannah already had the princess part down pat.

"I want you to tease me mercilessly. Don't hold anything back, princess slut."

* * *

Savannah had no clue how to behave like a slut. She'd never intentionally teased anyone, but she trusted him not to force her to do anything she wasn't ready for. Something he'd said resonated with her.

"You're safe to explore your sensuality."

His words reminded her of something her stripper-pole dance instructor had said to the women in her class. When she'd taken the first few classes at her therapist's insistence, she'd known the goal wasn't firmer thighs and better upper-body strength. Savannah had been one of the more self-conscious people in the class as she watched what the other women did.

She didn't have a dancer pole here. She looked around the bedroom. The closest thing she found was the cannonball bedpost. Not even close, but she needed a prop or she wouldn't be able to do this. Wiping her sweaty palms on her hot-pink pants, she took a deep breath and moved to the foot of the bed, turning her back to Damián. Shaking out her hands, she concentrated on the big round knob of the bedpost. Maybe if she kept her focus there, she could get through this. She certainly couldn't make eye contact with him.

This was so embarrassing and totally out of character. However, she wanted to try this. With Damián, she was safe to explore without having to go beyond her limits. She trusted him.

She closed her eyes and imagined the music from her pole-dancing practice video playing internally as she loosened up her neck and shoulders by pivoting her head. The muscles stretched and cartilage popped from a lack of exercise. She needed to work out the kinks.

She grinned, knowing she was actually about to get her kink on.

Grasping the cannonball with both hands, she bent over with her butt facing Damián and rotated her hips. His sharp intake of breath gave her confidence that she wasn't boring him, and she gyrated for all she was worth. She took one hand off the pole—er, ball—and stroked her ass. Her tongue darted across her lips, which had suddenly become dry. She realized Damián couldn't see her mouth.

Flinging her right leg around the post, she hooked her knee around the base of the ball. Savannah lowered her upper body backward toward him, anchored by the post. Damián's gaze zeroed in on her breasts. She took both hands, cupped each breast, and pushed them outward toward him. Unable to watch his reaction, she closed her eyes again. Remembering how one of the women in the videos had used her mouth and tongue as a seduction weapon, Savannah opened her mouth and stroked her upper lip from one corner to the other in a slow arc.

Picturing how ridiculous she must look playing at being a siren—no, a slut—she started to clamp her mouth shut.

"So fucking hot, *mamacita*."

Damián's appreciation gave her the courage to let her tongue skim across her lip again in the reverse direction, the way the actress had done in one of the videos this afternoon. She ventured a glance at him but was unable to tell if he was looking at her mouth or her boobs from this angle. Remembering that she'd been instructed to strip, as well as tease, she lowered her hands to the hem of the tank top and slowly pulled it up. Stopping just before she bared her breasts, she slipped her fingers inside the lower edge of the bra cup and pinched her nipples.

Zing!

Her eyes opened wide. The same kind of jolt she'd experienced when she'd pleasured herself for Damián zinged straight to her clit. Because she had no intention of taking her striptease dance to a full-blown orgasm, she released her nipples, but they were already swollen and straining against the fabric by the time she pulled the tank off the rest of the way.

"So pretty for me, *bebé*."

Wanting to please him even more, she lifted her torso and stood upright again. She let go of the post and took her boobs in her hands again. Swaying to the imaginary music as it ramped up in tempo, she tossed her head from side to side, causing her loosened hair to whip across her face. Again, she heard Damián's breathing change and became emboldened enough to open her eyes.

The lust she saw in his eyes stopped her in mid-motion. She felt as if a bucket of ice water had been dumped on her. What had gotten into her? She was acting like a—

Slut.

Her hands shook. She closed her eyes, unable to look at Damián. The bed creaked, and she was enveloped into the warmth of his arms.

"Where are you, Savannah?"

She blinked. She realized she hadn't been sucked into the past by her demons, as she had been so many times before. "I'm here, Sir. Your slut never left you."

"Good girl." He pressed her head to his chest and stroked her bare back in long, relaxing strokes. "That was the hottest thing I've ever seen. Thank you."

"But I couldn't finish."

He chuckled, and she felt the rumble of his laughter against her cheek. "I don't know if I could have taken much more, *bebé*."

He released her body and cupped her chin until he forced her to meet his gaze. "Now, strip out of those shorts and join me in bed."

Damián turned and walked back to the head of the bed. He still wore his leathers and his prosthesis.

"Sir, may I make you more comfortable first?"

He turned around with a puzzled frown on his face. "Comfortable?"

Savannah nodded, unable to speak. She'd never undressed a man before—ever. At least she didn't have to worry about triggers. She suspected she was just experiencing normal anxiety about the unknown. She'd talked with Angelina and Karla a lot in the past two days and knew what she needed to do. But could she pull it off?

Deep breath.

She walked over to him and pulled the tongue of his belt through the loop. Slowly, she released the buckle's prong before sliding the belt out of the loops. She unbuttoned his leathers and slowly drew the zipper downward.

Savannah hooked her thumbs inside his leathers and began working them down over his hips. She maneuvered them as far as his knees and stopped. "Sir. I have something to give you, but I can't do it while you have all these clothes on. Maybe you should sit on the bed."

* * *

"Savannah, you don't have to give me anything."

"No, I don't. That's what makes it possible for me to do this. My gift to you. My choice."

Her words wiped every thought from his head. What did she want to give him? Whatever it was, he knew it would be important for him to accept her gift.

Damián sat on the edge of the bed and watched as she knelt at his feet. His dick bobbed in his briefs at the sight of her kneeling before him. He'd never experienced having a woman kneel gracefully before him, but he imagined this must be what it felt like for Dad with Karla and Marc with Angelina. Fucking beautiful—and hot.

Whoa! Slow down. Savannah hadn't yet agreed to be his sub.

She pulled down his leathers, and he lifted his legs to let her remove them. She stared a moment at his prosthesis, and he reached out to stroke her hair, hoping to calm her fears. He'd never demand that she touch it, but Savannah surprised him when she unstrapped the device and slid it off. Next she removed the black stump sock.

He tried to see his stump the way Savannah would. He'd only shown her once, and she'd accepted it without a qualm, but the disfigurement had to be a turn-off for her, at the very least.

She gave him a querulous smile. "Is it okay if I massage it?"

He felt as if he'd been sucker punched. Seeing her kneeling at his feet definitely had given him ideas, but he quickly shifted his mindset to where it should be. Tonight wasn't about sex. Never had been. After the abuse he'd given his stump a month ago, a massage would feel great.

"Sure. I'd like that." None of the bottoms he'd worked with before Savannah had ever thought about what his needs might be. He swallowed hard and waited.

Without looking up at him again, she ran her hands lightly over his skin from his knee across his calf, brushing the coarse hairs aside. She lingered over the scar from the bullet he'd taken in the cabin raid. Every time he looked at it, he remembered how close the bullet had come to Savannah's severely battered body.

Her gentle, sensual touch brought him back to the moment, and his dick stirred. Chico sure as hell liked her touch, even though she'd come nowhere near him. He held his breath.

She laid her forehead against his thigh but continued to stroke his calf with both hands. Her fingers brushed his stump, tentatively at first, then with more pressure in all the right places. He'd abused the hell out of it these past few months and what she was doing felt so good. He closed his eyes and reveled in the feel of her magic hands. He didn't say anything to break the spell, but after a moment, she stopped.

"Damián."

He opened his eyes. "Yes, Savannah?" He loved having his blonde, blue-eyed princess back in his life.

"Let me know if I'm hurting you."

"Oh, *bebé*. What you've been doing felt so fucking good." Damián had never thought of his stump as being an erogenous zone, but she was killing him here.

She continued to massage the skin and muscle around his stump. He moaned.

Her hands stilled, and he thought he'd scared her off, but she soon resumed the tender ministrations. He'd tried to massage his stump himself every night like the physical therapists had instructed him to, but her hands were doing a better job than he ever could.

Her hands stopped once more, and he resigned himself that she might have had enough. Probably a good thing, given how Chico was responding to her.

She frowned up at him. "I…" She nibbled her lower lip and blushed before meeting his gaze. "I want to try something. Promise you won't laugh at me."

"*Querida*, nothing you could do at the moment would make me laugh. I'm at your mercy. Do whatever you're comfortable with."

"I'm tired of staying within my comfort zone."

Dios, what did she have in mind?

She got to her feet. "Lie down."

He gave her a puzzled look, but did as instructed, not sure getting horizontal at the moment was a good idea. She stared at his erection straining against his briefs. When he thought he might have frightened her off, she walked around the bed, grabbed two pillows, and tossed them to the bottom of the bed.

She crawled onto the bed with him and confused him by turning her backside to him, remaining on all fours. He enjoyed the view of her cute ass encased in the tight pink shorts, her lower cheeks flashing him. Knowing she wore no panties made him even harder. His dick went into another spasm.

Savannah seemed to be looking down at his stump. He felt exposed, having himself displayed to her like this. She turned perpendicular to his knees and, frowning, looked up at him and then back at his stump, assessing the situation on the ground…er, bed. The woman did act as if she was on a mission, though.

"Scoot up on the pillows. You need to be sitting upright." As if remembering their roles, she smiled sweetly and added, "*Sir*…please." He gawked like a teenager but didn't take his eyes off her as he followed her command.

She watched his stump move up the mattress and held up her left hand to halt him. "Perfect."

He guessed she just wanted to have better access to his stump to continue the massage. Maybe her back was hurting her from kneeling on the floor. She still had scars from the beating last month, and probably would carry some for life, although he'd applied the salves Marc had provided him with twice a day. At least some of the more superficial scars had faded.

Savannah broke into his thoughts when she stretched out lengthwise beside his lower body and laid her head on the pillows she'd placed at the foot of the bed. Before he could try to figure out what she had in mind, she took a deep breath and lifted his leg in the air. She brought it down on top of her chest, his stump nestled between her breasts. What the fuck was she trying to do to him? He wasn't a fucking eunuch.

Cupping her breasts, she encased his stump tightly between her firm breasts and squeezed. His dick throbbed as if she'd just taken it between her breasts for a boob job.

Santa Madre de Dios.

She lifted her hips, and his stump glided between her breasts. Developing a rhythm, she lowered and lifted her hips over and over. Chico bobbed, wanting his turn, too. *Dios*, Damián hoped he wouldn't embarrass himself, not that he was going to do anything to stop her.

No *way* was he going to stop his princess slut.

Savannah's breathing grew more rapid with her exertions, which just left him hotter than holy hell.

This isn't about sex. This isn't about you. Tonight is about Savannah's healing.

He needed to put an end to this. Now.

"Stop, *savita*. Look at me."

She stopped but continued to hold his stump in the warm embrace of her breasts. Damián felt her heart beating against the back of his calf, the gentle rise and fall of her chest as she caught her breath. He never could have planned for something like this to happen in a million years. She was going to kill him if she kept springing these surprises on him tonight, but he'd sure die one very, very happy man.

"Look. At. Me."

Her heart gave a little thump against him. Her body's response to his command caused a lump to form in his throat. He loved the beauty of her submission. His leg still resting on her chest, she lifted herself onto her elbows. Her cheeks were flushed, and he saw the vulnerability in her eyes.

"I hope that wasn't too weird. I just got the idea at the spur of the moment. Thanks for not laughing at me…"

Her chin began to quiver, and he motioned with his fingers for her to come to him. She set his leg back on the bed carefully, picked up her pillows, and tossed them to the spot beside his head. Still not sure he could speak, he opened his arms and Savannah stretched out beside him. He wrapped his arms around her, kissing the top of her head.

He cleared his throat. "That's the hottest…I mean sweetest thing anyone's ever done for me."

She lifted her head and stared into his eyes. "You thought it was hot, too?" She blushed. Did Savannah Gentry just admit she'd gotten hot playing with his stump?

"Woman, you're killing me, but, yeah, that was hotter than a fucking firecracker."

She beamed. "I was just practicing."

His eyes opened wider. *Did* she have a stump fetish—or was she practicing for something else? *Don't even think about Savannah giving you a boob job, Chico. Just fucking forget it.*

Fuck. Fuck. Fuck.

He needed to take back control of this scene and quick. At least they both still had the barrier of some of their clothing. *Dios,* but he wanted to go down on her pussy again in the worst way.

Chico bobbed against her hip, and she looked at him with fear in her eyes at first. Then she smiled. There was a tremor in her lips, but she most definitely smiled.

What the fuck was he in for tonight with his princess slut?

* * *

I can do this…for Damián.

Pulling away from his strong, safe arms, she ventured further into these uncharted waters. She kept her focus on his brown eyes, so warm and encouraging, but was unsure what to do next. That massage had worked out better than she'd expected. Could she go through with the rest of what she'd learned in the video?

"I'm not sure how to get started."

He pushed himself up, bracing on one elbow, and reached over with his free hand to tweak her nipple. She hissed at her body's response.

"*Bebé*, I'll do whatever you want me to. Start by giving me any hard limits here. You've gone OFP on me and…"

"OFP?"

"Sorry—an expression we use in the Corps. Means Own Fucking Program. I think you're going to have to at least give me the FragO here."

"Sir, could you use plain English, please? I'm already in over my head with all this kink vocabulary."

He grinned. "It's not kink. Sorry for reverting to jargon all of the sudden. In the Marine Corps, a Frag Order—fragmentary order—contains five paragraphs that spell out very basically the details, objectives, and logistics of a mission. You're in charge now. Issue the Frag Order. Tell me how far I can go."

"I don't even know how far *I* can go."

"Then you'll use your slow-down or safeword, if you need to."

"For sex?"

"Hell, when my niece and nephew were young, my sister gave them a safeword so she'd know when the play wasn't play anymore."

"Teresa's mom is into this, too? Is it hereditary?"

"I have no fucking clue what my sister is into and don't plan to ask. But I don't think safewords are strictly the property of those in the kink community."

"Damián, I'm afraid I'll get you all worked up and leave you hanging if I safeword."

His mouth twitched, and her eyes opened wider when she realized what she'd said. Her face grew heated.

"I can take care of myself. I've taken Chico in hand before."

Oh dear Lord. This conversation was getting more embarrassing by the minute. She glanced down at Chico's rigid length, barely contained by his briefs, and gulped. She was even less sure about taking this next step than before.

"I'm not sure how Chiquita feels about…"

"Chiquita?"

Her eyes darted up to Damián's puzzled face. *Had she said that aloud?*

Own it, Savannah. She held her chin higher. "Well, if you can have all these code words, so can I." She glanced away, then back at him. "I've never been comfortable saying pussy out loud, unless you make me. So if I'm in charge of the plan tonight, then I'm going to call my…pussy 'Chiquita.'" She found it easier to ask for what she needed when she referred to her privates by a silly name, even if it did sound ridiculous.

He chuckled. "*Bebé*, you can call her anything you like."

She relaxed. He was being very agreeable, letting her explore and set her own pace. But how far could she go with him? "What if Chiquita's not a good fit for Chico." The words had barely left her lips before her eyes opened wider. "I mean, not a good match!"

Oh, God. Take me now.

He grinned and tweaked her nose. "You forget that Chico and Chiquita fit together just fine before."

Memories of the day in the beach cave with Damián flooded over her, leaving her feeling safe and warm.

"So again, *bebé*, now that you've gone OFP on me, you're going to have to give *me* some direction. I shared my original plan for tonight—and sex wasn't even on the scope. Chico is standing by and ready to carry out any mission you come up with. If that means going back to my original plan of holding you in my arms all night long, then no worries. I can tell you right now, we *are* going to get to that part of my original plan eventually."

"That's really all you planned to do?"

"Well, that and touch you. Like this."

He traced his finger lightly along her collarbone, and her heart tripped over a few beats. Even though he hadn't touched them, her nipples became engorged. His gaze zeroed in on her breasts, igniting the peaks even more.

"Very pretty, princess."

The man must have sucked the oxygen out of the room, because she had to open her mouth to refill her lungs. His gaze moved to her mouth.

"This is unknown territory for me, Sir. I'd rather you take charge, and if I need to stop or slow down, I'll use one of my safewords."

"Fair enough." His finger skimmed along her shoulder and over her bicep. When she expected him to move over to her nipple, he pulled her into his arms and continued touching her shoulders and upper back. Most of the scars on her back had healed, but he avoided the two deeper ones that probably would never go away completely, despite the efforts of the plastic surgeon.

Savannah felt an increasingly familiar zing to her clit. She hadn't told Damián how her body had been responding to his touch the last couple of weeks, as he'd tenderly applied the healing salves. She'd been confused by her body's reaction, and even more by how he'd left her wanting more of his touches. She just hadn't known how to ask for what she needed.

Damián made her feel precious. Honored. Healed.

He made her *feel*. Period.

She'd never thought about it before, but she'd been healing little by little with Damián as far back as December.

"I like cuddling."

"Me, too, *bebé*."

Savannah realized she was taking and not giving—again. She reached around his side to run her hand up and down his back. The muscles were hard as rocks.

Strong.

He'd never use his strength to force her to do anything against her will. He wouldn't overpower her. She could submit to him consensually but he would always maintain control of himself. If she used her safeword, he would stop immediately.

Safe.

Her hand trailed down the valley of his spine to the waistband of his shorts. She hesitated a moment, not sure she could take the next step.

"No hands below the waist, *querida*."

She pulled away from him and cocked her head.

"We've got all night, *savita*, and we're taking this slow. To do that, you're going to have to keep your hands above my waist. That's *my* limit—until further notice."

"Oh." Some of her nervousness receded, knowing she wasn't under pressure to touch his—er, Chico—yet. "That sounds like a good plan, Sir."

He smiled at her, and her hand continued to stroke his back. Did her hands affect him the way his did her? The man's hands were seriously wicked. His focus was still on her shoulders and upper back, not exactly erogenous zones, but her response was purely carnal. She wanted more.

"I thought the rule was no hands below the waist."

"It is, *querida*."

"Then why aren't you touching my breasts?"

He pulled away and looked into her eyes, frowning. "I didn't want to rush you."

"I'm a patient woman, Damián, but you're driving me crazy. You're taking it *too* slowly."

Damián's eyes narrowed, and a slow smile curved his lips. He pressed her shoulder until she was lying on her back. Taking her hands by the wrists, he moved them up above her head and held them there. Her stomach flip-flopped as he took control of her body. She suddenly wanted his hands on every inch of her.

His face inched toward hers, and he captured her mouth, nibbling at her lower lip. He pulled away and whispered, "Open for me, *bebé*?"

Oh. She should have opened for him automatically. She knew how to kiss. "I'm sor—?"

He took advantage of her open mouth, his tongue plundering her like a pirate, taking her breath away. Her toes curled, and she drew her knees up to try and alleviate some of the building pressure.

When she thought she'd go insane from wanting him to touch her, his hand released her wrists and he ended the kiss. She gasped for air.

"Do not move your hands. *¿Comprendes?*"

She nodded, afraid her voice would betray her...neediness.

He trailed kisses to the hollow of her neck, nibbling the skin above her pulse. He must have felt her body's response. Her clit began to throb in syncopated rhythm with her heartbeat.

She wanted him to touch Chiquita but couldn't ask.

His lips blazed a trail to her chest, capturing her left nipple while his finger and thumb rolled her right one. His teeth bit at her peak and she hissed. The burning in her breasts bordered on painful. She wasn't sure, but thought Chiquita was getting wet.

Oh, my Lord!

How much more could she take before she exploded?

Damián released her nipples and rolled on top of her, his mouth descending on her once again.

Smothering. Father's weight pressed her into the mattress...

Her breathing became ragged as she fought for control, but panic won out. She lowered her hands and pushed at his shoulders. "Stop! Get off! Guacamole!"

Damián rolled off her immediately and lay on his side. Embarrassed at being such a failure, she turned away from him, gasping for air and hugging herself for comfort. His hand stroked her shoulder and back.

"Shhh. Deep breath, *savita*. Tell me where you are."

"I couldn't breathe. Your weight smothered me, just like…" Tears stung her eyes as she drew a deep breath. How could she ever have sex with Damián if she couldn't stand to have him on top of her? "I'm sorry. This isn't going to work."

"What are you apologizing for?"

"Freaking out on you. Being a failure at Foreplay 101."

He pulled her against his body and wrapped his arm around her waist where his hand rested on her abdomen. His lips tickled her ear as he spoke. "I don't want to hear you call yourself a failure ever again. We'll begin to map our course tonight, taking each trigger as it comes and talking about them. For starters, tell me where you went when I laid on top of you."

"My bedroom." Her voice sounded like a scared little girl's. She didn't want to be that tormented little girl anymore and made sure she sounded like a grown woman when she continued. "I flashed back to the age of eight or nine. My father came into my room at night and…"

His body tensed, but his voice remained calm. "Okay, we're going to put the missionary position on the hard-limits list."

The confident way he just proposed a solution to the problem made her wonder if there were any hang-ups too big for Damián. She scooted onto her back and looked up into his concerned face. "There are other positions?"

He grinned. "Hell, yeah. I look forward to showing *all* of them to you, *bebé*."

"Starting tonight?" How many positions could there be? Part of her wanted to learn more; part of her was scared to death.

"You're every man's dream."

But she didn't know where to start. "Sir, will you guide me?"

"We're going to take it one step at a time. First, let's get out of these clothes."

Savannah's heart pounded, and she glanced down at the dragon roaring at her, unable to meet Damián's gaze. She'd stopped at his briefs and hadn't completely removed her clothes either. She'd seen him naked before, but it had been so long ago. She'd grown curious lately to see what it had been too dark to see in that cave.

So why was she so nervous?

Trust him.

She drew a deep breath. "I'm ready to continue."

"That's my girl." He laid down on his back, never taking his eyes off her. "So who strips first? Lady's choice."

She grinned. "You've already seen me plenty of times, so I'm more comfortable starting with me."

Kneeling on the bed, she sat on her heels and faced Damián. He had his hands tucked behind his head, as if ready to watch a show. Did he notice her hesitation? Heck, Damián noticed everything.

"First, stroke your body—your chest, breasts, abdomen. Then work your way down to the shorts."

She hadn't intended to do another striptease but wanted to please him and appreciated his guidance so she could learn what he liked. Guessing what he would want based on her nonexistent knowledge of what men and women in loving relationships did in bed together would be impossible.

She began with her hands on the sides of her neck, realizing her palms were a little sweaty. Keeping her gaze on Damián's appreciative face gave her courage and she touched her body in what she hoped was a seductive way. When her hands reached her breasts, she pinched and pulled the nipples. Out of the corner of her eye, she saw Chico bob, and knew she must be doing something right.

After a few moments, she continued her journey across her abdomen to her belly button. She wasn't quite sure what to do, so she sat up off her heels, hooked her thumbs into the waistband, and wiggled her hips as she shimmied out of the tight shorts.

The cold air hit Chiquita full force, and without a doubt, Savannah knew she was wet. She smiled and laid down on the bed to finish removing the shorts. When she felt brave enough to look at him, she saw his gaze was focused on the pink, shaved skin of her mons.

She grew wetter. What was he doing to her?

"So fucking perfect."

Suddenly shy about meeting Chico again, she rolled over and got out of the bed. "I think it might be more…um, romantic without the lights." She turned off the overhead light and walked toward the bathroom. She shut the door partway, allowing just enough light into the room that they would be able to find each other.

When she returned to the bed, Damián had stretched out on his side facing her, still wearing his briefs. He patted the bed beside him and she crawled into the center and stretched out on her back.

"No. Lie on your side."

She started to turn toward him, but he motioned for her to face away. Confused, she followed his guidance, perfectly happy to have him calling the shots, but wondered what he had in mind. She couldn't touch him if he was behind her.

He spooned against her, his arm over her waist and his hand on her belly. He wanted to go to sleep? But she wasn't tired at all!

Chapter Twenty-Five

Savannah tried hard not to wiggle against Chico, pressed hard against her butt crack. She didn't want to encourage him. Damián needed his sleep.

His hand began stroking her abdomen, and she held her breath. Or maybe he didn't plan to go to sleep after all. Savannah had no clue what she was supposed to do in this position so she just gave in to the feel of his touch.

Damián's hand brushed against the underside of her breasts at the same time his lips came down on her shoulder in a tender kiss. She drew in a rapid breath. By the time his hand reached her nipple, it was rigid and waiting for him. He rolled it tenderly at first, then harder. Her hips bucked, not away from Chico, but toward him. Chiquita seemed to have a mind of her own.

"Oh. That feels so good." She didn't want him to stop.

His teeth nibbled on her shoulder sending a clear message to the area below her waist. Savannah ached, wanting his fingers, his lips, his teeth touching Chiquita, as well.

Damián seemed to be in no hurry with his slow, gentle exploration. Why didn't he touch her there? She wiggled her ass against Chico, who pulsated against her, but Damián hadn't moved his hips. Chiquita throbbed in response. She wanted him to touch her.

How could she get Damián to understand what she wanted?

"Sir?"

"Yes, Savannah?"

"I...you...um, what do you want me to be doing?"

"Feeling."

Oh, she was feeling all right—an overload of feelings. "I think I've achieved that objective. What's next?"

"This is your plan, *bebé*. I'm following the original Frag Order, but if you need to rip that one up and write a new one, just keep me informed."

"Oh." She couldn't ask for what she needed, though. How could she... "Sir...well then, Chiquita has lifted the ban on touches below the waist."

"Is she sure?"

"Are you questioning her orders, Marine?"

Did she need to draw him a road map here?

He chuckled. "No, ma'am. Tell General Chiquita I'm quite capable of following her FragO."

She held her breath, waiting for him to touch Chiquita, but instead he continued to drive her senses crazy by playing with her nipple. He took his sweet time pulling, squeezing, and rolling it, all the while making Chiquita wetter. When he let go, she nearly wept with joy. *Finally!* But he just moved his hand to the other and began torturing it the same way.

"Please, Damián. I want..." Remembering how he'd brought her to orgasm previously with his tongue, she wanted to experience that again.

Please don't make me beg.

"You want what, *bebé*?"

Savannah panted, her mouth slightly open to allow more air into her constricted lungs, as he continued to torment her.

"I want you to touch *mi chiquita!* I mean, Chiquita wants...oh, Sir, you know what I want. Why won't you give it to me?"

"Chiquita is a demanding little thing, but I'm here to follow orders. Now, define Chiquita's territory?"

"Sir?"

"I want to make sure I don't touch places that are off-limits. Tell me where I can touch you."

"Nothing is off-limits to your fingers, or...your tongue."

"Ahhh, I see."

Thank goodness the lights were out, although she was surprised her bright red face wasn't a beacon in here.

"On your back. Now." Her stomach seemed to drop through the mattress, and she rolled onto her back without hesitation. He reached up and grabbed a pillow. "Lift your hips."

Never taking her eyes off him, she bent her knees and did as he commanded. After he slid the pillow under her butt, he instructed her to do so again and tucked another pillow under her, raising her puss...*Chiquita* off the bed, positioning her for his mouth. Finally!

Instead, he lowered his mouth to her nipple. She groaned in frustration. While his mouth bit and pulled on one nipple, his fingers tormented the other. Her hips lifted into the air seeking his touch.

"Please, Sir. I can't take any more."

Damián pulled away, her nipple clamped between his teeth. He stretched her breast until the pain made her lift her chest, and then he pulled some more before releasing it with a plop. He grinned. "Oh, I think you can take much, much more, *savita*. And I plan to give it to you."

Chiquita responded by throbbing and growing even wetter.

She hadn't even caught her breath before his mouth descended again, blazing a trail across her belly. At last, he was advancing on Chiquita, who was growing even more impatient. She held her breath and clung to the sheets to keep from screaming as he drew closer and closer.

Pain burned in her chest before she remembered to breathe again. His teeth nibbled at her mons, driving her nearer to the edge. She bucked her hips and he bit her clit hood.

"Ouch!"

He kissed where he'd bitten her and stared up at her. "Lie still and you won't get hurt—as much."

Oh, dear Lord. She wasn't going to survive tonight.

Damián rose and crawled to the foot of the mattress and turned to face her. "Open yourself wider, *mi mariposa*."

She remembered feeling like a butterfly, spread open for him in the beach cave. She complied, and he crawled between her knees.

Oh, thank God. Maybe she'd make it, after all, if he put his tongue on her. Now!

Once more, he thwarted her and began placing kisses and nibbles on her feet, ankles, calves, alternating legs and taking his own time about it, too. She clutched the sheets and hung on. He placed a kiss on the inside of her knee joint, and her hip jolted upward. How much more did he expect her to take?

When he finally arrived at her thighs, she hyperventilated. He stopped.

"Slow, deep breaths, *savita*. I don't want you passing out on me."

"Passing out? Passing *out*? You're killing me, and you're worried I'm going to faint?"

He chuckled. "You've been so quiet, I wasn't sure you were awake."

She growled in frustration.

"Now, let's see if Chiquita is awake."

Her clit throbbed. She only nodded, unable to speak. At last. He'd run out of leg and was going to—

He spread her labia with his thumbs and blew warm breath on Chiquita. Savannah nearly wept. Her body began to shake. The pressure had built so far, she wasn't even sure he'd have to touch her for her to come.

"Please, Sir! I beg for mercy and release."

"I aim to give you only one of those."

"Release, Sir. Only release."

He chuckled and his tongue lapped at the juices flowing from her pussy. "So sweet. Thank you for getting wet for me, Chiquita."

How could she not get wet, the way he was bringing her body to life? Or maybe Chiquita was crying in frustration.

His tongue ventured up her cleft to the hood surrounding her clit. He stroked it several times before he took the entire hood between his teeth and nipped her. Rather than pull away, Chiquita moved closer.

"More. Please, don't stop."

He bit down again, not as hard as where he'd bitten her elsewhere, but she wouldn't have been able to take that much pressure. With his teeth holding the hood, he flicked his tongue against her until her clit came out and was overpowered by him.

"Yes! There!"

The movement of Damián's shoulders told her he was laughing, but she didn't care as long as he kept his teeth, tongue, and mouth where they belonged.

He pulled back, and she groaned. She looked down at him, tears springing to her eyes. "Why, Sir? Why won't you just let me come? I can't take any more."

He grinned and grabbed her right hip. "I'm going to hold you down with one hand so you won't flit away. Hang on, *bebé*."

He lowered his head, and she could only see his black hair nestled between her legs. His tongue flicked harder against her clit, and she bucked. She laid her head on the pillow and closed her eyes as he held her down with an even firmer hand and rammed his finger inside her. Chiquita clenched around his finger, welcoming him. The first finger was joined on the next stroke by another, and he began to palpate an area deep inside. Just when she thought the pressure couldn't get any worse, her entire body began shaking. Beads of sweat popped out on her skin, leaving her hot and cold at the same time.

His mouth left her.

"No!" *Don't stop now!*

"Come for me, Savannah."

Despite how long he'd taken to get her here, he held nothing back when he descended on her once more. His fingers and tongue assaulted her until every last defense was battered down.

"Yes! I'm coming! Don't stop. Oh, God, don't stop now!"

He didn't. She bucked against him, riding the tide of her physical and emotional release. "Yessss! Oh, Damián! I love you!" His movements stopped, and she realized what she'd said. A sob broke free. "I'm sorry. I can't help it. I do. But if you leave me hanging here any longer, you'll never get to visit Chiquita again."

He took her home.

"Yesss. Oh, oh, oh, don't stop!" The world disappeared for a moment as she rode his mouth, until the stimulation against her clit became painful. The earth moved again, then she realized it was just the mattress.

Damián stroked her sweat-dampened temple. "Did you mean that, or was it just the moment of passion?"

She batted her eyelashes. "What? About losing your visitation rights with Chiquita?"

He growled. "You know exactly what I mean."

She reached up and stroked his cheek. "I could answer that, but words are empty. Let me show you."

Remembering the video she'd watched, she inhaled deeply. She'd already used one of the ideas she'd seen in the video. She could do this.

"Remove your briefs, Sir."

* * *

Damián swallowed. The woman clearly was on a mission but was she ready to give him what he needed right now? In the heat of passion, she'd already fulfilled one of his fantasies, telling him she loved him. He wasn't sure he could take much more before he embarrassed himself—and scared the shit out of her.

"Savannah, I'm so close to losing it right now. I need to go take a shower and take Chico in hand first. Then why don't we get back to the original plan and just cuddle?"

"I. Said. Remove. Your. Briefs. And I mean now, Marine. *Muévete rapido.*"

Even if Damián hadn't learned to take orders very well, he was going to follow this one. He pulled his waistband over the painfully hard Chico and skimmed the briefs over his legs, tossing them to the floor. Her gaze went to his dick, and her eyes grew wide.

"What's that?"

Santa Madre de Dios, *had she blocked out what a dick looked like?*

She leaned closer and totally missed Chico, touching the spot between his dick and his hip joint instead. "Why, it's a butterfly."

Oh, hell. She was looking at the tattoo he'd gotten right before he'd enlisted in the Marines.

This tat meant a lot to him, but wasn't one very many people had seen. He cupped her chin and guided her head back until she met his gaze.

"You'd flitted out of my life, *mi mariposa*. This was my way of keeping you with me—turned out I didn't really need any reminders. I could never forget you."

She blinked rapidly, then squeezed her eyes shut a moment, fighting her emotions again. She opened her eyes again and grinned. "That's really sweet, but why would you put a tat there? It had to hurt like hell."

Not that he'd admit that to her. "I was getting ready to join the Marines. I couldn't exactly put a fucking butterfly tat on my chest."

She grinned. "I guess that might be a little awkward."

"Well, later I saw all kinds of tats I never thought I'd see on a Marine, but this one remained private from just about everyone."

She looked at it again and nibbled her lower lip. Chico bobbed, probably thinking she was looking at him. Damián's image of that sweet mouth on his dick, though, made him even harder.

Slow down, Chico. This is happening at her *speed, even if it kills you.*

She lay back down and steeled herself, meeting his gaze like some sacrificial virgin.

"Savannah, we don't have to…"

"Straddle me."

"I don't want to trigger you with my weight."

"I'm not totally sure how this works, but I think the only weight you'll have on me is Chico—and I don't think he's going to trigger me. You know I'll use my safeword if I need to."

Just what position did she have in mind? Before he could figure out what she wanted him to do, she guided him with her instructions.

"I want you facing me with your butt resting on my boobs and Chico between them."

Santa Madre de Dios.

Resting was the last thing on Chico's mind. Just hearing her command nearly made him cream. He didn't plan to mark her with his cum, but fuck, imagining feeling his dick between her breasts as they squeezed the life out of him…precum seeped from his dick. Not sure how long he could hold out, he assumed the position, knees inches from her armpits, barely brushing the sides of her breasts.

"I think you'll rest most of your weight on the headboard with your hands."

"You sure you haven't done this before?"

A guilty look passed over her face, and she shook her head.

"*Bebé*, none of those other men exist anymore. Just forget about what they…"

"No! I'm telling the truth. I've never lied to you."

He'd hurt her feelings. *Great.*

"Maybe I need to shut the fuck up and let you explain."

She grinned and glanced away once more, and her cheeks turned red. "While you were at work today, Karla and I—"

"Karla? I'm afraid she doesn't have the right parts for this position."

She took a deep breath, and her breasts brushed against his ass. Chico bobbed, drawing her attention for a moment. She licked her lips. Damián closed his eyes, no longer able to watch.

"We were watching online sex videos in Adam's office—"

His eyelids shot open. "You and Karla were watching porn on Dad's computer?" Now there was something he'd never thought he'd need to picture. *Whoever said the internet wasn't educational?*

"No! Not porn. Just free online videos."

What the fuck had they been learning down there? Hell, was she hotter than a habanero pepper tonight because she'd spent the day watching porn? "Did you enjoy figuring it out?"

"Enjoy? Of course not! The sex act was cold and disgusting. I already knew that, though."

Well, Chico, if she thinks that, you'd better hold on until I can get to you in the shower.

"The people in the videos were so mechanical, and they seemed to be seducing the camera more than each other. Total turn-off. Karla thought it was hot, though, and said she couldn't wait to try it after the baby's born."

"Whoa. The last thing I want to do right now is think about Karla and Dad having sex."

"Sorry. Please don't tell on her. And don't think badly of Karla. I'm sure she would never have looked at something like that if she wasn't trying to help me figure out how to make this work."

Think badly of her? He owed Karla dinner—Dad, too, for providing the computer—if Karla could help Savannah overcome some of her aversion to sex.

But they had a ways to go and hopefully a long lifetime to explore together. "*Savita*, tonight has been one of the best nights of my life. Just being able to touch you, to watch you come apart when I gave you an orgasm, is enough."

She shook her head. "It's not enough for me. I need…"

Her eyes squeezed shut.

"Tell me, *savita*. You know I'd give you anything within my power."

"I need…" She opened her eyes and made eye contact. "…for you to come, too."

He stopped breathing for a moment. "You're sure?"

"I think so, but I can't promise I won't get triggered by something I haven't anticipated."

He stroked her cheek. "The only promise I've ever asked you to make or ever will is that you'll try. You've always fulfilled every promise to me, Savannah. You could never disappoint me."

Her lip quivered, and he caged it, brushing his thumb over her lips.

"If I ever disappoint you, Sir, just know it wasn't intentional. I'm sorry I can't…you know."

"Say the words."

"I can't have sex. I'll never understand why people would want to—"

"What do you call what just happened here?"

"I think they call it foreplay."

He hadn't expected her to answer, but fuck, if *that* was foreplay, he was going to have one helluva ride with this woman. Someday soon, he hoped. He'd seen a lot of walls tumble down tonight.

The regret in her voice would have been funny if he didn't have Chico bobbing inches from her mouth.

"Foreplay is probably as far as I'll ever get. I do like the orgasms, but I don't want to have actual sex—intercourse, I mean."

If you throw down any more gauntlets, chica, *you're going to learn fast just how sexual you really are.*

"You and I will determine what our relationship—sexual and otherwise—will be, *bebé*. Only us. I learned long ago in this community there isn't a one-size-fits-all to kink—and the same goes for sex, whether it's kink or vanilla. Couples communicate about what works for them, and from time to time negotiate to see if they want to try something new. Hell, I'd die a happy man if you just let me kiss Chiquita at least once a day."

She smiled. "She'd like that, too." Looking down at his dick, she became serious again. "Now it's Chico's turn."

Without hesitation, her hand grabbed Chico with trembling fingers and squeezed. Hard. He hissed in a breath and reached for her hand wanting to slow her down before he exploded, but she yanked her hand away as if burned.

"Don't control my hand, Damián. I have to do this myself."

Another fucking trigger.

Damián placed both hands at the back of his head. "Take your time." He tried to grin in a wolfish way, and she grinned back. *Good.* The tension had been broken, well, for one of them, at least.

She wrapped her hand around him again, the pad of her thumb brushing the notch near the head. When he grew wetter there, she froze again.

Stay with me, savita. "That feels so good." She blinked, looked up at him, and smiled. "That's my girl."

She moved her hand down the column of his rigid penis, then released him. He wasn't going to survive tonight.

She nearly blew his mind when she lifted her head toward him and took the knob of his dick between her lips.

Damián leaned over and grabbed the top of the headboard. Her lips pressed against him, and she flicked her tongue on the underside of his dick.

Holy fuck.

Fuck, fuck, fuck.

No, Chico, you didn't get a FragO to fuck. She just said so.

But he planned to enjoy whatever the hell his princess slut had to offer.

He moved his hips, and Chico slipped a little farther into her mouth, but he pulled out quickly, not wanting to force himself on her. He waited to see if she'd come to him for the next stroke. *Fuck.* She did, taking him deeper inside her mouth, then releasing him, over and over. Watching her blonde head bobbing on his dick made his balls tighten.

Chico, don't even think *about shooting your load down her throat.* That would end this ecstasy before it even started.

She compressed her breasts around his dick with her hands as she pistoned him with her lips. He held onto the headboard for dear life. Sweat broke out on his upper lip, and he closed his eyes, focusing solely on the pressure of her lips and breasts caressing Chico.

"Oh, *bebé.* That feels so good."

She stopped moving and giggled. *Great. Maybe you should keep your fucking mouth shut and just let her do her thing.* On the other hand, he needed to slow down. He wouldn't last much longer.

"What's so fucking funny?"

"The hair on your legs is tickling the sides of my boobs."

Sweet Jesús. She was killing him.

When she took his dick even deeper into her mouth this time, he groaned. His grip tightened on the headboard making his fingers go numb. "I think you'd better stop, *bebé.* I'm close to coming."

She released him and looked up. Her gaze was direct, innocent, and unquestionably sexual.

"Newly issued Frag Order, Sir. Come on me."

He had to be dreaming. "Come again, *bebé?*"

"No, thanks, I'm fine. For now, anyway. And before you ask me to define 'fine,' I mean that I am one very satisfied *chica.*" She smiled.

She wasn't innocent at all; she knew exactly what she was fucking doing and enjoying the hell out of his shock and awe.

"I said, I want you to come on me." A shudder passed through her that he felt in his thighs. She grew serious. "On my boobs, though, not my face."

Mierda. Way to send him on an impossible mission. It had been so long for him, the explosion of his cum would probably give her whiplash.

"I can't promise that at this angle. Do you want to try another position?"

"No. This is the one I learned!"

Her distress was real. He grinned, hoping she wouldn't get too hung up on this position. He just needed to come without triggering her.

"Why don't you just watch while I jerk off?"

Tears came to her eyes. "No. I want to please you the way you've pleased me so many times." She took a deep breath. "Then just aim for my breasts. You're a sniper. You should have good aim."

The image of aiming his cum on her chest with precision made his balls ache. Chico needed no further invitation, but first sought the warm entrance of her mouth once more. This time, she took half the length of him and grazed the sides of his dick with her teeth.

His cum pulsated up his shaft, and he pulled his hips back. He hated for this to end, it felt so good. But he'd waited so long. He needed release. The tip of his dick pistoned in the tunnel of her breasts. Almost there. A few more strokes.

Madre de Dios!

He closed his eyes and heard a splintering sound that didn't make sense, but with his white-hot cum shooting into the tunnel she'd made for him between her breasts, he just kept pumping. Looking down to make sure she was okay, he watched his cum hitting her upper chest and jaw. "I'm sorry, *bebé*."

She smiled up at him and shook her head. "No! I'm fine. Don't stop." She cringed as each drop hit her. She was doing this for him.

She compressed her breasts even harder against him. *Fuck*. The cum kept pouring out of him. He'd never had an orgasm last this long in his fucking life.

After a few smaller spurts, he knew she'd boob-fucked him dry. Seeing his cum shooting onto her upper body like that beat missionary-position fucking all to hell. If she wanted to keep issuing new FragOs for experimental sex missions, he'd re-enlist for the rest of his life.

He tried to pry his fingers from their death-grip on the headboard and brought a piece of the decorative woodwork with him. *Mierda*.

"I think I broke the fucking bed!"

* * *

Savannah giggled, releasing some of the tension she'd been feeling.

Still straddling her breasts, he leaned over the side of the bed and laid the piece of broken headboard on the floor.

Damián Orlando had lost control one of the few times since she'd reunited with him last year. She'd done that for him.

She smiled at him. "The sex-video people should have you as the star in one of their films."

He cocked his head. "You want me to be a porn star?"

"No! I'm saying, if they had someone who put his heart into the act like you did, then maybe those movies wouldn't be so boring. They just focus on the mechanics of sliding Part A into Slot B."

He chuckled and bent down to kiss her again. "*Bebé*, whenever you want me to demonstrate how to slide Chico's Part A into Chiquita's Slot B, just issue the Frag Order, and I'm on it."

The suggestive words sent a jolt to Chiquita. Savannah grinned. She'd certainly knocked down a lot of walls tonight, ones that she'd slowly built up over decades.

Maybe she should stop worrying about what she couldn't do and focus on what she could. Look at what she'd just done. Savannah Gentry had just let a man—no, not just a man, but Damián, the love of her life—come all over her. Even more amazing was she hadn't been triggered by anything from the past. She still had demons she knew would attack from time to time, but if she'd tried to protect herself from that possible trigger, look what she would have missed.

Watching his face as he reached orgasm—the play of pain and pleasure over his features—brought her a sense of accomplishment unlike anything she'd imagined sex could be. Empowering and totally unexpected.

"*Bebé*, sex happens 90-percent or more in the mind and the heart. Believe me, what you and I shared here tonight is a helluva lot more exciting for us because it's real. We share a commitment to each other." He bent to brush a kiss across her lips. "Plus that was just fucking unbelievable, *mi mamacita*. Thank you for doing that for me. Now, let me go get something to clean you up."

She grabbed his wrist when he would have moved away from her. "Wait!"

He looked puzzled, and she tried to find the words to express the many things rolling through her mind, but this moment wasn't about speaking the words. She needed to demonstrate what was in her heart.

"Lie down. Please…Sir." She grinned as Damián stretched out beside her and placed a hand on her hip to roll her to face him.

Glancing at the cooling pools of his essence dotting her chest, she reached up and drew the shape of a heart over her left breast. She focused on his warm, chocolate eyes. "You won my heart, Damián Orlando, the first time on a hotel bed in La Jolla." Tears stung her eyes, and she swallowed past the lump growing in her throat. "And you've had a special place in my heart ever since. You gave me Mari, who is my very life's breath. I wouldn't be here today if not for the two of you."

Tears swam in Damián's eyes, too, not helping her at all to control her own. She glanced away.

"Damián, I love you more than I can say. I'll always be wounded and a little messed up—"

He placed a finger against her lips, and she glanced back at him. "*Mi sueño*, you are perfect. You always have been, from the first time I saw you sitting in that hotel restaurant."

He traced another heart, interlocked with hers. He lifted his gaze and grinned. "I like marking you with my cum more than with Karla's lipstick."

"Karla helped you with the scene in the dungeon?"

"*Querida*, you'd better get used to it. The people who frequent this club are one close-knit family. We laugh together, celebrate each other's joys, and cry over each other's pain. I've learned by the way I was accepted by the members here and at other clubs that's what the BDSM community is all about."

"I've noticed the members and owners here have a very special familial connection."

"Savannah, you were accepted into my family a long time ago. Dad would whip my ass if I did anything that caused you or Marisol to leave us. He loves you two like a daughter and a granddaughter."

More tears flowed. She'd fantasized about having a father—no, a real *Dad*—for most of her life. To find that at any time in one's life was a blessing. And now Mari had both a daddy and a grandpa, among so many others in Damián's family.

"I'd say it also sounds like Karla's accepted you into the sisterhood of submissives here at the club, if she had you over here watching porn with her all afternoon."

She laughed through the tears and thumped his chest. "You're not going to let me live that down, are you?"

"Not on your life, *chica*. I'll buy you a whole fucking video library if it gives you any more ideas."

"Fucking videos, huh? I think maybe we ought to make some of our own. They'd be more fun to watch."

The look on his face was priceless. Savannah Gentry and Damián Orlando starring in their own private skin flicks. Too funny."

Damián grew serious. "Now, I have a question I've wanted to ask you for a long time."

Damián got to his knees beside her, and Savannah's heart pounded. He pressed her shoulder back onto the mattress until she was looking up at him, and he reached his left index finger to her chest, where he wrote on her chest above their joined hearts as he spelled out the words MARRY ME?

The uncertainty in his expression as he met her gaze and awaited her response confused and warmed her heart.

Not giving her time to respond, he continued, "I asked Anita for her blessing back when you were in the hospital, but I wanted to give you time to heal before asking you to think about turning this page in our story."

Savannah reached up and pulled him into her arms until the hearts on her sticky chest devoured the dragon tat on his. "Earlier tonight, I told you I wasn't ready for happily ever after. But you've shown me there is no obstacle that can ever destroy or overcome what we feel for each other, unless we let it. I promise you, I won't do anything to allow that to happen."

She sealed their union with a kiss.

Epilogue

Cassie López squirmed in her seat. She tried to follow Kitty's latest plan to seduce Adam, but the last thing she wanted to talk about was sex. On top of that, Luke Denton kept watching her. She'd glanced at him across the room a couple of times, where he stood talking with Adam, but both times had found him scrutinizing her.

She shifted on the uncomfortable chair again. The tiny bar in Aspen Corners had opened especially so that they could hang out. Kitty and her husband Adam had followed Angelina back from Denver, and she'd arranged with her friend Rico Donati to have a private party, just the five of them. Well, until Marc had shown up an hour or so ago. He and Angelina had retreated to a booth in the back very seriously discussing something. They acted as if they hadn't seen each other in a long while and had a lot to catch up on.

Being in a bar again stressed her out enough—the smell of stale beer assaulting her senses as soon as she walked inside. She'd scanned the room quickly and had been relieved there was no pool table.

But Luke's focused gaze was disconcerting, to say the least. Not quite a leer but very intense.

Oh, no! Luke and Adam were coming this way, Luke holding a beer bottle. She shuddered.

I need to get out of here!

"Mind if we join you, girls?"

Without waiting for an answer—which for her would have been "yes, I mind"—Adam set his bottle of water on the table. Kitty looked up at him with an emotion akin to adoration. Cassie still couldn't believe her friend had succumbed to the man's *charms* so completely and in such a short time. In college, she'd never even looked at guys.

Cassie had been the wild one, dragging her to the clubs every weekend.

Kitty would rather be singing in the dives than drinking and flirting. Perhaps if she'd been more like Kitty…

Cassie blinked and looked at Adam, who certainly hadn't charmed her. Ever since he'd interrupted their annual cleansing ceremony on *his* deck and in *his* hot tub, she'd been upset about the way he'd treated Kitty. The man had a possessive streak a mile wide and seemed to have Kitty under his thumb.

If he ever did anything to hurt her friend, Cassie would make sure he paid. Kitty was like a sister to her—a sister of the soul. They'd probably been together in many lifetimes. In her heart, Cassie knew Kitty had been sent to her this time to help her through the attack in the bar during the college break between junior and senior years.

She probably should call her friend by her given name, Karla, now that she was married and about to become a mother, but she'd always be Kitty to her.

Adam took a seat next to Kitty at the square table for four, and Luke sat closer to Cassie. She sat back in her chair, putting distance between herself and both men. Adam gently rubbed Kitty's belly, as if to greet his baby, too.

The way they were always touching each other reminded her of her brother Eduardo and his wife, or Papá and Mamá.

She ached to see them sometimes, but she couldn't bring herself to go home to Peru—ever. Colorado was her home now. Eduardo was due to make his annual visit in a couple of weeks, but her sister-in-law, Susana, wanted to stay home in Peru with their three kids. Last year, he'd brought the whole family. She'd miss her nephews and niece this year, too.

In their last Skype call, he'd hinted there might be a fourth child before the year was over.

Kitty's eyes grew round. "Someone kicked." She grinned at Adam, who looked as if he'd been poleaxed. Kitty turned toward Cassie and Luke, "There's always a lot more activity in there whenever Adam is touching or talking to my belly. They…" Her friend stopped herself and amended, "He or she—it's just easier to say they, because we don't want to know the sex…"

Adam leaned closer to her ear. "Take a breath, Kitten." She did and calmed down.

Cassie must have missed something, but she was distracted by Luke holding the beer bottle to his lips. She turned away and took a sip of her margarita on the rocks.

"So, Cassie, what are you working on now?"

She nearly choked on her drink.

Luke leaned toward her and patted her hand. "You okay, darlin'?"

She snatched her hand away and coughed. "I'm fine. Went down the wrong way."

"As I was saying, any big projects we can look forward to? Exhibits?"

She'd nearly died when he'd shown up at a gallery showing in Denver last fall. The man knew art, though. It was the only thing they'd ever have in common.

"Actually, I've spent the winter preparing to work in a new medium—fiber art." Cassie relaxed. Talking about her latest loves and art calmed her nerves a bit. "I adopted a small herd of alpacas last fall. They've come through the harsh winter really well. Probably reminds them of their roots in the Andes."

Her Colorado cabin was located at over 12,000 feet in elevation, similar to the mountain peaks near where she'd grown up in the Andes. "I should be able to begin harvesting the fleece in another week or two if the temperatures stay warm like this."

"I'd love to see your llamas sometime. Maybe I can help with the harvest."

No man would ever invade her sanctuary. She didn't want that negative energy there. She was thankful she'd had to come down the mountain to see Kitty, but *he* wouldn't let her go over the rutted road to get to her isolated place. Not without him, at least, after what happened the last trip Kitty made over the pass. She didn't want him there anyway.

Cassie scowled at Luke. She needed to divest him of the notion that he'd ever see her *llamas*, as he called them. "They're *alpacas*. And I can manage them myself." Belatedly, she added, "But thanks for the offer."

Seeming to take the hint, he looked at Adam. "How about a round of pool? You and Karla taking on Cassie and me?"

Cassie's hand began to shake. She'd surveyed the bar the minute she'd entered. There hadn't been a pool table.

Adam's voice sounded as if he was speaking through a tunnel, distorted by the blood rushing in her ears. "Sounds…good…to…me."

Someone's hands were on her back and arm, making her throat close up even more. Luke.

Get your hands off me.

She pushed him away and retreated closer to Kitty, who reached out for her and squeezed her upper arm. "Deep breath, honey. You're safe."

Kitty directed her next words to Luke. "No, thanks. We don't play pool."

"Since when, Kitten?" Adam asked. "We just played over at…"

Cassie didn't miss Kitty's silent eye communication with Adam. "Not anymore. My…belly gets in the way."

They agreed upon something silently because Adam looked at Cassie and nodded. "Completely forgot."

The last thing she wanted was his pity, but she hadn't let Kitty or Angelina tell anyone about what had happened back then. She just wanted to bury and forget it.

Cassie needed out of here. She scooted the chair back and stood. "I'll be heading home now. I don't want to be out too late. It'll be dark soon."

Luke stood, as well. "There were some avalanche warnings issued for the passes after last night's snowfall." He pulled out his phone. "Let me check my app before you head out."

"No, really! I'll be fine. I know what to watch for."

Ignoring her, Luke checked anyway. After a moment, he reported, "No roads closed up that way." He cast a worried glance at her. "Why don't I follow you home, darlin'?"

"No!" *Don't panic, Cassie. Just get the hell out of here.* "I said, I'll be fine." Her hands grew clammy. She hadn't let her guard down around a man in a very long time. She wouldn't start now.

Knowing she might not see Kitty for a while, she hated leaving so abruptly, but her friend would understand. Adam stood and helped Kitty to her feet. "It's been great seeing you, Kitty. Good luck with the CD. I know you're going to top the indie charts. Maybe when I have my next gallery showing, we can play your music in the background and sell some of them there."

Kitty laughed. "I hope it doesn't jangle the nerves of your art patrons, but thanks. That would be fun."

Kitty hugged her. The baby kicked against Cassie's abdomen. "Oh! I almost forgot. Good luck with the baby, too. I'll come up to see you when I can."

Cassie looked up at Adam. He had his arm around Kitty, who seemed to melt into his body.

Their friendship was going to be further strained when Kitty became a mother and her interests and focus changed.

A deep sadness came over her. Cassie would never know the life of wife and mother. But maybe she could live vicariously through Kitty, who was glowing at the prospect of motherhood in just over two months.

Cassie wasn't jealous. She loved the solitary life she'd chosen to live up on her mountain, well, most of the time. The four alpacas had helped her get through this past winter with a little less loneliness, though. She couldn't wait to get home to see how her babies were doing. Graciela seemed nearly ready to drop her cria, although the owner she'd bought her from had said she wasn't due until early June. Cassie knew she wouldn't have to offer much assistance, but she didn't want to miss the happy event, either.

She waved at Angelina, who didn't notice because she was so deep in conversation with Marc. Was she crying?

Cassie couldn't check on her new friend right now. She needed to get away. She stepped out into the wind and took a deep breath. Then another.

Freedom.

She relaxed and walked to her SUV parked on a side street. A glance up at the mountain helped relax her further.

Home.

Soon she'd be in her haven. Nothing evil could invade her sanctuary. She sent positive energy and vibrations out every morning and every evening to prevent it.

The sun was setting as she made it through the pass and turned onto her rutted road. The huge chasms in the dirt road kept sightseers and interlopers away. Her four-wheel drive would manage fine. She glanced up at Iron Horse Peak and noticed a particularly dangerous-looking ledge of snow hanging near the crest of the mountaintop. Careful to take it slowly, not wanting to make a noise that might send it tumbling toward her, she maneuvered around the mountainside. When she'd gotten beyond where an avalanche could impede her getting home, she relaxed her grip on the steering wheel. At least, if the snowpack gave way in early May like this, she wouldn't be stranded for months like she had been the second year she'd lived up here.

As she came around the last bend in the road, her cabin loomed in front of her. She'd left the porch light on. Inviting.

The vintage log structure had been modified to accommodate her art studio, providing more light than the old cabin had offered originally, while remaining authentic.

Home.

She opened the door and got out. The slamming of the door resulted in a cacophony of welcoming hums and clucks from her precious babies in the barn. She smiled. They'd made life up here much less lonely—

The thundering roar of tumbling snow invaded her thoughts, and she looked up in time to watch the snowpack hurtle toward the roadway and the valley below. There weren't any cabins in its path, and it would be extremely unlikely anyone would hike or camp here, given all of the recent warnings.

Cassie watched in awe, appreciating the raw power of nature. Someday, she was going to capture the beauty of an avalanche on canvas.

When the air grew silent again, she trudged through last night's snowfall toward the front door. Good thing she'd stocked up. It would take a couple weeks for that amount of snow to melt. She had a small plow for her SUV, but she wasn't in any hurry to visit civilization again. She preferred to be with her alpacas and her art, far removed from regular human contact, which was…stressful.

Dusk had fallen by the time she'd gotten her supplies inside, fed the alpacas, and started back to work on the sketch for the fiber piece she planned to make from the first harvesting of their fleece. The wind had begun to pick up; it felt like more snow might fall before morning.

Her cell phone jarred her from her work some time later. Glancing at the clock, she saw that nearly an hour had passed. Caller ID showed Kitty's name. What could she want so soon?

"Hey, Kitty. What's up?"

"Are you okay? Marc said there was an avalanche up there."

"Obviously, I'm fine. I just made it through before the snowpack came down."

There was an awkward pause before Kitty continued. "Um, is Luke with you?"

"Luke? Why on earth would Luke be with *me*? I left him there with you."

"Oh, God, no!"

Cassie was bombarded by the impact of a wave of negative energy in the universe's aether. She knew with disturbing certainty her safe world was about to be invaded.

"Cassie, he followed you."

"Why? I told him I didn't *need* anyone."

"He just wanted to make sure you made it home safely. Adam agreed.

You know how Doms are."

She couldn't suppress the aggravation in her voice. "No, Kitty, I don't." And she didn't want to know. What little Kitty had told her about the kinky stuff she and Adam were into only reinforced for Cassie that *machismo* men would always try to subjugate women.

Although Karla didn't *seem* subjugated. She seemed very happy and fulfilled.

"But I didn't see anyone following me." Not that she'd looked. "He knew the conditions were ripe for an avalanche before venturing that far around the mountain. The man works in search-and-rescue, for heaven's sake."

"He was worried about you." Kitty's muffled voice was speaking with someone else now. "He's not there."

Adam's voice came through loud and clear next. "Marc, let's go!"

"Kitty. Kitty?"

"Sorry. Adam and Marc are going to go search for him."

"Why don't you just call his phone? He's probably beyond Fairchance by now on his way home."

"We tried that first. He's not answering."

Kitty sounded really worried. "Look, if it'll make you feel better, I'll go out, too, and see if I can see any sign of him."

"Is it safe?"

"Yeah, the ledge was gone after the snowpack broke loose."

"Would you? I'd feel better."

Only for you, Kitty, would I go out on a night like this looking for a man.

But if she could put her friend's mind at rest, she could do this. "I'll call you back in a few." She ended the call and sat on the cedar chest, pulling on her boots. She grabbed her parka and a flashlight from the hook in the mudroom as she went out the door.

The flashlight illuminated the tracks she'd made to and from where she parked her SUV. She got inside and started the engine, and then turned the vehicle around to head back the quarter-mile or however far she could get before the road became blocked.

What if she found him? What would she do with him? No one was going to get out of here anytime soon. The thought of being trapped here with him sent her heart jumping into her throat, and she swallowed to try and relieve the sensation of obstruction.

What if she *didn't* find him? If he really had followed her home, he could have been right in the middle of the treacherous snow's path. She shuddered but not from the cold. Luke seemed like a nice man, even if he did look at her the wrong way. She didn't want to see him hurt—or worse.

Fear caused her to drive a little faster until she reached the place where the snow had settled too deeply across the road. There weren't any trees above the roadway because of the altitude, so the snow was absent any debris. She didn't see any vehicles or people, either.

Casting the beam of the flashlight down the side of the mountain, she looked for anything out of the ordinary, other than a mountain of snow.

"Luke! Can you hear me?"

The wind howled, carrying her words into the valley, but there was no other sound.

She panned the light slowly down the mound of snow. White and more white. Surely she'd see if—

The beam flashed against something shiny, not a natural feature. She moved the light back until she saw it again—something gray amidst the white snow. Her heart stuttered once, twice, then thudded to life again. A truck's hood was embedded in the snow, the side of the truck, near the extended-cab passenger door, was wrapped around a spruce tree, which had withstood the force of the avalanche. Apparently, the snowslide had clipped the back of the vehicle, because there hadn't been time for him to turn around if he'd gotten as far as making sure she'd arrived home.

She needed to get down there and make sure he was okay.

Cassie sent positive vibrations out into the universe, attaching Luke's name to them. *Please let Luke Denton be all right.* She slid down the slope, coming to a thud against the back panel of the truck, then crawled her way to the door. She peered in and saw Luke slumped toward the passenger seat, still wearing his seatbelt.

She sent out healing vibrations this time, as she tried to pry open the door, but the snow was wedged against the lower third, and the wheel wells were completely covered with snow. She set the flashlight down on a nearby mound of snow to light the area. He'd been here over an hour. The night wasn't frigid, but if he'd gone into shock…

Cassie frantically clawed at the snow, thankful it hadn't settled to a sheet of ice yet as it would overnight. Her arms ached and the tips of her fingers were numb by the time she'd cleared enough snow to open the door. She picked up the flashlight and illuminated the cab of the truck.

Reaching in, she touched his denim shirt sleeve. Still warm. *Please don't let him be dead.* "Luke! Can you hear me?"

He moaned and, in a whoosh, she let out the breath she'd been holding. She whispered, "Thank you, goddess."

Cassie raised her voice again. "Luke, open your eyes. It's Cassie."

He groaned. "Hell, woman. Let me sleep. No more dreams, damn it."

At least he was talking, although he wasn't making any sense. This was no dream; it was a freaking nightmare.

* * *

Damián rolled the throttle, and the rented Harley roared to life as they pulled out of the gate at Camp Pendleton. He'd proudly shown off Savannah to some of his old buddies who'd just returned from their umpteenth deployment. Introducing his beautiful girl to the guys and their wives had been great, but the day wasn't over yet.

They'd flown in to San Diego yesterday with Marisol, primarily to meet with Father Martine for premarital counseling. Because of the distance issues, and the fact that the priest had known Damián and Savannah for so long, he had agreed to a single session. He said he was more than satisfied with their obvious commitment to each other.

Damián would have been happy with a simple wedding in Denver, because the sooner she made an honest man of him, the better. But Savannah wanted a Nuptial Mass at San Miguel's. No, she probably needed it. That church had done a lot toward helping her heal until she'd come to him last December.

Rosa had taken her kids and Marisol to San Diego for the day, giving Savannah and him the day and evening to themselves. He'd only told her they'd be going up to Pendleton, in case he chickened out. But if she could face as many demons as she had, he sure as hell wasn't going to be a pussy about his own.

When he turned north on the 5, rather than head back to Solana Beach, Savannah yelled in his ear, "Hey, where are we headed now?"

"You'll see, *bebé*! Anticipation is good for you."

She pinched his thigh but wrapped her arms around him and laid her helmeted head against his shoulder. He grinned. If she was his submissive, he'd have to work on discipline a little more. She'd never brought up the subject again after their date two weeks ago, but he'd give her time. Maybe they'd talk again after the wedding.

The closer they got to Laguna Beach, the more nervous he became. What if he made a fool of himself? He wanted today to be perfect, just like the last time they were here.

Don't think about that now. You have a beautiful woman plastered against your body, man. Focus.

The sense of *déjà vu* threatened to overwhelm him. Eight and a half years had passed. Sometimes it seemed like fifty, given all that had happened in his life since he'd met Savannah, but today he felt like a fucking teenager again.

All too soon, Damián pulled into a residential parking spot across the highway from the beach-access steps.

Savannah screamed, "Damián! You brought me back to Thousand Steps! Our special place! What a fantastic surprise!" She squeezed him around the waist and made him so glad he hadn't chickened out. Her excitement alone was worth any discomfort he might experience. The woman who once hated surprises had been full of them lately. Least he could do was surprise her in return.

She removed her helmet at the same time he did his. The smell of the salt air made him realize how much he'd missed coming to the beach. Rosa had decided recently she and the kids were moving to Denver after the school year ended, so Damián's ties to Southern California would pretty much be over soon. He'd better enjoy the beach while he could.

Damián retrieved a beach blanket, bottled waters, and some snacks from the rack bag. He was better prepared this time than he had been the last.

They crossed the busy highway, his anxiety and excitement building. What's the worst that could happen? He might stumble and fall on his ass. Hell, she'd *knocked* him on his ass before herself. Big deal. At the top of the long staircase, he turned to Savannah. The sparkle in her big blue eyes pushed aside some of his anxiety.

"I carried you down these stairs last time."

Damián glanced down the stairway and knew he'd never be able to do it.

She touched his cheek, bringing his attention back to her. "Damián, that was only because the soles of my feet had been beaten by the sadists. You were being my knight in shining armor. This time, we'll walk the stairs side-by-side."

Savannah took his hand and squeezed it. "You're even more my hero now. You rescued me again. Not just from my father but from the demons that had been ruling my life." She smiled. "Enough stalling. Let's get down to our cave."

She took the first step and pulled on his hand until he followed. Together, they started their journey, one step at a time. About halfway down, she said, "One of these days I'm going to count these steps."

"About two-hundred-and-thirty."

She stopped and looked at him. "That's like a skyscraper."

"Yeah, about seven or eight stories tall."

She frowned and looked back up the way they'd come. "Damián, we don't have to go to this beach. There are lots of them we could go to."

He reached up and cupped her cheek, stroking her soft skin with his thumb. "This is *our* special place. No other beach will do."

She stepped closer and wrapped her arms around his waist. "I love you so much, especially because you're so sentimental."

"If you tell the guys or Grant, I'll whip your ass."

"You'll do that anyway, I hope."

He swatted her ass.

"Thank you, Sir! May I have another?"

She grinned up at him, and his heart melted a little more, if possible. The change in her since they'd spent the night together at Dad's was nothing short of amazing.

"I'm just saying that, if you really don't want me to divulge your secrets, you'll have to come up with a punishment I wouldn't love."

"That can be arranged. How about making you climb up and down these stairs twice?"

Her smile faded. "You win. I'll behave."

They held hands and continued to walk side-by-side down more of the steps. His stump was holding up great, so far. About a third of the way from the bottom, she stopped again and turned to him.

"Let's stop." She didn't even sound winded, so he knew this was just for him.

"No, I'm good."

"If you stop for me a minute, I'll let you kiss me and…" She looked up and down the stairway and saw no other beach-goers. "…and I'll let you cop a feel, if you like."

Chico stirred. Damián pulled her into his arms and tipped her head back with a finger under her chin. He bent his head and captured her lips; then he caged her jaw and his tongue dove inside like a starving man. He moved his hands to cup her ass and pulled her against himself to let her know how excited Chico was to be here with her, too.

Damián's left hand slid up her side to her breast and squeezed her nipple between his finger and thumb. He felt her intake of breath with his mouth. No breath-play today, though. They were both going to need all the oxygen they could get to make it back up these stairs.

When he broke off the kiss, she looked a little dazed, and he held her in his arms to make sure she wasn't dizzy. She certainly was breathing hard now.

"Ready for more, *bebé*?"

"Always. You're a great kisser."

He chuckled. "More *stairs*. We'll have plenty of time for kissing later."

"Oh. I guess you've created a monster." She patted his ass.

"No, I've created a princess slut who can't keep her hands off me."

"That's just because you're a hot tamale."

They both grinned as he took her hand, and they made it down the rest of the stairs in record time. He didn't look forward to making the trip back to the top, but he knew she'd look out for his needs. It was nice having someone who wanted to take care of him like that, when she didn't go overboard, anyway.

Without saying a word, they headed across the sand toward the archway leading to their beach cave. Just before reaching it, they came upon the part he was most worried about. The uneven rocks were going to be a challenge with his prosthesis. Maybe it was time he got one that would allow him a little more flexibility and range of motion. Marisol was already asking when she could go skiing again with Uncle Marc. No way was she going to learn alone. All three of them could take lessons—and Damián would be the one to pick them up if they fell.

Savannah squeezed his hand. "I need to watch my footing or we're both going to be sprawled on those rocks."

He'd said something similar last time they were here, only then he was carrying her in his arms.

"Come on! Our cave is waiting."

She gave him a smile of encouragement and they started across the moss-covered rocks. The breeze cooled the sweat on his forehead, but he just put one foot in front of the other. When she slipped on a jagged rock near the tidal pool, he grabbed her around her waist, his other hand cupping her breast.

"You're getting to cop a feel and I'm not even wearing stilettos."

He bent down and gave her a kiss. "I love you."

She smiled, and they turned to walk under the jagged archway into the entrance to the cave. Their special place beckoned them inside.

*　*　*

Savannah took a little more care with her steps after nearly falling on her face. She was anxious to get back to the place that had been her refuge for so long. Memories of her last time here in real life weighed heavy on her mind. Damián seemed tense, too. He had to be remembering that time, as well. She hadn't been shut down sexually then. He hadn't seemed disappointed in her inability to take their relationship to that level these past two weeks, but if he kept igniting Chiquita's fire every chance he could when Mari was at school or with a sitter, it wouldn't take much to break down that last barrier.

Since the embrace-her-inner-slut date, as Damián referred to it now, usually right before he pulled her into his arms, she hadn't shied away from his sexual attentions. Together they'd discovered a number of ways to bring them each to orgasm—sometimes simultaneous ones—without actually having sex. He hadn't even had to resort to videos. True to his word, Damián didn't seem disappointed in her inability to have sex.

But she still kept it as a goal for herself.

She couldn't believe they'd be married in less than four weeks. She was planning a simple, weekday ceremony among her church family and her new family. She hoped Karla would be able to travel, but her friend had told her she would only be at the beginning of her eighth month and wouldn't miss it for the world.

Damián preceded her into the entrance of the beach cave, but before she could follow, she needed to do something.

"Damián, I need a few minutes alone. Wait for me inside?"

He frowned and stroked her arm but nodded. She turned and walked to the side of the archway, away from Damián's gaze, and looked out at the ocean.

The waves crashed against the rocks. Sea and sun. Marisol. She'd named her daughter for the memory of this special day with Damián.

But before Damián, this had been her special place with Maman. The last time she'd been here with her mother held bittersweet memories. Little Savannah had wished it could have just been she and her maman, but knowing what she knew now as an adult, Savannah was happy Maman had at least found someone who was good to her, however brief their time on earth together had been.

Tears burned the backs of her eyelids. She knew deep down that, all the times she'd prayed to Maman for guidance or help, she'd always interceded with God for her even if her prayers weren't always answered right away.

"Maman, I know you brought Damián into my life—twice. Thank you for always looking over me and protecting me. I'm so sorry you didn't get to live with the man of your dreams, but I hope you and John are together in heaven now."

She looked down at her sandals, unsure what else needed to be said to achieve closure. She'd said much of it at the funeral, but she couldn't be here again with Damián without first honoring the woman who had given birth to her.

A tear splashed onto her breast. She didn't know how long she stood there, but the sound of a gull squawking pulled her back into the moment.

A butterfly with almost translucent blue and white wings, edged in black, flitted from a hiding spot in the rocks and landed on her shoulder. She didn't think May was butterfly-migration season. Or could it be…?

Maman?

Had Maman found a way to let her know she was okay? Soon after, a second, slightly larger butterfly flitted toward her, but this one kept its distance, taking up a watchful place on the wall of the arch. Waiting, as if not wanting to invade her space.

She reached up and gently stroked the wing of the butterfly on her shoulder.

"Thank you, Maman. I hope this means you and John are together still. Forever." Another tear rolled down her cheek and splashed on her chest. The butterfly flew to her chest and its tiny tongue rolled out to lick away her tear.

More tears flowed freely now. "I'll always love you and will try to be as good a maman to my little girl as you were to me."

The second butterfly flitted away first, followed by the smaller one, and both soon disappeared behind the arch and out of sight.

Savannah smiled and brushed the tear tracks away before walking inside the cave. Damián had spread the blanket on the sand and was stretched out, waiting for her, his jacket, vest, and shirt removed. Shyly, she walked over to the blanket. She dropped to her knees beside him, not sure what to do. Memories of how tenderly he'd made love to her in this very cave so long ago made her ache for his touch.

"You okay?"

Unable to speak, she just nodded.

He held his arms out to her and she laid her head on his shoulder, placing her hand on his dragon tat. "I know this place carries a lot of memories for you. If you don't want to stay…"

She reached out, placed a finger on his lips, and smiled at him for worrying about her. "The memories I have here are some of the best ones of my life. This was a happy, safe place for me. I want to stay here with you as long as we can today."

He bent to kiss her gently. She didn't want to dwell on the past anymore. She wanted to be in the moment with Damián today. She opened her mouth, and his tongue accepted her invitation. His hand reached up and touched her breast through the "My Princess" tank's built-in bra, pinching her nipple. She drew a sharp breath, and both nipples responded immediately, becoming engorged.

He broke off the kiss. "You surprised me by wearing this top today."

"I'm proud to be your princess—and only you and some of our family know that behind this sweet persona, I'm really a princess slut." She grinned. "I told the wife of one of your buddies at Pendleton that my daughter made it for me."

He smiled. "Good thinking."

"You might have to make one for Mari, though. She wants to be your princess, too."

"She already is. You'll always be my only princess slut, but who says a commoner like me can't have two princesses in his life?"

Savannah hadn't known how special the bond could be between a loving daddy and his little girl, but Damián was totally besotted by Mari. Knowing without a doubt nothing inappropriate would ever happen between them, Savannah was able to relive her childhood vicariously through her daughter as she watched her interact with her daddy.

Damián took her hand and pulled her onto his chest. He flinched and closed his eyes, taking a deep breath. She remembered the story he'd told her about his own PTSD issues. Another position to check off the list, this time

Damián's limit. He opened his eyes, and she was wrapped in his warm, chocolate gaze until he rolled onto his side and positioned her facing him. They'd enjoyed discovering that lying side by side—whether spooning or like this—led to some creatively fun ways to touch without having actual intercourse.

His hands roamed down her back to her jeans, and he cupped her ass, pulling her closer as he ground his erection against her lower abdomen. One hand slid up between their bodies and under her tank. He cupped her bare breast. When he pinched her nipple, she felt a spark fly to her clit. Her hips bucked toward him, and she inhaled a sharp breath.

Suddenly, she wanted him to come inside Chiquita but didn't know how to ask for what she needed.

Make love to me again, Damián.

Damián searched her eyes, and she wondered if she'd spoken aloud. His lips captured hers in a tender kiss, but when she forced her tongue into his mouth, he grabbed her head with both hands and plunged his tongue back inside hers. Their tongues danced a sexy tango, and she met him stroke for stroke.

After several minutes, he broke away, breathing hard. "Get on top of me."

She wrinkled her brow. "But what about…?" She didn't want to trigger an episode.

"Get on top of me. Now."

She started to reach for the button on her jeans, but he stayed her hands. "Leave them on. You're not ready yet."

The promise of his "yet" stirred Chiquita once more. His fierce gaze told her he was on a mission to accomplish something and needed her help. Slowly, she straddled him—Chico meeting Chiquita for the first time today. They'd missed each other.

She rested her weight on her hands, trying not to put pressure on his chest, but he pulled her onto his chest. She felt his heart beating rapidly against her breast as he fought for control.

"Breathe, Damián. Breathe through it. You're with Savannah."

His gaze cleared, and he stared up at her, love and gratitude shining in his eyes. He pulled her by the hair until her lips hovered over his, the full weight of her now lying on him. He wrapped his arms around her and pulled her even closer.

She nibbled at his lower lip and he groaned, as he ground Chico against the juncture of her thighs.

She pulled away and stared into his eyes. If he could fight one of his demons head on, then so could she.

"I want you to make love to me, Damián."

"You're sure?"

"I want to try. That's all I can promise."

"That's all I'll ever ask. But I didn't bring protection."

"That hasn't stopped us before."

He gave her the stare he used to take her in hand at the club. "Strip."

Her stomach dropped, but she scrambled to her feet as quickly as she could, pulling off and discarding the tank before she'd even become fully upright. She didn't want to wait too long, in case the fear overtook her again. She unbuckled the sandals and shimmied the jeans off, baring herself to him.

"No panties?"

"Maybe Chiquita was hoping she'd get lucky today." She returned to him on the blanket.

Chico strained against Damián's leathers. Savannah reached out to unbuckle his belt and undo the button, and then he took over and unzipped them so he could shuck them. He seemed just as worried about the magic ending.

When Chico stood proudly above a cloud of black hair, Savannah's clit throbbed. Damián had gone commando.

He motioned with his fingers for her to join him on the blanket. She stretched out beside him again, curling up to his side, trying to draw courage from him. He pressed her onto her back and kissed her, but didn't linger. He trailed his lips down her neck, nipping at the skin above her collarbone.

Zing!

She nearly groaned when he turned her on her side, her back to him.

Please, touch me, Damián.

"Don't make me wait! I need this!"

"I know, *bebé*. I'll take care of you." His hand glided down her side, over her hip, and curled around to her mons. She bucked against him. He stroked her clit hood until she was on the verge of coming.

"Not like this!" She whimpered. "I want you inside me."

"I'm getting there. A little anticipation is good for my princess slut."

She groaned. How they'd gotten this far in such a short time, she didn't know or care. She only knew she needed him inside Chiquita—now!

"Lift your left leg."

She wasn't sure how he wanted her to lift it, so she tented it. He moved down the blanket a bit until she felt Chico gliding against her slick pussy—*Chiquita! Dear Lord!*

He stroked from her hole to her clit, back and forth, the pressure building. Then his hand came under her thigh and reached for her clit.

"Oh, God! Don't make me come yet! Please! I need you inside me!" She nearly whimpered with painful need and reached out to guide Chico to her opening. Damián sucked air into his mouth.

"You're in charge, *bebé*."

She pressed herself against him, taking him a little farther.

"You're so fucking tight."

"I'm sorry."

"Fuck, woman. That's something you don't ever have to apologize for."

He lay still, as if waiting for her to adjust to his size. His breathing was shallow and rapid, as was hers.

The only demon she fought now was the need for Chiquita to come. Raising up on her elbow, she found she had more leverage and pushed down more of Chico's length. She tilted her pelvis, taking him deeper.

"That's right, *bebé*. Fuck me."

She slammed herself down the length of him. "Oh, God!" He throbbed inside her, and she began to ride him harder. He took her hip in his firm hand and slowed down the rhythm.

"Chico's waited a long time to be here again and doesn't want it to end too soon."

She giggled and remembered to take a breath. She hadn't been this horny since, well, since she was nineteen and Damián had brought her here.

She felt so full. The pressure built beyond what she could stand.

"Damián, I don't think I can wait!"

"Come first. I'm right behind you."

"Ha-ha." This was no time for his teasing.

Chico throbbed inside her as Damián sank his teeth into her shoulder, as if to hold her steady. He pumped his hips against her backside, driving himself deeper inside her. She panted, trying to fill her lungs but not succeeding.

Reaching down, she stroked his balls, gently pulling the hairs. His teeth bit harder as he groaned.

His mouth released her. "I can't hold back any longer, *bebé*. Come. Now."

His hand stroked her clit faster, and the pressure built. Savannah had waited so long for Damián to possess her again, to claim her body and soul. He was the first, last, and only man who would ever receive the gift of her body.

"Ohh! Come with me, Damián! Don't stop!" She squeezed her eyes closed, the sweet agony of her release exploding between them.

"Give it all to me, *bebé!*" He pulsated inside her.

Savannah's screams reverberated throughout the walls of the cave. "I'm yours, Damián! Always."

"*Santa Madre de Dios!*" he gritted out through his teeth as he came.

His orgasm had been torn from him as painfully as hers had been, judging by the pain she heard in his voice. They both collapsed onto the blanket, chests heaving as they tried to breathe normally again.

She curled up against him and fell asleep.

* * *

Damián had no fucking clue how long they slept, but at some point, Savannah had rolled onto her back. He propped his head in his hand and watched the gentle rise and fall of her breasts.

His glance strayed lower, to her flat belly. What if he'd planted another baby in her today? He hoped so. He wanted to have lots of kids—and be able to be with her through every pregnancy until they were both old and gray and holding their great-grandchildren on their laps.

Mi mariposa. *I will never let you flit away from me again.*

He traced the almost invisible silvery marks low on her belly. The first time he'd seen her naked, when he'd restrained her to the St. Andrew's cross, he'd seen the marks made during her pregnancy.

She blinked herself awake and smiled up at him. "How long did I sleep?"

"As long as you needed to, I guess."

"How long have you been up?"

"Long enough to admire the beautiful marks on your belly."

She frowned. "I have stretch marks."

Damián hoped his expression conveyed how pissed he was that she was putting down his beautiful body. "Those are *my* stretch marks—from *my* baby—and they're the most beautiful marks I'll ever put on you—at least, until we have another baby."

She gave him a wobbly smile and blinked rapidly. "You can even make my stretch marks seem sexy."

His finger traced her jaw. "*Chica*, everything about you is sexy as hell."

She turned away, a pensive look on her face, and then met his gaze again. "I've been thinking more about becoming your submissive."

He grinned at her. "I wondered when you'd be ready to finish that discussion."

"I'd probably have finished sooner, if you'd prodded me nicely. Maybe with the evil stick."

He pinched her thigh to simulate the sting of the heart-shaped evil stick he'd used to help her focus. She yelped, then smiled. He was going to enjoy taking her deeper into sadomasochism and finding ways to turn pain into pleasure for her. First, she wanted to talk about submission.

"I'm not going to force you into something you aren't ready for. I figured you'd come back to it after you'd made your decision or when you had more questions."

"You're a very patient man, Damián." She traced the line of his jaw, brushing the tip of her finger across his lips. He opened and sucked her finger inside.

Her pupils dilated and nipples enlarged. The woman was such a fucking turn-on to him, and she was easier than ever to get turned on these past couple weeks. All that passion he'd seen years ago had lain dormant for so long, she needed release—and often.

She blinked a few times and pulled her hand away. "You're very distracting. If you want us to have this conversation, you'll need to stop doing things like that."

He chuckled.

She turned her face away. "Damián, what does being a bedroom submissive involve?" Her face flushed.

"It's just a label. The only rules are the ones we set, so it can mean whatever we want it to mean. More important than giving it a label is negotiating the hard limits, softer boundaries, wants, and needs. We can strictly be Dom/sub in the club, if you'd like, or at home, as well—in our bedroom."

Dios, he couldn't wait to move into their new house. Kissing her goodnight at his bedroom door and letting her sleep with Marisol instead of him had gotten fucking old, especially after she'd agreed to marry him.

He remembered the night he'd proposed and grinned. Dad had gifted them with the bedroom furniture in the room they'd shared at the club. Luke assured him the piece Damián had broken off could be glued back on, but Luke and Dad hadn't let him live it down yet.

"But if I'm your submissive, won't you want to control me all the time?"

He took her chin in his hand and turned her to face him. "I'm a Dom, Savannah. I try to be in control of *myself* at all times, sometimes to the extreme. That control allows me to be in a place where I am responsible enough to accept the submission of someone who wants me to control her. The only control I will ever have over you is what you grant to me."

"I don't want to give up what little control I have."

"What frightens you about giving up control?"

She shuddered. "My past."

"Your father, Lyle, and the others weren't Doms—they were abusers. If they'd come into my club or any other kink community, they'd have been taken care of long ago. We don't tolerate that behavior among our own."

"I've always felt safe in your club. I trust the people there."

"We run a pretty good club. Only one problem I can remember, when Angelina first came to the club. I think we owners learned then that letting someone that abusive off by withdrawing membership isn't good enough. Next time…"

He took a deep breath, still pissed the asshole had come back to attack Angelina again. If only they'd busted his balls the first time. But that didn't relate to this conversation.

"*Savita*, nothing is going to happen that you don't consent to, no matter what we call ourselves. Being a Dom isn't about me forcing my will on you or even having my own needs met."

"But I like to do things for you that I think you need."

He grinned. "Yes, that is the service part of submission. I've enjoyed how you've tried to anticipate and serve my needs as my bottom, but it's not something most of my bottoms have done. You didn't have to."

"I disagree—if that's okay…*Sir*."

He tweaked her impertinent nose. "We're negotiating. Now, if we were in a scene we'd negotiated and you got bratty and disagreeable, then there might be consequences. Right now, though, it's important that you continue to communicate honestly with me so I know what you like and don't like. I also need to know what you want our relationship to evolve into, if different from what we have now as Top and bottom."

Never having been in a Dom role before, he tried to think how else their relationship might change.

"Being a Dom gives me more of a chance to help train your mind to learn discipline that can help you cope. My dominance might spill over into other areas of our lives, as well, not just during a scene. Does that frighten you?"

"No, I think it would actually make me feel safer knowing you're protecting me."

"I would do that whether I was your Top or your Dom."

"Yes, you always have." Her hand played absently with the tat on his chest, causing his dick to stir.

"As your Dom, I would work with you to learn a deeper level of discipline, which would help you gain a better sense of control in your life—and help you learn what you can't control."

"The only thing I've ever felt in control of was raising Mari, but I enjoy sharing that responsibility with you now. It's hard to be a single parent."

"Hardest job in the world. I would be scared shitless if I had to do it all on my own. I don't know how you managed all those years, other than the fact that you're an amazingly strong woman. I've enjoyed sharing the responsibility of her upbringing with you these past months."

"You're an incredible daddy. I think I first realized I could trust you when I saw how you cared for Teresa when she was so vulnerable after her rape. You held her and comforted her. At first, I was a little nervous when she crawled into your lap in my office…"

He heard her voice go up in tone to become almost childlike and knew more memories of her own father's abuse and betrayal were surfacing. He wrapped her more tightly in his arms. "Most men would never even think what your father and Teresa's did was possible. Those *cabrones* are the exception. I know, in your line of work, you see the worst of mankind, but most men are honorable and decent."

"Maybe. All I know is that you are. And I trust Adam, Marc, Luke, Victor…I guess as I slowly get to know others, I'll grow to trust more men, but the net will never be cast far. It's so hard for me to trust anyone."

"For good reason. You're now under my protection, as well as the protection of other dominants at the club, including Grant. We take care of our own." His hand rested on her belly. "Family is everything."

"I'm glad to be part of your family, but also so happy we're a family now."

She continued to trace the jaw of his dragon tat as she thought things out. He held his emotions in check, not wanting to influence her decision of letting him become her Dom. This was something she had to want, not something she should do to serve his wants, although being her Dom also would fulfill a need deep inside him, he knew without a doubt.

"I love this tat."

He sighed. Clearly, she wasn't ready to make a decision.

"Why did you choose a dragon?"

Hmmm. How to answer this without looking even more like a sentimental pantywaist? When he didn't answer right away, she looked up at him. Drawing a page from the story books he liked to read to Marisol, he began, "Once upon a time, there was a blonde-haired princess who looked like a Barbie doll. She was being treated very badly by the evil, powerful men in her life…"

Savannah stopped breathing, waiting for him to continue the story.

"One day, a lowly peasant rescued her from the tower in a castle where she was being abused. They only spent one perfect day together before they were separated for many years by circumstances they couldn't control."

He brushed a hair from her forehead. "The peasant never forgot the sadness in the princess's pretty blue eyes and vowed to himself that one day he would return to slay her dragons. Unfortunately, he was sent to war and captured by a dragon from which he couldn't escape. The dragon began to eat away at him, starting with his foot, and ending with his pride and self-worth." Damián still had a ways to go in accepting his disability, but Savannah's acceptance of him helped a lot.

Realizing she was waiting for more of the story, he gathered his thoughts and continued.

"Even though he'd escaped to a mountain hideaway to start a new life, the dragon always found him, often late at night. He could never be what the beautiful princess needed, so he tried to forget about her."

Tears filled her eyes, and she reached up to stroke his cheek.

"Many years later, the princess and her equally beautiful daughter came to the peasant, who had some special skills she thought might help her slay the evil dragons pursuing them, as well." *There were too fucking many dragons in this fairy tale—and in their lives.* He cleared his throat. "The battle was fierce, but together with some of the peasant's family members, two of the princess's worst dragons were sent away where they could never hurt the two princesses again."

She smiled through her tears. "And they lived happily ever after?"

"Who can say until the ends of their lives, when the full tale can be revealed?"

She brushed the tears away and propped herself up on her elbow to glare at him. "That's a lousy way to end a fairy tale!"

Damián shrugged. "I'm pragmatic."

"Well, I'm an incurable romantic. I'll finish the tale."

She closed her eyes and took a deep breath. When she opened them again, she guided Damián to lay flat on his back and pressed her cheek against the head of the dragon. He made a pillow of his arm and waited to hear her vision for their future.

She cleared her throat. "The lonely princess found the love of her life in the heroic peasant and soon discovered he was really a noble knight who had been imprisoned at a young age by an evil dragon that should have been destroyed before he could hurt anyone else."

Her description of Teresa's father, Julio, was pretty accurate. Damián had been thrown in juvie for beating the man who nearly killed Rosa, only to have Damián wind up being the one punished. Life wasn't always fair.

"While the knight continued trying to make people think he was a peasant, those who knew and loved him saw the truth in his demeanor and actions. He married the maman-princess and protected both of his princesses, as well as the other children the knight and his lady were blessed with for the rest of their lives."

He grinned. "And they lived happily ever after?"

Savannah lifted her head and stared at him. "Yes, but that doesn't mean everything was perfect. There were times when the knight had to draw his sword and fight other cowardly dragons that tried to devour the princess and her knight while they slept."

Damián's eyes began to burn. She'd better not make him cry or he'd haul her ass over his knee. He was still her Top.

"But the silly dragons didn't realize they were up against *two* powerful warriors now. The knight fought with the sword, while the princess could knock a dragon on its ass with her magically powerful feet and legs."

He chuckled. "I think the knight got knocked on his ass once, too."

"Shhh. Don't interrupt."

He swatted her ass, and the smack against her bare skin made him realize they were lying in a cave on a public beach totally naked. Oh, well. He wasn't going to interrupt this tale again for anything. He wanted to know how it turned out.

"Besides, the knight needed to learn that his princess was a worthy warrior who would protect his child with her life."

Damián wrapped her in his arms and held her close, resting his chin on the top of her head, so she couldn't see the tears in his eyes. Savannah had done that with Marisol, and he had no doubt she'd do the same for any other children they were blessed with.

"After a while, the word on the street where the dragons hid was that this couple and their extended family members weren't to be messed with. The dragons became less and less powerful."

She placed a kiss on his pec, on the face of the dragon. "Princess Marisol made a pet of one of the baby dragons, and it grew to protect the young princess when she went away to college or was away from the knight and his lady.

"Heaven help any of the knights who come anywhere near my doll-baby princess, too."

"Our princess might not marry until she's thirty."

"Or forty."

They were both lost in their thoughts for a moment as Damián started to worry about how he was going to keep Marisol safe from the knights who might want to hurt her. Maybe she needed to have some martial-arts training.

"Sir…Damián."

"Yes, *bebé*?"

"That wasn't a question. I was trying it out to hear what it sounded like. Sir Damián."

His heart thudded against his chest. Was she still lost in the world of make-believe? He didn't realize he was holding his breath until his chest began to burn. Still, she hadn't said. "Well, how did it sound?"

"Nice. I think I like it."

"Is that the end?" If so, it was a lousy way to end the story. Where was the happily ever after she wanted so badly?

Savannah pushed herself up and knelt beside him, her knees spread to where he could see Chiquita peeking out. She sat on her heels, back straight, head bowed, and hands resting on her thighs. He hadn't taught her yet the kneeling position he liked for his bottoms, but she'd perfected it. Karla must have been instructing her in more than…

"One day, in a secluded cave by the peaceful sea, the princess had come full circle. She willingly submitted her body and mind fully to her noble knight. But not her heart."

She looked up at him, and he blinked away the sting in his eyes.

"Because she'd surrendered her heart to him, long, long ago."

(To be continued in *Somebody's Angel*, available now, where readers will share in some major events in the lives of Adam and Karla and Damian and Savannah, as well as learning more about Luke and Cassie as they watch the Masters at Arms Club family become stronger while helping Marc come to terms with what has kept him from committing to Angelina.)

Glossary of Terms for *Nobody's Perfect*

Aftercare—period of time after intense BDSM activity in which the dominant partner or a designee cares for the submissive partner. Some BDSM activities are physically challenging, psychologically intense, or both. After engaging in such activities, the submissive partner may need a safe psychological space to unwind and recover. Aftercare is the process of providing this safe space. (Source: xeromag.com)

Alive Day—the day a member of the armed forces is wounded and narrowly escapes death in combat; many commemorate the anniversary in some way

Bambolina—doll, in Italian

Bastinado—foot whipping; a form of corporal punishment in which the soles of a person's bare feet are repetitively beaten with an implement

Bottom—in a BDSM scene, the person to whom the action is being delivered by a "Top." (Also see **Top**.)

Breath Play—in the extreme, this is autoerotic asphyxiation, a form of dangerous edge play in the BDSM community. For a scene in this book, a much less dangerous form of breath play is used in which the Dom exerts control over the submissive by the exchange of breaths. But any form of breath play should be considered dangerous and not attempted without training and intense research.

Cabrón (pl., cabrones)—literally, a goat, in Spanish, but is used as a profanity in Mexico and other Latin American countries to mean bastard, scumbag, lowlife, and all things vile

Cara—dear, in Italian (*Cara mia* means my dear)

Catharsis by Whipping (sometimes Cathartic Whipping)—the purging of the emotions or relieving of emotional tensions through the BDSM practice of whipping (using a whip, cane, or other impact implement)

Chére—dear, in French

Chicano—a North American term for a person, especially a male, of Mexican origin or descent

Chica—girl, in Spanish

Chico—boy, in Spanish (a term Damián also uses for his penis)

Chiquita—little girl, in Spanish

¿Comprendes?—Understand? (in Spanish)

Corpsman—Navy personnel trained to administer medical aid in the field (similar to a medic in the Army); Navy hospital corpsmen served with both the Navy and the Marines. Often referred to as "Doc," when assigned to a Marine ground unit, the corpsman must train with the Marines and will be treated like a Marine by the unit.

Digitals—digital camouflage uniform, also referred to as MARPAT (Marine Pattern), Desert Digitals, cammies, or digis/diggis

Dios—God, in Spanish (also see *Madre de Dios* and *Sancta Madre de Dios*)

Doc—nickname for the Navy hospital corpsman attached to the Marines (also see **Corpsman**)

Dom/sub or D/s Dynamic in BDSM—a relationship in which the Dominant(s) is given control by consent of the submissive(s) or bottom(s) to make most, if not all, of the decisions in a play scene or in relationships with the submissive(s) or bottom(s).

Double-coin Knot—This knot looks like two overlapping round coins with a square hole in the center. It is not a tight knot.

Dungeon Monitor (DM)—volunteer usually at a play party or club who ensures the safety of those in scenes/activities; while on duty, a DM should not be engaging in play scenes. A Dungeon Monitor Supervisor, or DMS, oversees one or more Dungeon Monitors.

ETA—estimated time of arrival

F-Bomb—saying the word "fuck" (most likely at a time or in company it is inappropriate)

Feliz Navidad—Merry Christmas, in Spanish

FragO (aka Frag Order or Fragmentation Order)—a Marine Corps term for an addendum to published operational orders and contains five paragraphs spelling out in basic terms the 1) situation, 2) mission, 3) execution, 4) administration and logistics, and 5) command and signal for the mission under way. Fragmentation orders are issued when the time element precludes issuance of a complete order, usually in fast-moving situations.

Goth—a person who wears mostly black clothing, uses dark dramatic makeup, and often has dyed black hair

Grunt—term for an infantryman in the U.S. Marine Corps (once derogatory, now more neutral)

IED—Improvised Explosive Device, a bomb constructed, set, and detonated in unconventional warfare

Machismo—an attitude, quality, or way of behaving that agrees with traditional ideas about men being very strong and aggressive

Madre de Dios—Mother of God, in Spanish (also see ***Sancta Madre de Dios***)

Malditos Bastardos—fucking bastards, in Spanish

Mamacita—literally little mommy, in Spanish; but also can be used by a male to mean hot mamá

Maman—mother or mama, in French. NOTE: Savannah's mother was born in France and responded to Maman, as does Savannah with her daughter

Mariposa—butterfly, in Spanish (*mi mariposa* means my butterly)

Master Sergeant (MSgt)—The eighth enlisted rank in the U.S. Marine Corps, just above gunnery sergeant, below master gunnery sergeant, sergeant major, and Sergeant Major of the Marine Corps. It is equal in grade to first sergeant. It is abbreviated as MSgt. In the U.S. Marine Corps, master sergeants provide technical leadership as occupational specialists at the E-8 level. Also see "Top."

Master/slave Dynamic in BDSM—A BDSM relationship, usually a 24/7 TPE one, in which the Top is referred to as the Master and the bottom the slave. People in a "Master/slave" dynamic often see dominance or submission as a cornerstone of their identity and an essential part of who they are as people. This dynamic may affect and inform almost every aspect of their lives, but there is no one-size fits all and each member in such a relationship consents to enter into such an arrangement.

Merda—shit, in Italian

Mierda—shit, in Spanish

Mindfuck—Something that intentionally destabilizes, confuses or manipulates the mind of another person. Used in the BDSM lifestyle to make a submissive think something is happening that usually is much worse than what is actually happening.

Muévete Rapido—move very fast (or hurry up), in Spanish

Munchkins—another word for small children

Muñequita, mi—my little doll, in Spanish

Nipple nooses—a non-piercing form of tit torture in which the nipples are "lassoed" with string or wire which is then tightened to cut off sensation to the nipple; usually results in pain when the nooses are removed and circulation returns

No es nada—it's nothing or don't mention it, in Spanish

No la molestes—I won't hurt you, in Spanish

OFP—Own Fucking Plan, term for when a Marine does what he wants to, when he wants to, and gets away with it. Someone who is OFP might also use DGAF (Doesn't/Don't Give a Fuck).

Orgasm torture—The BDSM practice whereby a bottom or submissive is forced to orgasm multiple times in quick succession, usually under the control and command of a Dominant; a form of orgasm control

Pain Slut—a masochist or someone who enjoys feeling extreme pain in a BDSM scene

Papi—daddy, in Spanish; also see ***te quiero, papi***

Patriot Guard Riders—an all-volunteer, non-profit organization comprised primarily of motorcyclists/bikers and their friends and family whose mission it is to ensure dignity and respect at memorial services honoring Fallen Military Heroes, First Responders, and Honorably Discharged Veterans.

PDQ—pretty damned/darn quick

Père Noël—Father Christmas or Santa Claus, in French

Petit mort—literally means little death, in French; a term for orgasm

Phantom Pain—sensations of pain experienced by an individual relating to a limb or organ that is no longer physically part of the body

Princesa—princess, in Spanish

PT—physical therapy. **PTs** refers to the uniform worn for doing workouts while in the Marine Corps

PTSD—Post Traumatic Stress Disorder, is a mental health condition that's triggered by a terrifying, often life-threatening, event (combat, attack, rape, abuse, incest)

Puta Madre—an expletive meaning motherfucker or holy fuck, in Spanish

Que Idiota Soy—I'm an idiot, in Spanish

Querida—darling, in Spanish

Rack Bag—term used by bikers for the saddlebag or storage area on a Harley or other motorcycle

Recon—reconnaissance. In the Marine Corps, trainees in the recon unit are referred to as "ropers" because of the ropes attached to the backs of their uniforms during training.

Rehab—rehabilitation. In this saga, refers to the period of time Damián spends in recovery from his combat injuries.

RPG—Rocket-Propelled Grenade, is a shoulder-fired, anti-tank weapon system that fires rockets equipped with an explosive warhead. These warheads are affixed to a rocket motor and stabilized in flight with fins. The RPG became a favorite weapon of the insurgent forces fighting U.S. troops in Iraq and was sometimes used in place of mortar, as happened on the rooftop attack.

Sadomasochism—sexual behavior that involves giving or receiving pleasure from causing or feeling pain

Sancta Madre de Dios—Holy Mother of God, in Spanish (also see ***Madre de Dios***)

SAR—Search and Rescue

Safephrase—a phrase agreed upon prior to a BDSM scene that can be used to end (temporarily or completely) a play scene

Safeword—a word agreed upon prior to a BDSM scene that can be used to end (temporarily or completely) a play scene

Savita—a Spanish endearment meaning "little Savi"; also one of the aliases used by Savi Baker

Seabag—term used by sailors and Marines to describe their duffel bag for storing their gear

Semper Fidelis **(usually shortened to *Semper Fi*)**—Marine Corps motto; Latin for "always faithful"

Service Top—a Dominant who provides a service, often an area of mastery or expertise he or she possesses, in consensual scenes with submissives, slaves, and bottoms in the BDSM community

Shibari—A type of bondage originating in Japan and characterized by extremely elaborate and intricate patterns of rope, often used both to restrain the subject and to stimulate the subject by binding or compressing the breasts and/or genitals. Shibari is an art form; the aesthetics of the bound person and the bondage itself are considered very important. Also sometimes called kinbaku. Most technically, shibari is the act of tying, and kinbaku is artistic bondage. In general use, however, shibari and kinbaku are often used as synonyms. (Source: Xeromag.com)

Skype—a software used to have video conferences or calls via the internet

Slut—literally, a woman who has many casual sexual partners, however in the BDSM community it can be used to describe someone who enjoys a certain practice (pain slut, anal slut, etc.); can be used as a term of humiliation or of endearment in the community

Soldier—Term to describe a member of the U.S. Army. Also considered a derogatory term to a U.S. Marine (Although Adam let's it slide when Karla calls him one because her brother is a U.S. Army soldier and she wouldn't know about this being an insult, he isn't too pleased that the pimp in the bus station uses the term to refer to Adam.)

SNAFU—Marine acronym meaning Situation Normal, All Fucked Up

SSC—Safe, Sane, and Consensual kink scenes with a safeword that doesn't carry the level of risk some edgeplay does

Stump Sock—tubular medical or clothing accessory with a blind end fashioned similar to a sock, usually without a heel. It is worn on an amputation stump, typically on body parts that do not contain a foot, to protect the stump from heat, cold, or chafing

Subspace—A state of mind that a submissive may enter, particularly after intense activities and/or (depending on the person) intense pain play, characterized by euphoria, bliss, a strong feeling of well-being, or even a state similar to intoxication. Thought to be related to the release of endorphins in the brain. The euphoria associated with subspace may last for hours or sometimes even days after the activity ceases. (Source: Xeromag.com)

Sueño, Mi—My dream, in Spanish

Te quiero, papi—I love you, daddy, in Spanish

Tighter than a Gnat's Ass—an expression used by Marines to describe something as being very tight

Top—1) In the U.S. Marine Corps, master sergeants may be referred to by the nickname of "Top." This usage is an informal one, however, and would not be used in an official or formal setting. Use of this nickname by Marines of subordinate rank is at the rank holder's discretion. 2) In a BDSM scene, the person delivering the action to a submissive or "bottom." (Also see **Bottom** and **Master Sergeant**)

Twentynine Palms—a Marine Corps training base in Twentynine Palms, Calif.; sometimes referred to by the derogatory term Twentynine Stumps.

Uniform Code of Military Justice (UCMJ)—the Congressional Code of Military Criminal Law applicable to all military members worldwide

USMC—United States Marine Corps

Violet Wand—a modern electrical sexual or kink stimulation toy used to apply low current, high voltage, high-frequency electricity to the body. They are most commonly used in BDSM though erotic sensation play is also possible with them. The name comes from the color of the light emitted from many of the wands.

About the Author

Kallypso Masters writes emotional, realistic Romance novels with dominant males (for the most part) and the strong women who can bring them to their knees. She also has brought many readers to their knees—having them experience the stories right along with her characters in the Rescue Me Saga. Kally knows that Happily Ever After takes maintenance, so her couples don't solve all their problems and disappear at "the end" of their Romance, but will continue to work on real problems in their relationships in later books in the saga.

Kally has been writing full-time since May 2011, having quit her "day job" the month before. She lives in rural Kentucky and has been married for 30 years to the man who provided her own Happily Ever After. They have two adult children, one adorable grandson, and a rescued dog.

Kally enjoys meeting readers at national romance-novel conventions, book signings, and informal gatherings (restaurants, airports, bookstores, wherever!), as well as in online groups (including Facebook's "The Rescue Me Saga Discussion Group"—send a friend request to Karla Montague on Facebook to join if you are 18 or older and don't mind spoilers. Kally also visits the Fetlife "Rescue Me! discussion group" regularly). She hopes to meet you in her future travels whether virtually or in-person! If you meet her face to face, be sure to ask for a Kally's friend button!

To contact or interact with Kally,

go to Facebook (http://www.facebook.com/kallypsomasters),
her Facebook Author page
(https://www.facebook.com/KallypsoMastersAuthorPage),
or Twitter (@kallypsomasters).

To join the secret Facebook group Rescue Me Saga Discussion Group, please send a friend request to Karla Montague and she will open the door for you. Must be 18 to join.

Keep up with news on her **Ahh, Kallypso…the stories you tell** blog at
KallypsoMasters.blogspot.com
Or on her Web site (KallypsoMasters.com).

You can sign up for her newsletter (e-mailed monthly) at her Web site or blog, e-mail her at kallypsomasters@gmail.com, or write to her at

Kallypso Masters
PO Box 206122
Louisville, KY 40250

Get your Kally Swag!

Want merchandise from the Rescue Me Saga? T-shirts and aprons inspired by a scene in *Nobody's Angel* that read: "Master Marc can put me in culinary bondage anytime." A beaded evil stick similar to the one used in *Nobody's Perfect*. Items from other books in the series will be added in coming months. With each order, you will receive a bag filled with other swag items, as well, including a 3-inch pin-back button that reads "I'm a Masters Brat," two purple pens, bookmarks, and trading cards. Kally ships internationally. To shop, go to http://kallypsomasters.com/kally_swag.

Excerpt from
Dungeon Royale (Masters and Mercenaries, Book 6)
Now Available!

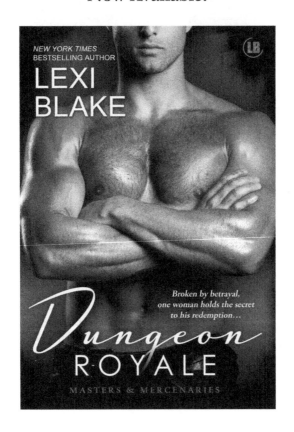

Dungeon Royale (excerpt)

Copyright 2014, Lexi Blake

An agent broken

MI6 agent Damon Knight prided himself on always being in control. His missions were executed with cold, calculating precision. His club, The Garden, was run with an equally ordered and detached decadence. But his perfect world was shattered by one bullet, fired from the gun of his former partner. That betrayal almost cost him his life and ruined his career. His handlers want him to retire, threatening to revoke his license to kill if he doesn't drop his obsession with a shadowy organization called The Collective. To earn their trust, he has to prove himself on a unique assignment with an equally unusual partner.

A woman tempted

Penelope Cash has spent her whole life wanting more. More passion. More adventure. But duty has forced her to live a quiet life. Her only excitement is watching the agents of MI6 as they save England and the world. Despite her training, she's only an analyst. The closest she is allowed to danger and intrigue is in her dreams, which are often filled with one Damon Knight. But everything changes when the woman assigned to pose as Damon's submissive on his latest mission is incapacitated. Penny is suddenly faced with a decision. Stay in her safe little world or risk her life, and her heart, for Queen and country.

An enemy revealed

With the McKay-Taggart team at their side, Damon and Penny hunt an international terrorist across the great cities of Northern Europe. Playing the part of her Master, Damon begins to learn that under Penny's mousy exterior is a passionate submissive, one who just might lay claim to his cold heart. But when Damon's true enemy is brought out of the shadows, it might be Penny who pays the ultimate price.

* * * *

"I'm going to kiss you now, Penelope."

"What?"

"You seem to have an enormously hard time understanding me today. We're going to have to work on our communication skills." He moved right between her legs, spreading her knees and making a place for himself there. One minute she was utterly gobsmacked by the chaos he'd brought into her life in a couple of hours' time, and the next, she couldn't manage to breathe. He invaded her space, looming over her. Despite the fact that she was sitting on the counter, he still looked down at her. His hands slid her skirt up, making her gasp a little. "You said yes. That means you're mine, Penelope. You're my partner and my submissive. I take care of what's mine."

She swallowed, forcing herself to look into those stormy eyes of his. He was so close she could smell the scent of his aftershave, feel the heat his big body gave off. "For the mission."

"I don't know about that," he returned, his voice deepening. "If this goes well, I get to go back out in the field. It's always good to have a cover. Men are less threatening when they have a woman with them. If you like fieldwork, there's no reason you can't come with me. Especially if you're properly trained. Tell me how much your siblings know."

She shook her head before finally realizing what he was asking. His fingers worked their way into her hair, smoothing it back, forcing her to keep eye contact with him. "Oh, about work, you mean. Everyone in my family thinks I work for Reeding Corporation in their publishing arm. They think I translate books."

Reeding Corporation was one of several companies that fronted for SIS. When she'd hired on, she'd signed documentation that stated she would never expose who she truly worked for.

"Excellent. If they research me they'll discover I'm an executive at Reeding. We've been having an affair for the last three months. You were worried about your position at the company and the fact that I'm your superior, but I transferred to another department and now we're free to be open about our relationship."

"I don't know that they'll believe we're lovers."

"Of course, they will. I'm very persuasive, love. Now, I'm going to kiss you and I'm going to put my hand in your knickers. You are wearing knickers, aren't you?"

"Of course."

He shuddered. "Not anymore. Knickers are strictly forbidden. I told you I would likely get into your knickers, but what I really meant was I can't tolerate them and you're not to wear them at all anymore. I've done you the enormous service of making it easy on you and tossing the ones you had in the house out."

His right hand brushed against her breast. The nipple responded by peaking immediately, as if it were a magnet drawn to Damon's skin.

"You can't toss my knickers out, Damon. And you can't put your hand there. We're in the ladies' room for heaven's sake."

"Here's the first rule, love. Don't tell me what I can't do." His mouth closed over hers, heat flashing through her system.

His mouth was sweet on hers, not an outright assault at first. This was persuasion. Seduction. His lips teased at hers, playing and coaxing.

And his hand made its way down, skimming across her waist to her thigh.

"Let me in, Penelope." He whispered the words against her mouth.

Drugged. This was what it felt like to be drugged. She'd been tipsy before, but no wine had ever made her feel as out of control as Damon's kiss.

Out of control and yet oddly safe. Safe enough to take a chance.

On his next pass, she opened for him, allowing him in, and the kiss morphed in a heartbeat from sweet to overpowering.

She could practically feel the change in him. He surged in, a marauder gaining territory. His tongue commanded hers, sliding over and around, his left hand tangling in her hair and getting her at the angle he wanted. Captured. She felt the moment he turned from seduction to Dominance, and now she understood completely why they capitalized the word. Damon didn't merely kiss her. She'd been kissed before, casual brushes of lips to hers, fumblings that ended in embarrassment, long attempts at bringing up desire.

This wasn't a kiss. This was possession.

He'd said she belonged to him for the course of the mission, and now she understood what he meant. He meant to invade every inch of her life, putting his stamp on her. If she proceeded, he would take over. He would run her life and she would be forced to fight him for every inch of freedom she might have.

"That's right, love. You touch me. I want you to touch me. If you belong to me, then my body is yours, too."

She hadn't realized her hands were moving. She'd cupped his bum even as his fingers slid along the leg band of her knickers, under and over, tickling against her female flesh.

He'd said exactly the right thing. He hadn't made her self-conscious. He'd told her he would give as good as he got. It wasn't some declaration of love, but she'd had that before and it proved false. Damon Knight was offering her something different. He was offering her the chance to explore without shame.

* * * *

For more information visit www.lexiblake.net.

The *Rescue Me* Saga

Masters at Arms & Nobody's Angel (Combined Volume)
(First in the *Rescue Me* Saga)

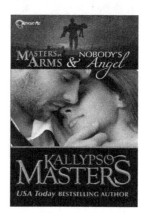

Masters at Arms is an introduction to the *Rescue Me* Saga, which needs to be read first. The book begins the journey of three men, each on a quest for honor, acceptance, and to ease his unspoken pain. Their paths cross at one of the darkest points in their lives. As they try to come to terms with the aftermath of Iraq—forging an unbreakable bond—they band together to start their own BDSM club. But will they ever truly become masters of their own fates? Or would fate become master of them?

Nobody's Angel: Marc d'Alessio might own a BDSM club with his fellow military veterans, Adam and Damián, but he keeps all women at a distance. However, when Marc rescues beautiful Angelina Giardano from a disastrous first BDSM experience at the club, an uncharacteristic attraction leaves him torn between his safe, but lonely world, and a possible future with his angel.

Angelina leaves BDSM behind, only to have her dreams plagued by the Italian angel who rescued her at the club. When she meets Marc at a bar in her hometown, she can't shake the feeling she knows him—but has no idea why he reminds her of her angel.

Nobody's Hero
(Second in the *Rescue Me* Saga)

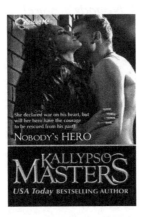

The continuing romantic journey of Adam and Karla from *Masters at Arms & Nobody's Angel*, which ended in a dramatic cliffhanger that sets up the opening scene of *Nobody's Hero*.

Retired Marine Master Sergeant Adam Montague has battled through four combat zones, but now finds himself running from Karla Paxton, who has declared war on his heart. With a twenty-five year age difference, he feels he should be her guardian and protector, not her lover. But Karla's knack for turning up in his bed at inopportune times is killing his resolve to do the right thing. Karla isn't a little girl anymore—something his body reminds him of every chance it gets.

Karla Paxton fell in love with Adam nine years ago, when she was a 16-year-old runaway and he rescued her. Now 25, she's determined to make Adam see her as a woman. But their age difference is only part of the problem. Fifty-year-old Adam has been a guardian and protector for lost and vulnerable souls most of his life, but a secret he has run from for more than three decades has kept him emotionally unable to admit he can love anyone. Will she be able to lower his guard long enough to break down the defenses around his heart and help him put the ghosts from his past to rest? In her all-out war to get Adam to surrender his heart, can the strong-willed Goth singer offer herself as his submissive—and at what cost to herself?

Damián Orlando and Savannah (Savi) Baker also will reunite in this book and begin their journey to a happy ending in *Nobody's Perfect*.

Nobody's Perfect
(Third in the *Rescue Me* Saga)

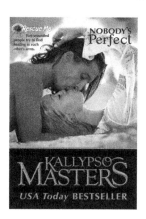

The continuing story of Savannah Gentry (now Savi Baker) and Damián Orlando from *Masters at Arms & Nobody's Angel* and *Nobody's Hero*.

Savannah/Savi escaped eleven years of abuse at the hands of her father and finally made a safe life for herself and her daughter. But when her father once again threatens her peace of mind—and her daughter's safety—Savi runs to Damián Orlando for protection. Eight years earlier, Savannah shared one perfect day with Damián that changed both their young lives and resulted in a secret she no longer can hide. But being with Damián reawakens repressed memories and feelings she wants to keep hidden—buried. After witnessing a scene with Damián on Savi's first night at his private club, she begins to wonder if he could help her regain control of her life and reclaim her sexuality and identity.

Damián, a wounded warrior, has had his own dragons to fight in life, but has never forgotten Savannah. He will lay down his life to protect her and her daughter, but doesn't believe he can offer more than that. She deserves a whole man, something he can never be after a firefight in Iraq. Damián has turned to SM to regain control of his life and emotions and fulfills the role of Service Top to "bottoms" at the club. However, he could never deliver those services to Savi, who needs someone gentle and loving, not the man he has become.

Will two wounded people find love and healing in each other's arms?

Somebody's Angel
(Fourth in the *Rescue Me* Saga)

The continuing story of Marc D'Alessio and Angelina Giardano.

When Marc d'Alessio first rescued the curvaceous and spirited Italian Angelina Giardano at the Masters at Arms Club, he never expected her to turn his safe, controlled life upside down and pull at his long-broken heartstrings. Months later, the intense fire of their attraction still rages, but something holds him back from committing to her completely. Worse, secrets and memories from his past join forces to further complicate his relationships with family, friends, and his beautiful angel.

Angelina cannot give all of herself to someone who hides himself from her. She loves Marc, the BDSM world he brought her into, and the way their bodies respond to one another, but she needs more. Though she destroyed the wolf mask he once wore, only he can remove the mask he dons daily to hide his emotions. In a desperate attempt to break through his defenses and reclaim her connection to the man she loves, she attempts a full frontal assault that sends him into a fast retreat, leaving her nobody's angel once again.

Marc finds that running to the mountains no longer gives him solace but instead leaves him empty and alone. Angelina is the one woman worth the risk of opening his heart. Will he risk everything to become the man she deserves and the man he wants to be?

CPSIA information can be obtained at www.ICGtesting.com
Printed in the USA
LVOW04s2345210814

400292LV00029B/1186/P